Thomas Wolfe

From Death
to Morning

Thomas Wolfe

From Death to Morning

Illustrated by Uldis Klavins

A LIMITED EDITION

THE FRANKLIN LIBRARY
Franklin Center, Pennsylvania
1979

Contents

No Door

I t is wonderful with what warm enthusiasm well-kept people who have never been alone in all their life can congratulate you on the joys of solitude. I know whereof I speak. I have been alone a great deal in my life—more than anyone I know—and I also knew, for one short period, a few of these well-kept people. And their passionate longing for the life of loneliness is astonishing. In the evening they are driven out to their fine houses in the country where their wives and children eagerly await them; or to their magnificent apartments in the city where their lovely wife or charming mistress is waiting for them with a tender smile, a perfumed, anointed, and seductive body, and the embrace of love. And all of this is as a handful of cold dust and ashes, and a little dross.

Sometimes one of them invites you out to dinner: your host is a pleasant gentleman of forty-six, a little bald, healthily plump, well-nourished-looking, and yet with nothing gross and sensual about him. Indeed he is a most æsthetic-looking millionaire, his features, although large and generous, are full of sensitive intelligence, his manners are gentle, quietly subdued, his smile a little sad, touched faintly with a whimsy of ironic humor, as of one who has passed through all the anguish, hope, and tortured fury youth can know, and now knows what to expect from life and whose "eyelids are a little weary," patiently resigned, and not too bitter about it.

Yet life has not dealt over-harshly with our host: the evidence of his interest in unmonied, precious things is quietly, expensively, all around him. He lives in a penthouse apartment near the East River: the place is furnished with all the discrimination of a quiet but distinguished taste, he has several of Jacob Epstein's heads and figures, including one of himself which the sculptor made "two years ago when I was over there," and he also has a choice collection of rare books and first editions, and after admiring these treasures appreciatively, you all step out upon the roof for a moment to admire the view you get there of the river.

Evening is coming fast, and the tall frosted glasses in your hands make a thin but pleasant tinkling, and the great city is blazing there in your vision in its terrific frontal sweep and curtain of star-flung towers, now sown with the diamond pollen of a million lights, and the sun has set behind them, and the red light of fading day is painted upon the river—and you see the boats, the tugs, the barges passing, and the winglike swoop of bridges with exultant joy— and night has come, and there are ships there—there are ships—and a wild intolerable longing in you that you cannot utter.

When you go back into the room again, you feel very far away from Brooklyn, where you live, and everything you felt about the city as a child, before you ever saw or knew it, now seems not only possible, but about to happen.

The great vision of the city is burning in your heart in all its enchanted colors just as it did when you were twelve years old and thought about it. You think that same glorious happiness of fortune, fame, and triumph will be yours at any minute, that you are about to take your place among great men and lovely women in a life more fortunate and happy than any you have ever known—that it is all here, somehow, waiting for you and only an inch away if you will touch it, only a word away if you will speak it, only a wall, a door, a stride from you if you only knew the place where you may enter.

And somehow the old wild wordless hope awakes again that you will find it—the door that you can enter—that this man is going to tell you. The very air you breathe now is filled with the thrilling menace of some impossible good fortune. Again you want to ask him what the magic secret is that has given his life such power, authority, and ease, and made all the brutal struggle, pain, and ugliness of life, the fury, hunger, and the wandering, seem so far away, and you think he is going to tell you—to give this magic secret to you—but he tells you nothing.

Then, for a moment the old unsearchable mystery of time and the city returns to overwhelm your spirit with the horrible sensations of defeat and drowning. You see this man, his mistress, and all the other city people you have known, in shapes of deathless brightness, and yet their life and time are stranger to you than a dream, and you think that you are doomed to walk among them always as a phantom who can never grasp their life or make their time your own. It seems to you now that you are living in a world of creatures who have learned to live without weariness or agony of the soul, in a life which you can never touch, approach or apprehend; a strange city race who have never lived in a dimension of time that is like your own, and that can be measured in minutes, hours, days, and years, but in dimensions of fathomless and immemorable sensation; who can be remembered only at some moment in their lives nine thousand enthusiasms back, twenty thousand nights of drunkenness ago, eight hundred parties, four million cruelties, nine thousand treacheries or fidelities, two hundred love affairs gone by—and whose lives therefore take on a fabulous and horrible age of sensation, that has never known youth or remembered innocence and that induces in you the sensation of drowning in a sea of horror, a sea of blind, dateless, and immemorable time. There is no door.

But now your host, with his faintly bitter and ironic smile, has poured himself out another good stiff drink of honest rye into a tall thin glass that has some ice in it, and smacked his lips around it with an air of rumination, and, after two or three reflective swallows, begins to get a trifle sorrowful about the life harsh destiny has picked out for him.

While his mistress sits prettily upon the fat edge of an upholstered chair, stroking her cool and delicate fingers gently over his knit brows, and while his good man Ponsonby or Kato is quietly "laying out his things" for dinner, he stares gloomily ahead, and with a bitter smile congratulates you on the blessed luck that has permitted you to live alone in the Armenian section of South Brooklyn.

Well, you say, living alone in South Brooklyn has its drawbacks. The place you live in is shaped just like a Pullman car, except that it is not so long and has only one window at each end. There are bars over the front window that your landlady has put there to keep the thugs in that sweet neighborhood from breaking in; in winter the place is cold and dark, and sweats with clammy water, in summer you do all the sweating yourself, but you do plenty of it, quite enough for anyone; the place gets hot as hell.

Moreover—and here you really begin to warm up to your work—when you get up in the morning the sweet aroma of the old Gowanus Canal gets into your nostrils, into your mouth, into your lungs, into every-

thing you do, or think, or say! It is, you say, one huge
gigantic Stink, a symphonic Smell, a vast organ note
of stupefying odor, cunningly contrived, compacted,
and composted of eighty-seven separate several pu-
trefactions; and with a rich and mounting enthusiasm, you name them all for him. There is in it, you
say, the smell of melted glue and of burned rubber. It
has in it the fragrance of deceased, decaying cats, the
odor of rotten cabbage, prehistoric eggs, and old to-
matoes; the smell of burning rags and putrefying
offal, mixed with the fragrance of a boneyard horse,
now dead, the hide of a skunk, and the noisome
stenches of a stagnant sewer; it has as well the——

But at this moment your host throws his head back
and, with a look of rapture on his face, draws in upon
the air the long full respiration of ecstatic satisfaction, as if, in this great panoply of smells, he really
had found the breath of life itself, and then cries:

"Wonderful! Wonderful! Oh, simply *swell!* *Mar-
velous!*" he cries and then throws back his head
again, with a shout of exultant laughter.

"Oh, John!" his lady says at this point with a troubled look upon her lovely face, "I don't think you'd
like a place like that at *all*. It sounds simply *dreadful!*
I don't like to hear of it," she says, with a pretty little
shudder of distaste. "I think it's simply terrible that
they let people live in places like that!"

"Oh!" he says, "it's wonderful! The power, the
richness, and the beauty of it all!" he cries.

Well, you agree, it's wonderful enough. And it's
got power and richness—sure enough! As to the
beauty—that's a different matter. You are not so sure
of that—but even as you say this you remember many
things. You remember a powerful big horse, slow-
footed, shaggy in the hoof, with big dappled spots of
iron gray upon it that stood one brutal day in August
by the curb. Its driver had unhitched it from the

wagon and it stood there with its great patient head bent down in an infinite and quiet sorrow, and a little boy with black eyes and a dark face was standing by it holding some sugar in his hand, and its driver, a man who had the tough seamed face of the city, stepped in on the horse with a bucket full of water which he threw against the horse's side. For a second, the great flanks shuddered gratefully and began to smoke, the man stepped back on to the curb and began to look the animal over with a keen deliberate glance, and the boy stood there, rubbing his hand quietly into the horse's muzzle, and talking softly to it all the time.

Then you remember how a tree that leaned over into the narrow little alley where you lived had come to life that year, and how you watched it day by day as it came into its moment's glory of young magic green. And you remember a raw, rusty street along the waterfront, with its naked and brutal life, its agglomeration of shacks, tenements, and slums and huge grimy piers, its unspeakable ugliness and beauty, and you remember how you came along this street one day at sunset, and saw all of the colors of the sun and harbor, flashing, blazing, shifting in swarming motes, in an iridescent web of light and color for an instant on the blazing side of a proud white ship.

And you start to tell your host what it was like and how the evening looked and felt—of the thrilling smell and savor of the huge deserted pier, of the fading light upon old rusty brick of shambling houses, and of the blazing beauty of that swarming web of light and color on the ship's great prow, but when you start to tell about it, you cannot, nor ever recapture the feeling of mystery, exultancy, and wild sorrow that you felt then.

8

*　*　*

Yes, there has been beauty enough—enough to burst the heart, madden the brain, and tear the sinews of your life asunder—but what is there to say? You remember all these things, and then ten thousand others, but when you start to tell the man about them, you cannot.

Instead you just tell him about the place you live in: of how dark and hot it is in summer, how clammy cold in winter, and of how hard it is to get anything good to eat. You tell him about your landlady who is a hardbitten ex-reporter. You tell him what a good and liberal-hearted woman she is; how rough and ready, full of life and energy, how she likes drinking and the fellowship of drinking men, and knows all the rough and seamy side of life which a newspaper reporter gets to know.

You tell how she has been with murderers before their execution, got the story from them or their mothers, climbed over sides of ships to get a story, forced herself in at funerals, followed burials to the graveyard, trampled upon every painful, decent, sorrowful emotion of mankind—all to get that story; and still remains a decent woman, an immensely good, generous, and lusty-living person, and yet an old maid, and a puritan, somehow, to the roots of her soul.

You tell how she went mad several years before, and spent two years in an asylum; you tell how moments of this madness still come back to her, and of how you went home one night several months before, to find her stretched out on your bed, only to rise and greet you as the great lover of her dreams—Doctor Eustace McNamee, a name, a person, and a love she had invented for herself. Then you tell of her fantastic family, her three sisters and her father, all touched with the same madness, but without her energy, power, and high ability; and of how she has kept the whole crowd going since her eighteenth year.

You tell about the old man who is an inventor who does not invent; of how he invented a corkscrew with the cork attached that would not cork; an unlockable lock; an unbreakable looking glass that wouldn't look. And you tell how the year before, he inherited $120,000—the first money he had ever had—and promptly took it down to Wall Street where he was as promptly shorn of it, meanwhile sending his wife and daughters to Europe in the nuptial suite of a palatial liner and cabling them when they wanted to come back: "Push on to Rome, my children! Push on, push on! Your father's making millions!"

Yes, all this, and a hundred other things about this incredible, mad, fantastic, and yet high-hearted family which I had found in a dingy alleyway in Brooklyn I could tell my host. And I could tell him a thousand other things about the people all about me —of the Armenians, Spaniards, Irishmen in the alley who came home on weekdays and turned on the radio, until the whole place was yelling with a hundred dissonances, and who came home on Saturday to get drunk and beat their wives—the whole intimate course and progress of their lives published nakedly from a hundred open windows with laugh, shout, scream, and curse.

I could tell him how they fought, got drunk, and murdered; how they robbed, held up, and blackjacked, how they whored and stole and killed—all of which was part of the orderly and decent course of life for them—and yet, how they could howl with outraged modesty, complain to the police, and send a delegation to us when the young nephew of my landlady lay for an hour upon our patch of backyard grass clad only in his bathing trunks.

10

"Yuh gotta nekkid man out deh!" they said, in tones of hushed accusatory horror.

Yes, we—good sir, who are so fond of irony—we, old Whittaker, the inventor, and Mad Maude, his oldest daughter, who would grumble at a broken saucer, and then stuff lavish breakfasts down your throat, who would patiently water twenty little feet of backyard earth from April until August, and until the grass grew beautifully, and then would turn twenty skinny, swarthy, and half-naked urchins loose into it to stamp it into muddy ruin in twenty minutes while she played the hose upon their grimy little bodies; we, this old man, his daughters, and his grandson, three bank clerks, a cartoonist, two young fellows who worked for Hearst, and myself; we, good sir, who sometimes brought a girl into our rooms, got drunk, wept, confessed sinful and unworthy lives, read Shakespeare, Milton, Whitman, Donne, the Bible—and the sporting columns—we, young, foolish, old, mad, and bewildered as we were, but who had never murdered, robbed, or knocked the teeth out of a woman; we, who were fairly decent, kind, and liberal-hearted people as the world goes, were the pariahs of Balcony Square—called so because there was neither square nor balconies, but just a little narrow alleyway.

Yes, we were suspect, enemies to order and the public morals, shameless partakers in an open and indecent infamy, and our neighbors looked at us with all the shuddering reprehension of their mistrustful eyes as they beat their wives like loving husbands, cut one another's throats with civic pride, and went about their honest toil of murder, robbery, and assault like the self-respecting citizens they were.

Meanwhile a man was murdered, with his head bashed in, upon the step of a house three doors below me; and a drunken woman got out of an automobile

one night at two o'clock, screaming indictments of
her escort to the whole neighborhood.

"Yuh gotta pay me, ya big bum!" she yelled. "Yuh
gotta pay me now! Give me my t'ree dollehs, or I'll go
home an' make my husband beat it out of yuh!"

"Staht actin' like a lady!" said the man in lower
tones. "I won't pay yuh till yuh staht actin' like a lady!
Yuh gotta staht actin' like a lady!" he insisted, with a
touching devotion to the rules of gallantry.

And this had continued until he had started the
engine of his car and driven off at furious speed, leaving her to wander up and down the alleyway for
hours, screaming and sobbing, cursing foully and
calling down the vengeance of her husband on this
suitor who had thus misused her—an indictment
that had continued unmolested until three young
ambitious thugs had seized the opportunity to go out
and rob her; they passed my window running, in the
middle of the night, one fearful and withdrawing,
saying, "Jeez! I'm sick! I don't feel good! Wait a minute! Youse guys go on an' do it by yourself! I want a
cup of coffee!"—And the others snarling savagely:

"Come on! Come on, yuh yellah bastad! If yuh
don't come on, I'll moiduh yuh!" And they had gone,
their quick feet scampering nimbly in the dark, while
the woman's drunken and demented howls came
faintly from the other end, and then had ceased.

Your host has been enchanted by that savage
chronicle. He smites himself upon the brow with
rapture, crying "Oh, grand! *Grand*! What a lucky fellow you are! If I were in your place I'd be the happiest man alive!"

You take a look about you and say nothing.

"To be free! To go about and see these things!" he
cries. "To live among real people! To see life as it is,
in the raw—the *real* stuff, not like this!" he says with

a weary look at all the suave furnishings of illusion that surround him. "And above all else to be *alone!*"

You ask him if he has ever been alone, if he knows what loneliness is like. You try to tell him, but he knows about this too. He smiles faintly, ironically, and dismisses it and you, with a wise man's weary tolerance of youth: "I know! I know!!" he sighs. "But all of us are lonely, and after all, my boy, the real loneliness for most of us is *here*"—and he taps himself a trifle to the left of the third shirt stud, in the presumptive region of his heart. "But you! Free, young, and footloose, with the whole world to explore— You have a fine life! What more, in God's name, could a man desire?"

Well, what is there to say? For a moment, the blood is pounding at your temples, a hot retort springs sharp and bitter to your lips, and you feel that you could tell him many things. You could tell him, and not be very nice or dainty with it, that there's a hell of a lot more that a man desires: good food and wonderful companions, comfort, ease, security, a lovely woman like the one who sits beside him now, and an end to loneliness—but what is there to say?

For you are what you are, you know what you know, and there are no words for loneliness, black, bitter, aching loneliness, that gnaws the roots of silence in the night.

So what is there to say? There has been life enough, and power, grandeur, joy enough, and there has also been beauty enough, and God knows there has been squalor and filth and misery and madness and despair enough; murder and cruelty and hate enough, and loneliness enough to fill your bowels with the substance of gray horror, and to crust your lips with its hard and acrid taste of desolation.

And oh, there has been time enough, even in

Brooklyn there is time enough, strange time, dark secret time enough, dark million-visaged time enough, forever flowing by you like a river, even in cellar depths in Brooklyn there is time enough, but when you try to tell the man about it you cannot, for what is there to say?

For suddenly you remember how the tragic light of evening falls even on the huge and rusty jungle of the earth that is known as Brooklyn and on the faces of all the men with dead eyes and with flesh of tallow gray, and of how even in Brooklyn they lean upon the sills of evening in that sad hushed light. And you remember how you lay one evening on your couch in your cool cellar depth in Brooklyn, and listened to the sounds of evening and to the dying birdsong in your tree; and you remember how two windows were thrown up, and you heard two voices—a woman's and a man's—begin to speak in that soft tragic light. And the memory of their words came back to you, like the haunting refrain of some old song—as it was heard and lost in Brooklyn.

"Yuh musta been away," said one, in that sad light.

"Yeah, I been away. I just got back," the other said.

"Yeah? Dat's just what I was t'inkin'," said the other. "I'd been t'inkin' dat yuh musta been away."

"Yeah, I been away on my vacation. I just got back."

"Oh, yeah? Dat's what I t'ought meself. I was t'inkin' just duh oddeh day dat I hadn't seen yuh f'r some time, 'I guess she's gone away,' I says."

And then for seconds there was silence—save for the dying birdsong, voices in the street, faint sounds and shouts and broken calls, and something hushed in evening, far, immense, and murmurous in the air.

14

"Well, wat's t' noos sinct I been gone?" the voice

went out in quietness in soft soft tragic light. "Has anyt'ing happened sinct I was away?"

"Nah! Nuttin's happened," the other made reply. "About duh same as usual—*you* know?" it said with difficult constraint, inviting intuitions for the spare painfulness of barren tongues.

"Yeah, I know," the other answered with a tranquil resignation—and there was silence then in Brooklyn.

"I guess Fatheh Grogan died sinct you was gone," a voice began.

"Oh, yeah?" the other voice replied with tranquil interest.

"Yeah."

And for a waiting moment there was silence.

"Say, dat's too bad, isn't it?" the quiet voice then said with comfortless regret.

"Yeah. He died on Sattiday. When he went home on Friday night, he was OK."

"Oh, yeah?"

"Yeah."

And for a moment they were balanced in strong silence.

"Gee, dat was tough, wasn't it?"

"Yeah. Dey didn't find him till duh next day at ten o'clock. When dey went to look for him he was lyin' stretched out on duh bat' room floeh."

"Oh, yeah?"

"Yeah. Dey found him lyin' deh," it said.

And for a moment more the voices hung in balanced silence.

"Gee, dat's too bad. . . . I guess I was away when all dat happened."

"Yeah. Yuh musta been away."

"Yeah, dat was it, I guess. I musta been away. Oddehwise I woulda hoid. I was away."

15

"Well, so long, kid. . . . I'll be seein' yuh."

"Well, so long!"

A window closed, and there was silence; evening and far sounds and broken cries in Brooklyn, Brooklyn, in the formless, rusty, and unnumbered wilderness of life.

And now the red light fades swiftly from the old red brick of rusty houses, and there are voices in the air, and somewhere music, and we are lying there, blind atoms in our cellar depths, gray voiceless atoms in the man-swarm desolation of the earth, and our fame is lost, our names forgotten, our powers are wasting from us like mined earth, while we lie here at evening and the river flows . . . and dark time is feeding like a vulture on our entrails, and we know that we are lost, and cannot stir . . . and there are ships there! there are ships! . . . and Christ! we are all dying in the darkness! . . . and yuh musta been away . . . yuh musta been away. . . .

And that is a moment of dark time, that is one of strange million-visaged time's dark faces.

Death
the Proud
Brother

The face of the night, the heart of the dark, the tongue of the flame—I had known all things that lived or stirred or worked below her destiny. I was the child of night, a son among her mighty family, and I knew all that moved within the hearts of men who loved the night. I had seen them in a thousand places and nothing that they ever did or said was strange to me. As a child, when I had been a route boy on a morning paper, I had seen them on the streets of a little town—that strange and lonely company of men who prowl the night. Sometimes they were alone, and sometimes they went together in a group of two or three, forever in midwatches of the night in little towns prowling up and down the empty pavements of bleak streets, passing before the ghastly waxen models in the windows of the clothing stores, passing below hard bulbous clusters of white light, prowling before the façades of a hundred darkened stores, pausing at length in some little lunchroom to drawl and gossip quietly, to thrust snout, lip, and sallow jowl into the stained depths of a coffee mug, or dully to wear the slow gray ash of time away without a word.

The memory of their faces, and their restless prowling of the night, familiar and unquestioned at the time, returned now with the strangeness of a dream. What did they want? What had they hoped to find as they prowled past a thousand doors in those little, bleak, and wintry towns?

Their hope, their wild belief, the dark song that the night awoke in them, this thing that lived in darkness while men slept and knew a secret and exultant triumph, and that was everywhere across the land, were written in my heart. Not in the purity and sweetness of dawn with all the brave and poignant glory of its revelation, nor in the practical and homely lights of morning, nor in the silent stature of the corn at noon, the drowsy hum and stitch of three o'clock across the fields, nor in the strange magic gold and green of its wild lyric wooded earth, nor even in the land that breathed quietly the last heat and violence of day away into the fathomless depth and brooding stillness of the dusk—as brave and glorious as these times and lights had been—had I felt and found the mystery, the grandeur, and the immortal beauty of America.

I had found the dark land at the heart of night, of dark, proud, secret night: the immense and lonely land lived for me in the brain of night. I saw its plains, its rivers, and its mountains spread out before me in all their dark immortal beauty, in all the space and joy of their huge sweep, in all their loneliness, savagery, and terror, and in all their immense and delicate fecundity. And my heart was one with the hearts of all men who had heard the strange wild music that they made, filled with unknown harmonies and a thousand wild and secret tongues crying to men the exultant and terrible music of wild earth, triumph and discovery, singing a strange and bitter prophecy of love and death.

For there was something living on the land at night. There was a dark tide moving in the hearts of men. Wild, strange and jubilant, sweeping on across the immense and sleeping earth, it had spoken to me in a thousand watches of the night, and the language of all its dark and secret tongues was written in my heart. It had passed above me with the rhythmical sustentions of its mighty wing, it had shot away with bullet cries of a demonic ecstasy on the swift howlings of the winter wind, it had come softly, numbly, with a dark impending prescience of wild joy in the dull soft skies of coming snow, and it had brooded, dark and wild and secret, in the night, across the land, and over the tremendous and dynamic silence of the city, stilled in its million cells of sleep, trembling forever in the night with the murmurous, remote and mighty sound of time.

And I was joined in knowledge and in life with an indubitable certitude to the great company of men who lived by night and had known and loved its mystery. I had known all joys and labors and designs that such men know. I had known all things living on the earth by night, and finally, I had known by night the immortal fellowship of those three with whom the best part of my life was passed —proud Death, and his stern brother, Loneliness, and their great sister, Sleep. I had lived and worked and wrought alone with Loneliness, my friend, and in the darkness, in the night, in all the sleeping silence of the earth, I had looked a thousand times into the visages of Sleep, and had heard the sound of her dark horses when they came. And I had watched my brother and my father die in the dark midwatches of the night, and I had known and loved the figure of proud Death when he had come.

Three times already I had looked upon the visage of death in the city, and now that spring I was to see it once again. One night—on one of those kaleidoscopic nights of madness, drunkenness, and fury that I knew that year, when I prowled the great

street of the dark from light to light, from midnight until morning—I saw a man die in the city
subway.

He died so quietly that most of us would not
admit at first that he was dead, so quietly that his
death was only an instant and tranquil cessation of
life's movement, so peaceable and natural in its action, that we all stared at it with eyes of fascination
and unbelief, recognizing the face of death at once
with a terrible sense of recognition which told us
we had always known him, and yet, frightened and
bewildered as we were, unwilling to admit that he
had come.

For although each of the three city deaths that I
had seen had come terribly and by violence, there
would remain finally in my memory of this one a
quality of terror, majesty, and grandeur which the
others did not have.

The first of these deaths had occurred four years
before in the month of April of my first year in the
city. It had happened upon the corner of one of the
dingy, swarming streets of the upper East Side, and
in the way it had happened there had been a merciless, accidental, and indifferent quality which was
far more terrible than any calculated or deliberate
cruelty could have been, which spoke terribly and
at once through the shining air, the joy and magic of
the season, obliterating all the hope and exultancy
in the hearts of men who saw it.

I was coming along one of the dingy cross-streets
in the upper East Side district—a street still filled
with the harsh and angular fronts of old brownstone
houses, which once no doubt had been the homes
of prosperous people but were now black with the
rust and grime of many years. These streets were
seething with the violent and disorderly life of

22

dark-faced, dark-eyed, strange-tongued people, who
surged back and forth, innumerably, namelessly,
with the tidal, liquid, and swarming fluency that all
dark bloods and races have, so that the lean precision, the isolation, and the severe design char-
acteristic of the lives of northern peoples—like
something lonely, small, pitifully yet grandly itself
—are fractured instantly by this tidal darkness. The
numberless and ageless man-swarm of the earth is
instantly revealed in all its fathomless horror, and
will haunt one later in dreams, even if one sees only
a half-dozen of these dark faces in a street.

Upon the corner of this swarming street, where it
joined one of the great grimy streets that go up and
down the city, and that are darkened forever by the
savage violence and noise of the elevated structure,
so that not only the light which swarms through the
rusty iron webbing, but all the life and movement
underneath it seems harsh, driven, beaten, violent,
bewildered, and confused—on such a corner the
man was killed. He was a little middle-aged Italian
who had a kind of flimsy cart which was stationed at
the curb, and in which he had a shabby and miscel-
laneous stock of cigarettes, cheap candies, bottled
drinks, a big greasy-looking bottle of orange juice
turned neck downward into a battered cylinder of
white enamelled tin, and a small oil stove on which
several pots of food—sausages and spaghetti—
were always cooking.

The accident occurred just as I reached the corner
opposite the man's stand. The traffic was roaring
north and south beneath the elevated structure. At
this moment an enormous covered van—of the kind
so powerful and cumbersome that it seems to be as
big as a locomotive and to engulf the smaller machines around it, to fill up the street so completely

that one wonders at the skill and precision of the driver who can manipulate it—came roaring through beneath the elevated structure. It curved over and around, in an attempt to get ahead of a much smaller truck, and as it did so, swiped the little truck a glancing blow that wrecked it instantly, and sent it crashing across the curb into the vendor's wagon with such terrific force that the cart was smashed to splinters, and the truck turned over it completely and lay beyond it in a stove-in wreckage of shattered glass and twisted steel.

The driver of the truck, by the miracle of chance, was uninjured, but the little Italian vendor was mangled beyond recognition. As the truck smashed over him the bright blood burst out of his head in an instant fountain so that it was incredible so small a man could have such fountains of bright blood in him; and he died there on the sidewalk within a few minutes, and before the ambulance could reach him. A great crowd of shouting, dark-faced people gathered around the dying man at once, police appeared instantly in astonishing numbers, and began to thrust and drive in brutally among the excited people, cursing and mauling them, menacing them with their clubs, and shouting savagely:

"Break it up, deh! Break it up! On your way, now!" . . . "Where yuh goin'?" one snarled suddenly, grabbing a man by the slack of his coat, lifting him and hurling him back into the crowd as if he were a piece of excrement. "Break it up, deh! Break it up! G'wan, youse guys—yuh gotta move!"

Meanwhile the police had carried the dying man across the curb, laid him down on the sidewalk, and made a circle around him from the thrusting mob. Then the ambulance arrived with its furious and dreadful clangor of bells, but by this time the man was dead. The body was taken away, the police drove and lashed the crowds before them, whipping and mauling them along, as if they were surly and stupid animals, until at length the whole space around the wreck was clear of people.

Then two policemen, clearing the street again for its unceasing traffic, half pushed, half carried the twisted wreckage of the vendor's cart to the curb, and began to pick up his strewn stock, boxes, broken cups and saucers, fragments of broken glass, cheap knives and forks, and finally his tin spaghetti pots, and to throw them into the heap of wreckage. The spaghetti, pieces of brain, and fragments of the skull were mixed together on the pavement in a horrible bloody welter. One of the policemen looked at it for a moment, pushed the thick toe of his boot tentatively into it, and then turned away with a grimace of his brutal red face, as he said, "Jesus!"

At this moment, a little gray-faced Jew, with a big nose, screwy and greasy-looking hair that roached backward from his painful and reptilian brow, rushed from the door of a dismal little tailor's shop across the sidewalk, breathing stertorously with excitement, and carrying a bucket full of water in his hand. The Jew ran swiftly out into the street, with a funny bandy-legged movement, dashed the water down upon the bloody welter and then ran back into the shop as fast as he had come. Then a man came out of another shop with a bucket full of sawdust in his hand which he began to strew upon the bloody street until the stain was covered over. Finally, nothing was left except the wreckage of the truck and the vendor's cart, two policemen who conferred quietly together with notebooks in their hands, some people staring with dull fascinated eyes upon the bloodstain on the pavement, and little groups of people on the corners talking to one another in low, excited tones, saying:

"Sure! I seen it! I seen it! Dat's what I'm tellin' yuh! I was talkin' to 'm myself not two minutes before it happened! I saw duh whole t'ing happen! I was standin' not ten feet away from 'im when it hit him!"—as they revived the bloody moment, going over it again and again with an insatiate and feeding hunger.

Such was the first death that I saw in the city. Later, the thing I would remember most vividly, after the horror of the blood and brains and the hideous mutilation of man's living flesh were almost forgotten, was the memory of the bloody and battered tins and pots in which the vendor had cooked his spaghetti, as they lay strewn on the pavement, and as the policeman picked them up to fling them back into the pile of wreckage. For later it seemed these dingy and lifeless objects were able to evoke, with a huge pathos, the whole story of the man's life, his kindly warmth and smiling friendliness— for I had seen him many times—and his pitiful small enterprise, to eke out shabbily, but with constant hope and as best he could, beneath an alien sky, in the heart of the huge indifferent city, some little reward for all his bitter toil and patient steadfastness—some modest but shining goal of security, freedom, escape, and repose, for which all men on this earth have worked and suffered.

And the huge indifference with which the vast and terrible city had in an instant blotted out this little life, soaking the shining air and all the glory of the day with blood, the huge and casual irony of its stroke—for the great van which had wrecked the truck and killed the man, had thundered ahead and vanished, perhaps without its driver even knowing what had happened—was evoked unforgettably, with all its pity, pathos, and immense indifference, by the memory of a few battered pots and pans. This, then, was the first time I saw death in the city.

The second time I saw death in the city, it had come by night, in winter, in a different way.

About midnight of a night of still bitter cold in February, when the moon stood cold and blazing in the white-blue radiance of the frozen skies, a group of people were huddled together upon the sidewalk of one of those confusing and angular streets which join Seventh Avenue near Sheridan Square. The people were standing before a new building which was being put up there, whose front stood raw and empty in the harsh brown-livid light a few feet away. Upon the curb, the watchman of the building had made a fire in a rusty ashcan, and this fire now whipped and blazed in the frozen air with a crackling flame to which some of the people in the group would go from time to time to warm their hands.

Upon the icy pavement before the building, a man was stretched out on his back and a hospital interne, with the tubes of a stethoscope fastened to his ears, was kneeling beside him moving the instrument from place to place on the man's powerful chest, which was exposed. An ambulance, its motor throbbing with a quiet and reduced power that was somehow ominous, was drawn up at the curb.

The man on the pavement was about forty years old and had the heavy shambling figure, the brutal and powerful visage, of the professional bum. On the scarred and battered surface of that face it seemed that every savage violence of weather, poverty, and physical degradation had left its mark of iron, during the years the vagabond had wandered back and forth across the nation, until now the man's features had a kind of epic brutality in which a legend of lonely skies and terrible distances, of pounding wheel and shining rail, of rust and steel and bloody brawl, and of the wild and savage earth, was plainly written.

The man lay on his back, as still and solid as a rock, eyes closed, his powerful, brutal features upthrust in the rigid and stolid attitude of death. He was still living, but one side of his head, at the temple, had been bashed in—a terrible, gaping wound which he had got when he wandered, drunk and almost blind with the cheap alcohol or "smoke" which he had been drinking, into the building, and had fallen forward across a pile of iron beams, against one of which he had smashed his head. The great black stain of the wound had run down across one side of his face and on the ground, but it had almost ceased to bleed, and in the freezing air the blood was clotting rapidly.

The man's rag of dirty shirt had been torn open and his powerful breast also seemed to swell forward with the same rigid and stolid immobility. No movement of breath was visible: he lay there as if carved out of rock, but a dull, flushed, unwholesome looking red was still burning on his broad and heavy face, and his hands were clenched beside him. His old hat had fallen off and his bald head was exposed. This bald head, with its thin fringe of hair upon each side, gave a final touch of dignity and power to the man's strong and brutal face, that was somehow terrible. It was like the look of strength and stern decorum that one sees on the faces of those powerful men who do the heavy work in the trapeze act at the circus, and who are usually baldheaded men.

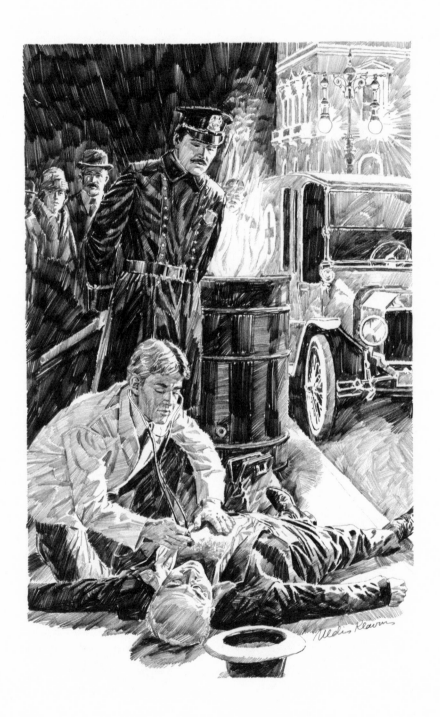

None of the people who had gathered there about the man showed any emotion whatever. Instead, they just stood looking at him quietly with an intent yet indifferent curiosity, as if there were in the death of this vagabond something casual and predictable which seemed so natural to them that they felt neither surprise, pity, nor regret. One man turned to the man next to him, and said quietly, but with assurance, and a faint grin:

"Well, dat's duh way it happens to dem in duh end. Dey all go like dat sooner or later. I've neveh known it to fail."

Meanwhile, the young interne quietly and carefully, yet indifferently, moved his stethoscope from place to place, and listened. A policeman with a dark, heavy face, pitted, seamed, and brutal-looking, stood over him, surveying the scene calmly as he gently swung his club, and ruminating slowly on a wad of gum. Several men, including the night watchman and a newsdealer on the corner, stood quietly, staring. Finally, a young man and a girl, both well dressed, and with something insolent, naked, and ugly in their speech and manner that distinguished them as being a cut above the others in education, wealth, position—as young college people, young city people, young Village, painting, writing, art-theatre people, young modern "postwar generation" people—were looking down at the man, observing him with the curiosity with which, and with less pity than, one would regard a dying animal, and laughing, talking, jesting with each other with a contemptible and nasty callousness that was horrible, and that made me want to smash them in the face.

They had been drinking, but they were not drunk: 30 something hard and ugly was burning nakedly in them—yet, it was not anything forced or deliberate, it was just hard-eyed, schooled in arrogance, dry and false, and fictional, and carried like a style. They had an astonishing literary reality, as if they might have stepped out of the pages of a book, as if there really were a new and desolate race of youth upon the earth that men had never known before—a race hard, fruitless, and unwholesome, from which man's ancient bowels of mercy, grief, and wild exultant joy had been eviscerated as out of date and falsely sentimental to bright arid creatures who breathed from sullen preference an air of bitterness and hate, and hugged desolation to the bone with a hard fatality of arrogance and pride.

Their conversation had in it something secret, sweet, and precious. It was full of swift allusions, little twists and quirks and subtleties of things about which they themselves were in the know, and interspersed with all the trademarks of the rough-simple speech that at that time was in such favor with this kind of people: the "swell," the "grand," the "fine," the "simply marvellous."

"Where can we go?" the girl was asking him. "Will Louie's still be open? I thought that he closed up at ten o'clock."

The girl was pretty, and had a good figure, but both face and body had no curve or fullness; body and heart and soul, there was no ripeness in her, she was something meager of breast, hard, sterile, and prognathous.

"If he's not," the young man said, "we'll go next door to Steve's. He's open all night long." His face was dark and insolent, the eyes liquid, the mouth soft, weak, pampered, arrogant, and corrupt. When he laughed, his voice had a soft welling burble in it, loose, jeering, evilly assured.

31

"Oh, swell!" the girl was saying in her naked tone. "I'd love to go there! Let's have another party! Who can we get to go? Do you think Bob and Mary would be in?"

"Bob might be, but I don't think that you'll find Mary," said the young man, adroitly innocent.

"*No!*" the girl exclaimed incredulously. "You don't mean that she's"—and here their voices became low, eager, sly, filled with laughter, and the young man finally could be heard saying with the burble of soft laughter in his voice:

"Oh, I don't know! It's just another of those things! It happens in the best of families, you know."

"No!" the girl cried with a little scream of incredulous laughter. "You *know* she hasn't! After all she said about him, too! . . . I think—that's—simply—priceless!" She then said slowly: "Oh—I—think—that's—simply—*swell!*" She cried: "I'd give anything to see Bob's face when he finds out about it!"—and for a moment they laughed and whispered knowingly together, after which the girl cried once more, with her little shout of incredulous laughter:

"Oh, this is too good to be true! Oh—I think that's *marvellous*, you know!"—then added quickly and impatiently:

"Well, who can we get to go, then? Who *else* can we get?"

"I don't know," the young man said, "it's getting late now. I don't know who we can get unless"— and here his soft dark mouth began to smile, and the burble of laughter appeared in his throat as he nodded towards the man upon the ground "—unless you ask our friend here if he'd like to come along."

"Oh, that would be *grand!*" she cried with a glee-

32

ful little laugh. Then for a moment she stared down seriously at the silent figure on the pavement. "I'd *love* it!" the girl said. "Wouldn't it be swell if we could get someone like that to go with us!"

"Well—" the young man said, indefinitely. Then, as he looked down at the man, his soft wet flow of laughter welled up and he spoke softly and slyly to the girl, "I hate to disappoint you, but I don't think we'll get our friend here to go. He looks as if he's going to have a bad head in the morning," and again his dark mouth began to smile, and the burble of soft laughter welled up in his throat.

"Stop!" the girl cried with a little shriek. "Aren't you mean!" she said reproachfully. "I think he's sweet. I think it would be simply marvellous to take someone like that on a party! He looks like a swell person," she continued, looking down at the man curiously. "He really does, you know."

"Well, you know how it is," the young man said. "He was a great guy when he had it!" The burble welled up richly in his soft throat. "Come on," he said. "We'd better go. I think you're trying to make him!"—and laughing and talking together in their naked and arrogant young voices, they went away.

Presently the interne got up, took the ends of the stethoscope from his ears, and spoke a few quiet and matter-of-fact words to the policeman, who scrawled something down in a small book. The interne walked over to the curb, climbed up into the back of the ambulance and sat down on one seat with his feet stretched out upon the other one, meanwhile saying to the driver: "All right, Mike, let's go!" The ambulance moved off smoothly, slid swiftly around the corner with a slow clangor of bells, and was gone.

Then the policeman folded his book, thrust it into

33

his pocket, and, turning on us suddenly, with a weary expression on his heavy, dark, nighttime face, stretched out his arms and began to push us all back gently, meanwhile saying in a patient and weary tone of voice: "All right, you guys! On your way, now. Yuh gotta move. It's all oveh."

And obedient to his weary and tolerant command, we moved on and departed. Meanwhile, the dead man lay, as solid as a rock, upon his back, with that great brutal face of power and fortitude, upthrust and rigid, bared with a terrible stillness, an awful dignity, into the face of the cold and blazing moon.

This was the second time that I saw death in the city.

The third time that I saw death in the city, it had come like this:

One morning in May the year before, I had been on my way uptown, along Fifth Avenue. The day was glorious, bright and sparkling, the immense and delicate light of the vast blue-fragile sky, was firm and almost palpable. It seemed to breathe, to change, to come and go in a swarming web of iridescent and crystalline magic, and to play and flash upon the spires of the great shining towers, the frontal blaze and sweep of the tremendous buildings, and on the great crowd which swarmed and wove unceasingly on the street, with vivid and multifarious points of light and color, as if the light were shining on a lake of sapphires.

Up and down the great street as far as the eye could reach, the crowd was surging in the slow yet sinuous convolutions of an enormous brilliantly colored reptile. It seemed to slide, to move, to pause, to surge, to writhe here and to be motionless there in a gigantic and undulant rhythm that was infinitely

34

complex and bewildering, but that yet seemed to move to some central and inexorable design and energy. So did the great surge of the man-swarm look from afar, but when one passed it by at close range it all broke up into a million rich, brilliant, and vivid little pictures and histories of life, all of which now seemed so natural and intimate to me that I felt I knew all the people, that I had the warm and palpable substance of their lives in my hands, and knew and owned the street itself as if I had created it.

At one place, a powerful motor with a liveried chauffeur would snake swiftly in toward the curb, and a uniformed doorman of some expensive shop would scramble with obsequious haste across the sidewalk and open the door for some rich beauty of the upper crust. The woman would get out swiftly with a brisk sharp movement of her well-shod little feet and slender ankles, speak a few incisive words of command to her attentive driver, and then walk swiftly across the sidewalk towards the shop with a driving movement of her shapely but rather tailored-looking hips and a cold impatient look on her lovely but hard little face. To her, this great affair of seduction, attraction, and adornment for which she lived—this constant affair of clothing her lovely legs to the best advantage, setting off her solid shapely little buttocks in the most persuasive fashion, getting varnished, plucked, curled, perfumed, and manicured until she smelled like an exotic flower and glittered like a rare and costly jewel— was really as stern a business as her husband's job of getting money, and not to be trifled with or smiled at for a moment.

Again, some lovely and more tender, simple, and good-natured girl would come by on the pavements, jaunty and rich with some glowing spot of color—a scarf of red or blue, or a gay hat—her hair fine-spun and blown by light airs, her clear eyes fathomless and luminous with a catlike potency and health, her delicate loins undulant with a long full stride, and her firm breasts rhythmical with each step she took, her mouth touched by a vague and tender smile as she passed by.

Elsewhere, dark-eyed, dark-faced, gray-faced, driven, meager, harassed and feverish-looking men and women would be swarming along, but the shining light and magic of the day seemed to have touched them all with its sorcery, so that they, too, all seemed filled with hope, gayety, and good nature, and to drink in as from some source of central and exultant energy the glorious intoxication of the day.

Meanwhile in the street the glittering projectiles of machinery were drilling past incredibly in their beetle-bullet flight, the powerful red-faced police stood like towers in the middle of the street stopping, starting, driving them on or halting them with an imperious movement of their mastlike hands.

Finally, even the warm odors of the hot machinery, the smells of oil, gasoline, and worn rubber which rose up from the bluish surface of the furious street, seemed wonderful, mixed as they were with the warm, earthy and delicious fragrance of the trees, grass, and flowers in the park, which was near by. The whole street burst into life for me immediately as it would on such a day for every young man in the world. Instead of feeling crushed down and smothered beneath its cruel and arrogant blaze of power, wealth, and number, until I seemed to drown in it, a nameless atom, it now seemed to me to be a glorious pageantry and carnival of palpable life, the great and glamorous Fair of all the earth, in which I was moving with certitude as one of the most honored and triumphant figures.

At this moment, with the park in view, with the sight of the trees, in their young magic green, and all the flash and play of movement, color, and machinery, in the square before the park, I halted and began to look with a particular interest at the people working on a building which was being erected there across the street. The building was not large, and neither very tall nor wide: it rose up ten flights with its steel girders set against the crystal air with a graceful and almost fragile delicacy, as if already, in this raw skeleton, the future elegance and style of the building were legible.

For I knew that this building was to house the great business which was known as Stein and Rosen and, like the man who once had shaken the hand of John L. Sullivan, I had a feeling of joy, pride, and familiarity when I looked at it. For the sister of a woman that I loved was a director of this mighty shop, its second-in-command, its first in talent and in knowledge, and from that woman's merry lips I had often heard the fabulous stories of what took place daily there. She told of the glittering processions of rich women who came there for their finery; of actresses, dancers, millionaires' wives, moving-picture women, and of all the famous courtesans, who would pay as they bought, and would plank down the ransom of a king in thousand-dollar bills for a coat of chinchilla fur; and of the stupendous things these legendary creatures said.

Through the portals of this temple in the daytime would move the richest women and the greatest harlots in the country. And an exiled princess would be there to sell them underwear, an impoverished duchess would be there to sell perfumery, and Mr.

Rosen himself would be there to greet them. He would bend before them from the waist, he would give his large firm hand to them, he would smile and smile with his large pearly teeth, as his eyes went back and forth about his place continually. He would wear striped trousers and he would walk up and down upon rich carpets, he would be splendid and full of power like a well-fed bull, and somehow he would be like that magnificent horse in Job who paweth in the valley and saith among the trumpets, "Ha! Ha!"

And all day long they would be calling all over the place for her sister, who seldom spoke and rarely smiled. They could not get along without her, they would be asking for her everywhere, the rich woman would demand her, and the famous courtesan would say she had to speak to her. And when she came to them, they would say: "I wanted to speak to you, because the rest of them know nothing. You are the only one who understands me. You are the only one I can talk to," and yet they could not talk to her, because she never spoke. But they would want to be near her, to confess to her, to pour their words into her silence: her large still eyes would look at them and make them want to speak. Meanwhile the Rosens smiled.

Thus, while the countless man-swarm of the earth thronged all around me I stood there thinking of these things and people. I thought of Mr. Rosen, and of the woman and her sister, and of a thousand strange and secret moments of our lives. I thought how great Cæsar's dust could patch a wall, and how our lives touch every other life that ever lived, how every obscure moment, every obscure life, every lost voice and forgotten step upon these pavements had somewhere trembled in the air about us.

"'Twere to consider too curiously, to consider so."
"No! faith, not a jot!—" the step that passed there in
the street rang echoes from the dust of Italy, and
still the Rosens smiled.

And it seemed to me that all the crowded and various life of this great earth was like a Fair. Here
were the buildings of the Fair, the shops, the
booths, the taverns, and the pleasure places. Here
were the places where men bought and sold and
traded, ate, drank, hated, loved, and died. Here
were the million fashions that they thought eternal,
here was the ancient, everlasting Fair, tonight
bereft of people, empty and deserted, tomorrow
swarming with new crowds and faces in all its million lanes and passages, the people who are born,
grow old and weary, and who die here.

They never hear the great dark wing that beats in
the air above them, they think their moment lasts
forever, they are so intent that they scarcely see
themselves falter and grow old. They never lift their
eyes up to the deathless stars above the deathless
Fair, they never hear the immutable voice of time
that lives in the upper air, that never ceases, no matter what men live or die. The voice of time is distant
and remote and yet it has all of the voice of million-
noted life within its murmur, it feeds on life and yet
it lives above it and apart from it, it broods forever
like the flowing of a river round the Fair.

Therefore when I looked at the spare webbing of
this building on that shining day, and knew that
those ingots of lean steel, those flat blocks of
fashionable limestone which already sheeted the
building's basal front, and which in their slender
elegance were somehow like the hips of the women
that the building would adorn, had been spun marvellously from the gossamer substance of Parisian

frocks, distilled out of the dearest perfumes in the world, shaped from the cunning in man's brain, and from the magic in a woman's hands—it all seemed good and wonderful to me.

For above, beyond, and through that web of steel, and over the whole pulse and surge of life in the great street, over all the sparkling surge and shift of the great Fair, I saw suddenly the blazing image of my mistress's jolly, delicate, and rosy face of noble beauty. And the image of that single face seemed to give a tongue to joy, a certitude to all the power and happiness I felt, to resume into its small circle, as into the petals of a flower, all of the glory, radiance, and variousness of life and of the street, until a feeling of such triumph and belief surged up in me that I thought I could eat and drink the city, and possess the earth.

Quite suddenly, as I stood there looking at the little figures of the men who were working on the building, walking along high up against the crystal air with a corky and scuttling movement as they swarmed back and forth across the girders, the thing happened with the murderous nonchalance of horror in a dream. Nine floors above the earth, a little figure was deftly catching in a bucket the nails or rivets of red-hot steel which a man with tongs was tossing to him from the forge. For a moment, the feeder had paused in his work, had turned, tongs in hand, for a breather, and had spoken to a man upon another girder. The catcher, meanwhile, grateful for this respite, had put his bucket down and stood erect, a cigarette between his lips, the small flame of a match held in the cave of his brown cupped hands. Then the feeder, his throat still loud with laughter from some scrap of bawdry irrelevant to steel, turned to his forge, gripped with his tongs a glowing rivet, and his throat still trembling with its laughter, tossed deftly, absently, casually, in its accustomed arc, that nail of fire. His scream broke in upon the echoes of his laughter, carrying to the glut of faultless and accurate machinery in the street below him its terrible message of human error.

His scream was "Christ!" and at that word so seldom used for love and mercy the startled eyes of the other man leaped from his match upon the death that whizzed toward him. Even in the six feet of life that still remained to him, his body had its time for several motions. It half turned, the knees bent as if for a spring out into space, the shoulder stooped, the big brown hands groping in a futile, incompleted gesture for the bucket. Then, half crouched and rigid with palms curved out in a kind of grotesque and terrible entreaty, and one foot groping horribly into thin air, he met his death squarely, fronting it. For a moment after the rivet struck him, his body paused, crouched, rigid, like a grotesque image, groping futilely and horribly into space with one clumsy foot, and with a wire of acrid smoke uncoiling at his waist. Then his shabby garments burst into a flame, the man pawed blindly out in sickening vacancy and fell, a blazing torch lit by a single scream.

So that rich cry fell blazing through the radiant and living air. It seemed to me that the cry had filled up life—for a moment I had the sense that all life was absolutely motionless and silent save for that one cry. Perhaps this was true. It is certain that all life in that building had ceased—where but a moment before there had been the slamming racket of the riveting machines, the rattling of the winches, and the hammering of the carpenters, there was now the silence of a cataleptic trance.

Above the street, delicate and spare in the blue weather, two girders swung gently in the clasp of the chain, but all machinery had stopped. The signal-man leaned over bent, staring, his hands still stretched in warning for his mate. The feeder sat astride a girder, gripping it in his curved hands, his face bent forward sightlessly in an oblivion of horror. The body had fallen, like a mass of blazing oil waste, upon the wooden structure that covered the sidewalk, then bounced off into the street.

Then the illusion of frozen silence, which seemed to have touched all the world, was broken. That crowd, which in the city seems to be created on the spot, to spring up from the earth like Gorgon seed for every calamity, had already grown dense at the spot where the man had fallen. Several policemen were there, mauling, cursing, thrusting back the thickening ring that terribly suggested flesh flies that work on something dead or sweet. And all the gleaming machinery in the street—which had been halted by the traffic lights—was again in motion.

There had been threat of a longer halt, a disruption of that inevitable flow, because several of the human units in the foremost squadrons of motors, who had witnessed the accident, refused now, under the strong drug of horror, to "click" as good machinery ought. But they were whipped into action after a moment's pause by a ponderous traffic cop, who stood in the center of the street, swinging his mighty arm back and forth like a flail, sowing the air with rich curses, his accents thickened in the long apelike upper lip. So, the lights burned green again, the clamors in the street awoke, the hot squadrons of machinery crawled up and down: an army of great beetles driven by an ape. Then the racket of the riveters began anew, high up above the

42

street in the blue air the long arm of the derrick moved, a chain with its balanced weight of steel swung in and down.

Already the body had been carried inside the building, the police were charging like bulls into the persistent crowd, dispersing them. In a closed car, a young woman, bright with the hard enamel of city elegance, stared through the window, her little gloved hand clenched upon the glass, her face full of manicured distress. And as she looked, she kept murmuring sharply and monotonously: "Quick! quick! be quick!" Before her, her driver bent stolidly over his work. He was upset, but he could not show it. Perhaps he was thinking: "Jesus! I've got to get her out of this quick. What'll *he* say if she tells him about it? He can't blame me. I can't help what the *other* guy does! That's *his* lookout. You never know what's gonna happen. A guy's got to think of everything at once."

He took a chance. Smoothly, swiftly, he skirted into the first rank between cursing drivers, just as the lights changed. The lady settled back in her seat with a look of relief. Thank heaven, that was over! George was so smart. He got in ahead of everyone: you never knew how he did it! He had done *that* beautifully.

I leaned against a building. I felt empty and dizzy. It seemed to me suddenly that I had only two dimensions—that everything on earth was like something cut out of stiff paper, with no thickness.

"Brightness falls from the air." Yes, brightness had fallen suddenly from the air, and with it all the marrowy substance of life. The vitality of life and air and people was gone. What remained to me was only a painting of warmth and color that my sick

43

eyes viewed with weariness and disbelief. Everything in that street went up and down. It seemed to me suddenly that everything was thin, two-dimensioned, without body and fullness. The street, the people, the tall thin buildings: these were all plane lines and angles. There were no curves in the street—the only thing that curved had been that one rich cry.

And just as the light of noon had gone out of the day so had the image of that woman's face, struck by the casual horror of this death with all its evocations of a life she knew, now suffered a transforming and sorrowful change.

For where that radiant, good, and lovely face had just the moment before wrought for me its magic certitude and unity of exultant joy, now all this magic world of health and life was shattered by this nameless death, was drowned out in the torrent of this man's nameless blood, and I could see her face no longer as it had looked at noon.

Rather that man's blood and death had awakened the whole black ruin in my heart, the hideous world of death-in-life had instantly returned with all its thousand phantom shapes of madness and despair and, intolerably, unanswerably, like the unsearchable mystery of love and death, the bitter enigma of that face of radiant life was now fixed among these shapes of death to drive me mad with its unsearchable mystery.

For in the image of that face was held all the pity and the wild regret of love that had to die and was undying, of beauty that must molder into age and wither to a handful of dry dust and yet was high as a star, as timeless as a river, undwarfed beneath the whole blind horror of the universe, and taller than man's tallest towers, and more enduring than steel and stone.

And then the shapes of death would wake and move around her, and I could only see her now fixed and secure in an infamous and arrogant power, which could not be opposed or beaten by any man, and against which, like a maddened animal, I could do nothing but batter my life and brains out on the pavements, as this man had done, or madden horribly into a furious death among the other nameless, faceless, man-swarm atoms of the earth.

I saw her, impregnably secure in an immense, complex, and corrupt city life—a life poisonous, perverse, and sterile that moved smoothly in great chambers of the night ablaze with baleful suavities of vanity and hate, where the word was always fair and courteous, and the eye forever old and evil with the jubilation of a filthy consent. It was a world of the infamous dead so powerful in the entrenchments of its obscene wealth, its corruption that was amorous of death and faithlessness, its insolence of a jaded satiety, and its appalling weight of number and amount that it crushed man's little life beneath its ramified assault and killed and mutilated every living thing it fed upon—not only the heart and spirit of youth, with all the hope and pride and anguish in him, but also the life and body of some obscure worker whose name it did not know, whose death, in its remote impregnability, it would never hear or care about.

I tried to get the fingers of my hate upon that immense and shifting world of shapes and phantoms, but I could not. I could track nothing to its tangible source, trace nothing to some fatal certitude. Words, whispers, laughter, even an ounce of traitorous flesh, all the immense and moving tapestry of that cruel and phantasmal world were all impalpable and hovered above me, the deathless and invincible legend of scorn and defeat.

45

*   *   *

Then, even as I stood there in the street, the blind horror left me with the magic instancy in which it always came and went; all around me people seemed to live and move, and it was noon, and I could see her face the way it was again, and thought that it was the best face in the world, and knew that there was no one like her.

Two men came rapidly back across the street from the dispersing crowd and one of them was talking in a low earnest tone to the other:

"Jeez!" he said. "Dat gul! Did yuh see her? Sure, sure, he almost fell on top of her! . . . Sure, dat's what I'm tellin' yuh! . . . She fainted! . . . Dey had to carry her into a stoeh! . . . Jeez!" he said. In a moment, and in a quietly confidential tone, he added: "Say—dat makes duh fourt' one on dat building—did yuh know dat?"

Then I saw a man beside me with a proud, shrinking, and sensitive face, set in a blind sightless stare that kept looking through people, feeding on something that could not be seen. As I looked, he moved, turned his head slowly, and presently in the dull voice of someone who has had an opiate he said "What? The fourth? The fourth?"—although no one had spoken to him. Then he moved his thin hand slowly, and with an almost meditative gesture over his forehead and eyes, sighed wearily and slowly like someone waking from a trance or some strong drug, and then began to walk ahead uncertainly.

This was the third time I saw death in the city.

Later, the thing I was to remember vividly about these three deaths, in contrast to the fourth one, was this: That, where the first three deaths had come by violence, where almost every circumstance of horror, sudden shock, disgust and terror, was present to convulse the hearts and sicken and wither up the flesh of those who saw death come, the city people, when their first surprise was over, had responded instantly to death, accepting its violence, bloody mutilation, and horror calmly, as one of the natural consequences of daily life. But the fourth time that I saw death come, the city people were stunned, awed, bewildered, and frightened, as they had not been before; and yet the fourth death had come so quietly, easily, and naturally that it seemed as if even a child could have looked at it without terror or surprise.

This is the way it happened:

At the heart and core of the most furious center of the city's life—below Broadway at Times Square— a little after one o'clock in the morning, bewildered, aimless, having no goal or place to which I wished to go, with the old chaos and unrest inside me, I had thrust down the stairs out of the great thronging street, the tidal swarm of atoms who were pressing and hurrying forward in as fierce a haste to be hurled back into their cells again as they had shown when they had rushed out into the streets that evening.

Thus, we streamed down from free night into the tunnel's stale and fetid air again, we swarmed and hurried across the floors of gray cement, we thrust and pushed our way along as furiously as if we ran a race with time, as if some great reward were to be won if only we could save two minutes, or as if we were hastening onward, as fast as we could go, toward some glorious meeting, some happy and fortunate event, some goal of beauty, wealth, or love on whose shining mark our eyes were fastened.

Then, as I put my coin into the slot, and passed on

through the wooden turnstile, I saw the man who was about to die. The place was a space of floor, a width of cement which was yet one flight above the level of the trains, and the man was sitting on a wooden bench which had been placed there to the left, as one went down the incline to the tunnel.

The man just sat there quietly at one end of the bench, leaned over slightly to his right with his elbow resting on the arm of the bench, his hat pulled down a little, and his face half lowered. At this moment, there was a slow, tranquil, hardly perceptible movement of his breath—a flutter, a faint sigh—and the man was dead. In a moment, a policeman who had watched him casually from a distance walked over to the bench, bent down, spoke to him, and then shook him by the shoulder. As he did so, the dead man's body slipped a little, his arm slid over the end of the bench and stayed so, one hand hanging over, his shabby hat jammed down, a little to one side, upon his head, his overcoat open, and his short right leg drawn stiffly back. Even as the policeman shook him by the shoulder, the man's face was turning gray. By this time a few people, out of the crowds that swarmed constantly across the floor, had stopped to look, stared curiously and uneasily, started to go on, and then had come back. Now, a few of them were standing here, just looking, saying nothing, casting uneasy and troubled looks at one another from time to time.

And yet I think that we all knew the man was dead. By this time another policeman had arrived, was talking quietly to the other one, and now he, too, began to look curiously at the dead man, went over and shook him by the shoulder as the other one had done, and then after a few quiet words with his comrade, walked off rapidly. In a minute or two he

came back again and another policeman was with
him. They talked together quietly for a moment.
One of them bent over and searched the man's
pockets, finding a dirty envelope, a wallet, and a
grimy-looking card. After prying into the purse and
taking notes upon their findings they just stood beside the dead man, waiting.

The dead man was a shabby-looking fellow of an
age hard to determine, but he was scarcely under
fifty, and hardly more than fifty-five. And, had one
sought long and far for the true portrait of the
pavement cipher, the composite photograph of the
man-swarm atom, he could have found no better
specimen than this man. His only distinction was
that there was nothing to distinguish him from a
million other men. He had the kind of face that one
sees ten thousand times a day upon the city streets,
and cannot remember later.

This face, which even when alive, it is true, was
of a sallow, sagging, somewhat paunchy and unwholesome hue and texture, was dryly and unmistakably Irish—city Irish—with the mouth thin,
sunken, slightly bowed, and yet touched with something loose and sly, a furtive and corrupt humor.
And the face was also surly, hangdog, petulant, and
servile—the face of one of those little men—a doorman at a theatre, a janitor in a shabby warehouse,
office building, or cheap apartment house, the father-in-law of a policeman, the fifth cousin of a desk
sergeant, the uncle of a ward heeler's wife, a pensioned door opener, office guarder, messenger, or
question evader for some Irish politician, schooled
to vote dutifully for "the boys" upon election day,
and to be flung his little scrap of patronage for service rendered and silence kept, apt at servility,
fawning, cringing to those sealed with the mark of

49

privilege and favor, and apt at snarling, snapping, gratuitous and impudent discourtesy to those who had no power, no privilege, no special mark of favor or advancement to enlarge them in his sight. Such was indubitably the man who now sat dead upon the subway bench.

And that man's name was legion, his number myriad. On his gray face, on his dead sunken mouth, the ghost of his still recent life and speech sat incredibly, until it seemed we heard him speak, listened to the familiar tones of his voice again, knew every act and quality of his life, as certainly as if he were yet alive, as he snarled at one man: "I can't help dat, I don't know nuttin' about dat, misteh. All I know is dat I got my ordehs, an' my ordehs is to keep everyone out unless dey can prove dey've gotta date wit' Misteh Grogan. How do *I* know who you are? How can *I* tell what yoeh business is? What's dat got to do wit' me? No, seh! Unless you can prove you gotta date wit' Misteh Grogan, I can't let yuh in. . . . Dat may be true . . . and den again it may not be. . . . Wat t' hell am *I* supposed t' be? A mind readeh, or somp'n? . . . No, misteh! Yuh can't come in! . . . I got my ordehs an' dat's all I know."

And yet, the next moment, this same voice could whine, with a protesting servility, its aggrieved apology to the same man, or to another one: "W'y didn't yuh say yuh was a friend of Misteh Grogan's? . . .W'y didn't yuh tell me befoeh you was his brudder-in-law? . . . If yuh'd told me dat, I'd 'a' let yuh by in a minute. *You* know how it is," here the voice would drop to cringing confidence, "so many guys come in here every day an' try to bust dere way right in to Misteh Grogan's office when dey got no bizness dere. . . . Dat's duh reason dat I gotta be kehful. . . . But now dat I know dat you're **OK** wit' Misteh Grogan," it would say fawningly, "you can go on in any time yuh like. Anyone dat's **OK** wit' Misteh Grogan is *all right*," that voice would say with crawling courtesy. "*You* know how it is," it whispered, rubbing sly, unwholesome fingers on one's sleeve, "I didn't mean nuttin'—but a guy in my position has gotta be kehful."

Yes, that was the voice, that was the man, as certainly as if that dead mouth had just moved, that dead tongue stirred and spoken to us its language. There he was, still with the sallow hue of all his life upon his face, as it faded visibly, terribly before us to the gray of death. Poor, shabby, servile, fawning, snarling, and corrupted cipher, poor, meager, cringing, contriving, cunning, drearily hopeful, and dutifully subservient little atom of the million-footed city. Poor, dismal, ugly, sterile, shabby little man— with your little scrabble of harsh oaths, and cries, and stale constricted words, your pitiful little designs and feeble purposes, with your ounce of brain, your thimbleful of courage, the huge cargo of your dull and ugly superstitions. Oh, you wretched little thing of dough and tallow, you eater of poor foods and drinker of vile liquors. Joy, glory, and magnificence were here for you upon this earth, but you scrabbled along the pavements rattling a few stale words like gravel in your throat, and would have none of them, because the smell of the boss, the word of the priest, the little spare approvals of Mike, Mary, Molly, Kate, and Pat were not upon them— and tonight the stars shine, great ships are blowing from the harbor's mouth, and a million more of your own proper kind and quality go stamping on above your head, while you sit here *dead* in your gray tunnel!

We look at your dead face with awe, with pity, and

with terror, because we know that you are shaped from our own clay and quality. Something of us all, the high, the low, the base, and the heroic, the rare, the common, and the glorious lies dead here in the heart of the unceasing city, and the destiny of all men living, yes, of the kings of the earth, the princes of the mind, the mightiest lords of language, and the deathless imaginers of verse, all the hope, hunger, and the earth-consuming thirst that can incredibly be held in the small prison of a skull, and that can rack and rend the little tenement in which it is confined, is written here upon this shabby image of corrupted clay.

The dead man was wearing nondescript clothing, and here again, in these dingy garments, the whole quality, the whole station of his life was evident, as if the clothes he wore had had a tongue, a character, and a language of their own. They said that the man had known poverty and a shabby security all his life, that his life had been many degrees above the moment-by-moment desperation of the vagabond and pauper, and many degrees below any real security, substance, or repose. His garments said that he had lived from month to month rather than from day to day, always menaced by the fear of some catastrophe—sickness, the loss of his job, the coming on of age—that would have dealt a ruinous blow to the slender resources which he had built between him and the world, never free from the fear of these calamities, but always just escaping them.

He wore an unpressed baggy gray suit which he filled out pretty well, and which had taken on the whole sagging, paunchy, and unshapely character of his own body. He had a small potbelly, a middling fleshiness and fullness which showed he had known

52

some abundance in his life, and had not suffered much from hunger. He was wearing a dingy old brown felt hat, a shabby gray overcoat, and a ragged red scarf—and in all these garments there was a quality of use and wear and shabbiness that was inimitable and that the greatest costume artist in the world could never have duplicated by intent.

The lives of millions of people were written in these garments. In their sag and hang and worn dingy textures, the shabby lives of millions of pavement ciphers were revealed, and this character was so strong and legible that as the dead man sat there and his face took on the corpsen gray of death, his body seemed to shrink, to dwindle, to withdraw visibly before our eyes out of its last relationship with life, and the clothes themselves took on a quality and character that were far more living than the shape they covered.

And now the dead man's face had grown ghastly with the strange real unreality of death that has such terrible irony in it, for, as one looks, the face and figure of the dead seem to have no more of the substance of mortal flesh than a waxen figure in a museum, and to smile, to mock, to stare, to mimic life in the same ghastly and unreal manner that a waxen figure would.

The turnstiles kept clicking with their dull wooden note, the hurrying people kept swarming past over the gray cement floor, the trains kept roaring in and out of the station below with a savage grinding vibrance, and from time to time, out of these swarming throngs, someone would pause, stare curiously for a moment, and stay. By this time, a considerable number of people had gathered in a wide circle about the bench on which the dead man sat, and curiously, although they would not go away, they did not press in, or try to thrust their way up close, as people do when some violent, bloody, or fatal accident has occurred.

Instead, they just stood there in that wide semicircle, never intruding farther, looking at one another in an uneasy and bewildered manner, asking each other questions in a low voice from time to time which, for the most part, went unanswered since the person asked would squirm, look at his questioner uneasily and with wavering eyes, and then, muttering "I don't know," with a slight gesture of his arms and shoulders, would sidle or shuffle away. And from time to time the policemen, whose number by this time had grown to four, and who just stood around the man's body with a waiting and passive vacancy, would suddenly start, curiously and almost comically, into violent activity, and would come thrusting and shoving at the ring of people, pushing them back and saying in angry and impatient voices: "All right, now! Break it up! Break it up! Break it up! Go on! Go on! Go on! Yuh're blockin' up duh passageway! Go on! Go on! Break it up, now! Break it up!"

And the crowd obediently would give ground, withdraw, shuffle around, and then with the invincible resiliency of a rope of rubber or a ball of mercury would return, coming back once more into their staring, troubled, uneasily whispering circle.

Meanwhile, the wooden stiles kept clicking with their dull, dead, somewhat thunderous note, the people kept thronging past to get their trains, and in their glances, attitudes, and gestures when they saw the ring of staring people and the man upon the bench, there was evident all of the responses which it is possible for men to have when they see death.

Some people would come by, pause, stare at the

man, and then begin to whisper to one another in low uneasy tones: "What's wrong with him? Is he sick? Did he faint? Is he drunk—or something?" to which a man might answer, looking intently for a moment at the dead man's face, and then crying out heartily, with a hard derisive movement of his hand, and yet with something troubled and uncertain in his voice: "Nah! He's not sick. Duh guy is drunk! Dat's all it is. Sure! He's just passed out. . . . Look at dem all standin' dere, lookin' at duh guy!" he jeered. "Yuh'd t'ink dey neveh saw a drunk befoeh. Come on!" he cried. "Let's go!" And they would hurry on, while the man mocked at the crowd with hard derisive laughter.

And indeed, the dead man's posture and appearance as he sat there on the bench with his shabby old hat pushed forward over his head, one leg drawn stiffly back, his right hand hanging over the edge of the bench, and his thin, sunken Irish mouth touched by a faint, loose, rather drunken smile, was so much like the appearance of a man in a drunken stupor that many people, as soon as they saw his gray ghastly face, would cry out with a kind of desperate relief in their voices: "Oh! He's only drunk. Come on! Come on! Let's go!"—and would hurry on, knowing in their hearts the man was dead.

Others would come by, see the dead man, start angrily, and then look at the crowd furiously, frowning, shaking their head in a movement of strong deprecation and disgust, and muttering under their breath before they went on, as if somehow the crowd were guilty of some indecent and disorderly act which their own decent and orderly souls abhorred.

Three little Jewesses and a young Jewish boy had come in together, and pressed up in a group into the circle of the crowd. For a moment the girls stood there, staring, frightened, huddled in a group, while the boy looked in a rather stupid and bewildered manner at the dead man, finally saying nervously in a high stunned tone of voice: "What's wrong wit' him? Have dey called duh ambulance yet?"

No one in the ring of silent people answered him, but in a moment a taxi driver, a man with a brutal heavy nighttime face, a swarthy, sallow, pitted skin, black hair and eyes, a cap, a leather jacket, and a shirt of thick black wool—this man turned and, jerking his head contemptuously toward the boy without looking at him, began to address the people around him in a jeering and derisive tone:

"Duh *ambulance!*" he cried. "Duh *ambulance!* Wat t' hell's duh use of duh *ambulance!* Jesus! Duh guy's dead an' he wants t' know if anyone has called duh ambulance!" he cried, jerking his head contemptuously toward the boy again, and evidently getting some kind of security and assurance from his own jeering and derisive words. "Jesus!" he snorted. "Duh guy's dead an' he wants to know w'y someone don't call duh ambulance!" And he went off snorting and sneering by himself, saying "Jesus!" and shaking his head, as if the stupidity and folly of people were past his powers of understanding or consent.

The boy kept staring at the dead man on the bench with a fascinated eye of horror and disbelief. Presently he moistened his dry lips with his tongue, and spoke nervously and dully in a bewildered tone:

"I don't see him breathe or nuttin'," he said. "He don't move or nuttin'."

Then the girl beside him, who had been holding

to his arm all this time, and who was a little Jewess
with red hair, thin meager features, and an enormous nose that seemed to overshadow her whole
face, now plucked nervously and almost frantically
at the boy's sleeve, as she whispered:

"Oh! Let's go! Let's get away from heah! . . .
Gee! I'm shakin' all oveh! Gee! I'm tremblin'—
look!" she whispered, holding up her hand which
was trembling visibly. "Let's go!"

"I don't see him breathe or nuttin'," the boy muttered dully, staring.

"Gee! Let's go!" the girl whispered pleadingly
again. "Gee! I'm so noivous I'm tremblin' like a
leaf—I'm shakin' all oveh! Come on!" she whispered. "Come on! Let's go!" And all four of them,
the three frightened girls and the stunned bewil-
dered-looking boy, hurried away in a huddled
group, and went down the incline into the tunnel.

And now the other people who up to this time had
only stood, looked uneasily at one another, and
asked perplexed and troubled questions which no
one answered, began to talk quietly and whisper
among themselves, and one caught the sound of the
word "dead" several times. Having spoken and
heard this word, all the people grew very quiet and
still, and turned their heads slowly toward the figure of the dead man on the bench, and began to
stare at him with a glance full of curiosity, fascination, and a terrible feeding hunger.

At this moment a man's voice was heard speaking
quietly, and with an assurance and certainty which
seemed to say for everyone what they had been un-
able to say for themselves.

"Sure, he's dead. The man's dead." The quiet and
certain voice continued. "I knew all the time that he
was dead."

57

And at the same time a big soldier, who had the seamed and weathered face of a man who has spent years of service in the army, turned and spoke with a quiet and familiar assurance to a little dish-faced Irishman who was standing at his side.

"No matter where they kick off," he said, "they always leave that little black mark behind them, don't they?" His voice was quiet, hard, and casual as he spoke these words, and at the same time he nodded toward a small wet stain upon the cement near the dead man's foot where it had been drawn stiffly back.

The little dish-faced Irishman nodded as soon as the soldier had spoken, and with an air of conviction and agreement, said vigorously:

"You said it!"

At this moment, there was a shuffling commotion, a disturbance in the crowd near the gate beside the turnstiles, the people pressed back respectfully on two sides, and the ambulance doctor entered followed by two attendants, one of whom was bearing a rolled stretcher.

The ambulance surgeon was a young Jew with full lips, a somewhat receding chin, a little silky moustache, and a rather bored, arrogant and indifferent look upon his face. He had on a blue jacket, a flat blue cap with a visor which was pushed back on his head, and even as he entered and came walking slowly and indifferently across the cement floor, he had the tubes of the stethoscope fastened in his ears and was holding the end part in his hand. The two attendants followed him.

About every movement which the ambulance doctor made there was an air of habit, boredom, even weariness, as if he had been summoned too

58

many times on errands such as this to feel any emotion. As he approached the policemen, they separated and opened up a path for him. Without speaking to them he walked over to the dead man, unbuttoned his shirt and pulled it open, bent, and then began to use the stethoscope, listening carefully and intently for some seconds, then moving it to another place upon the dead man's tallowy, hairless, and ghastly looking breast, and listening carefully again.

During all this time his face showed no emotion whatever of surprise, regret, or discovery. Undoubtedly, the doctor had known the man was dead the moment that he looked at him, and his duties now were only a part of that formality which law and custom demanded. But the people during all this time surged forward a little, with their gaze riveted on the doctor's face with awe, respect, and fascinated interest as if they hoped to read there the confirmation of what they already knew themselves, or as if they expected to see there a look of developing horror, pity, or regret which would put the final stamp of conviction on their own knowledge. But they saw nothing in the doctor's face but deliberation, dutiful intentness, and a look almost of weariness and boredom.

When he had finished with the stethoscope, he got up, took it out of his ears, and then casually opened the half-shut eyelids of the dead man for a moment. The dead eyes stared with a ghastly bluish glitter. The doctor turned and spoke a few words quietly to the police who were standing around him with their notebooks open, with the same air of patience, custom, and indifference, and for a moment they wrote dutifully in their little books. One of them asked him a question and wrote down what he said, and then the doctor was on his way out again, walking slowly and indifferently away, followed by his two attendants, neither of whom showed any curiosity or surprise. The dead man, in fact, seemed to be under the control of a régime which worked with a merciless precision, which could not be escaped or altered by a jot, and whose operations all of its servants—doctors, stretcher-bearers, policemen, and even the priests of the church—knew with a weary and unarguable finality.

The police, having written in their books and put the books away, turned and came striding toward the crowd again, thrusting and pushing them back, and shouting, as they had before: "Go on! Go on! Break it up, now! Break it up!"—but even in the way they did this, there was this same movement of régime and custom, a sense of weariness and indifference, and when the people surged back into their former positions with maddening mercurial resiliency, the police said nothing and showed no anger or impatience. They took up their station around the dead man again, and waited stolidly, until the next move in their unalterable program should occur.

And now the people, as if the barriers of silence, restraint, and timidity had been broken, and the confusion and doubt in their own spirits dispersed by a final acknowledgment, and the plain sound of the word "death," which had at last been spoken openly, began to talk to one another easily and naturally as if they had been friends or familiar associates for many years.

A little to one side, and behind the outer ring of the crowd, three sleek creatures of the night and of the great street which roared on above our heads—a young smooth Broadwayite wearing a jaunty gray hat and a light spring overcoat of gray, cut inward toward the waist, an assertive and knowing-looking Jew, with a large nose, an aggressive voice, and a vulturesque smile, and an Italian, smaller, with a vulpine face, a ghastly yellow nighttime skin, glittering black eyes and hair—all three smartly dressed and overcoated in the flashy Broadway manner—now gathered together as if they recognized in one another men of substance, worldliness, and knowledge. They began to philosophize in a superbly knowing manner, bestowing on life, death, the brevity of man's days, and the futility of man's hopes and aspirations, the ripe fruit of their experience. The Jew was dominantly the center of this little group, and did most of the talking. In fact, the other two served mainly as a chorus to his harangue, punctuating it whenever he paused to draw breath with vigorous nods of agreement, and such remarks as "You said it!" "And I don't mean maybe!" or "Like I was sayin' to a guy duh otheh day—" an observation which was never completed, as the philosopher would be wound up and on his way again:

"And they ask us, f'r Christ's sake, to save for the future!" he cried, at the same time laughing with jeering and derisive contempt. "For the future!" Here he paused to laugh scornfully again. "When you see a guy like that you ask what for? Am I right?"

"You said it!" said the Italian, nodding his head with energetic assent.

"Like I was sayin' to a guy duh otheh day"—the other younger man began.

"Christ!" cried the Jew. "Save for the *future*! W'y the hell should *I* save for the future?" he demanded in a dominant and aggressive tone, tapping himself on the breast belligerently, glancing around as if someone had just tried to ram this vile proposal

61

down his throat. "What's it goin' to getcha? You may be dead tomorrow! What the hell's the use in saving, f'r Christ's sake! We're only here for a little while. Let's make the most of it, f'r Christ's sake!— Am I right?" he demanded pugnaciously, looking around, and the others dutifully agreed that he was.

"Like I was sayin' to a guy duh otheh day," the young man said, "it only goes to show dat yuh——"

"Insurance!" the Jew cried at this point, with a loud scornful laugh. "The insurance companies, f'r Christ's sake! W'y the hell should anyone spend their dough on insurance?" he demanded.

"Nah, nah, nah," the Italian agreed gutturally, with a smile of vulpine scorn, "dat's all a lotta crap."

"A lotta boloney," the young man said, "like I was sayin' to a guy duh otheh——"

"Insurance!" said the Jew. "W'y to listen to *those* bastuds talk you'd think a guy was gonna live forever! Save for the future, f'r Christ's sake," he snarled. "Put something by f'r your old age—your *old* age, f'r Christ's sake," he jeered, "when you may get what this guy got at any minute! Am I right?"

"You said it!"

"Put something by for a rainy day! Leave something for your children when you kick off!" he sneered. "W'y the hell should *I* leave anything for *my* children, f'r Christ's sake?" he snarled, as if the whole pressure of organized society and the demands of fifteen of his progeny had been brought to bear on him at this point. "No, sir!" he said. "Let my children look out for themselves the way *I* done!" he said. "Nobody ever did anything f'r me!" he said. "W'y the hell should *I* spend *my* life puttin' away jack for a lot of bastuds to spend who wouldn't appreciate it, noway! Am I right?"

"You said it!" said the Italian nodding. "It's all a lotta crap!"

"Like I was sayin' to dis guy—" the young man said.

"No, sir," said the Jew in a hard positive tone, and with a smile of bitter cynicism. "No, sir, misteh! Not for me! When I kick off and they all gatheh around the big cawfin," he continued with a descriptive gesture, "I want them *all* to take a good long look," he said. "I want them all to take a good long look at me and say: 'Well, he didn't bring nothing with him when he came, and he's not taking anything with him when he goes—but *there* was a guy,'" the Jew said loudly, and in an impressive tone, "'there was a guy who spent it when he had it—and *who didn't miss a thing!*'" Here he paused a moment, grasped the lapels of his smart overcoat with both hands, and rocked gently back and forth from heel to toe, as he smiled a bitter and knowing smile.

"Yes, sir!" he said presently in a tone of hard assurance.

"Yes, sir! When I'm out there in that graveyahd pushin' daisies, I don't want no bokays! I want to get what's comin' to me here and now! Am I right?"

"You said it!" the Italian answered.

"Like I was sayin' to a guy duh otheh day," the young man now concluded with an air of triumph, "yuh neveh can tell. No, sir! Yuh neveh can tell what's goin' t' happen. You're here one day an' gone duh next—so wat t' hell!" he said. "Let's make duh most of it."

And they all agreed that he was right, and began to search the dead man's face again with their dark, rapt, fascinated stare.

Elsewhere now, people were gathering into little groups, beginning to talk, to discuss, debate, philosophize, even to smile and laugh, in an earnest and animated way. One man was describing his experience to a little group that pressed around him eagerly, telling again and again, with unwearied repetition, the story of what he had seen, felt, thought and done when he first saw the dead man.

"Sure! Sure!" he cried. "Dat's what I'm tellin' yuh. I seen him when he passed out. I was standin' not ten feet away from 'im! Sure! I watched 'im when he stahted gaspin' t' get his bret'. I was standin' dere. Dat's what I'm sayin'. I tu'ns to duh cop an' says, 'Yuh'd betteh look afteh dat guy,' I says. 'Deh's somet'ing wrong wit' 'im,' I says. Sure! Dat's when it happened. Dat's what I'm tellin' yuh. I was standin' dere," he cried.

Meanwhile, two men and two women had come in and stopped. They all had the thick clumsy figures, the dull-red smouldering complexions, the thick taffy-colored hair, bleared eyes, and broad, blunted, smeared features of the Slavic races—of Lithuanians or Czechs—and for a while they stared stupidly and brutally at the figure of the dead man, and then began to talk rapidly among themselves in coarse thick tones, and a strange tongue.

And now, some of the people began to drift away, the throng of people swarming homeward across the cement floor had dwindled noticeably, and the circle of people around the dead man had thinned out, leaving only those who would stay like flesh flies feeding on carrion, until the body was removed.

A young Negro prostitute came through the gate and walked across the floor, glancing about her quickly with every step she took, and smiling a hideous empty smile with her thin encarmined lips.

When she saw the circle of men she walked over to it and after one vacant look toward the bench where the dead man sat, she began to glance swiftly about her from right to left, displaying white, shining, fragile-looking teeth.

The thin face of the young Negress, which was originally of a light coppery color, had been so smeared over with rouge and powder that it was now a horrible, dusky yellow-and-purplish hue, her black eyelashes were coated with some greasy substance which made them stick out around her large dark eyes in stiff oily spines, and her black hair had been waved and was also coated with this grease.

She was dressed in a purple dress, wore extremely high heels which were colored red, and had the wide hips and the long thin ugly legs of the Negress. There was something at once horrible and seductive in her figure, in her thin stringy lower legs, her wide hips, her mongrel color, her meager empty little whore's face, her thin encarmined lips, and her thin shining frontal teeth, as if the last atom of intelligence in her bird twitter of a brain had been fed into the ravenous maw of a diseased and insatiable sensuality, leaving her with nothing but this thin varnished shell of face, and the idiot and sensual horror of her smile which went brightly and impudently back and forth around the ring of waiting men.

The Italian with the vulpine face, whose former companions, the Jew and the sleek young Broadwayite, had now departed, sidled stealthily over toward the Negress until he stood behind her. Then he eased up on her gently, his glittering eye feeding on her all the time in a reptilian stare, until his body was pressed closely against her buttocks, and his breath was hot upon her neck. The Negress said

65

nothing but looked swiftly around at him with her bright smile of idiot and sensual vacancy, and in a moment started off rapidly, stepping along on her high red heels and long stringy legs, and looking back swiftly toward the Italian, flashing her painted lips and shining teeth at him in a series of seductive invitations to pursuit. The man craned his neck stealthily at the edges of his collar, looked furtively around with glittering eyes and vulpine face, and then started off rapidly after the girl. He caught up with her in the corridor beyond the stiles and they went on together.

The stiles still turned with their blunt, dull, wooden note, belated travellers came by with a lean shuffle of steps upon the cement floors, in the newsstand the dealer sold his wares, giving only an occasional and wearily indifferent glance at the dead man and the people, and in the cleared space round the bench the police were standing, waiting, with a stolid and impassive calm. A man had come in, walked across the space and was now talking to one of the police. The policeman was a young man with a solid strong-necked face that was full of dark color. He talked quietly out of the side of his mouth to the man who questioned him, and who was taking notes in a small black book. The man had a flabby yellowish face, weary eyes, and a flabby roll of flesh beneath his chin.

The people who remained, having greedily sucked the last drop of nourishment from conversation, now stood silent, staring insatiably at the dead man with a quality of vision that had a dark, feeding, glutinous and almost physical property, and that seemed to be stuck upon the thing they watched.

By this time an astonishing thing had happened. Just as the dead man's figure had appeared to shrink and contract visibly within its garments, as if before our eyes the body were withdrawing out of a life with which it had no further relationships, so now did all the other properties of space and light, the dimensions of width, length, and distance that surrounded him undergo an incredible change.

And it seemed to me that this change in the dimensions of space was occurring visibly and momently under my eyes, and that just as the man's body seemed to dwindle and recede so did the gray cement space around him grow tremendously. The space that separated him from the place where the police stood, and the gray space which separated us from the police, together with the distance of the tiled subway wall behind, all grew taller, wider, longer, enlarged themselves terrifically while I looked. It was as if we were all looking at the man across an immense and lonely distance. The dead man looked like a lonely little figure upon an enormous stage, and by his very littleness and loneliness in that immense gray space, he seemed to gain an awful dignity and grandeur.

And now, as it seemed to me, just as the living livid gray-faced dead men of the night were feeding on him with their dark and insatiate stare, so did he return their glance with a deathless and impassive irony, with a terrible mockery and scorn, which were as living as their own dark look, and would endure forever.

Then, as suddenly as it had come, that distorted vision was gone, all shapes and things and distances swam back once more into their proper focus. I could see the dead man sitting there in the gray space, and the people as they looked and were. And the police were driving forward again and thrusting at the people all about me.

But they could not bear to leave that little lonely

image of proud death, that sat there stiffly with its grotesque, drunken dignity, its thin smile—as men are loyal to a lifeless shape, and guard and watch and will not leave it till the blind earth takes and covers it again. And they would not leave it now because proud death, dark death, the lonely dignity of proud dark death sat grandly there upon man's shabby image, and because they saw that nothing common, mean, or shabby on earth, nor all the fury, size, and number of the million-footed city could alter for an instant the immortal dignities of death, proud death, even when it rested on the poorest cipher in the streets.

Therefore they would not leave it from a kind of love and loyalty they bore it now; and because proud death was sitting grandly there and had spoken to them, and had stripped them down into their nakedness; and because they had built great towers against proud death, and had hidden from him in gray tunnels, and had tried to still his voice with all the brutal stupefactions of the street, but proud death, dark death, proud brother death, was striding in their city now, and he was taller than their tallest towers, and triumphant even when he touched a shabby atom of base clay, and all their streets were silent when he spoke.

Therefore they looked at him with awe, with terror and humility, and with love, for death, proud death, had come into their common and familiar places, and his face had shone terribly in gray tainted air, and he had matched his tongue, his stride, his dignities against the weary and brutal custom of ten million men, and he had stripped them down at length, and stopped their strident and derisive tongues, and in the image of their poorest fellow had shown them all the way that they must

go, the awe and terror that would clothe them—and
because of this they stood before him lonely, silent,
and afraid.

Then, the last rituals of the law and church were
observed, and the dead man was taken from their
sight. The dead wagon of the police had come. Two
men in uniform came swiftly down the stairs and
entered carrying a rolled stretcher. The stretcher
was rolled out upon the cement floor, swiftly the
dead man was lifted from the bench and laid down
on the stretcher, and at the same moment, a priest
stepped from the crowd, and knelt there on the floor
beside the body.

He was a young man, plump, well kept, and very
white, save for his garments, pork-faced, worldly,
and unpriestly, and on his full white jaws was the
black shaved smudge of a heavy beard. He wore a
fine black overcoat with a velvet collar, and had on a
scarf of fine white silk, and a derby hat, which he removed carefully and put aside when he knelt down.
His hair was very black, fine-spun as silk, and getting thin on top. He knelt swiftly beside the dead
man on the stretcher, raised a white, hairy hand, and
as he did so, the five policemen straightened suddenly, whipped off their visored hats with a military
movement, and stood rigidly for a moment, with
their hats upon their hearts as the priest spoke a few
swift words above the body, which no one could
hear. In a moment a few of the people in the crowd
also took off their hats awkwardly, and presently the
priest got up, put on his derby hat carefully, ad-
justed his coat and scarf, and stepped back into the
crowd again. It was all over in a minute, done with
the same inhuman and almost weary formality that
the ambulance doctor had shown.

Then the two uniformed stretcher men bent   **69**

down, took the handles of the stretcher, and, speaking in low voices to each other, lifted it. They started off at a careful step, but as they did so, the dead man's gray-tallow hands flapped out across the edges of the stretcher, and began to jog and jiggle in a grotesque manner with every step the stretcher-bearers took.

One of the men spoke sharply to another, saying, "Wait a minute! Put it down! Someone get his hands!"

The stretcher was laid down upon the floor again, a policeman knelt down beside the body and quickly stripped the dead man's necktie from his collar, which had been opened by the doctor and now gaped wide, showing a brass collar button in the neckband of the shirt, and the round greenish discoloration of the brass collar button in the dead yellowed tissues of the neck. The policeman took the dead man's necktie, which was a soiled, striped, and stringy thing of red and white, and quickly tied it in a knot around the dead man's wrists in order to keep his hands from jerking.

Then the stretcher-bearers lifted him again, and started off, the police striding before them toward the gateway, thrusting the people back, and crying:

"Get back, there! Get back! Make way! Make way! Make way!"

The dead man's hands were silent now, tied together across his stomach, but his shabby old garments trembled, and his gray-yellow cheek flanks quivered gently with every step the stretcher-bearers took. The gaping collar ends flapped stiffly as they walked and his soiled white shirt was partially unbuttoned revealing a dead, bony, tallowy-yellow patch of breast beneath, and his battered old

brown hat was now pushed down so far over his face

that it rested on his nose, and, together with the thin sunken smile of his mouth, intensified the grotesque and horrible appearance of drunkenness.

As for the rest of him—the decaying substance that had been his body—this seemed to have shrunk and dwindled away almost to nothing. One was no longer conscious of its existence. It seemed lost, subsided to nothing and indistinguishable in a pile of shabby old garments—an old gray overcoat, baggy old trousers, an old hat, a pair of scuffed and battered shoes. This in fact was all he now seemed to be: a hat, a thin grotesquely drunken smile, two trembling cheek flanks, two flapping collar ends, two gray-grimy claws tied with a stringy necktie, and a shabby heap of worn, dingy, and nondescript garments that moved and oscillated gently with every step the stretcher-bearers took.

The stretcher men moved carefully yet swiftly through the gate and up the stairs of an obscure side opening which was marked "Exit." As they started up the grimy iron steps, the body sloped back a little heavily and the old brown hat fell off, revealing the dead man's thin, disordered, and gray-grimy hair. One of the policemen picked up the hat, saying to one of the stretcher-bearers, "OK, John, I've got it!" then followed him upstairs.

It was now early morning, about half-past three o'clock, with a sky full of blazing and delicate stars, an immense and lilac darkness, a night still cool, and full of chill, but with all the lonely and jubilant exultancy of spring in it. Far-off, half heard, immensely mournful, wild with joy and sorrow, there was a ship lowing in the darkness, a great boat blowing at the harbor's mouth.

The street looked dark, tranquil, almost de-

serted—as quiet as it could ever be, and at that brief
hour when all its furious noise and movement of the
day seemed stilled for a moment's breathing space,
and yet preparing for another day. The taxis drilled
past emptily, sparely, and at intervals, like projectiles, the feet of people made a lean and picketing
noise upon the pavements, the lights burned green
and red and yellow with a small hard lonely radiance that somehow filled the heart with strong joy
and victory, and belonged to the wild exultancy of
the night, the ships, the springtime, and of April. A
few blocks farther up the street where the great
shine and glitter of the night had burned immensely
like a huge censer steaming always with a dusty,
pollenated, immensely brilliant light, that obscene
wink had now gone dull, and shone brownly, still
livid but subdued.

When the stretcher men emerged from the subway exit, the green dead wagon of the police was
waiting at the curb, and a few taxi drivers with dark
dingy faces had gathered on the sidewalk near the
door. As the stretcher men moved across the pavement with their burden, one of the taximen stepped
after them, lifted his cap obsequiously to the dead
man, saying eagerly:

"Taxi, sir! Taxi!"

One of the policemen, who was carrying the dead
man's hat, stopped suddenly, turned around laughing, and lifted his club with jocular menace, saying
to the taximan:

"You son-of-a-bitch! Go on!"

Then, still laughing, saying "Jesus!" he tossed the
dead man's hat into the green wagon, into which the
stretcher men had already shoved the body. One of
the stretcher men closed the doors, went around to

the driver's seat where the other was already sitting,

took out a cigarette and lit it between a hard cupped palm and a twisted mouth, climbed up beside the driver saying "OK, John," and the wagon drove off swiftly. The police looked after it as it drove off. Then they all talked together for a moment more, laughed a little, spoke quietly of the plans, pleasures, and duties of the future, said good night all around, and walked off, two up the street toward the dull brown-livid smoulder of the lights, and three down the street, where it was darker, quieter, more deserted, and where the lights would shift and burn green, yellow, red.

The jesting taximan who had offered his services to the dead man on the stretcher turned briskly to his fellows with an air of something ended, saying sharply and jocosely:

"Well, whattya say, boy! Whattya say!"—at the same time sparring sharply and swiftly at one of the other drivers with his open hands. Then the taxi drivers walked away toward their lines of shining, silent machines, jesting, debating, denying, laughing in their strident and derisive voices.

And again, I looked and saw the deathless sky, the huge starred visage of the night, and heard the boats then on the river. And instantly an enormous sanity and hope of strong exultant joy surged up in me again; and like a man who knows he is mad with thirst, yet sees real rivers at the desert's edge, I knew I should not die and strangle like a mad dog in the tunnel's dark. I knew I should see light once more and know new coasts and come into strange harbors, and see again, as I had once, new lands and morning.

* * *

73

Therefore, immortal fellowship, proud Death, stern Loneliness, and Sleep, dear friends, in whose communion I shall live forever, out of the passion and the substance of my life, I have made this praise for you:

To you, proud Death, who sit so grandly on the brows of little men—first to you! Proud Death, proud Death, whom I have seen by darkness, at so many times, and always when you came to nameless men, what have you ever touched that you have not touched with love and pity, Death? Proud Death, wherever we have seen your face, you came with mercy, love, and pity, Death, and brought to all of us your compassionate sentences of pardon and release. For have you not retrieved from exile the desperate lives of men who never found their home? Have you not opened your dark door for us who never yet found doors to enter, and given us a room who, roomless, doorless, unassuaged, were driven on forever through the streets of life? Have you not offered us your stern provender, Death, with which to stay the hunger that grew to madness from the food it fed upon, and given all of us the goal for which we sought but never found, the certitude, the peace, for which our overladen hearts contended, and made for us, in your dark house, an end of all the tortured wandering and unrest that lashed us on forever? Proud Death, proud Death, not for the glory that you added to the glory of the king, proud Death, nor for the honor you imposed upon the dignities of famous men, proud Death, nor for the final magic you have given to the lips of genius, Death, but because you come so gloriously to us who never yet knew glory, so proudly and sublimely to us whose lives were nameless and obscure, because you give to all of us—the nameless, faceless, voiceless atoms of the earth—the awful chrysm of your grandeur, Death, because I have seen and known you so well, and have lived alone so long with Loneliness, your brother, I do not fear you any longer, friend, and I have made this praise for you.

Now, Loneliness forever and the earth again! Dark brother and stern friend, immortal face of darkness and of night, with whom the half-part of my life was spent, and with whom I shall abide now till my death forever, what is there for me to fear as long as you are with me? Heroic friend, blood brother of proud Death, dark face, have we not gone together down a million streets, have we not coursed together the great and furious avenues of night, have we not crossed the stormy seas alone, and known strange lands, and come again to walk the continent of night, and listen to the silence of the earth? Have we not been brave and glorious when we were together, friend, have we not known triumph, joy, and glory on this earth—and will it not be again with me as it was then, if you come back to me? Come to me, brother, in the watches of the night, come to me in the secret and most silent heart of darkness, come to me as you always came, bringing to me once more the old invincible strength, the deathless hope, the triumphant joy and confidence that will storm the ramparts of the earth again.

Come to me through the fields of night, dear friend, come to me with the horses of your sister, Sleep, and we shall listen to the silence of the earth and darkness once again, we shall listen to the heartbeats of the sleeping men, as with soft and rushing thunder of their hooves the strange dark horses of great Sleep come on again.

They come! Ships call! The hooves of night, the

horses of great Sleep, are coming on below their manes of darkness. And forever the rivers run. Deep as the tides of Sleep the rivers run. We call!

They come: My great dark horses come! With soft and rushing thunder of their hooves they come, and the horses of Sleep are galloping, galloping over the land.

Oh, softly, softly the great dark horses of Sleep are galloping over the land. The great black bats are flying over us. The tides of Sleep are moving through the nation; beneath the tides of Sleep and time strange fish are moving.

For Sleep has crossed the worn visages of day, and in the nighttime, in the dark, in all the sleeping silence of the towns, the faces of ten million men are strange and dark as time. In Sleep we lie all naked and alone, in Sleep we are united at the heart of night and darkness, and we are strange and beautiful asleep; for we are dying in the darkness, and we know no death, there is no death, there is no life, no joy, no sorrow and no glory on the earth but Sleep.

Come, mild and magnificent Sleep, and let your tides flow through the nation. Oh, daughter of unmemoried desire, sister of Death, and my stern comrade, Loneliness, bringer of peace and dark forgetfulness, healer and redeemer, dear enchantress, hear us: come to us through the fields of night, over the plains and rivers of the everlasting earth, bringing to the huge vexed substance of this world and to all the fury, pain, and madness of our lives the merciful anodyne of your redemption. Seal up the porches of our memory, tenderly, gently, steal our lives away from us, blot out the vision of lost love, lost days, and all our ancient hungers; great Transformer, heal us!

Oh, softly, softly, the great dark horses of Sleep are galloping over the land. The tides of Sleep are moving in the hearts of men, they flow like rivers in the night, they flow with glut and fullness of their dark unfathomed strength into a million pockets of the land and over the shores of the whole earth. They flow with the full might of their advancing and inexorable flood across the continent of night, across the breadth and sweep of the immortal earth, until the hearts of all men living are relieved of their harsh weight, the souls of all men who have ever drawn in the breath of anguish and of labor are healed, assuaged, and conquered by the vast enchantments of dark, silent, all-engulfing Sleep.

Sleep falls like silence on the earth, it fills the hearts of ninety million men, it moves like magic in the mountains, and walks like night and darkness across the plains and rivers of the earth, until low upon lowlands, and high upon hills, flows gently sleep, smooth-sliding sleep—oh, sleep—sleep—sleep!

The Face
of the War

Heat-brutal August the year the war ended: here are four moments from the face of the war. One—at Langley Field: a Negro retreating warily out of one of the rude shedlike offices of the contracting company on the flying field, the white teeth bared in a horrible grimace of fear and hatred, the powerful figure half crouched, apelike, ready to leap or run, the arms, the great black paws, held outward defensively as he retreats under the merciless glazed brutality of the August sun, over the barren, grassless horror of hard dry clay, the white eyeballs fixed with an expression of mute unfathomable hatred, fear and loathing upon the slouchy, shambling figure of a Southern white—a gang boss or an overseer—who advances upon him brandishing a club in his meaty hand, screaming the high thick throat scream of bloodlust and murder: "I'll stomp the guts out of you, you Goddamned black bastard! I'll beat his Goddamn brains out!"—and smashing brutally with his club, coming down across the Negro's skull with the sickening resilient thud, heard clear across the field, of wood on living bone. Behind the paunch-gut white, an office clerk, the little meager yes-man of the earth, a rat in shirt-sleeves, quick as a rat to scamper to its hiding, quick as a rat to come in to the kill when all is safe, with rat's teeth bared—advancing in the shambling wake of his protector, fear's servile seconder, murder's cringing aide, coming in behind with rat's teeth bared, the face white as a sheet, convulsed with fear and with the coward's lust to kill without mercy or reprisal, the merciless sun blazing hot upon the armband buckles on the crisp shirt-sleeve, and with a dull metallic glint upon the barrel of the squat blue automatic that he clutches with a trembling hand, offering it to his blood-mad master, whispering frantically—"Here! . . . Here, Mister Bartlett! . . . Shoot the bastard if he tries to hit you!"

Meanwhile, the Negro retreating slowly all the time, his terrible white stare of fear and hatred no longer fixed upon his enemy, but on the evil glint of that cylinder of blue steel behind him, his arms thrust blindly, futilely before him as his hated foe comes on, his black face, rilled and channelled first with lacings of bright red, then beaten to a bloody pulp as the club keeps smashing down with its sickening and resilient crack:

"You . . . Goddamn . . . black . . . son-of-a-bitch!" the voice, thick, high, phlegmy, choked with murder. "I'll teach ye—" Smash! the cartilage of the thick black nose crunches and is ground to powder by the blow "—if a Goddamned Nigger can talk back to a white man!"—Smash. A flailing, horribly clumsy blow across the mouth which instantly melts into a bloody smear through which the Negro, eyes unmoving from the blue glint of the steel, mechanically spits the shattered fragments of his solid teeth—"I'll bash in his Goddamned head—the damned black bastard—I'll show him if he can—" Smash! Across the wooly center of the skull and now, the scalp ripped open to the base of the low forehead, the powerful black figure staggering drunkenly, bending at the knees, the black head sagging, going down beneath the blows, the arms still blindly thrust before him, upon one knee now on the barren clay-baked earth, the head sunk down completely on the breast, blood over all, the kneeling figure blindly rocking, swaying with the blows, the arms still out until he crashes forward on the earth, his arms outspread, face to one side and then, the final nausea of horror—the murderous kick of the shoe into the blood-pulp of the unconscious face, and then silence, nothing to see or hear now but the heavy, choked and labored breathing of the paunch-gut man, the white rat face behind him with the bared rat's fangs of terror, and the dull blue wink of the envenomed steel.

Again, the coward's heart of fear and hate, the coward's lust for one-way killing, murder without danger to himself, the rat's salvation from the shipwreck of his self-esteem—armed with a gun now, clothed in khaki, riding the horse of his authority, as here. Three boys, all employed by the contracting company, are walking after supper on the borders of the flying field in the waning light of evening, coming dark. They are walking down near the water's edge, across the flat marshy land, they are talking about their homes, the towns and cities they have known and come from, their colleges and schools, their plans for an excursion to the beach at the weekend, when they draw their pay. Without knowing it, they have approached a hangar where one of the new warplanes with which the government is experimenting has been housed. Suddenly, the soldier who is there on guard has seen them, advances on them now, one hand upon the revolver in his holster, his little furtive eyes narrowed into slits. Face of the city rat, dry, gray, furtive, pustulate, the tallowy lips, the rasping voice, the scrabble of a few harsh oaths, the stoney gravel of a sterile, lifeless, speech:

"What are ya doin' here ya f—— little bastards!—
Who told ya t'come f—— round duh hangah?"

One of the boys, a chubby red-cheeked young-
ster from the lower South, fair-haired, blue-eyed,
friendly and slow of speech, attempts to answer:

"Why, mister, we just thought——"

Quick as a flash, the rat has slapped the boy across
the mouth, the filthy fingertips have left their mottled
print upon the boy's red cheek, have left their loath-
some, foul and ineradicable print upon the visage of
his soul forever:

"I don't give a f—— what ya t'ought, ya little
p——! Anuddeh woid out a ya f—— trap an' I'll
shoot the s—— outa ya!" He has the gun out of its
holster now, ready in his hand; the eyes of the three
boys are riveted on the dull wink of its blue barrel
with a single focal intensity of numb horror, fascinated disbelief.

"Now get t' f—— hell outa here!" the hero cries,
giving the boy he has just slapped a violent shove
with his free hand. "Get t' f—— hell away from heah,
all t'ree of youse! Don't f—— aroun' wit me, ya little
p——," the great man snarls now, eyes a-glitter, narrow as a snake's, as he comes forward with deadly
menace written in his face. "Anuddeh woid outa ya
f—— traps, an' I'll shoot t' s—— outa youse! On yuh
way, now, ya p——! Get t' hell away from me befoeh
I plug yah!"

And the three boys, stunned, bewildered, filled
with shame, and sickened out of all the joy and hope
with which they had been speaking of their projects
just a moment before, have turned, and are walking
silently away, with the dull shame, the brutal and
corrosive hatred which the war has caused, aching
and rankling in their hearts.

* * *

Again, an image of man's naked desire, brutal and imperative, stripped down to his raw need, savage and incurious as the harsh pang of a starved hunger which takes and rends whatever food it finds—as here: Over the bridge, across the railway track, down in the Negro settlement of Newport News—among the dives and stews and rusty tenements of that grimy, dreary and abominable section, a rude shack of unpainted pine boards, thrown together with the savage haste which war engenders, to pander to a need as savage and insatiate as hunger, as old as life, the need of friendless, unhoused men the world over.

The front part of this rawly new, yet squalid place, has been partitioned off by rude pine boards to form the semblance of a lunch room and soft-drink parlor. Within are several tables, furnished with a few fly-specked menu cards, on which half a dozen items are recorded, and at which none of the patrons ever look, and a wooden counter, with its dreary stage property of lukewarm soda pop, a few packages of cigarettes and a box of cheap cigars beneath a dingy little glass case; and beneath a greasy glass humidor, a few stale ham-and-cheese sandwiches, which have been there since the place was opened, which will be there till the war is done.

Meanwhile, all through the room, the whores, in their thin and meager mummers, act as waitresses, move patiently about among the crowded tables and ply their trade. The men, who are seated at the tables, belong for the most part to that great group of un-classed creatures who drift and float, work, drift, and starve, are now in jail, now out again, now foul, filthy, wretched, hungry, out of luck, riding the rods, the rusty box cars of a freight, snatching their food at night from the boiling slum of hoboes' jungle, now

85

swaggering with funds and brief prosperity—the floaters, drifters, and half-bums, that huge nameless, houseless, rootless and anomalous class that swarm across the nation.

They are the human cinders of the earth. Hard, shabby, scarred and lined of face, common, dull and meager of visage as they are, they have the look of having crawled that morning from the boxcar in the train yard of another city or of having dropped off a day coach in the morning, looking casually and indifferently about them, carrying a cardboard suitcase with a shirt, two collars and a tie. Yet a legend of great distances is written on them—a kind of atomic desolation. Each is a human spot of moving rust, naked before the desolation of the skies that bend above him, unsheltered on the huge and savage wilderness of the earth, across which he is hurled—a spot of grimy gray and dingy brown, clinging to the brake rods of a loaded freight.

He is a kind of human cinder hurled through space, naked, rootless, nameless, with all that was personal and unique in its one life almost emptied out into that huge vacancy of rust and iron and waste, and lonely and incommunicable distances, in which it lives, through which it has so often been bombarded.

And this atom finds its end at length, perhaps, at some unknown place upon the savage visage of the continent, exploded, a smear of blood on the rock ballast, a scream lost in the roar of pounding wheels, a winding of entrails round the axle rods, a brief indecipherable bobbing of blood and bone and brains upon the wooden ties, or just a shapeless bundle of old soiled brown and gray slumped down at morning in a shabby doorway, on a city street, beneath the elevated structure, a bundle of rags and bone, now cold and lifeless, to be carted out of sight by the police, nameless and forgotten in its death as in its life.

Such, for the most part, were the men who now sat at the tables in this rude house of pleasure, looking about them furtively, warily, with an air of waiting calculation, or indecision, and sometimes glancing at one another with sly, furtive, rather sheepish smiles.

As for the women who attended them, they were prostitutes recruited, for the most part, from the great cities of the North and Middle West, brutally greedy, rapacious, weary of eye, hard of visage, overdriven, harried and exhausted in their mechanical performance of a profession from which their only hope was to grasp and clutch as much as they could in as short a time as possible. They had the harsh, rasping and strident voices, the almost deliberately exaggerated and inept extravagance of profanity and obscenity, the calculated and overemphasized style of toughness which one often finds among poor people in the tenement sections of great cities—which one observes even in small children—the constant oath, curse, jeer, threat, menace, and truculent abuse, which really comes from the terrible fear in which they live, as if, in that world of savage aggression and brute rapacity, from which they have somehow to wrest their bitter living, they are afraid that any betrayal of themselves into a gentler, warmer and more tolerant kind of speech and gesture, will make them suspect to their fellows, and lay them open to the assaults, threats, tyrannies, and dominations they fear.

So was it with these women now: one could hear their rasping voices everywhere throughout the smoke-filled room, their harsh jeering laughter, and the extravagant exaggeration and profusion with which they constantly interlarded their strident speech with a few oaths and cries repeated with a brutal monotony—such phrases as "Christ!"— "Jesus!"—"What t' Goddamn hell do I care?"—

"Come on! Whatcha goin' t' do now! I got no time t'—— around wit' yuh! If ya want t' —— come on an' pay me—if ya don't, get t' Goddamn hell outa here" —being among the expressions one heard most frequently.

Yet, even among these poor, brutally exhausted and fear-ridden women, there was really left, like something pitiably living and indestructible out of life, a kind of buried tenderness, a fearful, almost timid desire to find some friendship, gentleness, even love among the rabble-rout of lost and ruined men to whom they ministered.

And this timid, yet inherent desire for some warmer and more tender relation even in the practice of their profession, was sometimes almost ludicrously apparent as they moved warily about among the tables soliciting patronage from the men they served. Thus, if a man addressed them harshly, brutally, savagely, with an oath—which was a customary form of greeting—they would answer him in kind. But if he spoke to them more quietly, or regarded them with a more kindly smiling look, they might respond to him with a pathetic and ridiculous attempt at coquetry, subduing their rasping voices to a kind of husky, tinny whisper, pressing against him intimately, bending their bedaubed and painted faces close to his, and cajoling him with a pitiable pretense at seductiveness, somewhat in this manner:

"Hello there, big boy! . . . Yuh look lonesome sittin' there all by yourself. . . . Whatcha doin' all alone? . . . Yuh want some company? Huh?" —whispered hoarsely, with a ghastly leer of the smeared lips, and pressing closer—"Wanta have some fun, darling? . . . Come on!"—coaxingly, imperatively, taking the patron by the hand—"I'll show yuh a big time."

It was in response to some such blandishment as

this that the boy had got up from his table, left the smoke-filled room accompanied by the woman, and gone out through a door at one side into the corridor that led back to the little partitioned board compartments of the brothel.

Here, it was at once evident that there was nothing to do but wait. A long line of men and women that stretched from one end of the hallway to another stood waiting for their brief occupancies of the little compartments at the other end, all of which were now obviously and audibly occupied.

As they came out into the hall, the woman with the boy called out to another woman at the front end of the line: "Hello, May! . . . Have ya seen Grace?"

"Aah!" said the woman thus addressed, letting cigarette smoke coil from her nostrils as she spoke, and speaking with the rasping, exaggerated and brutal toughness that has been described: "I t'ink she's in number seven here havin' a ——."

And having conveyed the information in this delicate manner, she then turned to her companion, a brawny, grinning seaman in the uniform of the United States Navy, and with a brisk, yet rather bantering humor, demanded:

"Well, whatcha say, big boy? . . . Gettin' tired of waitin'? . . . Well, it won't be long now . . . Dey'll be troo in dere in a minute an' we're next."

"Dey better had be!" the sailor replied with a kind of jocular savagery. "If dey ain't, I'll tear down duh —— joint! . . . Christ!" he cried in an astounded tone, after listening attentively for a moment. "Holy Jeez!" he said with a dumbfounded laugh. "What t' hell are dey doin' in deh all dis time? Who is dat guy, anyway?—A whole regiment of duh Marines, duh way it sounds t' me! Holy *Je-sus*!" he cried with an astounded laugh, listening again—"Christ!"

"Ah, c'mon, Jack!" the woman said with a kind of

brutal, husky tenderness, snuggling close to his brawny arm meanwhile, and lewdly proposing her heavy body against his. "Yuh ain't gonna get impatient on me now, are yuh? . . . Just hold on a minute moeh an' I'll give ya somet'ing ya neveh had befoeh!——"

"If yuh do," the gallant tar said tenderly, drawing his mighty fist back now in a gesture of savage endearment that somehow seemed to please her, "I'll come back here and smack yuh right in duh puss, yuh son-of-a-bitch!" he amorously whispered, and pulled her to him.

Similar conversations and actions were to be observed all up and down the line: there were lewd jests, ribald laughter, and impatiently shouted demands on the noisy occupants of the little compartments to "come on out an' give some of duh rest of us a chanct, f'r Chris' sake!" and other expressions of a similar nature.

It was a brutally hot night in the middle of August: in the hallway the air was stifling, weary, greasily humid. The place was thick, dense, stale and foul with tobacco smoke, the stench of the men, the powder and cheap perfume of the women and over all, unforgettable, overpowering, pungent, resinous, rude and raw as savage nature and man's naked lust, was the odor of the new, unpainted, white-pine lumber of which the whole shambling and haphazard place had been constructed.

Finally, after a long and weary wait in that stifling place, during which time the door of the compartments had opened many times, and many men and women had come out, and many more gone in, the boy and the woman with him had advanced to the head of the line, and were next in the succession of that unending and vociferous column.

90

Presently, the door of the room for which they waited opened, a man came out, shut the door behind him, and then went quickly down the hall. Then for a moment there was silence, impatient mutters in the line behind them, and at length the woman with the boy, muttering:

"I wondeh what t' hell she's doin' all dis time!—Hey!" she cried harshly, and hammered on the door, "Who's in dere? . . . Come on out, f'r Chris' sake! . . . Yuh're holding up duh line!"

In a moment, a woman's voice answered wearily:

"All right, Fay! . . . Just a moment, dear. . . . I'll be there."

"Oh," the woman with the boy said, in a suddenly quiet, strangely tender kind of voice. "It's Margaret. . . . I guess she's worn out, poor kid." And knocking at the door again, but this time gently, almost timidly, she said in a quiet voice:

"How are yuh, kid? . . . D'ya need any help?"

"No, it's all right, Fay," the girl inside said in the same tired and utterly exhausted tone. "I'll be out in a moment. . . . Come on in, honey."

The woman opened the door softly and entered the room. The only furnishings of the hot, raw, and hideous little place, besides a chair, an untidy and rumpled looking bed, and a table, was a cheap dresser on which was a doll girdled with a soiled ribbon of pink silk, tied in a big bow, a photograph of a young sailor inscribed with the words, "To Margaret, the best pal I ever had—Ed"—and a package of cigarettes. An electric fan, revolving slowly from left to right, droned incessantly, and fanned the close stale air with a kind of sporadic and sweltering breeze.

And from moment to moment, as it swung in its half-orbit, the fan would play full upon the face and head of the girl, who was lying on the bed in an

attitude of utter pitiable weariness. When this happened, a single strand of her shining hair, which was
straight, lank, fine spun as silk, and of a lovely red-
bronze texture, would be disturbed by the movement of the fan and would be blown gently back and
forth across her temple.

The girl, who was tall, slender, and very lovely
was, save for her shoes and stockings, naked, and she
lay extended at full length on the untidy bed, with
one arm thrust out in a gesture of complete exhaus-
tion, the other folded underneath her shining hair,
and her face, which had a fragile, transparent, almost
starved delicacy, turned to one side and resting on
her arm, the eyelids closed. And the eyelids also had
this delicacy of texture, were violet with weariness,
and so transparent that the fine network of the veins
was plainly visible.

The other woman went softly over to the bed, sat
down beside her, and began to speak to her in a low
and tender tone. In a moment the girl turned her
head towards the woman, opened her eyes, and
smiled, in a faint and distant way, as of someone who
is just emerging from the drugged spell of an opiate:

"What? . . . What did you say, darling? . . . No,
I'm all right," she said faintly, and sitting up, with the
other woman's help, she swiftly pulled on over her
head the cheap one-piece garment she was wearing,
which had been flung back over the chair beside the
bed. Then smiling, she stood up, took a cigarette out
of the package on the dresser, lighted it, and turning
to the boy, who was standing in the door, said ironically, with something of the rasping accent which the
other women used, beneath which, however, her
pleasant rather husky tone was plainly evident.

"All right, 'Georgia'! Come on in!"

He went in slowly, still looking at her with an as-

tounded stare. He had known her the first moment he had looked at her. She was a girl from the little town where the state university, at which he was a student, was situated, a member of a family of humble decent people, well known in the town: she had disappeared almost two years before, there had been rumor at the time that one of the students had "got her in trouble," and since that time he had neither seen nor heard of her.

"How are all the folks down home?" she said. "How's everyone in Hopewell?"

Her luminous smoke-gray eyes were hard and bright as she spoke, her mouth, in her thin young face, was hard and bitter as a blade, and her voice was almost deliberately hard and mocking. And yet, beneath this defiant scornfulness, the strange, husky tenderness of the girl's tone persisted, and as she spoke, she put her slender hand lightly on his arm, with the swift, unconscious tenderness of people in a world of strangers who suddenly meet someone they know from home.

"They're all right," he stammered in a confused and bewildered tone, his face beginning to smoulder with embarrassment as he spoke.

"Well, if you see anyone I know," she said in the same ironic tone, "say hello for me. . . . Tell 'em that I sent my love."

"All right," be blurted out stupidly. "I—I—certainly will."

"And I'm mad at you, 'Georgia,'" she said with a kind of mocking reproachfulness, "I'm mad at you for not telling me you were here. . . . The next time you come here you'd better ask for me—or I'll be mad! . . . We homefolks have got to stick together. . . . So you ask for Margaret—or I'll be mad at you—do you hear?"

"All right!" he stammered confusedly again, "I certainly will."

She looked at him a moment longer with her hard bright stare, her bitter, strangely tender smile. Then thrusting her fingers swiftly through his hair, she turned to the other woman and said:

"Be nice to him, Fay. . . . He's one of the folks from down my way. . . . Good-bye, 'Georgia.' . . . When you come back again you ask for Margaret."

"Good-bye," he said, and she was gone, out the door and down that stifling little hall of brutal, crowding, and imperative desire, into the marketplace again, where for the thousandth time she would offer the sale of her young slender body to whoever would be there to buy; to solicit, take, accept the patronage of any of the thousand nameless and unknown men that the huge cylinder of chance and of the night might bring to her.

He never saw her after that. She was engulfed into the great vortex of the war, the huge dark abyss and thronging chaos of America, the immense, the cruel, the indifferent and the magic land, where all of us have lived and walked as strangers, where all of us have been so small, so lonely, and forsaken, which has engulfed us all at length, and in whose dark and lonely breast so many lost and nameless men are buried and forgotten.

This, then, was the third visage of calamity, the image of desire, the face of war.

Again, the speed, haste, violence, savage humor and the instant decisiveness of war:—A sweltering noon on one of the great munition piers at Newport News where now the boy is working as material checker. Inside the great shed of the pier, a silent, suffocating heat of one hundred ten degrees, a grimy, mote-filled air, pollenated with the golden dust of oats which feed through a gigantic chute into the pier in an unending river, and which are sacked and piled in tremendous barricades all up and down the length of that enormous shed.

Elsewhere upon the pier, the towering geometries of war munitions: the white hard cleanliness of crated woods containing food and shot provender of every sort—canned goods, meat, beans, dried fruits, and small-arms ammunitions—the enormous victualling of life and death fed ceaselessly into the insatiate and receiving maw of distant war.

The sweltering air is impregnated with the smells of all these things—with smell of oats and coarse brown sacking, with the clean fresh pungency of crated boxes, and with the huge, drowsy and nostalgic compact of a pier—the single blend of a thousand multiform and mixed aromas, the compacted fragrance of the past, sharp, musty, thrilling, unforgettable, as if the savor of the whole huge earth's abundance had slowly stained, and worn through, and soaked its mellow saturation into the massive and encrusted timbers.

But now all work has ceased: all of the usual sounds of work—the unceasing rumble of the trucks, the rattling of winches and the hard, sudden labor of the donkey engines on the decks of ships, the great nets swinging up and over with their freight of boxes, the sudden rattling fall, and rise again, the shouts and cries of the black sweating stevedores, the sharp commands of the gang bosses, overseers, and loading men—all this has stopped, has for the moment given over to the measured stamp of marching men, the endless streams of men in khaki uniforms who have all morning long, since early light, been tramping

through the pier and filing up a gangplank into the

side of a great transport which waits there to engulf them.

The Negro stevedores sprawl lazily on loaded oat sacks round the grain chute, the checkers doze upon the great walled pile of grain or, kneeling in a circle down behind some oaty barricade, they gamble feverishly with dice.

Meanwhile, the troops come through. The sweltering brown columns tramp in, pause, are given rest, wearily shift the brutal impediment of the loaded knapsacks on their shoulders, take off their caps, wipe their sleeves across their red sweating faces, curse quietly among themselves, and then wait patiently for the lines to move again.

Down by the shipside, at the gangplank's end, a group of officers are seated at a table as the troops file by them, examining each man's papers as he comes to them, passing them on from hand to hand, scrawling signatures, filing, recording, putting the stamp of their approval finally on the documents that will release each little khaki figure to its long-awaited triumph of the ship, the voyage, the new land, to all the joy and glory it is panting for, and to the unconsidered perils of battle, war, and death, disease or mutilation, and the unknown terror, horror, and disgust.

But now a column of black troops is coming by. They are a portion of a Negro regiment from Texas, powerful big men, naïve and wondering as children, incorrigibly unsuited to the military discipline. Something, in fact, is missing, wrong, forgotten, out of place, with everyone's equipment: one has lost his cap, another is without a belt, another is shy two buttons on his jacket, still another has mislaid his canteen, one is shy a good part of his knapsack equipment, and dumbly, ignorantly bewildered at his loss —everyone has lost something, left something behind, done something wrong, now misses something which he has to have.

And now, in one of the pauses of their march along the pier, each one of them pours out the burden of his complaint; into the sweltering misery of the heated air, the babel of black voices mounts. And the target of their bewilderment, the object on whom this whole burden of mischance and error is now heaped, the overburdened and exhausted ruler to whom each now turns in his distress, and, with the naïve and confident faith of a child, asks for an instant solution of the tangled web of error in which he is enmeshed —is an infuriated little bullock of a white man, a first lieutenant, their commander, who during the mountainous accumulations of that catastrophic morning has been driven completely out of his head.

Now he stamps up and down the pier like a maddened animal, the white eyeballs, and the black, sweat-rilled faces follow him back and forth on his stamping and infuriated lunges with the patient, dutiful, and all-confiding trustfulness of children.

His red solid little face is swollen with choked fury and exasperation: as the unending chronicle of their woes mounts up he laughs insanely, clutches violently at the neckband of his coat as if he is strangling, and stamps drunkenly and blindly about like a man maddened with the toothache.

And still they petition him, with the confident hope and certitude of trusting children that one word from their infallible governor will settle everything: —one tells about his missing belt, another of his forgotten canteen, another of his lost cap, his depleted and half-furnished knapsack—affectionately, incorrigibly, they address him as "Boss!" in spite of his curses, threats, entreaties, his final maddened screams that they must address him in a military manner, and the man stamps up and down, out of his wits with choking and unutterable exasperation, cursing vilely:

"You Goddamned black boneheaded gang of sausage-brained gorillas!" he yells chokingly, and clutches at his throat—"Oh, you damned thick-skulled solid-ivory idiot brothers of a one-eyed mule! You sweet stinking set of ape-faced sons of bitches, you! If your brains were made of dynamite you wouldn't have enough to blow your nose, you poor dumb suffering second cousins of an owl! . . . Oh, you just wait, you ink-complected bastards, you!" he now shouts with a kind of fiendish and anticipatory pleasure. "Just wait until I get you in the front-line trenches—I'll line you up there till those German bastards shoot you full of daylight if it's the last thing I ever live to do, you . . . damned . . . ignorant . . . misbegotten . . . cross . . . between a . . . a . . . a . . . wall-eyed possum and a camel's hump—why, you low-down, ignorant bunch of . . . of——"

"Boss?"

"Don't call me Boss!" in a high, choking, almost strangled gurgle. "You dumb son-of-a-bitch, how often have I got to tell you not to call me BOSS!" he yells.

"I know, Boss—" in a plaintive tone—"but my belt buckle's busted. Is you got a piece of string?"

"*A piece of string!*" he chokes. "Why you damned —you—you—a piece of string!" he squeaks, and finally defeated, he takes off his cap, throws it on the floor and, sobbing, stamps upon it.

But an even greater affliction is in store for this unhappy man. Down at the shipside now, where the examining officers are sitting at the table, there has come a sudden pause, a disturbing interruption in the swift and mechanical dispatch with which the troops have been filing in before them. Six of the big black soldiers in a group have been stopped, sharply questioned, and then brusquely motioned out of line.

The officer picks up his cap, yells, "What in Christ's name is the matter now?" and rushes down to where they stand, in an attitude of crushed dejection, with tears rolling down their ebony cheeks. A moment's excited interrogation of the officers seated at the table informs him of the trouble: the six Negroes, all of whom are members of his command, have been under treatment for venereal diseases, but have somehow managed to sneak away from camp without a clean bill of health. Now their delinquency and stratagem of escape has been discovered, they have been denied their embarkation papers and weeping and begging, with the pitiable confidence which all these blacks put in their commanding officer, they are fairly grovelling before him, pleading with him that they be allowed to take ship with the rest of their companions.

"We ain't done nothin', Boss!" their leader, a huge ape of a man, black as ebony, is sniffling, pawing at the officer's sleeve. "Dey ain't nothin' wrong with us!"—"We don't want to stay heah in dis Gawddamn hole, Boss!" another sniffles. "We want to go to France wheah you is! . . . Don't leave us behind, Boss! . . . We'll do anyt'ing you say if you'll jest take us along wid you!——"

"Why, you black clappy bastards!" he snarls—"I wish you were in hell, the lot of you! . . . How the hell do you expect *me* to do anything now at the last moment?" he yells, and filled with a frenzy that can find no stay or answer he goes stamping back and forth like a man gone mad with the very anguish of exasperation and despair. He charges into the midst of that small group of tainted and dejected blacks like a maddened little bull. He raves at them, he reviles them and curses them most foully, for a moment it seems that he is going to assault them physically. And they gather around him, weeping, entreating, crying, begging him for rescue and release, until at length, as if driven frantic by their clamor, he claps both hands to his ears and screaming, "All right, all right, all right!—I'll try—but if they let you go I hope they kill every clappy son-of-a-bitch in the first attack"—he rushes away to the table where the examining officers are seated at their work, engages them long and earnestly in a passionate and persuasive debate and finally wins them over to his argument.

It is decided that the infected Negroes shall be given a physical examination here and now upon the pier and a tall medical officer, delegated for this task, rises from the table, signs briefly to the rejected men, and accompanied by their red-faced little officer, marches them away behind the concealing barrier of the great wall of sacked oats.

They are gone perhaps ten minutes: when they return the Negroes are cavorting with glee, their black faces split by enormous ivory grins, and they are scraping around their little officer like frantic children. They fairly fawn upon him, they try to kiss his hands, they pat his shoulders with their great black paws—the story of their triumphant restoration to the fold is legible in every move they make, in everything they do.

The tall medical officer marches sternly ahead, but with a faint grin playing round the corners of his mouth, and the little red-faced officer is still cursing bitterly, but in his curses now there is a gentler note, the suggestion almost of a lewd tenderness.

And at length that brown, enormous, apparently **101**

interminable column has filed into the ship's great side, and there is nothing on the pier now but far lost sounds and silence, the breath of coolness, evening, the oncoming, undulant stride of all-enfolding and deep-breasted night.

Only
the Dead
Know
Brooklyn

D ere's no guy livin' dat knows Brooklyn t'roo an' t'roo, because it'd take a guy a lifetime just to find his way aroun' duh f—— town.

So like I say, I'm waitin' for my train t' come when I sees dis big guy standin' deh—dis is duh foist I eveh see of him. Well, he's lookin' wild, y'know, an' I can see dat he's had plenty, but still he's holdin' it; he talks good an' is walkin' straight enough. So den, dis big guy steps up to a little guy dat's standin' deh, an' says, "How d'yuh get t' Eighteent' Avenoo an' Sixty-sevent' Street?" he says.

"Jesus! Yuh got me, chief," duh little guy says to him. "I ain't been heah long myself. Where is duh place?" he says. "Out in duh Flatbush section somewhere?"

"Nah," duh big guy says. "It's out in Bensonhoist. But I was neveh deh befoeh. How d'yuh get deh?"

"Jesus," duh little guy says, scratchin' his head, y'know—yuh could see duh little guy didn't know his way about—"yuh got me, chief. I neveh hoid of it. Do any of youse guys know where it is?" he says to me.

"Sure," I says. "It's out in Bensonhoist. Yuh take duh Fourt' Avenoo express, get off at Fifty-nint' Street, change to a Sea Beach local deh, get off at Eighteent' Avenoo an' Sixty-toid, an' den walk down foeh blocks. Dat's all yuh got to do," I says.

"G'wan!" some wise guy dat I neveh seen befoeh pipes up. "Whatcha talkin' about?" he says—oh, he was wise, y'know. "Duh guy is crazy! I tell yuh what yuh do," he says to duh big guy. "Yuh change to duh West End line at Toity-sixt'," he tells him. "Get off at Noo Utrecht an' Sixteent' Avenoo," he says. "Walk two blocks oveh, foeh blocks up," he says, "an' you'll be right deh." Oh, a *wise* guy, y'know.

"Oh, yeah?" I says. "Who told *you* so much?" He got me sore because he was so wise about it. "How long you been livin' heah?" I says.

"All my life," he says. "I was bawn in Williamsboig," he says. "An' I can tell you t'ings about dis town you neveh hoid of," he says.

"Yeah?" I says.

"Yeah," he says.

"Well, den, you can tell me t'ings about dis town dat nobody else has eveh hoid of, either. Maybe you make it all up yoehself at night," I says, "befoeh you go to sleep—like cuttin' out papeh dolls, or somp'n."

"Oh, yeah?" he says. "You're pretty wise, ain't yuh?"

"Oh, I don't know," I says. "Duh boids ain't usin' my head for Lincoln's statue yet," I says. "But I'm wise enough to know a phony when I see one."

"Yeah?" he says. "A wise guy, huh? Well, you're so wise dat someone's goin' t'bust yuh one right on duh snoot someday," he says. "Dat's how wise *you* are."

Well, my train was comin', or I'da smacked him den and dere, but when I seen duh train was comin', all I said was, "All right, mugg! I'm sorry I can't stay to take keh of you, but I'll be seein' yuh sometime, I hope, out in duh cemetery." So den I says to duh big guy, who'd been standin' deh all duh time, "You come wit me," I says. So when we gets onto duh train I says to him, "Where yuh goin' out in Bensonhoist?" I says. "What numbeh are yuh lookin' for?" I says. *You* know—I t'ought if he told me duh address I might be able to help him out.

"Oh," he says, "I'm not lookin' for no one. I don't know no one out deh."

"Then whatcha goin' out deh for?" I says.

"Oh," duh guy says, "I'm just goin' out to see duh place," he says. "I like duh sound of duh name— Bensonhoist, y'know—so I t'ought I'd go out an' have a look at it."

"Whatcha tryin' t'hand me?" I says. "Whatcha tryin' t'do—kid me?" *You* know, I t'ought duh guy was bein' wise wit me.

"No," he says, "I'm tellin' yuh duh troot. I like to go out an' take a look at places wit nice names like dat. I like to go out an' look at all kinds of places," he says.

"How'd yuh know deh was such a place," I says, "if yuh neveh been deh befoeh?"

"Oh," he says, "I got a map."

"A *map*?" I says.

"Sure," he says, "I got a map dat tells me about all dese places. I take it wit me every time I come out heah," he says.

And Jesus! Wit dat, he pulls it out of his pocket, an' so help me, but he's *got* it—he's tellin' duh troot—a big map of duh whole f—— place with all duh different pahts mahked out. You know—Canarsie an' East Noo Yawk an' Flatbush, Bensonhoist, Sout' Brooklyn, duh Heights, Bay Ridge, Greenpernt—duh whole Goddamn layout, he's got it right deh on duh map.

"You been to any of dose places?" I says.

"Sure," he says, "I been to most of 'em. I was down in Red Hook just last night," he says.

"Jesus! Red Hook!" I says. "Whatcha do down deh?"

"Oh," he says, "nuttin' much. I just walked aroun'. I went into a coupla places an' had a drink," he says, "but most of the time I just walked aroun'."

"Just walked aroun'?" I says.

"Sure," he says, "just lookin' at t'ings, y'know."

"Where'd yuh go?" I asts him.

"Oh," he says, "I don't know duh name of duh place, but I could find it on my map," he says. "One time I was walkin' across some big fields where deh ain't no houses," he says, "but I could see ships oveh deh all lighted up. Dey was loadin'. So I walks across duh fields," he says, "to where duh ships are."

"Sure," I says, "I know where you was. You was down to duh Erie Basin."

"Yeah," he says, "I guess dat was it. Dey had some of dose big elevators an' cranes an' dey was loadin' ships, an' I could see some ships in drydock all lighted up, so I walks across duh fields to where dey are," he says.

"Den what did yuh do?" I says.

"Oh," he says, "nuttin' much. I came on back across duh fields after a while an' went into a coupla places an' had a drink."

"Didn't nuttin' happen while yuh was in dere?" I says.

"No," he says. "Nuttin' much. A coupla guys was drunk in one of duh places an' started a fight, but dey bounced 'em out," he says, "an' den one of duh guys stahted to come back again, but duh bartender gets his baseball bat out from under duh counteh, so duh guy goes on."

"Jesus!" I said. "Red Hook!"

"Sure," he says. "Dat's where it was, all right."

"Well, you keep outa deh," I says. "You stay away from deh."

"Why?" he says. "What's wrong wit it?"

"Oh," I says, "it's a good place to stay away from, dat's all. It's a good place to keep out of."

"Why?" he says. "Why is it?"

Jesus! Whatcha gonna do wit a guy as dumb as dat? I saw it wasn't no use to try to tell him nuttin', he wouldn't know what I was talkin' about, so I just says to him, "Oh, nuttin'. Yuh might get lost down deh, dat's all."

"Lost?" he says. "No, I wouldn't get lost. I got a map," he says.

A map! Red Hook! Jesus!

So den duh guy begins to ast me all kinds of nutty questions: how big was Brooklyn an' could I find my way aroun' in it, an' how long would it take a guy to know duh place.

"Listen!" I says. "You get dat idea outa yoeh head right now," I says. "You ain't neveh gonna get to know Brooklyn," I says. "Not in a hunderd yeahs. I been livin' heah all my life," I says, "an' I don't even know all deh is to know about it, so how do you expect to know duh town," I says, "when you don't even live heah?"

"Yes," he says, "but I got a map to help me find my way about."

"Map or no map," I says, "yuh ain't gonna get to know Brooklyn wit no map," I says.

"Can you swim?" he says, just like dat. Jesus! By dat time, y'know, I begun to see dat duh guy was some kind of nut. He'd had plenty to drink, of course, but he had dat crazy look in his eye I didn't like. "Can you swim?" he says.

"Sure," I says. "Can't you?"

"No," he says. "Not more'n a stroke or two. I neveh loined good."

"Well, it's easy," I says. "All yuh need is a little confidence. Duh way I loined, me older bruddeh pitched me off duh dock one day when I was eight yeahs old, cloes an' all. 'You'll swim,' he says. 'You'll swim all right—or drown.' An', believe me, I *swam*! When yuh know yuh got to, you'll do it. Duh only t'ing yuh need is confidence. An' once you've loined," I says, "you've got nuttin' else to worry about. You'll neveh forget it. It's somp'n dat stays wit yuh as long as yuh live."

"Can yuh swim good?" he says.

"Like a fish," I tells him. "I'm a regulah fish in duh wateh," I says. "I loined to swim right off duh docks wit all duh oddeh kids," I says.

"What would you do if yuh saw a man drownin'?" duh guy says.

"Do? Why, I'd jump in an' pull him out," I says. "Dat's what I'd do."

"Did yuh eveh see a man drown?" he says.

"Sure," I says. "I see two guys—bot' times at Coney Island. Dey got out too far, an' neider one could swim. Dey drowned befoeh anyone could get to 'em."

"What becomes of people after dey've drowned out heah?" he says.

"Drowned out where?" I says.

"Out heah in Brooklyn."

"I don't know whatcha mean," I says. "Neveh hoid of no one drownin' heah in Brooklyn, unless you mean a swimmin' pool. Yuh can't drown in Brooklyn," I says. "Yuh gotta drown somewhere else—in duh ocean, where dere's wateh."

"Drownin'," duh guy says, lookin' at his map.

110 "Drownin'." Jesus! I could see by den he was some

kind of nut, he had dat crazy expression in his eyes when he looked at you, an' I didn't know what he might do. So we was comin' to a station, an' it wasn't my stop, but I got off anyway, an' waited for duh next train.

"Well, so long, chief," I says. "Take it easy, now."

"Drownin'," duh guy says, lookin' at his map. "Drownin'."

Jesus! I've t'ought about dat guy a t'ousand times since den an' wondered what eveh happened to 'm goin' out to look at Bensonhoist because he liked duh name! Walkin' aroun' t'roo Red Hook by himself at night an' lookin' at his map! How many people did I see get drowned out heah in Brooklyn! How long would it take a guy wit a good map to know all deh was to know about Brooklyn!

Jesus! What a nut *he* was! I wondeh what eveh happened to 'im, anyway! I wondeh if someone knocked him on duh head, or if he's still wanderin' aroun' in duh subway in duh middle of duh night wit his little map! Duh poor guy! Say, I've got to laugh, at dat, when I t'ink about him! Maybe he's found out by now dat he'll neveh live long enough to know duh whole of Brooklyn. It'd take a guy a lifetime to know Brooklyn t'roo an' t'roo. An' even den, yuh wouldn't know it all.

Dark in the Forest, Strange as Time

Some years ago, among the people standing on one of the platforms of the Munich railway station, beside the Swiss express, which was almost ready to depart, there were a woman and a man—a woman so lovely that the memory of her would forever haunt the mind of him who saw her, and a man on whose dark face the legend of a strange and fatal meeting was already visible.

The woman was at the flawless summit of a mature and radiant beauty, packed to the last red ripeness of her lip with life and health, a miracle of loveliness in whom all the elements of beauty had combined with such exquisite proportion and so rhythmical a balance that even as one looked at her he could scarcely believe the evidence of his eyes.

Thus, although not over-tall, she seemed at times to command a superb and queenly height, then to be almost demurely small and cozy as she pressed close to her companion. Again, her lovely figure seemed never to have lost the lithe slenderness of girlhood, yet it was ripe, lavish, undulant with all the voluptuous maturity of womanhood, and every movement she made was full of seductive grace.

The woman was fashionably dressed; her little toquelike hat fitted snugly down over a crown of coppery reddish hair and shaded her eyes which had a smoke-blue and depthless quality that could darken almost into black, and change with every swiftest shade of feeling that passed across her face. She was talking to the man in low and tender tones, smiling a vague voluptuous smile as she looked at him. She spoke eagerly, earnestly, gleefully to him, and from time to time burst into a little laugh that came welling low, rich, sensual, and tender from her throat.

As they walked up and down the platform talking, the woman thrust her small gloved hand through the arm of his heavy overcoat and snuggled close to him, sometimes nestling her lovely head, which was as proud and graceful as a flower, against his arm. Again they would pause, and look steadfastly at each other for a moment. Now she spoke to him with playful reproof, chided him, shook him tenderly by the arms, pulled the heavy furred lapels of his overcoat together, and wagged a small gloved finger at him warningly.

And all the time the man looked at her, saying little, but devouring her with large dark eyes that were burning steadily with the fires of death, and that seemed to feed on her physically, with an insatiate and voracious tenderness of love. He was a Jew, his figure immensely tall, cadaverous, and so wasted by disease that it was lost, engulfed, forgotten in the heavy and expensive garments that he wore.

His thin white face, which was wasted almost to a fleshless integument of bone and skin, converged to an immense hooked nose, so that his face was not so much a face as a great beak of death, lit by two blazing and voracious eyes and colored on the flanks with two burning flags of red. Yet, with all its ugliness of disease and emaciation it was a curiously memorable and moving face, a visage somehow nobly tragic with the badge of death.

But now the time had come for parting. The guards were shouting warnings to the passengers, all up and down the platform there were swift serried movements, hurried eddyings among the groups of friends. One saw people embracing, kissing, clasping hands, crying, laughing, shouting, going back for one hard swift kiss, and then mounting hastily into their compartments. And one heard in a strange tongue the vows, oaths, promises, the jests and swift allusions, that were secret and precious to each group and that sent them off at once in roars of laughter, the words of farewell that are the same the whole world over:

"Otto! Otto! . . . Have you got what I gave you? . . . Feel! Is it still there?" He felt, it was still there: fits of laughter.

"Will you see Else?"

"How's that? Can't hear"—shouting, cupping hand to ear, and turning head sideways with a puzzled look.

"I—say—will—you—see—Else?" fairly roared out between cupped palms above the tumult of the crowd.

"Yes. I think so. We expect to meet them at St. Moritz."

"Tell her she's got to write."

"Hey? I can't hear you." Same pantomime as before.

"I—say—tell—her—she's got—to write"—another roar.

"Oh, yes! Yes!" Nodding quickly, smiling, "I'll tell her."

"—or I'll be mad at her!"

"What? Can't hear you for all this noise"—same business as before.

"I—say—tell—her—I'll—be—mad—if she—doesn't—write" roared out again deliberately at the top of his lungs.

Here, a man who had been whispering slyly to a woman, who was trembling with smothered laughter, now turned with grinning face to shout something at the departing friend, but was checked by the woman who seized him by the arm and with a face reddened by laughter, gasped hysterically.

"No! No!"

But the man, still grinning, cupped his hands around his mouth and roared:

"Tell Uncle Walter he has got to wear his——"

"How's that? Can't hear!"—cupping ear and turning head to one side as before.

"I—say," the man began to roar deliberately.

"No! No! No! Sh-h!" the woman gasped frantically, tugging at his arm.

"—to—tell—Uncle Walter—he—must—wear—his woolen——"

"No! No! No!—Heinrich! . . . Sh-h!" the woman shrieked.

"—The—heavy—ones—Aunt—Bertha embroidered with his—initials!" the man went on relentlessly.

Here the whole crowd roared, and the women screamed with laughter, shrieking protests, and saying:

"Sh-h! Sh-h!" loudly.

"Ja—I'll tell him!" the grinning passenger yelled back at him as soon as they had grown somewhat quieter. "Maybe—he hasn't—got—'em—any—more," he shouted as a happy afterthought. "Maybe—one—of—the—Fräuleins—down—there—" he gasped and choked with laughter.

"Otto!" the women shrieked. "Sh-h!"

"Maybe—one—of—the—Fräuleins—got them—away—from"—he began to gasp with laughter.

"O-o-o-t-to! . . . Shame on you—Sh-h!" the

118 women screamed.

"Souvenir—from—old—München," roared back his fellow wit, and the whole group was convulsed again. When they had recovered somewhat, one of the men began in a wheezing and faltering tone, as he wiped at his streaming eyes:

"Tell—Else"—here his voice broke off in a feeble squeak, and he had to pause to wipe his eyes again.

"What?"—the grinning passenger yelled back at him.

"Tell—Else," he began again more strongly, "that Aunt—Bertha—oh! my God!" he groaned weakly again, faltered, wiped at his streaming eyes, and was reduced to palsied silence.

"What?—What?" shouted the grinning passenger sharply, clapping his hand to his attentive ear. "Tell Else what?"

"Tell—Else—Aunt—Bertha—is—sending—her —recipe—for—layer—cake," the man fairly screamed now as if he would get it out at any cost before his impending and total collapse. The effect of that apparently meaningless reference to Aunt Bertha's layer cake was astonishing: nothing that had gone before could approach the spasmodic effect it had upon this little group of friends. They were instantly reduced to a shuddering paralysis of laughter, they staggered drunkenly about, clasped one another feebly for support, tears streamed in torrents from their swollen eyes, and from their wide-open mouths there came occasionally feeble wisps of sound, strangled gasps, faint screams from the women, a panting palsied fit of mirth from which they finally emerged into a kind of hiccoughing recovery.

What it was—the total implication of that apparently banal reference which had thrown them all into such a convulsive fit of merriment—no stranger could ever know, but its effect upon the other people was infectious; they looked toward the group of

119

friends, and grinned, laughed, and shook their heads at one another. And so it went all up and down the line. Here were people grave, gay, sad, serious, young, old, calm, casual, and excited; here were people bent on business and people bent on pleasure; here people sharing by every act, word, and gesture the excitement, joy, and hope which the voyage wakened in them, and people who looked wearily and indifferently about them, settled themselves in their seats and took no further interest in the events of the departure—but everywhere it was the same.

People were speaking the universal language of departure, that varies not at all the whole world over —that language which is often banal, trivial, and even useless, but on this account curiously moving, since it serves to hide a deeper emotion in the hearts of men, to fill the vacancy that is in their hearts at the thought of parting, to act as a shield, a concealing mask to their true feeling.

And because of this there was for the youth, the stranger, and the alien who saw and heard these things, a thrilling and poignant quality in the ceremony of the train's departure. As he saw and heard these familiar words and actions—words and actions that beneath the guise of an alien tongue were identical to those he had seen and known all his life, among his own people—he felt suddenly, as he had never felt before, the overwhelming loneliness of familiarity, the sense of the human identity that so strangely unites all the people in the world, and that is rooted in the structure of man's life, far below the tongue he speaks, the race of which he is a member.

 But now that the time had come for parting, the woman and the dying man said nothing. Clasped arm to arm they looked at each other with a stare of burning and voracious tenderness. They embraced, her arms clasped him, her living and voluptuous body drew toward him, her red lips clung to his mouth as if she could never let him go. Finally, she fairly tore herself away from him, gave him a desperate little push with her hands, and said. "Go, go! It's time!"

Then the scarecrow turned and swiftly climbed into the train, a guard came by and brutally slammed the door behind him, the train began to move slowly out of the station. And all the time the man was leaning from a window in the corridor looking at her, and the woman was walking along beside the train, trying to keep him in sight as long as she could. Now the train gathered motion, the woman's pace slowed, she stopped, her eyes wet, her lips murmuring words no one could hear, and as he vanished from her sight she cried, "Auf Wiedersehen!" and put her hand up to her lips and kissed it to him.

For a moment longer the younger man, who was to be this specter's brief companion of the journey, stood looking out the corridor window down the platform toward the great arched station sheds, seeming to look after the group of people departing up the platform, but really seeing nothing but the tall, lovely figure of the woman as she walked slowly away, head bent, with a long, deliberate stride of incomparable grace, voluptuous undulance. Once she paused to look back again, then turned and walked on slowly as before.

Suddenly she stopped. Someone out of the throng of people on the platform had approached her. It was a young man. The woman paused in a startled manner, lifted one gloved hand in protest, started to go on, and the next moment they were locked in a savage embrace, devouring each other with passionate kisses.

When the traveller returned to his seat, the dying   **121**

man who had already come into the compartment from the corridor and had fallen back into the cushions of his seat, breathing hoarsely, was growing calmer, less exhausted. For a moment the younger man looked intently at the beaklike face, the closed weary eyes, wondering if this dying man had seen that meeting on the station platform, and what knowledge such as this could now mean to him. But that mask of death was enigmatic, unrevealing; the youth found nothing there that he could read. A faint and strangely luminous smile was playing at the edges of the man's thin mouth, and his burning eyes were now open, but far and sunken and seemed to be looking from an unspeakable depth at something that was far away. In a moment, in a profound and tender tone, he said:

"Zat vas my vife. Now in ze vinter I must go alone, for zat iss best. But in ze spring ven I am better she vill come to me."

All through the wintry afternoon the great train rushed down across Bavaria. Swiftly and powerfully it gathered motion, it left the last scattered outposts of the city behind it, and swift as dreams the train was rushing out across the level plain surrounding Munich.

The day was gray, the sky impenetrable and somewhat heavy, and yet filled with a strong, clean Alpine vigor, with that odorless and yet exultant energy of cold mountain air. Within an hour the train had entered Alpine country, now there were hills, valleys, the immediate sense of soaring ranges, and the dark enchantment of the forests of Germany, those forests which are something more than trees—which are a spell, a magic, and a sorcery, filling the hearts of men, and particularly those strangers who have some racial kinship with that land, with a dark music, a haunting memory, never wholly to be captured.

It is an overwhelming feeling of immediate and impending discovery, such as men might have who come for the first time to their father's country. It is like coming to that unknown land for which our spirits long so passionately in youth, which is the dark side of our soul, the strange brother and the complement of the land we have known in our childhood. And it is revealed to us instantly the moment that we see it with a powerful emotion of perfect recognition and disbelief, with that dreamlike reality of strangeness and familiarity which dreams and all enchantment have.

What is it? What is this wild fierce joy and sorrow swelling in our hearts? What is this memory that we cannot phrase, this instant recognition for which we have no words? We cannot say. We have no way to give it utterance, no ordered evidence to give it proof, and scornful pride can mock us for a superstitious folly. Yet we will know the dark land at the very moment that we come to it, and though we have no tongue, no proof, no utterance for what we feel, we have what we have, we know what we know, we are what we are.

And what are we? We are the naked men, the lost Americans. Immense and lonely skies bend over us, ten thousand men are marching in our blood. Where does it come from—the sense of strangeness, instant recognition, the dream-haunted, almost captured, memory? Where does it come from, the constant hunger and the rending lust, and the music, dark and solemn, elfish, magic, sounding through the wood? How is it that this boy, who is American, has known this strange land from the first moment that he saw it?

How is it that from his first night in a German town

he has understood the tongue he never heard before, has spoken instantly, saying all he wished to say, in a strange language which he could not speak, speaking a weird argot which was neither his nor theirs, of which he was not even conscious, so much did it seem to be the spirit of a language, not the words, he spoke, and instantly, in this fashion, understood by everyone with whom he talked?

No. He could not prove it, yet he knew that it was there, buried deep in the brain and blood of man, the utter knowledge of this land and of his father's people. He had felt it all, the tragic and insoluble admixture of the race. He knew the terrible fusion of the brute and of the spirit. He knew the nameless fear of the old barbaric forest, the circle of barbaric figures gathered round him in their somber and unearthly ring, the sense of drowning in the blind forest horrors of barbaric time. He carried all within himself, the slow gluttony and lust of the unsated swine, as well as the strange and powerful music of the soul.

He knew the hatred and revulsion from the never-sated beast—the beast with the swine face and the quenchless thirst, the never-ending hunger, the thick, slow, rending hand that fumbled with a smouldering and unsated lust. And he hated the great beast with the hate of hell and murder because he felt and knew it in himself and was himself the prey of its rending, quenchless, and obscene desires. Rivers of wine to drink, whole roast oxen turning on the spit, and through the forest murk, the roaring wall of huge beast bodies and barbaric sound about him, the lavish flesh of the great blonde women, in brutal orgy of the all-devouring, never-sated maw of the huge belly, without end or surfeit—all was mixed into his blood, his spirit, and his life.

It had been given to him somehow from the dark **125**

time-horror of the ancient forest together with all
that was magical, glorious, strange and beautiful: the
husky horn notes sounding faint and elfin through
the forests, the infinite strange weavings, dense mu-
tations of the old Germanic soul of man. How cruel,
baffling, strange, and sorrowful was the enigma of the
race: the power and strength of the incorruptible and
soaring spirit rising from the huge corrupted beast
with such a radiant purity, and the powerful enchantments of grand music, noble poetry, so sorrowfully
and unalterably woven and inwrought with all the
blind brute hunger of the belly and the beast of man.

It was all his, and all contained in his one life. And
it could, he knew, never be distilled out of him, no
more than one can secrete from his flesh his father's
blood, the ancient and immutable weavings of dark
time. And for this reason, as he now looked out the
window of the train at that lonely Alpine land of snow
and dark enchanted forest he felt the sense of familiar
recognition instantly, the feeling that he had always
known this place, that it was home. And something
dark, wild, jubilant, and strange was exulting, swelling in his spirit like a grand and haunting music
heard in dreams.

And now, a friendly acquaintance having been established, the specter, with the insatiate, possessive
curiosity of his race, began to ply his companion
with innumerable questions concerning his life, his
home, his profession, the journey he was making, the
reason for that journey. The young man answered
readily, and without annoyance. He knew that he
was being pumped unmercifully, but the dying
man's whispering voice was so persuasive, friendly,
gentle, his manner so courteous, kind, and insinuat-
ing, his smile so luminous and winning, touched

126

with a faint and yet agreeable expression of weariness, that the questions almost seemed to answer themselves.

The young man was an American, was he not? . . . Yes. And how long had he been abroad—two months? Three months? No? Almost a year! So long as that! Then he liked Europe, yes? It was his first trip? No? His fourth?—The specter lifted his eyebrows in expressive astonishment, and yet his sensitive thin mouth was touched all the time by his faint, wearily cynical smile.

Finally, the boy was pumped dry: the specter knew all about him. Then for a moment he sat staring at the youth with his faint, luminous, subtly mocking, and yet kindly smile. At last, wearily, patiently, and with the calm finality of experience and death, he said:

"You are very young. Yes. Now you vant to see it all, to haf it all—but you haf nothing. Zat iss right— yes?" he said with his persuasive smile. "Zat vill all change. Someday you vill vant only a little—maybe, den, you *haf* a little—" and he flashed his luminous, winning smile again. "Und zat iss better—Yes?" He smiled again, and then said wearily, "I know. I know. Myself I haf gone eferyvere like you. I haf tried to see eferyt'ing—und I haf had nothing. Now I go no more. Eferyvere it iss ze same," he said wearily, looking out the window, with a dismissing gesture of his thin white hand. "Fields, hills, mountains, riffers, cities, peoples—you vish to know about zem all. Vun field, vun hill, vun riffer," the man whispered, "zat iss enough!"

He closed his eyes for a moment: when he spoke again his whisper was almost inaudible—"Vun life, vun place, vun time."

* * *

Darkness came, and the lights in the compartment were turned on. Again that whisper of waning life made its insistent, gentle, and implacable demand upon the youth. This time it asked that the light in the compartment be extinguished, while the specter stretched himself out upon the seat to rest. The younger man consented willingly and even gladly: his own journey was near its end and outside, the moon, which had risen early, was shining down upon the Alpine forests and snows with a strange, brilliant, and haunting magic which gave to the darkness in the compartment some of its own ghostly and mysterious light.

The specter lay quietly stretched out on the cushions of the seat, his eyes closed, his wasted face, on which the two bright flags of burning red now shone with vermilion hue, strange and ghastly in the magic light as the beak of some great bird. The man scarcely seemed to breathe: no sound or movement of life was perceptible in the compartment except the pounding of the wheels, the leathery stretching and creaking sound of the car, and all that strange-familiar and evocative symphony of sounds a train makes—that huge symphonic monotone which is itself the sound of silence and forever.

For some time held in that spell of magic light and time, the youth sat staring out the window at the enchanted world of white and black that swept grandly and strangely past in the phantasmal radiance of the moon. Finally he got up, went out into the corridor, closing the door carefully behind him, and walked back down the narrow passageway through car after car of the rocketing train until he came to the dining car.

Here all was brilliance, movement, luxury, sensual warmth and gaiety. All the life of the train now seemed to be concentrated in this place. The waiters, surefooted and deft, were moving swiftly down the aisle of the rocketing car, pausing at each table to serve people from the great platters of well-cooked food which they carried on trays. Behind them the *sommelier* was pulling corks from tall frosty bottles of Rhine wine: he would hold the bottle between his knees as he pulled, the cork would come out with an exhilarating pop, and he would drop the cork then into a little basket.

At one table a seductive and beautiful woman was eating with a jaded-looking old man. At another a huge and powerful-looking German, with a wing collar, a shaven skull, a great swine face and a forehead of noble and lonely thought, was staring with a concentrated look of bestial gluttony at the tray of meat from which the waiter served him. He was speaking in a guttural and lustful tone, saying, "Ja! . . . Gut! . . . und etwas von diesem hier auch. . . ."

The scene was one of richness, power and luxury, evoking as it did the feeling of travel in a crack European express, which is different from the feeling one has when he rides on an American train. In America, the train gives one a feeling of wild and lonely joy, a sense of the savage, unfenced, and illimitable wilderness of the country through which the train is rushing, a wordless and unutterable hope as one thinks of the enchanted city toward which he is speeding; the unknown and fabulous promise of the life he is to find there.

In Europe, the feeling of joy and pleasure is more actual, ever present. The luxurious trains, the rich furnishings, the deep maroons, dark blues, the fresh, well-groomed vivid colors of the cars, the good food and the sparkling, heady wine, and the worldly, wealthy, cosmopolitan look of the travellers—all of this fills one with a powerful sensual joy, a sense of expectancy about to be realized. In a few hours' time one goes from country to country, through centuries of history, a world of crowded culture and whole nations swarming with people, from one famous pleasure city to another.

And, instead of the wild joy and nameless hope one feels as he looks out the window of an American train, one feels here (in Europe) an incredible joy of realization, an immediate sensual gratification, a feeling that there is nothing on earth but wealth, power, luxury, and love, and that one can live and enjoy this life, in all the infinite varieties of pleasure, forever.

When the young man had finished eating, and paid his bill, he began to walk back again through corridor after corridor along the length of the rocketing train. When he got back to his compartment, he saw the specter lying there as he had left him, stretched out upon the seat, with the brilliant moonlight still blazing on the great beak of his face.

The man had not changed his position by an inch, and yet at once the boy was conscious of some subtle, fatal change he could not define. What was it? He took his seat again and for some time stared fixedly at the silent ghostly figure opposite him. Did he not breathe? He thought, he was almost sure, he saw the motion of his breathing, the rise and fall of the emaciated breast, and yet he was not sure. But what he plainly saw now was that a line, vermilion in its moon-dark hue, had run out of the corner of the firm set mouth and that there was a large vermilion stain upon the floor.

What should he do? What could be done? The

haunted light of the fatal moon seemed to have

steeped his soul in its dark sorcery, in the enchantment of a measureless and inert calmness. Already,
too, the train was slackening its speed, the first lights
of the town appeared, it was his journey's end.

And now the train was slowing to a halt. There
were the flare of rails, the switch lights of the yard,
small, bright, and hard, green, red, and yellow,
poignant in the dark, and on other tracks he could see
the little goods cars and the strings of darkened
trains, all empty, dark, and waiting with their strange
attentiveness of recent life. Then the long station
quays began to slide slowly past the windows of the
train, and the sturdy goatlike porters were coming on
the run, eagerly saluting, speaking, calling to the
people in the train who had already begun to pass
their baggage through the window.

Softly the boy took his overcoat and suitcase from
the rack above his head and stepped out into the
narrow corridor. Quietly he slid the door of the compartment shut behind him. Then, for a moment, still
unsure, he stood there looking back. In the semidark-
ness of the compartment the spectral figure of the
cadaver lay upon the cushions, did not move.

Was it not well to leave all things as he had found
them, in silence, at the end? Might it not be that in
this great dream of time in which we live and are the
moving figures, there is no greater certitude than
this: that, having met, spoken, known each other for a
moment, as somewhere on this earth we were hurled
onward through the darkness between two points of
time, it is well to be content with this, to leave each
other as we met, letting each one go alone to his
appointed destination, sure of this only, needing
only this—that there will be silence for us all and
silence only, nothing but silence, at the end?

Already the train had come to a full stop. The boy

131

went down the corridor to the end, and in a moment, feeling the bracing shock of the cold air upon his flesh, breathing the vital and snow-laden air into his lungs, he was going down the quay with a hundred other people, all moving in the same direction, some toward certitude and home, some toward a new land, hope, and hunger, the swelling prescience of joy, the promise of a shining city. He knew that he was going home again.

The Four
Lost Men

S uddenly, at the green heart of June, I heard my
father's voice again. That year I was sixteen; the
week before I had come home from my first
year at college, and the huge thrill and menace of
the war, which we had entered just two months before, had filled our hearts. And war gives life to men
as well as death. It fills the hearts of young men with
wild song and jubilation. It wells up in their throats
in great-starred night, the savage cry of all their pain
and joy. And it fills them with a wild and wordless
prophecy not of death, but life, for it speaks to them
of new lands, triumph, and discovery, of heroic
deeds, the fame and fellowship of heroes, and the
love of glorious unknown women—of a shining triumph and a grand success in a heroic world, and of a
life more fortunate and happy than they have ever
known.

So was it with us all that year. Over the immense
and waiting earth, the single pulse and promise of
the war impended. One felt it in the little towns at
dawn, with all their quiet, casual, utterly familiar
acts of life beginning. One felt it in the route boy
deftly flinging the light folded block of paper on a
porch, a man in shirt-sleeves coming out upon the
porch and bending for the paper, the slow-clopping
hoofs of the milk horse in a quiet street, the bottle-
clinking wagon, and the sudden pause, the rapid
footsteps of the milkman and the clinking bottles,

then clopping hoof and wheel, and morning, stillness, the purity of light, and the dew-sweet birdsong rising in the street again.

In all these ancient, ever-new, unchanging, always magic acts of life and light and morning one
felt the huge impending presence of the war. And
one felt it in the brooding hush of noon, in the ring
of the ice tongs in the street, the cool whine of the
ice saws droning through the smoking block, in leaf,
and blade and flower, in smell of tar, and the sudden
haunting green-gold summer absence of a streetcar
after it had gone.

The war had got in everything: it was in things
that moved, and in things that were still, in the ani-
mate red silence of an old brick wall as well as in all
the thronging life and traffic of the streets. It was in
the faces of the people passing, and in ten thousand
familiar moments of man's daily life and business.

And lonely, wild, and haunting, calling us on forever with the winding of its far lost horn, it had got
into the time-enchanted loneliness of the magic
hills around us, in all the sudden, wild and lonely
lights that came and passed and vanished on the
massed green of the wilderness.

The war was in far cries and broken sounds and
cowbells tinkling in the gusty wind, and in the far,
wild, wailing joy and sorrow of a departing train, as
it rushed eastward, seaward, warward through a valley of the South in the green spell and golden magic
of full June, and in the houses where men lived, the
brief flame and fire of sheeted window panes.

And it was in field and gulch and hollow, in the
sweet green mountain valleys fading into dusk, and
in the hill flanks reddened with the ancient light,
and slanting fast into steep cool shade and lilac silence. It was in the whole huge mystery of earth

that, after all the dusty tumult of the day, could lapse with such immortal stillness to the hush, the joy, the sorrow of oncoming night.

The war had got into all sounds and secrecies, the sorrow, longing, and delight, the mystery, hunger and wild joy that came from the deep-breasted heart of fragrant, all-engulfing night. It was in the sweet and secret rustling of the leaves in summer streets, in footsteps coming quiet, slow, and lonely along the darkness of a leafy street, in screen doors slammed, and silence, the distant barking of a dog, far voices, laughter, faint pulsing music at a dance, and in all the casual voices of the night, far, strangely near, most intimate and familiar.

And suddenly, as I sat there under the proud and secret mystery of huge-starred, velvet-breasted night, hearing my father's great voice sounding from the porch again, the war, with a wild and intolerable loneliness of ecstasy and desire came to me in the sudden throbbing of a racing motor, far-away silence, an image of the cool sweet darkness of the mountainside, the white flesh and yielding tenderness of women. And even as I thought of this I heard the rich, sensual welling of a woman's voice, voluptuous, low, and tender, from the darkness of a summer porch across the street.

What had the war changed? What had it done to us? What miracle of transformation had it wrought upon our lives? It had changed nothing; it had heightened, intensified, and made glorious all the ancient and familiar things of life. It had added hope to hope, joy to joy, and life to life; and from that vital wizardry it had rescued all our lives from hopelessness and despair, and made us live again who thought that we were lost.

The war seemed to have collected in a single

image of joy, and power, and proud compacted might all of the thousand images of joy and power and all-exulting life which we had always had, and for which we had never had a word before. Over the fields of silent and mysterious night it seemed that we could hear the nation marching, that we could hear, soft and thunderous in the night, the million-footed unison of marching men. And that single glorious image of all-collected joy and unity and might had given new life and new hope to all of us.

My father was old, he was sick with a cancer that flowered and fed forever at his entrails, eating from day to day the gaunt sinew of his life away beyond a hope or remedy, and we knew that he was dying. Yet, under the magic life and hope the war had brought to us, his life seemed to have revived again out of its grief of pain, its death of joy, its sorrow of irrevocable memory.

For a moment he seemed to live again in his full prime. And instantly we were all released from the black horror of death and time that hung above him, from the nightmare terror that had menaced us for years. Instantly we were freed from the evil spell of sorrowful time and memory that had made his living death more horrible than his real one could ever be.

And instantly the good life, the golden and jubilant life of childhood, in whose full magic we had been sustained by the power of his life, and which had seemed so lost and irrecoverable that it had a dreamlike strangeness when we thought of it, had, under this sudden flare of life and joy and war, returned in all its various and triumphant colors. And for a moment we believed that all would be again for us as it had been, that he never could grow old and die, but that he must live forever, and that the summertime, the orchard and bright morning, would be ours again, could never die.

138

I could hear him talking now about old wars and ancient troubles, hurling against the present and its leaders the full indictment of his soaring rhetoric that howled, rose, fell, and swept out into the night, piercing all quarters of the darkness with the naked penetration which his voice had in the old days when he sat talking on his porch in summer darkness, and the neighborhood attended and was still.

Now as my father talked, I could hear the boarders on the porch attending in the same way, the stealthy creak of a rocker now and then, a low word spoken, a question, protest or agreement, and then their hungry, feeding, and attentive silence as my father talked. He spoke of all the wars and troubles he had known, told how he had stood, "a barefoot country boy," beside a dusty road twelve miles from Gettysburg, and had watched the ragged rebels march past upon the road that led to death and battle and the shipwreck of their hopes.

He spoke of the faint and ominous trembling of the guns across the hot brooding silence of the countryside, and how silence, wonder, and unspoken questions filled the hearts of all the people, and how they had gone about their work upon the farm as usual. He spoke of the years that had followed on the war when he was a stonecutter's apprentice in Baltimore, and he spoke of ancient joys and labors, forgotten acts and histories, and he spoke then with familiar memory of the lost Americans—the strange, lost, time-far, dead Americans, the remote, voiceless, and bewhiskered faces of the great Americans, who were more lost to me than Egypt, more far from me than the Tartarian coasts, more haunting strange than Cipango or the lost faces of the first dynastic kings that built the pyramids—and whom he had seen, heard, known, found familiar in the full pulse, and passion, and

139

proud glory of his youth: the lost, time-far, voiceless faces of Buchanan, Johnson, Douglas, Blaine—the proud, vacant, time-strange and bewhiskered visages of Garfield, Arthur, Harrison, and Hayes.

"Ah, Lord!" he said—his voice rang out in darkness like a gong, "Ah, Lord!—I've known all of 'em since James Buchanan's time—for I was a boy of six when he took office!" Here he paused a moment, lunged forward violently in his rocking chair, and spat cleanly out a spurt of strong tobacco juice across the porch rail into the loamy earth, the night-sweet fragrance of the geranium beds. "Yes, sir," he said gravely, lunging back again, while the attentive, hungry boarders waited in the living darkness and were still, "I remember all of them since James Buchanan's time, and I've seen most of them that came since Lincoln!—Ah, Lord!" he paused briefly for another waiting moment, shaking his grave head sadly in the dark. "Well do I remember the day when I stood on a street in Baltimore—poor friendless orphan that I was!" my father went on sorrowfully, but somewhat illogically, since at this time his mother was alive and in good health, upon her little farm in Pennsylvania, and would continue so for almost fifty years—"a poor friendless country boy of sixteen years, alone in the great city where I had come to learn my trade as an apprentice—and heard Andrew Johnson, then the president of this *great* nation," said my father, "speak from the platform of a horsecar—and he was so drunk—so *drunk*—" he howled, "the president of this country was so *drunk* that they had to stand on each side of him, and hold him as he spoke—or he'd a-gone head over heels into the gutter!" Here he paused, wet his great thumb briefly, cleared his throat with considerable satisfaction, lunged forward violently again in his rocking chair and spat strongly a wad of bright to- bacco juice into the loamy fragrance of the dark geranium bed.

"The first vote I ever cast for president," my fa- ther continued presently, as he lunged back again, "I cast in 1872, in Baltimore, for that *great* man— that brave and noble soldier—U. S. Grant! And I have voted for every Republican nominee for presi- dent ever since. I voted for Rutherford Hayes of Ohio in 1876—that was the year, as you well know, of the great Hayes-Tilden controversy, in 1880 for James Abram Garfield—that *great* good man," he said passionately, "who was so foully and brutally done to death by the cowardly assault of a murder- ous assassin." He paused, wet his thumb, breathing heavily, lunged forward in his rocking chair, and spat again. "In 1884, I cast my vote for James G. Blaine in the year that Grover Cleveland defeated him," he said shortly, "for Benjamin Harrison in 1888, and for Harrison again in 1892, the time that Cleveland got in for his second term—a time we will all remember to our dying days," my father said grimly, "for the Democrats were in and we had soup kitchens. And, you can mark my words," he howled, "you'll have them again, before these next four years are over—your guts will grease your back- bone, as sure as there's a God in heaven, before that fearful, that awful, that cruel, inhuman and blood- thirsty Monster who kept us out of war," my father jeered derisively, "is done with you—for hell, ruin, misery, and damnation commence every time the Democrats get in. You can rest assured of that!" he said shortly, cleared his throat, wet his thumb, lunged forward violently and spat again. And for a moment there was silence and the boarders waited.

141

"Ah, Lord!" my father said at length sadly, gravely, in a low, almost inaudible tone. And suddenly, all the old life and howling fury of his rhetoric had gone from him: he was an old man again, sick, indifferent, dying, and his voice had grown old, worn, weary, sad.

"Ah, Lord!" he muttered, shaking his head sadly, thinly, wearily in the dark. "I've seen them all. . . . I've seen them come and go . . . Garfield, Arthur, Harrison, and Hayes . . . and all . . . all . . . all of them are dead. . . . I'm the only one that's left," he said illogically, "and soon I'll be gone, too." And for a moment he was silent. "It's pretty strange when you come to think of it," he muttered. "By God it is!" And he was silent, and darkness, mystery, and night were all about us.

Garfield, Arthur, Harrison, and Hayes—time of my father's time, blood of his blood, life of his life, had been living, real, and actual people in all the passion, power, and feeling of my father's youth. And for me they were the lost Americans: their gravely vacant and bewhiskered faces mixed, melted, swam together in the sea depths of a past intangible, immeasurable, and unknowable as the buried city of Persepolis.

And they were lost.

For who was Garfield, martyred man, and who had seen him in the streets of life? Who could believe his footfalls ever sounded on a lonely pavement? Who had heard the casual and familiar tones of Chester Arthur? And where was Harrison? Where was Hayes? Which had the whiskers, which the burnsides: which was which?

Were they not lost?

Into their ears, as ours, the tumults of forgotten

crowds, upon their brains the million printings of
lost time, and suddenly upon their dying sight the
brief bitter pain and joy of a few death-bright, fixed
and fading memories: the twisting of a leaf upon a
bough, the grinding felloe rim against the curb, the
long, distant and retreating thunder of a train upon
the rails.

Garfield, Hayes, and Harrison were Ohio men;
but only the name of Garfield had been brightened
by his blood. But at night had they not heard the
howlings of demented wind, the sharp, clean,
windy raining to the earth of acorns? Had all of
them not walked down lonely roads at night in winter and seen a light and known it was theirs? Had all
of them not known the wilderness?

Had they not known the smell of old bound calf
and well-worn leathers, the Yankee lawyer's smell
of strong tobacco spit and courthouse urinals, the
smell of horses, harness, hay, and sweating country
men, of jury rooms and courtrooms—the strong
male smell of Justice at the county seat, and heard a
tap along dark corridors where fell a drop in darkness with a punctual crescent monotone of time,
dark time?

Had not Garfield, Hayes, and Harrison studied
law in offices with a dark brown smell? Had not the
horses trotted past below their windows in wreaths
of dust along a straggling street of shacks and buildings with false fronts? Had they not heard below
them the voices of men talking, loitering up in
drawling heat? Had they not heard the casual, rich-
fibered, faintly howling country voices, and heard
the rustling of a woman's skirt, and waiting silence,
slyly lowered tones of bawdry and then huge guf-
faws, slapped meaty thighs, and high fat choking
laughter? And in the dusty dozing heat, while time

143

buzzed slowly, like a fly, had not Garfield, Arthur, Harrison, and Hayes then smelled the river, the humid, subtly fresh, half-rotten river, and thought of the white flesh of the women then beside the river, and felt a slow impending passion in their entrails, a heavy rending power in their hands?

Then Garfield, Arthur, Harrison, and Hayes had gone to war, and each became a brigadier or major general. All were bearded men: they saw a spattering of bright blood upon the leaves, and they heard the soldiers talking in the dark of food and women. They held the bridgehead in bright dust at places with such names as Wilson's Mill and Spangler's Run, and their men smashed cautiously through dense undergrowth. And they had heard the surgeons cursing after battles, and the little rasp of saws. They had seen boys standing awkwardly holding their entrails in their hands, and pleading pitifully with fear-bright eyes: "Is it bad, General? Do you think it's bad?"

When the canister came through it made a ragged hole. It smashed through tangled leaves and boughs, sometimes it plunked solidly into the fiber of a tree. Sometimes when it struck a man it tore away the roof of his brain, the wall of his skull, raggedly, so that his brains seethed out upon a foot of wilderness, and the blood blackened and congealed, and he lay there in his thick clumsy uniform, with a smell of urine in the wool, in the casual, awkward, and incompleted attitude of sudden death. And when Garfield, Arthur, Harrison, and Hayes saw these things they saw that it was not like the picture they had had, as children, it was not like the works of Walter Scott and William Gillmore Sims. They saw that the hole was not clean and small and in the central front, and the field was not

144

green nor fenced, nor mown. Over the vast and immemorable earth the quivering heated light of afternoon was shining, a field swept rudely upward to a lift of rugged wood, and field by field, gulley by gulch by fold, the earth advanced in rude, sweet, limitless convolutions.

Then Garfield, Arthur, Harrison, and Hayes had paused by the bridgehead for a moment and were still, seeing the bright blood at noon upon the trampled wheat, feeling the brooding hush of six o'clock across the fields where all the storming feet had passed at dawn, seeing the way the rough field hedge leaned out across the dusty road, the casual intrusions of the coarse field grasses and the hot dry daisies to the edges of the road, seeing the rock-bright shallows of the creek, the sweet cool shade and lean of river trees across the water.

They paused then by the bridgehead looking at the water. They saw the stark blank flatness of the old red mill that somehow was like sunset, coolness, sorrow, and delight, and looking at the faces of dead boys among the wheat, the most-oh-most-familiar plain, the death-strange faces of the dead Americans, they stood there for a moment, thinking, feeling, thinking, with strong, wordless wonder in their hearts:

"As we leaned on the sills of evening, as we stood in the frames of the marvellous doors, as we were received into silence, the flanks of the slope and the slanted light, as we saw the strange hushed shapes upon the land, the muted distances, knowing all things then—what could we say except that all our comrades were spread quietly around us and that noon was far?

"What can we say now of the lonely land—what can we say now of the deathless shapes and substances—what can we say who have lived here with our lives, bone, blood, and brain, and all our tongue-less languages, hearing on many a casual road the plain-familiar voices of Americans, and who tomorrow will be buried in the earth, knowing the fields will steep to silence after us, the slant light deepen on the slopes, and peace and evening will come back again—at one now with the million shapes and single substance of our land, at one with evening, peace, the huge stride of the undulant oncoming night, at one, also, with morning?

"Silence receive us, and the field of peace, hush of the measureless land, the unabated distances; shape of the one and single substance and the million forms, replenish us, restore us, and unite us with your vast images of quietness and joy. Stride of the undulant night, come swiftly now; engulf us, silence, in your great-starred secrecy; speak to our hearts of stillness, for we have, save this, no speech.

"There is the bridge we crossed, the mill we slept in, and the creek. There is a field of wheat, a hedge, a dusty road, an apple orchard, and the sweet wild tangle of a wood upon that hill. And there is six o'clock across the fields again, now and always, as it was and will be to the world's end forever. And some of us have died this morning coming through the field—and that was time—time—time. We shall not come again, we never shall come back again, we never shall come back along this road again as we did once at morning—so, brothers, let us look again before we go. . . . There is the mill, and there the hedge, and there the shallows of the rock-bright waters of the creek, and there the sweet and most familiar coolness of the trees—and surely we have been this way before!" they cried.

"Oh, surely, brothers, we have sat upon the

bridge, before the mill, and sung together by the rock-bright waters of the creek at evening, and come across the wheatfield in the morning and heard the dew-sweet birdsong rising from the hedge before! You plain, oh-most-familiar and most homely earth, proud earth of this huge land unutterable, proud nobly swelling earth, in all your delicacy, wildness, savagery, and terror—grand earth in all your loneliness, beauty and wild joy, terrific earth in all your limitless fecundities, swelling with infinite fold and convolution into the reaches of the West forever—American earth!—bridge, hedge, and creek and dusty road—you plain tremendous poetry of Wilson's Mill, where boys died in the wheat this morning—you unutterable far-near, strange-familiar, homely earth of magic, for which a word would do if we could find it, for which a word would do if we could call it by its name, for which a word would do that never can be spoken, that can never be forgotten, and that will never be revealed—oh, proud, familiar, nobly swelling earth, it seems we must have known you before! It seems we must have known you forever, but all we know for certain is that we came along this road one time at morning, and now our blood is painted on the wheat, and you are ours now, we are yours forever— and there is something here we never shall remember—there is something here we never shall forget!"

Had Garfield, Arthur, Harrison, and Hayes been young? Or had they all been born with flowing whiskers, sideburns, and wing collars, speaking gravely from the cradle of their mother's arms the noble vacant sonorities of far-seeing statesmanship? It could not be. Had they not all been young men in the thirties, the forties, and the fifties? Did they not, as we, cry out at night along deserted roads into demented winds? Did they not, as we, cry out in ecstasy and exultancy, as the full measure of their hunger, their potent and inchoate hope, went out into that single wordless cry?

Did they not, as we, when young, prowl softly up and down in the dark hours of the night, seeing the gaslamps flare and flutter on the corner, falling with livid light upon the corners of old cobbled streets of brownstone houses? Had they not heard the lonely rhythmic clopping of a horse, the jounting wheels of a hansom cab, upon those barren cobbles? And had they not waited, trembling in the darkness till the horse and cab had passed, had vanished with the lonely recession of shod hoofs, and then were heard no more?

And then had Garfield, Arthur, Harrison, and Hayes not waited, waited in the silence of the night, prowling up and down the lonely cobbled street, with trembling lips, numb entrails, pounding hearts? Had they not set their jaws, made sudden indecisive movements, felt terror, joy, a numb impending ecstasy, and waited, waited then—for what? Had they not waited, hearing sounds of shifting engines in the yards at night, hearing the hoarse, gaseous breaths of little engines through the grimy fan-flare of their funnels? Had they not waited there in that dark street with the fierce lone hunger of a boy, feeling around them the immense and moving quietness of sleep, the heartbeats of ten thousand sleeping men, as they waited, waited in the night?

Had they not, as we, then turned their eyes up and seen the huge starred visage of the night, the immense and lilac darkness of America in April? Had they not heard the sudden, shrill, and piping whistle of a departing engine? Had they not waited, thinking, feeling, seeing then the immense mysterious continent of night, the wild and lyric earth, so casual, sweet, and strange-familiar, in all its space and savagery and terror, its mystery and joy, its limitless sweep and rudeness, its delicate and savage fecundity? Had they not had a vision of the plains, the mountains, and the rivers flowing in the darkness, the huge pattern of the everlasting earth and the all-engulfing wilderness of America?

Had they not felt, as we have felt, as they waited in the night, the huge, lonely earth of nighttime and America, on which ten thousand lonely sleeping little towns were strewn? Had they not seen the fragile network of light, racketing, ill-joined little rails across the land, over which the lonely little trains rushed on in darkness, flinging a handful of lost echoes at the river's edge, leaving an echo in the cut's resounding cliff, and being engulfed then in huge lonely night, in all-brooding, all-engulfing night? Had they not known, as we have known, the wild secret joy and mystery of the everlasting earth, the lilac dark, the savage, silent, all-possessing wilderness that gathered in around ten thousand lonely little towns, ten million lost and lonely sleepers, and waited, and abode forever, and was still?

Had not Garfield, Arthur, Harrison, and Hayes then waited, feeling wild joy and sorrow in their hearts, and a savage hunger and desire—a flame, a fire, a fury—burning fierce and lean and lonely in the night, burning forever while the sleepers slept? Were they not burning, burning, burning, even as the rest of us have burned? Were Garfield, Arthur, Harrison, and Hayes not burning in the night? Were they not burning forever in the silence of the little towns, with all the fierce hunger, savage passion,

149

limitless desire that young men in this land have known in the darkness?

Had Garfield, Arthur, Harrison, and Hayes not waited then, as we have waited, with numb lips and pounding hearts and fear, delight, strong joy and terror stirring in their entrails as they stood in the silent street before a house, proud, evil, lavish, lighted—certain, secret, and alone? And as they heard the hoof, the wheel, the sudden whistle and the immense and sleeping silence of the town, did they not wait there in the darkness, thinking:

"Oh, there are new lands, morning, and a shining city. Soon, soon, soon!"

Did not Garfield, Arthur, Harrison, and Hayes, those fierce and jubilant young men, who waited there, as we have waited, in the silent barren street, with trembling lips, numb hands, with terror, savage joy, fierce rapture alive and stirring in their entrails—did they not feel, as we have felt, when they heard the shrill departing warning of the whistle in the dark, the sound of great wheels pounding at the river's edge? Did they not feel, as we have felt, as they waited there in the intolerable sweetness, wildness, mystery, and terror of the great earth in the month of April, and knew themselves alone, alive and young and mad and secret with desire and hunger in the great sleep-silence of the night, the impending, cruel, all-promise of this land? Were they not torn, as we have been, by sharp pain and wordless lust, the asp of time, the thorn of spring, the sharp, the tongueless cry? Did they not say:

"Oh, there are women in the East—and new lands, morning, and a shining city! There are forgotten fume-flaws of bright smoke above Manhattan, the forest of masts about the crowded isle, the proud cleavages of departing ships, the soaring web, the

winglike swoop and joy of the great bridge, and men
with derby hats who come across the bridge to greet
us—come, brothers, let us go to find them all! For
the huge murmur of the city's million-footed life,
far, beelike, drowsy, strange as time, has come to
haunt our ears with all its golden prophecy of joy
and triumph, fortune, happiness and love such as no
men before have ever known. Oh, brothers, in the
city, in the far-shining, glorious, time-enchanted
spell of that enfabled city we shall find great men
and lovely women, and unceasingly ten thousand
new delights, a thousand magical adventures! We
shall wake at morning in our rooms of lavish brown
to hear the hoof and wheel upon the city street
again, and smell the harbor, fresh, half-rotten, with
its bracelet of bright tides, its traffic of proud sea-
borne ships, its purity and joy of dancing morning
gold.

"Street of the day, with the unceasing promise of
your million-footed life, we come to you!" they
cried. "Street of the thunderous wheels at noon,
street of the great parades of marching men, the
band's bright oncoming blare, the brave stick-candy
whippings of a flag, street of the cries and shouts,
the swarming feet,—street of the jounting cabs, the
ringing hooves, the horsecars and the jingling bells,
the in-horse ever bending its sad nodding head toward its lean and patient comrade on the right—
great street of furious life and movement, noon, and
joyful labors, your image blazes in our hearts forever, and we come!

"Street of the morning, street of hope!" they
cried. "Street of coolness, slanted light, the frontal
cliff and gulch of steep blue shade, street of the
dancing morning gold of waters on the flashing
tides, street of the rusty weathered slips, the blunt-

151

nosed ferry foaming in with its packed wall of small white staring faces, all silent and intent, all turned toward *you*—proud street! Street of the pungent sultry smells of new-ground coffee, the good green smell of money, the fresh half-rotten harbor smells with all its evocation of your mast-bound harbor and its tide of ships, great street!—Street of the old buildings grimed richly with the warm and mellow dinginess of trade—street of the million morning feet forever hurrying onward in the same direction—proud street of hope and joy and morning, in your steep canyon we shall win the wealth, the fame, the power and the esteem which our lives and talents merit!

"Street of the night!" they cried, "great street of mystery and suspense, terror and delight, eagerness and hope, street edged forever with the dark menace of impending joy, an unknown happiness and fulfillment, street of gaiety, warmth, and evil, street of the great hotels, the lavish bars and restaurants, and the softly golden glow, the fading lights and empetalled whiteness of a thousand hushed white thirsty faces in the crowded theatres, street of the tidal flood of faces, lighted with your million lights and all thronging, tireless and unquenched in their insatiate searching after pleasure, street of the lovers coming along with slow steps, their faces turned toward each other, lost in the oblivion of love among the everlasting web and weaving of the crowd, street of the white face, the painted mouth, the shining and inviting eye—oh, street of night, with all your mystery, joy, and terror—we have thought of you, proud street.

"And we shall move at evening in the noiseless depths of sumptuous carpets through all the gaiety, warmth, and brilliant happiness of great lighted chambers of the night, filled with the mellow thrum and languor of the violins, and where the loveliest and most desirable women in the world—the beloved daughters of great merchants, bankers, millionaires, or rich young widows, beautiful, loving, and alone—are moving with a slow proud undulance, a look of depthless tenderness in their fragile, lovely faces. And the loveliest of them all," they cried, "is ours, is ours forever, if we want her! For, brothers, in the city, in the far-shining, magic, golden city, we shall move among great men and glorious women and know nothing but strong joy and happiness forever, winning by our courage, talent, and deserving the highest and most honored place in the most fortunate and happy life that men have known, if only we will go and make it ours!"

So thinking, feeling, waiting as we have waited in the sleeping silence of the night in silent streets, hearing, as we have heard, the sharp blast of the warning whistle, the thunder of great wheels upon the river's edge, feeling, as we have felt, the mystery of nighttime and of April, the huge impending presence, the wild and secret promise, of the savage, lonely, everlasting earth, finding, as we have found, no doors to enter, and being torn, as we were torn, by the thorn of spring, the sharp, the wordless cry, did they not carry—these young men of the past, Garfield, Arthur, Harrison, and Hayes—even as we have carried, within their little tenements of bone, blood, sinew, sweat, and agony, the intolerable burden of all the pain, joy, hope and savage hunger that a man can suffer, that the world can know?

Were they not lost? Were they not lost, as all of us have been who have known youth and hunger in this land, and who have waited lean and mad and lonely in the night, and who have found no goal, no wall, no dwelling, and no door?

*　*　*

The years flow by like water, and one day it is spring again. Shall we ever ride out of the gates of the East again, as we did once at morning, and seek again, as we did then, new lands, the promise of the war, and glory, joy, and triumph, and a shining city?

O youth, still wounded, living, feeling with a woe unutterable, still grieving with a grief intolerable, still thirsting with a thirst unquenchable—where are we to seek? For the wild tempest breaks above us, the wild fury beats about us, the wild hunger feeds upon us—and we are houseless, doorless, unassuaged, and driven on forever; and our brains are mad, our hearts are wild and wordless, and we cannot speak.

Gulliver

S omeday someone will write a book about a man who was too tall—who lived forever in a dimension that he did not fit, and for whom the proportions of everything—chairs, beds, doors, rooms, shoes, clothes, shirts and socks, the berths of Pullman cars, and the bunks of transatlantic liners, together with the rations of food, drink, love, and women which most men on this earth have found sufficient to their measure—were too small.

He should write the story of that man's journey through this world with the conviction of incontrovertible authority, and with such passion, power, and knowledge that every word will have the golden ring of truth; and he will be able to do this because that man's life has been his own, because he has lived it, breathed it, moved in it, and made it his with every sinew of his life since he was fifteen years of age, and because there is no one on earth who understands that world, in all the joy and pain and strangeness of its incommunicable loneliness, as well as such a man.

The world this man would live in is the world of six feet six, and that is the strangest and most lonely world there is. For the great distances of this world are the fractional ones, the terrific differences are those which we can measure by a hand, a step, a few short inches, and that shut us as completely from the world we see, the life we love, the room, the door we want to enter, as if we saw them from the star-flung planetary distances of bridgeless and unmeasured vacancy. Yes, that world we see and want is even more remote from us than Mars, for it is almost ours at every instant, intolerably near and warm and palpable, and intolerably far because it is so very near—only a foot away if we could span it, only a word, a wall, a door away if we could utter, find, and enter it—and we are lashed on by our fury and devoured by our own hunger, captives in the iron and impregnable walls of our own loneliness.

To be a giant, to be one of those legendary creatures two miles high in the old stories—that is another thing. For a giant lives in his own world and needs and wants no other: he takes a mountain at a stride, drinks off a river in one gulp of thirst, wanders over half a continent in a day, and then comes home at night to dine in friendship with his fellow Titans, using a shelf of mountain as a table, a foothill as a stool, and the carcasses of whole roast oxen as the dainty morsels of his feast.

And to be a giant in a world of pygmy men—to be a mile-high creature in a world of foot-high men—that also is another thing. For sometimes his huge single eye is blinded by their cunning, he will make the mountains echo with his wounded cries, tear up a forest in his pain and fury, and will lash about him with an oak tree, and hurl ten-ton boulders torn from granite hills after the little ships of terror-stricken men.

He awakes at morning in a foreign land, his ship is wrecked, his comrades drowned, and he forsaken: a regiment of tiny creatures are swarming up across his body, they shoot their tiny arrows at his face and bind him down with countless weavings of a thread-like cord, and the terrific legend of his life among the pygmies becomes the instrument by which another giant whipped the folly, baseness, and corruption in the lives of men with the scorpion lash of the most savage allegory ever written.

And to be a pygmy in a world of pygmy men, that also is another thing. For where we all are inches tall, our size is only measured by proportion. We live elf-close and midget-near the earth, and desperately explore the tropic jungle of the daisy fields while monstrous birds—huge buzzing flies and booming bees and tottering butterflies unfurl the enormous velvet sails of their slashed wings as they soar over us. We think we are as tall, as big, as strong as any men that ever lived, and in our three-inch world our corn and wheat is good but is no higher than the grass. We wander through great gloomy forests no taller than scrub pine, there are no Atlantic depths and Himalayan heights, our grandest mountain ranges are just molehill high, and if the stars seem far, most far, to us, they are no farther than they seem to other men.

Finally, to be one of those poor giants and midgets of the time in which we live—one of these paltry eight- and nine-foot Titans, two-foot dwarfs of circuses—that also is a different thing. For now they live the life, and love the lights of carnival, and the world beyond those lights is phantom and obscure. Each day the world throngs in to sit beneath the canvas top and feed its fascinated eye on their deformities, and they display themselves before that world and are not moved by interest, touched by desire, from what they see of it. Instead they live together in the world of freaks, and this world seems to them to have been framed inevitably by nature. They love, hate, plot, contrive, betray, and hope, are happy, sorrowful, and ambitious like all other men.

159

The eight-foot giant and the two-foot dwarf are bosom friends. And three times a day they sit down and eat at table in an interesting and congenial society given charm and romance by The Fat Girl and The Bearded Lady and piquant zest by the witty repartee of Jo-Jo-What-Is-It, The Living Skeleton, and The Tattooed Man. But that, as well, is not a tall man's world: it is another door he cannot enter.

For he is earthy, of the earth, like every man. Shaped from the same clay, breathing the same air, fearing the same fears, and hoping the same hopes as all men in the world, he walks the thronging streets of life alone—those streets that swarm forever with their tidal floods of five feet eight. He walks those streets forever a stranger, and alone, having no other earth, no other life, no other door than this, and feeding upon it with an eye of fire, a heart of intolerable hunger and desire, yet walled away from all the dimensional security of that great room of life by the length of an arm, the height of a head, the bitter small denial of a foot—seeing, feeling, knowing, and desiring the life that blazes there before his eyes, which is as near as his heart, and as far as heaven, which he could put his hand upon at every moment, and which he can never enter, fit, or make his own again, no more than if he were phantasmal substances of smoke.

It is a strange adventure—the adventure of being very tall—and in its essence it comes to have a singular and instinctive humanity. In an extraordinary way, a tall man comes to know things about the world as other people do not, cannot, know them. And the reason for this lies mainly in the purely fortuitous quality of a tall man's difference from average humanity. In no respect, save in respect to his unusual height, is a tall man different from other men. In no way is he less his brother's brother, or his father's son. In fact—astonishing as that fact may seem—the overwhelming probability is that a tall man never thinks of being tall, never realizes indeed, that he *is* tall until other people remind him of his height.

Thus, there was a tall man once and when he was alone he never thought of his great height; it never occurred to him that his dimensions were in any way different from those of most of the people that he saw around him every day upon the streets. In fact, he was the victim of an extraordinary delusion: for some reason which he could not define, he had a secret and unspoken conviction—an image of himself that was certainly not the product of his conscious reasoning, but rather the unconscious painting of his desire—that he was really a person of average height and size—a man of five feet eight or nine, no more. A moment's reflection would, of course, instantly tell him that this picture of himself was wrong, but his natural and instinctive tendency was to think—or rather *feel*—himself in this perspective. It was, therefore, only natural, that when his attention was rudely and forcibly brought to a realization of his unusual height—as it was a hundred times a day now by people on the street—he should receive the news with a sense of shocked surprise, bewilderment, and finally with quick flaring anger and resentment.

He would be going along a street at five o'clock when the city was pouring homeward from its work, and suddenly he would become conscious that people were watching him: would see them stare at him and nudge each other, would see their surprised looks travelling curiously up his frame, would hear them whisper to each other in astonished voices, **161** and see them pass him, laughing, and hear their oaths and words of astounded disbelief, hilarious surprise. When this happened, he could have strangled them. As he heard their scoffs and jokes and exclamations—those dreary husks of a stale and lifeless humor which are the same the world over, which never change, and which have worn their weary rut into a tall man's heart and brain until he knows them as no one else can ever know them— he felt almost that he could *choke* them into wisdom, seize them, knock their heads together, snarl at them:

"Goddamn you, but I'll show you that I am the same as you if I have to shake you into owning it!"

Thus he was the butt, a hundred times a day, of those clumsy, tiresome but well-intentioned jocularities to which, in course of time, a tall man becomes so patiently accustomed, so wearily resigned. And his own response to them was probably the same as that of every other tall man who ever lived and had to weather the full measure of man's abysmal foolishness. At first, he felt only the fierce and quick resentment of youth, the truculent sensitivity of youth's wounded pride, its fear of ridicule, its swift readiness to take offense, to feel that it was being flouted, mocked, insulted, its desire to fight and to avenge its wounded honor.

And then he felt a kind of terrible shame and self-abasement: a feeling of personal inferiority that made him envy the lot of average men, that made him bitterly regret the accident of birth and nature that had imprisoned a spirit fierce and proud and swift as flight, and burning as a flame, in such a grotesque tenement. And this feeling of shame and self-abasement and hatred of his flesh is the worst

162

thing that a tall man knows, the greatest iniquity
that his spirit suffers. For it is during this period that
he comes to hate the body that has been given him
by birth and nature, and by this act of hatred, he de-
grades himself and dishonors man. For this loathing
for his body is like the ignoble hatred that a man
may have for a loyal and ugly friend whose destiny
is coherent with his own, and who must endure.
And endure he does—this loyal ugly friend that is
man's grotesque tenement—and goes with him
everywhere in all his mad and furious marchings,
and serves man faithfully like no other friend on
earth, and suffers the insults and injuries that man
heaps upon him, the frenzy, passion, and brute ex-
haustion, the scars, the sickness, and the pain, the
surfeits of his master's intolerable hunger, and at
the end, all battered, scarred, debased, befouled,
and coarsened by his master's excess, is still with
him, inseparable as his shadow, loyal to the end—a
friend homely, true, devoted, good as no one else
can ever be, who sticks with us through every trouble, stays by us through every brawl, bears the brunt
of all our drinking, eating, and our brutal battery,
reels in and out of every door with us, and falls with
us down every flight of stairs, and whom we one day
find again before us—as a madman may discover
light and sanity again and see the comrade, the protector and the victim of his madness steady there
before him, grinning at him wryly through his
puffed and battered lips, and saying with a rueful
but an all-forgiving humor:

"Well—here we are again."

It is a strange adventure, a hard but precious education, that a tall man knows. For finally he comes to
learn, through sweat and toil and bitter anguish, a
stern but not a desolate humanity. He gets a kind of   **163**

lonely wisdom that no one else on earth can get. And by the strange and passionate enigma of his destiny, he is drawn close to man by the very circumstance that shuts him out. He enters life through the very door that once he thought was shut against him, is of the earth, more earthy, by the fact of his exclusion. A tall man could not escape from life, or flee the world, even if he desired it: he is at once life's exile and life's prisoner; wherever he goes life reaches out and pulls him to it, will not let him go. And at the end, he learns the truth of Ernest Renan's bitter observation—that the only thing that can give one a conception of the infinite is the extent of human stupidity. And in the jibes, the jests, the drolleries that are shouted after him a dozen times a day in the streets because of his great height, in the questions that are asked concerning it, and in the innumerable conversations that it provokes, he acquires a huge and damning accumulation of evidence concerning man's fatal unity, the barren paucity of his invention, the desolate consonance of his wit.

For one such man, at least, it never changed, it was always the same: it went on day by day and month by month in the narrow crowded streets around him, and it would go on year after year in a hundred cities, a dozen countries, amid a thousand scattered places in all quarters of the world, and it would always be the same—a barren formula endlessly renewed with the unwearied pertinacity of an idiot monotony—it would always be the same.

He never found the slightest deviation in that barren formula. No one ever made an interesting or amusing observation about his height—and ten thousand people talked to him about it. No one ever said a funny or a witty thing about his height, and ten thousand people had their fling about it. No one ever showed the slightest understanding of the nature of a tall man's life, or asked a single shrewd and penetrating question about it—and yet the curiosity that his tallness caused was almost incredible, the conversations that he had, the questions that he had to answer were innumerable.

The barren formula was so endlessly repeated that at length it had worn its dull grooves into his brain, and he answered without thinking, replied without listening, giving mechanically the answers that they wished to hear, the tried and trusted formula that had served its purpose so many thousand times before, knowing in advance what everyone would say.

Was it wit? Then let the diligent historian of the nation's wit give ear and pay attention to these drolleries which were shouted after one man's tall receding figure as he trod the pavements of ten thousand streets:

"Hey-y!"

"Hey-y! Youse guy!"

"Hey-y-y! . . . Holy   Jeez! . . . Chizzus! . . . Look ut duh guy!"

"Hey-y, Mis-teh! . . . Is it rainin' up deh? . . . Cheezus! . . . Ho-lee Chee! . . . Will yuh lookut duh guy?"

"Hey-y—Mis-teh! . . . How's duh weatheh up deh? . . . Ho-lee Chee! . . . Take a lookut duh size of 'm, will yah?"

Such, then, were the evidences of the popular humor upon this subject—by a high authority it can solemnly be affirmed that these evidences were all there were.

Or was it conversation of a more polite and genteel sort—well-bred consolation, soothing affirmations, suave flatteries meant to hearten and give cheer? The formula in this kind of conversation ran as follows:

"You're ver-ee tall, aren't you?"

"Yes—hah! hah!—yes—hah! hah!—I suppose I am—hah! hah!—I suppose you noticed it!"

"Yes, I did—when you got up, it did seem ra-ther overwhelming the first time—(with hasty correction)—only of course, one doesn't notice it at *all* later . . . I *mean* one forgets all about it . . . I *ree-lee* think you'd be *awf-lee* glad you *are* that way . . . I *mean*, that's the way most people would like to be . . . it does give you such an advantage, doesn't it?. . . I *mean*, after *all*, everyone would be that way if they could—no one wants to be *short*, do they? . . . Everyone would much rather be *tall* . . . I *mean*, it makes everyone look *up* to you, doesn't it, wherever you go. . . . *Ree-lee*, I shouldn't think you'd *mind* at all . . . I should think you'd be glad you *are* that way . . . I *mean*, after *all*, it does give you a great advantage, *doesn't it?* . . . Do you see what I *mean?*"

"Yes . . . ah-hah-hah! . . . I certainly do! . . . ah-hah-hah! . . . Yes, I certainly do see what you mean . . . ah-hah-hah! . . . You're right about it . . . ah-hah-hah! . . . I certainly do!"

Or was it friendly banter, now, a kindly curiosity of a rougher sort, among a simple yet good-natured kind of men? Suppose a scene, then: such a scene as one has found ten thousand times within the labyrinth of night upon the seaboard of the continent. It is an airless groove in an old wall behind blind windows set in rotting brick: within, a slab of bar, its wet shine puddled here and there with rings of glasses; a battered rail of brass, not polished recently; and a radiance of hard dead light; Leo, the barman, with his jowled, swart face of night, professionally attentive; and at the end, the dead stamped visages of night, the rasping snarl of drunken voices, the elbows of the barflies puddled in beer slop.

The buzzer rings, good Leo peers with hard mistrust through opened slot, the door is opened, and the tall man enters, to whom at once Pat Grogan— wit by nature, Kelt by birth, and now the antic of good Leo's bar—approaches, with the small red eyes of rheum and murder comically astare, ape shoulders stooped, ape knees bowed and tucked under, and jowled ape visage comically turned upwards in a stare of apelike stupefaction—all most comical to see—while good Leo looks and chuckles heavily and all the barflies grin. So, now, as follows:

Grogan (still crouching): *"Je-zus . . . Christ! . . . Ho-lee Jeez! . . .* What's dat guy *standin'* on, anyway? . . . (Leo and all the grinning barflies chortle with appreciative delight, and thus encouraged, Jolly Grogan carries on) . . . Jee-zus! (with a slow bewildered lifting of his red-jowled face, he calculates the visitor from foot to head—a delicate stroke, not lost by any means on grinning Leo and his appreciative clientele) . . . Say-y! . . . When I first saw dat guy I t'ought he was standin' on a box or somep'n . . . (turning to Leo with an air of fine bewilderment) . . . Take a look ut 'im, will yuh? *Ho-lee* Chee! . . . Who *is* dis guy, anyway? . . . (turning to all the grinning others) . . . When I foist sees duh guy, I says t' myself . . . What *is* dis, anyway? . . . Is duh *coicus* in town or somep'n? (turns again, gesturing to tall visitor with air of frank bewilderment) . . . Take a look at 'm, will yah? . . .(satisfied with his success, he rejoins his grinning and appreciative comrades, and for some time further regales them by taking astounded

167

glances at the tall visitor, shaking his head in a bewildered way, and saying in an unbelieving tone) . . . But *Je-sus*! . . . Take a look at 'm, will yah?" etc.

And now Leo, shaking his head slowly to himself with appreciative admiration of his client's wit, approaches the tall visitor and still chuckling heartily at the recollection, leans over the bar and whispers confidingly:

"Dat's Mistuh Grogan. . . . (a trifle apologetically) He's been drinkin' a little so don't pay no attention to anyt'ing he says. . . . He didn't mean nuttin' by it—(with ponderous assurance) Nah-h! . . . He's one of duh nicest guys you eveh saw when he's not drinkin' . . . he's only kiddin' anyway . . . he don't mean nuttin' by it . . . but *Je-sus*! (suddenly laughs heartily at the recollection, a heavy, swarthy, and deliberate hah-hah-hah that sets all of his nighttime jowls a-quiver) . . . I had t' laff when he pulled dat one about yuh standin' on a box or somep'n . . . hah! hah! hah! hah! hah! . . . But he don't mean nuttin' by it! . . . Nah-h! . . . One of duh nicest guys yuh eveh saw when he's not drinkin'! . . . When he pulled dat one aboutcha standin' on a box or somep'n, I had t' laugh . . . duh way he said it! . . . Standin' on a box or somep'n—dat's a good one! . . . Hah! Hah! Hah! Hah! Hah!" . . . (and goes heavily away, heaving with slow nocturnal laughter, shaking his head slowly to himself).

Now, as the visitor stands drinking by himself, the barflies cluster at the other end in excited controversy, from which disputatious murmurs may be heard from time to time—such vehement scraps of affirmation or denial as the following:

"Nah-h! . . . Guh-*wan*! . . . Watcha givin' me? . . . He's more'n dat . . . I'll betcha on it! . . .

Nah-h! . . .Guh-*wan*! . . . He's oveh *seven* if he's
an inch! . . . Guh-*wan*! . . . I'll betcha on it! . . .
All right! All right! . . . Guh-wan and *ast* him
den! . . . But he's more'n dat! I'll betcha on
it!" . . .

One of the debaters now detaches himself from
his disputatious group, and beer glass in hand, approaches the lone visitor. . . . A face not bad, not
vicious, not unfriendly: face of a city man in the late
forties—the face of the cartoonist drawing—lean,
furrowed, large-nosed, deeply seamed, a little
sunken around the mouth, almost metallically
stamped, and wisely knowing, cynically assured—
the nerve ends stunned, the language strident, utterly, unmistakably, the city's child.

The City's Child (grinning amiably, a trifle apologetically, lowering his voice, and speaking with a
natural tension of his lips, out of the corners of his
mouth): . . . "Podden me, Mac . . . I hope yuh
don't mind my astin' yuh a question . . . but my
frien's an' me has been havin' a leetle oggument
aboutcha . . . an' I gotta little question dat I'd like
t' ast yuh. . . . Yuh don't mind, do yuh?"

The Tall Stranger (grinning mechanically and
laughing an agreeable and complaisant laugh of
utter falseness): "Why, no! . . . ah-hah-hah! . . .
Not at all! . . . ah-hah-hah! . . . Go right ahead, it's
perfectly all right. . . . Ah-hah-hah."

The City's Child: "Because if yuh do I wantcha t'
say so . . . I guess a lotta guys ast yuh duh same
question an' I t'ought mebbe yuh might get tired
hearin' it—you know what I mean? . . . A lotta
guys might get tired of bein' ast duh same question
so many times . . . (with an expression of difficulty
on his face, shrugs his shoulders expressively and
says hopefully) *You* know?"

The Tall Stranger: "Why . . . ah-hah-hah! . . .

169

Yes . . . I think I do. . . . That is to say, go right ahead . . . ah-hah-hah . . . it's quite all right."

The City's Child: "I guess so many guys have ast yuh dis same question dat yuh can guess already what it is —can't yuh?"

The Tall Stranger: "Why, yes—no—ah-hah-hah! . . . That is to say—*Yes!* . . . I think I can!"

The City's Child: "Well, den, Mac . . . if yuh *don't* mind . . . if it's all right . . . I was just goin' t' ast yuh . . . (whispering persuasively) . . . just t' settle a little oggument I been havin' wit' my frien's—*How tall are yuh?* . . . (hastily). Now if yuh don't want t' tell me, it's OK. . . . Yuh know how it is, *some* guys . . ."

The Tall Stranger: "Not at all—ah-hah-hah—that is to say, *yes*—ah-hah-hah . . . it's quite all right . . . I don't mind at all. . . . I'm between six feet five and six feet six . . . that is, I haven't measured for some time . . . but I was between six feet five and six feet six the last time that I measured. . . . (Apologetically) That's been some time ago . . . several years ago since I last measured . . . but . . . ah-hah-hah . . . it was between six feet five and six feet six and I don't think I've grown much since then . . . ah-hah-hah. . . . Between six feet five and six feet six."

The City's Child (with an astonished but somewhat disappointed air): "Is *dat* a fact? . . . I t'ought you was more'n dat! . . . I t'ought you was aroun' seven foot . . . but anotheh guy oveh heah said you wasn't more'n six foot seven or eight . . . (reflectively). . . . Six foot five or six, eh? . . . Is dat a fact? . . . I t'ought you was more'n dat!"

The Tall Stranger: "No . . . ah-hah-hah . . . a lot of people think so . . . but I guess that's right . . . about six feet five or six."

171

The City's Child (jocularly): "Say! . . . Yuh know watta guy like *you* oughta do! . . . Yuh know what *I'd* do if I was big as you——"

The Tall Stranger: "Why, no . . . ah-hah-hah— What's that?"

The City's Child: "I'd go in duh ring an' fight Dempsey . . . I'd fight *all* dose guys. . . . Dat's what I'd do. . . . A guy as big as you could hit an awful wallop . . . and wit' your reach dey couldn't touch yuh. . . . Dat's what I'd do if I had yoeh size! I'd go in duh ring—yes, sir!—Dat's just duh t'ing I'd do if I was big as *you*."

The Tall Stranger (rising glibly and mechanically to the occasion): "Well, you'd better be glad you're not. . . . You don't know how lucky you are."

The City's Child (in a slow, interested voice): "Oh yeah?"

The Tall Stranger (getting off his little speech rapidly and glibly): "Sure. A guy like me has nothing but trouble everywhere he turns."

The City's Child (with awakened interest): "Oh yeah?"

The Tall Stranger: "Sure. They don't make anything big enough to fit you."

The City's Child (with an air of slow, surprised revelation): "Say! I guess dat's right, at dat!"

The Tall Stranger: "Sure it is! You can't get a bed long enough to sleep in——"

The City's Child (curiously): "I guess yuh got to sleep all doubled up, heh?"

The Tall Stranger: "Sure I have. Like this, see!" (Here he makes a zigzag movement with his hand and the City's Child laughs hoarsely.)

The City's Child: "Wat d' yuh do about clo'es? I guess yuh gotta have everyt'ing made to ordeh, huh?"

The Tall Stranger: "Sure." (And according to the formula, now tells his fascinated listener that the cot he sleeps on is a foot too short for him, that he cannot stretch out straight in a berth or a steamer bunk, that he cracks his head against the rafters as he descends a steep flight of stairs, that he cannot find room for his knees in theatres or buses—and all the rest of it. When he has finished, the City's Child strokes his head with a movement of slow and almost disbelieving revelation, and then saying slowly, "Well, what d'yuh t'ink of dat?" returns to impart the fascinating information he has gathered to the waiting group of his expectant and interested friends.)

So, in ten thousand streets and towns and places of the earth, ran the undeviating formula: a formula that never changed, that was the same forever—and that showed the tall and lonely man the barren unity of life, and that finally, curiously, in a poignant and inexplicable fashion, gave him a faith in man, a belief in man's fundamental goodness, kindliness, and humanity, as nothing else on earth could do.

The Bums
at Sunset

S lowly, singly, with the ambling gait of men who have just fed, and who are faced with no pressure of time and business, the hoboes came from the jungle, descended the few feet of clay embankment that sloped to the roadbed, and in an unhurried manner walked down the tracks toward the water tower. The time was the exact moment of sunset, the sun indeed had disappeared from sight, but its last shafts fell remotely, without violence or heat, upon the treetops of the already darkening woods and on the top of the water tower. That light lay there briefly with a strange unearthly detachment, like a delicate and ancient bronze, it was no part of that cool, that delicious darkening of the earth which was already steeping the woods—it was like sorrow and like ecstasy and it faded briefly like a ghost.

Of the five men who had emerged from the "jungle" above the tracks and were now advancing, in a straggling procession, toward the water tower, the oldest was perhaps fifty, but such a ruin of a man, such a shapeless agglomerate of sodden rags, matted hair, and human tissues, that his age was indeterminable. He was like something that has been melted and beaten into the earth by a heavy rain. The youngest was a fresh-skinned country lad with bright wondering eyes: he was perhaps not more than sixteen years old. Of the remaining three, one was a young man not over thirty with a ferret face and very few upper teeth. He walked along gingerly on tender feet that were obviously unaccustomed to the work he was now putting them to: he was a triumph of dirty elegance—he wore a pinstripe suit heavily spattered with grease stains and very shiny on the seat: he kept his coat collar turned up and his hands thrust deeply into his trouser pockets—he walked thus with his bony shoulders thrust forward as if, in spite of the day's heat, he was cold. He had a limp cigarette thrust out of the corner of his mouth, and he talked with a bare movement of his lips, and a curious and ugly convulsion of his mouth to the side: everything about him suggested unclean secrecy.

Of the five men, only the remaining two carried on them the authority of genuine vagabondage. One was a small man with a hard seamed face, his eyes were hard and cold as agate, and his thin mouth was twisted slantwise in his face, and was like a scar.

The other man, who might have been in his mid-fifties, had the powerful shambling figure, the seamed face of the professional vagabond. It was a face and figure that had a curious brutal nobility; the battered and pitted face was hewn like a block of granite and on the man was legible the tremendous story of his wanderings—a legend of pounding wheel and thrumming rod, of bloody brawl and brutal shambles, of the savage wilderness, the wild, cruel and lonely distances of America.

This man, somehow obviously the leader of the group, walked silently, indifferently, at a powerful shambling step, not looking at the others. Once he paused, thrust a powerful hand into the baggy pocket of his coat, and drew out a cigarette, which he lit with a single motion of his cupped hand. Then his face luxuriously contorted as he drew upon the cigarette, he inhaled deeply, letting the smoke trickle slowly out through his nostrils after he had drawn it into the depths of his mighty lungs. It was a powerful gesture of sensual pleasure that suddenly gave to the act of smoking and to the fragrance of tobacco all of their primitive and pungent relish. And it was evident that the man could impart this rare quality to the simplest physical acts of life—to everything he touched—because he had in him somehow the thrilling qualities of exultancy and joy.

All the time, the boy had been keeping step behind this man, his eyes fixed steadily upon the broad back. Now, as the man stopped, the boy came abreast of him, and also stopped, and for a moment continued to look at the man, a little uncertainly, but with the same expression of steadfast confidence.

The bum, letting the smoke coil slowly from luxurious nostrils, resumed his powerful swinging stride, and for a moment said nothing to the boy. Presently, however, he spoke, roughly, casually, but with a kind of coarse friendliness:

"Where yuh goin', kid?" he said. "To duh Big Town?"

The boy nodded dumbly, seemed about to speak, but said nothing.

"Been there before?" the man asked.

"No," said the boy.

"First time yuh ever rode the rods, huh?"

"Yes," said the boy.

"What's the matter?" the bum said, grinning. "Too many cows to milk down on the farm, huh? Is that it?"

The boy grinned uncertainly for a moment, and then said, "Yes."

"I t'ought so," the bum said, chuckling coarsely, "Jesus! I can tell one of youse fresh country kids a mile off by duh way yuh walk. . . . Well," he said with a rough blunt friendliness, in a moment, "stick wit me if you're goin' to duh Big Town. I'm goin' dat way, too."

"Yeah," the little man with the mouth like a scar now broke in, in a rasping voice, and with an ugly jeering laugh:

"Yeah. You stick to Bull, kid. He'll see yuh t'roo. He'll show yuh de——woild, I ain't kiddin' yuh! He'll take yuh up to Lemonade Lake an' all t'roo Breadloaf Valley—won't yuh, Bull? He'll show yuh where de ham trees are and where de toikeys grow on bushes—won't yuh, Bull?" he said with ugly yet fawning insinuations. "You stick to Bull, kid, an' you'll be wearin' poils. . . . A-a-a-ah! yuh punk kid!" he now said, with a sudden turn to snarling viciousness.

"Wat t'hell use do yuh t'ink we got for a punk kid like you—Dat's duh trouble wit dis racket now! . . . We was all right until all dese kids begin to come along! . . . Wy t'hell should we be boddered wit him!" he snarled viciously. "Wat t'hell am I supposed to be—a noicemaid or sump'n? . . . G'wan, yuh little punk," he snarled once more, and lifted his fist in a sudden backhand movement, as if to strike the boy. "Scram! We got no use fer yuh! . . . G'wan, now. . . . Get t'hell away from here before I smash yuh one."

The man named Bull turned for a moment and looked silently at the smaller bum.

"Listen, Mug!" he said quietly, in a moment. "You leave duh kid alone. Duh kid stays, see?"

"A-a-a-ah!" the other man snarled sullenly. "What

is dis anyway?—A——noic'ry, or sump'n?"

"Listen," the other man said, "yuh hoid me, didn't yuh?"

"A-a-ah, t'hell wit it!" the little man muttered. "I'm not goin' t' rock duh——cradle f'r no punk kid."

"Yuh hoid what I said, didn't yuh?" the man named Bull replied in a heavy menacing tone.

"I hoid yuh. Yeah!" the other muttered.

"Well, I don't want to hear no more outa your trap. I said duh kid stays—and he stays."

The little man muttered sullenly under his breath, but said no more. Bull continued to scowl heavily at him a moment longer, then turned away and went over and sat down on a handcar which had been pushed up against a toolhouse on the siding.

"Come over here, kid," he said roughly, as he fumbled in his pocket for another cigarette. The boy walked over to the handcar.

"Got any smokes?" the man said, still fumbling in his pocket. The boy produced a package of cigarettes and offered them to the man. Bull took a cigarette from the package, lighted it with a single movement, between his tough seamed face and his cupped paw, and then dropped the package of cigarettes in his pocket, with the same spacious and powerful gesture.

"T'anks," he said as the acrid smoke began to coil luxuriously from his nostrils. "Sit down, kid."

The boy sat down on the handcar beside the man. For a moment, as Bull smoked, two of the bums looked quietly at each other with sly smiles, and then the young one in the soiled pinstripe suit shook his head rapidly to himself, and, grinning toothlessly with his thin sunken mouth, mumbled derisively:

"Cheezus!"

Bull said nothing, but sat there smoking, bent forward a little on his knees, as solid as a rock.

It was almost dark; there was still a faint evening light, but already great stars were beginning to flash and blaze in cloudless skies. Somewhere in the wood there was a sound of water. Far off, half heard, and half suspected, there was a faint dynamic throbbing on the rails. The boy sat there quietly, listening, and said nothing.

One of
the Girls in
Our Party

The midday meal was ended and "the tour"—
a group of thirty women, all of them teachers
from the public schools of the American Middle West—had got up from their tables and left the
dining room of the sedate little Swiss hotel where
they were quartered. Now they were gathered in
the hall beyond: their voices, shrill, rasping and metallic, were united in a clamor of strident eagerness.
In a moment one of the older women, who wore an
air of authority, returned to the dining room, and
looking through the door at two young women who
were still seated at one of the tables hastily bolting a
belated luncheon, called imperatively:

"Miss Turner! Miss Blake! Aren't you coming?
The bus is here."

"All right!" Miss Turner, the smaller of the two
women, was the one who answered. "In a moment."

"Well, you hurry then," the woman said in an ad-
monishing tone as she turned to go. "Everyone else
is ready: we're waiting on you."

"Come on," Miss Turner said quickly, in a
lowered tone, as she turned to Miss Blake, "I guess
we'd better go. You know how cranky they get if you
keep them waiting."

"Well, you go on then," said Miss Blake calmly.
"I'm not coming." Miss Turner looked at her with
some surprise. "I've decided to pass this one up.
I've got some letters to answer, and if I don't do it
now, they just won't get answered."

"I know," said Miss Turner. "I haven't written a word to anyone in two weeks. The way they keep you on the go there's no time to write." The two women got up from the table, moved toward the door, and there faced each other in a gesture of instinctive farewell. Then for a moment each stood in a constrained and awkward silence, as if waiting for the other one to speak. It was Miss Turner who first broke the pause:

"Well," she said, "I guess that means I won't see you again, will I?"

"Why?" Miss Blake said. "You'll come back here before you get your train, won't you?"

"No," said Miss Turner, "I don't think so. They've taken our baggage to the station and I think we're going to get out there on the way back—I mean, all the girls in *my* party."

"Well," Miss Blake said, in her curiously flat and toneless way, "I guess I won't see you, then—not until we get to Vienna, anyway. I'll see you there."

"Yes," Miss Turner agreed, "and I want to hear all about it, too. I almost wish I were going along with you—I've always wanted to see Italy—I'd almost rather go there than where we're going, but then you can't take in everything at one time, can you?"

"No," Miss Blake agreed, "you certainly can't."

"But I think it's just wonderful how much you do see!" Miss Turner went on with considerable enthusiasm. "I mean, when you consider that the whole tour only lasts six weeks from the time you leave home, it's wonderful how much you do take in, isn't it?"

"Yes," Miss Blake said, "it certainly is."

"Well, good-bye. I guess I'd better go."

"Yes, you'd better," Miss Blake answered. "I wouldn't want you to miss the bus. Good-bye."

"Good-bye," Miss Turner answered, "I'll see you in Vienna. Have a good time, and take care of yourself, now."

"All right," Miss Blake said flatly. "You do the same."

Miss Blake watched the bus go, then turned and went quickly upstairs to her room and set to work on her unfinished letters. She wrote:

England was the first place we went to when we left the ship. We were in England a whole week, but it rained all the time we were in London. The coffee that they drink is awful. All the traffic goes to the left in London, and none of the girls could get used to this. Miss Cramer, who is one of the girls in our party, came within an inch of being run over one day because she was looking in the wrong direction; I know they have a lot of accidents. London was also the place where Miss Jordan slipped and fell and sprained her ankle when getting out of the bus. She is one of the girls in our party. She didn't get to see anything of London because she was in bed all the time we were there and has been walking on a cane with her ankle taped ever since. But we took two bus tours while we were in London that covered the whole city. In the morning we saw the Bank of England and the Tower of London and the Crown Jewels and came back for lunch to an old inn where Doctor Johnson, who was a good friend of Shakespeare's, used to eat. Miss Barrett was especially interested in this as she teaches English literature in the senior high at Moline. She is one of the girls in our party. After lunch we saw Trafalgar Square with Nelson's Monument and the National Gallery. We didn't stay long at the National Gallery, we just stopped long enough to say we'd seen it. Then we visited the Houses of Parliament, Westminster Abbey with the Poets' Corner, and Buckingham Palace with the sentinels on duty walking up and down. We got there just as the King and Queen were driving out; we got a good look

187

at her but you could hardly see the King because of that big hat she was wearing. You couldn't help feeling sorry for the poor man. As Miss Webster said, he did look so small and henpecked peeking out from behind the edges of that big hat. Miss Webster is one of the girls in our party.

We also spent a day at Oxford. We had good weather there, it didn't rain at all the day we were there. Then we spent a day at Stratford-on-Avon where Shakespeare was born. But as Miss Webster said, they've fixed that house up a lot since he lived in it. It didn't rain the morning of the day we went to Stratford-on-Avon but it started in again as we were coming back. It rained most of the time we were in England. No wonder everything is so green.

The next country that we visited was Holland. Of all the countries we have been to I like Holland best. Everything was so clean in Holland. We spent three days in Holland, and it didn't rain the whole time we were there. We were in Amsterdam for a day, and we went out to the Island of Marken where all the people were dressed up in their quaint costumes and even the children wore wooden shoes just the same as they have done for hundreds of years. Miss Turner took some pictures of some children. She is making a collection to show to her classes when she gets back home. It is a very interesting collection, and most of the pictures came out very well. Miss Turner is one of the girls in our party.

We spent another whole day at Haarlem and The Hague. We saw the Palace of Peace and some pictures by Rembrandt, including "The Anatomy Lesson," which of course was interesting to me and some more "grist for the mill" as I will be able to make use of all this material in my drawing class when school takes up again.

In Holland we had the nicest guide we met on the whole trip. Everyone was crazy about him, we have thought so often of him, and laughed so much about him, since. He was an old man named Singvogel, and when Miss Watson, who is one of the girls in our party, asked him what that name meant, he said the name meant

Songbird, so after that we called him our Songbird. You couldn't get the best of Mr. Singvogel, no matter what you said. He always had an answer ready for you. We have laughed so much about it since whenever we thought of Mr. Singvogel.

Singvogel iss my name unt dat means Sonkbirt. Sonkbirt by name, sonkbirt by nature; if you are nice to me perhaps I sink for you. Now ve are coming to de olt shot tower. It vas conshtructed in de year uff sixteen hundert unt t'venty-nine mit contributions mait by all de burghers uff de town. De roof is uff golt unt silfer conshtructed vich vas gifen by de laities from deir chewells, ornaments unt odder brecious bossessions. De two fickures dat you see on top uff de olt glock iss subbosed to represent de burgermeister uff dat beriod, Pieter Van Hondercoetter, unt his vife Matilda. Upon de shtroke uff t'ree o'glock you vill see dem come out on de blatform, turn unt shtrike mit golten mallets on de bell——so! it comes now, vatch it!—so! *vun!* de burgermeister shtrikes upon his seit vun time—you see?——so! now! *two!*—de laity shtrikes upon her seit vun time—so! now! *t'ree!*—de burgermeister shtrikes upon his seit—now it iss t'ree o'glock—! all iss ofer for anodder hour—unt laities, dat's de only time dat a man has effer been known to haf de last vort mit a vooman.

Oh, you couldn't get the best of Mr. Singvogel, we used to tease him but he always had an answer ready for you.

Now, laities, dis tower vas erected at a cost of t'welluf million guilders vich iss fife million dollars in real money. It took ofer sixteen years to built it, de golt, chewells unt odder brecious metals in de roof alone is vort ofer vun million two hundert unt fifty t'ousand dollars. De tower is two hundert unt sixty-t'ree feet tall from top to bottom unt dere iss t'ree hundert sixty-fife shtone steps in de shtaircase, vun for effery day in de year, engrafed mit de name uff a citizen who gafe money for de tower. If you vould like to gount de shteps yourself you gan now glimb to de top but ass for me I t'ink I shtay here. For ald'ough my name iss Sonkbirt, I am now too olt to fly.

Mr. Singvogel always had a joke for everything. Well, we all climbed up to the top of the tower then and when we got back down Miss Powers said that Mr. Singvogel was wrong because she had counted three hundred and sixty-seven steps both ways, and Miss Turner swore that he was right, that she had made it three hundred and sixty-five both up and down. And then Mr. Singvogel said: "Vell, laities, I tell you how it iss. You are both wronk because I liet to you. I forgot to tell you dis iss leap year, unt ven leap year gomes dere is alvays vun shtep more. Dis year you find dat dere is t'ree hundert sixty-six if you gount again."

Well, we had to laugh then because you couldn't get the best of Mr. Singvogel. But Miss Powers was awfully mad and swore that she was right, that she had counted three hundred and sixty-seven both ways. She and Miss Turner had an argument about it and that's why they've hardly spoken to each other since. But we all liked Holland, it didn't rain there, and everyone was crazy about Mr. Singvogel.

We were in Paris for four days, and it only rained once. We were really only there three days, we got there late at night, and we were all so tired that we went to bed as soon as we got to the hotel. But we didn't get much sleep, it was the noisiest place you ever saw, and those little taxi horns they have kept tooting all night long right under your window until it almost drove you crazy. Some of the girls thought they'd lost their baggage, it failed to arrive when we did, they almost had a fit. It didn't get there until the day we left for Switzerland and Miss Bradley said her whole stay in Paris was ruined by worrying about it. Miss Bradley is one of the girls in our party.

We took a bus tour the first day and saw Notre Dame and the Latin Quarter, the Eiffel Tower and the Arch de Triumph, and came back and had lunch at the hotel. After lunch some of the girls went shopping, but the rest of us went to the Louvre. We didn't stay long, just long enough to see what it was like, and to see the Mona Lisa. One night we all had tickets for the Opera, where we saw Faust. The next night we went to the Folies Bergères and the last night we went up to Montmartre in buses to see the night life there.

Today we are in Montreux: this is the place where the tour splits up, some of the party leaving us to take the trip along the Rhine, and then to Munich, Salzburg, and the Bavarian Alps, while the rest of us are seeing Switzerland and Italy. After visiting Milan, Venice, Florence, Rome, and the Austrian Tyrol, we will join up with the other group in Vienna two weeks from now.

All of us were sorry to say good-bye to most of the girls, but we know it will only be for two weeks' time, and we are all looking forward eagerly to our meeting in Vienna and relating our experiences to one another. But, frankly, there are one or two of the girls we wouldn't miss if we never saw them again. There are always one or two on a party like this who can't adjust themselves to the group, and do their best to spoil the trip for everyone. That Miss Powers was one of them. She was always losing her baggage, or forgetting something, and leaving it behind; we got so tired of having her yapping all the time that there were three hundred and sixty-seven steps in that old shot tower, that she was right and Miss Turner wrong, until Miss Turner finally said: "All right, have it your own way —there were three hundred and sixty-seven—who cares about it? Only, for heaven's sake forget about it, and give the rest of us some peace."

Of course, that only made Miss Powers madder than **191**

ever, she was furious about it. She was certainly a pest, if I ever saw one. She was forever coming up to one of the girls and asking her to write something in her memory book. She carried that memory book with her wherever she went; I believe she slept with it under her pillow.

Now when one of the girls wants to be funny, she says, "Won't you please write something in my memory book?"—It's become a regular joke with us. But Miss Powers was certainly a nuisance, and none of the girls are sorry to say good-bye to her.

We have been spending the day in Switzerland. We all visited the League of Nations in Geneva and the famous castle of Chillon this morning. This afternoon, while I am writing this letter, everyone has gone for a bus tour through the Alps. We are leaving for Rome tonight.

Well, it has been a wonderful trip and a wonderful experience, as well as being very educational. I can hardly wait now until I get home and have time to think over the many beautiful things I have seen.

The tour has been well run and well conducted from start to finish. And on the whole the girls are enthusiastic about the way the trips have been managed. Of course when you have to cover so many countries—we will have covered nine countries—England, Holland, Belgium, France, Switzerland, Italy, Austria, Czechoslovakia, and Germany—by the time we set sail for home again, just thirty-one days after we disembarked—it is wonderful to think of all you do take in in such a short space of time.

I get a little confused sometimes when I try to remember all the places we have been to and all the wonderful things we've seen, and if I come back again I think I will take it a little more slowly and travel in a smaller party, with just a friend or two. But I'm certainly glad I took this tour, it gives you a chance to look around and pick out the high spots, so you will know what you want to see when you come back a second time. And it has certainly been very educational. Still, I won't be sorry to see home again. I am looking forward to it already.

I'm dying to see you and have a good long talk with you as soon as I get back. I'm starved for news. What has happened? Is Ted still going with the Trumbull girl, or has he found himself a new "innamorata"? ("Ain't love grand?" Especially when you are seventeen—hah! hah!) Have you been out to the lodge this summer, and were Bill and Lola there? Couldn't we get them to take us out the first weekend after I get back? It will be good to get a cup of real coffee for a change. Summer has come and gone before I knew it, and soon autumn will be here again.

. . . and the smell of the woodsmoke in Ohio and the flaming maples, the nights of the frosty stars, the blazing moons that hang the same way in a thousand streets, slanting to silence on the steeple's slope; nights of the wheel, the rail, the bell, the wailing cry along the river's edge, and of the summer's ending, nights of the frost and silence and the barking of a dog, of people listening, and of words unspoken and the quiet heart, and nights of the old October that must come again, must come again, while we are waiting, waiting, waiting in the darkness for all of our friends and brothers who will not return.

I'll see you in September.

The
Far and
the Near

O n the outskirts of a little town upon a rise of land that swept back from the railway there was a tidy little cottage of white boards, trimmed vividly with green blinds. To one side of the house there was a garden neatly patterned with plots of growing vegetables, and an arbor for the grapes which ripened late in August. Before the house there were three mighty oaks which sheltered it in their clean and massive shade in summer, and to the other side there was a border of gay flowers. The whole place had an air of tidiness, thrift, and modest comfort.

Every day, a few minutes after two o'clock in the afternoon, the limited express between two cities passed this spot. At that moment the great train, having halted for a breathing space at the town nearby, was beginning to lengthen evenly into its stroke, but it had not yet reached the full drive of its terrific speed. It swung into view deliberately, swept past with a powerful swaying motion of the engine, a low smooth rumble of its heavy cars upon pressed steel, and then it vanished in the cut. For a moment the progress of the engine could be marked by heavy bellowing puffs of smoke that burst at spaced intervals above the edges of the meadow grass, and finally nothing could be heard but the solid clacking tempo of the wheels receding into the drowsy stillness of the afternoon.

Every day for more than twenty years, as the train had approached this house, the engineer had blown on the whistle, and every day, as soon as she heard this signal, a woman had appeared on the back porch of the little house and waved to him. At first she had a small child clinging to her skirts, and now this child had grown to full womanhood, and every day she, too, came with her mother to the porch and waved.

The engineer had grown old and gray in service. He had driven his great train, loaded with its weight of lives, across the land ten thousand times. His own children had grown up and married, and four times he had seen before him on the tracks the ghastly dot of tragedy converging like a cannon ball to its eclipse of horror at the boiler head—a light spring wagon filled with children, with its clustered row of small stunned faces; a cheap automobile stalled upon the tracks, set with the wooden figures of people paralyzed with fear; a battered hobo walking by the rail, too deaf and old to hear the whistle's warning; and a form flung past his window with a scream —all this the man had seen and known. He had known all the grief, the joy, the peril and the labor such a man could know; he had grown seamed and weathered in his loyal service, and now, schooled by the qualities of faith and courage and humbleness that attended his labor, he had grown old, and had the grandeur and the wisdom these men have.

But no matter what peril or tragedy he had known, the vision of the little house and the women waving to him with a brave free motion of the arm had become fixed in the mind of the engineer as something beautiful and enduring, something beyond all change and ruin, and something that would always be the same, no matter what mishap, grief or error might break the iron schedule of his days.

The sight of the little house and of these two women gave him the most extraordinary happiness he had ever known. He had seen them in a thousand lights, a hundred weathers. He had seen them through the harsh bare light of wintry gray across the brown and frosted stubble of the earth, and he had seen them again in the green luring sorcery of April.

He felt for them and for the little house in which they lived such tenderness as a man might feel for his own children, and at length the picture of their lives was carved so sharply in his heart that he felt that he knew their lives completely, to every hour and moment of the day, and he resolved that one day, when his years of service should be ended, he would go and find these people and speak at last with them whose lives had been so wrought into his own.

That day came. At last the engineer stepped from a train onto the station platform of the town where these two women lived. His years upon the rail had ended. He was a pensioned servant of his company, with no more work to do. The engineer walked slowly through the station and out into the streets of the town. Everything was as strange to him as if he had never seen this town before. As he walked on, his sense of bewilderment and confusion grew. Could this be the town he had passed ten thousand times? Were these the same houses he had seen so often from the high windows of his cab? It was all as unfamiliar, as disquieting as a city in a dream, and the perplexity of his spirit increased as he went on.

Presently the houses thinned into the straggling outposts of the town, and the street faded into a country road—the one on which the women lived. And the man plodded on slowly in the heat and dust. At length he stood before the house he sought.

He knew at once that he had found the proper place. He saw the lordly oaks before the house, the flower beds, the garden and the arbor, and farther off, the glint of rails.

Yes, this was the house he sought, the place he had passed so many times, the destination he had longed for with such happiness. But now that he had found it, now that he was here, why did his hand falter on the gate; why had the town, the road, the earth, the very entrance to this place he loved turned unfamiliar as the landscape of some ugly dream? Why did he now feel this sense of confusion, doubt and hopelessness?

At length he entered by the gate, walked slowly up the path and in a moment more had mounted three short steps that led up to the porch, and was knocking at the door. Presently he heard steps in the hall, the door was opened, and a woman stood facing him.

And instantly, with a sense of bitter loss and grief, he was sorry he had come. He knew at once that the woman who stood there looking at him with a mistrustful eye was the same woman who had waved to him so many thousand times. But her face was harsh and pinched and meager; the flesh sagged wearily in sallow folds, and the small eyes peered at him with timid suspicion and uneasy doubt. All the brave freedom, the warmth and the affection that he had read into her gesture, vanished in the moment that he saw her and heard her unfriendly tongue.

And now his own voice sounded unreal and ghastly to him as he tried to explain his presence, to tell her who he was and the reason he had come. But he faltered on, fighting stubbornly against the horror of regret, confusion, disbelief that surged up in his spirit, drowning all his former joy and making his act of hope and tenderness seem shameful to him.

At length the woman invited him almost unwillingly into the house, and called her daughter in a harsh shrill voice. Then, for a brief agony of time, the man sat in an ugly little parlor, and he tried to talk while the two women stared at him with a dull, bewildered hostility, a sullen, timorous restraint.

And finally, stammering a crude farewell, he departed. He walked away down the path and then along the road toward town, and suddenly he knew that he was an old man. His heart, which had been brave and confident when it looked along the familiar vista of the rails, was now sick with doubt and horror as it saw the strange and unsuspected visage of an earth which had always been within a stone's throw of him, and which he had never seen or known. And he knew that all the magic of that bright lost way, the vista of that shining line, the imagined corner of that small good universe of hope's desire, was gone forever, could never be got back again.

In the Park

That year I think we were living with Bella; no, we weren't, I guess we were living with Auntie Kate—well, maybe we were staying with Bella: I don't know, we moved around so much, and it's so long ago. It gets all confused in my mind now; when Daddy was acting he was always on the go, he couldn't be still a minute; sometimes he was playing in New York, and sometimes he went off on a tour with Mr. Mansfield and was gone for months.

Anyway, that night when the show was over we went out onto the street and turned up Broadway. We were both so happy and excited that we fairly bounded along, and that was the way it was that night. It was one of the first fine days in spring, the air was cool and delicate and yet soft, and the sky was of a velvety lilac texture, and it was glittering with great stars. The streets outside the theatre were swarming with hansoms, four-wheelers, private carriages and victorias; they kept driving up in front of the theatre all the time and people kept getting into them.

All of the men looked handsome, and all of the women were beautiful: everyone seemed to be as happy and elated as we were, it seemed as if a new world and new people had burst out of the earth with the coming of spring—everything ugly, dull, sour, and harsh had vanished—the streets were flashing with life and sparkle. I saw all of it, I felt myself a part of it all, I wanted to possess it all, and there was something I wanted to say so much it made my throat ache, and yet I could not say it because I could not find the words I wanted. I could not think of anything else to say—it sounded foolish, but suddenly I seized my father's arm and cried: "Oh, to be in April, now that England's there."

"Yes!" he shouted, "Also in Paris, Naples, Rome, and Dresden! Oh, to be in Budapest!" cried Daddy, "now that April's here and the frost is on the pumpkin, and the dawn comes up like thunder out of the night that covers me."

He seemed to have grown young again; he was the way he used to be when I was a little girl and I would knock at his study door and he would call out in a wonderful actor's voice, "Enter, Daughter of Des-o-la-tion, into this abode of mis-er-ee."

His eyes sparkled, and he threw back his head and laughed his wild and happy laugh.

I think that must have been the year before he died; I was about eighteen: I was a beauty—I was like peaches and cream——

In those days when he was acting I used to meet him after the theatre and we would go somewhere to eat. *There* was a fellow after your heart: the very best was *just* about good enough for him. New York was awfully nice in those days. They had such nice places to go to—I don't know, they didn't have all this noise and confusion; it seems like another world sometimes. You could go to White's or Martin's or Delmonico's—there were a lot of nice places. There was also a place called Mock's; I never went there, but one of the first things I remember as a child was hearing Daddy come home late at night and say he'd been to Mock's. When he came home, I would listen at the grating of the heater in my room and I could hear him and the other actors talking to my mother: it was fascinating; and sometimes it was all about Mock's. "Oh, have you been to Mock's?" I thought I heard my mother say. "Oh, yes! I have been to Mock's," my father said. "And what did you have at Mock's?" my mother said. "Oh, I had some oysters and a glass of beer and some mock-turtle soup at Mock's," my father said.

We used to go to White's almost every night after the show, with two priests who were friends of Daddy's: Father Dolan and Father Chris O'Rourke. Father Dolan was a big man with the bluest eyes I ever saw, and Father Chris O'Rourke was a little man with a swarthy and greasy face: it was all full of black marks, it was one of the strangest faces I ever saw; but there was something very powerful and sweet about it. Father Dolan was a very fine, high sort of man: he was very kind and jolly, but he also had a fine mind and he was very outspoken and honest. He loved the theatre, he knew a great many actors, a great many of them went to his church, and he loved my father. He was a great scholar, he knew the plays of Shakespeare almost by heart—he and Daddy used to tag each other's lines, to see who knew the most. I never knew my father to catch him up but once and that was on a line from *King Lear*, "The prince of darkness is a gentleman"—Father Dolan said it came from *As You Like It*.

How those fellows loved to eat and drink: if one of them had to say Mass the next day we had to hurry, because you can't eat or drink after midnight if you are saying Mass the next day. Because of this, both these priests would immediately take out their watches and lay them on the table before them

when they sat down. Father Chris O'Rourke drank
nothing but beer and as soon as he sat down a waiter
would bring him a half-dozen glasses which he
would drink at once. But if these two priests had a
glass of beer on the table before them when midnight came, they left it: no matter what it was, no
matter whether they'd finished eating or drinking or
not, when the stroke of midnight came these fellows
quit, if they were going to say Mass the morning
after.

Father Chris O'Rourke would eat and drink for almost an hour as if his life depended on it: he was
very nearsighted, he wore thick glasses, and from
time to time he would seize his watch and bring it
right under his nose while he peered and squinted
at it. Because of his own hurry to get through before
twelve o'clock, he thought everyone else must be
the same way: he was afraid someone would not get
fed, and he was always urging and belaboring people to hurry up and eat. Father Dolan loved to eat,
too, but he was a great talker: sometimes he would
get to talking to Daddy and forget to eat: when he
did this Father Chris O'Rourke would almost go out
of his head, he would keep nudging and poking at
Father Dolan and pointing at his watch with a look
of agony on his face, leaning over and muttering at
him in an ominous sort of way, "You're going to be
late! It's almost *twelve*!"

"Bedad, then!" said Father Dolan, "I'll be late!"
He was a big man, but he had a funny little Irish
voice; it was very crisp and jolly and had a little
chuckling lilt in it, and it seemed to come from a
long way off. "I never saw a man like ye, Chris, to
be always thinkin' of his belly! Did the great saints
of the Church spend their time guzzlin' and cram-
min', or did they spend it in meditatin' and prayin'

an' mortifyin' their flesh? Did ye never hear of the sin of gluttony?"

"Yis," said Father Chris O'Rourke, "that I have, an' I've also heard of the wicked sin of wanton waste. Shame on ye, Dan Dolan, wit yer talk about the great saints of the Church: there was niver a great saint yit that would praise a man fer wastin' what the Lord had set before him. Do ye think I'll sit here an' see good food go to waste whin there's poor people all over the world tonight that's goin' witout?"

"Well," said Father Dolan, "I've read most of the argyments of the learned reasoners of the Church, as well as the damnable heresies of the infidels, all the way from St. Thomas Aquinas to Spinozey, an' in me young days I could split a hair meself wit the best of them, but in all me life I niver heard the beat of that one: it makes Aristotle look like Wordsworth's Idiot Boy. Bedad, if ye can prove that what ye're doin' wit yer gorgin' is feedin' the poor all over the earth, I won't put anything past yer powers of reasonin', Chris—ye could show the pope that Darwin was a Jesuit, an' he'd believe ye!"

Well, as I say, when we got to the restaurant the first thing Father Chris O'Rourke would do was to lay his watch upon the table, and the first thing Daddy would do was to order two or three bottles of champagne: they used to know we were coming and it would be waiting for us in great silver buckets full of ice. Then Daddy would pick up the menu—it was a great big card simply covered with the most delicious things to eat, and he would frown and look serious and clear his throat, and say to Father Dolan, "What does the pontifical palate crave, Dan?"

* * *

209

After the play, that night, we went to White's and these two priests were waiting for us when we got there. A little later Mr. Gates came in—he's still alive, I saw him on the street the other day, he's getting quite old. He was married to one of the most beautiful women you ever saw, and she was burned to death in an automobile accident. He saw the thing happen right under his eyes: isn't that the most horrible thing you ever heard of? Well, you could tell by the way Mr. Gates walked that he was awfully excited about something: he was another of these great fat fellows, and you could see his old jowls quivering as he came.

"Good God!" said Daddy, "here comes Bunny with a full head of steam on!"

Mr. Gates began to speak to Daddy half across the room, all of the people stopped and stared at him.

"Joe! Joe!" he said—he had a funny hoarse kind of voice, one of those foggy whiskey voices; I think he drank a good deal. "Joe, do you know what I've done? I've just bought a horseless carriage. Come on! You're going for a ride with me!"

"Now, wait! Wait! Wait!" said Daddy, holding up his hand just like an actor. "Not so fast, Bunny! Sit down and have a bite to eat first, and tell us about it. When did you do this desperate deed?"

"Today," Mr. Gates said in a sort of hoarse whisper. "Do you suppose I've done right?"

He looked around at us with his old eyes simply bulging out of his head and with a sort of scared look on his face. Oh! We laughed so much about it: Father Dolan began to laugh, and Daddy had to pound him on the back, he got to coughing so!

* * *

Mr. Gates was an awfully nice man: he was a great
fat fellow, but he was so handsome; there was something so delicate about him, his mouth kept trembling and twitching so when he was excited and
wanted to say something. I think that was why they
called him Bunny.

So Daddy said, "Sit down and have something to
eat and then we'll see."

Mr. Gates said, "Say, Joe, I've got the mechanic
outside here, and I don't know what to do with
him."

"You mean you hired him for keeps?" Daddy said.

"Yes," Mr. Gates said, "and I'm damned if I'm not
embarrassed! I don't know what to do with him. I
mean, what is his social standing?"

"Does he wash?" Daddy said.

"Well," said Mr. Gates, looking at Father Dolan,
"I think he uses holy water."

"Oh, Mr. Gates!" I said. "How awful! Right before Father Dolan, too!"

But Father Dolan laughed just as I knew he
would: he was another great fat fellow, he was an
awfully nice man. Father Chris O'Rourke laughed,
too, but I don't think he liked it so much.

"I mean," Mr. Gates said, "I don't know how to
treat the man. Is he above me, or below me, or
what?"

"It looks to me," Daddy said, "as if he were on top
of you. I think you've gone and got yourself saddled
with a black elephant."

Daddy was so wonderful like that, everybody
loved him. Mr. Gates was so worried about the
driver: it all seems so funny now to think back on
it—he didn't know whether the man was to eat at
the table with his family, and be treated like one of
them, or what. There was something so delicate

about Mr. Gates: he was big and fat, but a very sensitive, fine person.

"It looks like a neat little problem in social etiquette, Bunny," Daddy said. "Well, let's have him in here for a bite to eat. We'll see what he looks like."

So Mr. Gates went out and got him, and pretty soon he came back with him, and he was really an awfully nice young fellow: he had a little mustache, and he wore a Norfolk jacket and a flat cap, and everybody stared so, and nudged each other, he was awfully embarrassed. But Daddy was wonderful with people, he made him feel right at home. He said, "Sit down, young fellow. If we're going to run an engine we've got to feed the driver."

So he sat down, and we had a wonderful meal: you'd get great juicy chops in that place, cooked in butter, and steaks an inch thick, and the most marvellous oysters and seafood.

I know it was pretty late in the season, but we started off with oysters and champagne: I don't think the young fellow was used to drinking. Daddy kept filling up the young fellow's glass, and he got quite drunk. He was awfully funny, he kept talking about his responsibility.

"It's a terrible responsibility to know that all these lives are dependent on you," he said; then Daddy would fill up his glass again.

"A moment's hesitation in a crisis," he said, "and all is lost."

"A truer word was never spoken," said Daddy, and he filled his glass up again.

"A man must have a clear brain and a steady hand," he said.

"Right you are," said Daddy. "This will make you so steady, son, that you will get practically paralyzed."

Mr. Gates and Father Dolan laughed so much that the tears began to trickle down their cheeks. Oh, we had an awfully good time in those days, there was something so innocent about everything.

Then we all got up to go, and I was really quite nervous: the poor kid could hardly stand up, and I didn't know what was going to happen. Daddy was so happy and excited, there was something so wild about him, his eyes danced like devils, and he threw back his head and laughed, and you could hear him all over the place.

Father Chris O'Rourke had to hold Mass the next morning, and he left us, but Father Dolan came along. We all went outside, with the young man being helped along by Daddy and Mr. Gates, and everyone in the restaurant followed us outside, and Mr. Gates told me to sit up front beside the driver. God, I was proud! And Daddy and Mr. Gates and Father Dolan got in behind; how they ever did it I don't know, it must have been awfully small—I think Daddy must have sat on Father Dolan's lap. Oh, yes! I know he did.

And everybody cheered as we started off: the actors followed us out of the restaurant and stood looking after us as we drove off into the lilac and velvet darkness, and I can still remember how I looked back and saw their smiling and unnatural faces, their bright masks, their lonely and haunted eyes. They kept shouting funny things at Daddy and asking if he had any last messages, and De Wolfe Hopper was there and he ran around pretending to be a horse and neighing, and trying to climb up a lamppost. Oh, it was thrilling!

So Mr. Gates said, "Whither away, Joe?"

And Daddy said, "To the Golden Gate and may she never stop!"

213

Then Daddy said to the young fellow who was driving, "How fast can she go, son?" and the young fellow said, "She can do twenty miles an hour without any trouble."

"Downhill, you mean," said Daddy just to tease him, so we started to go, and God! I was thrilled! It seemed to me we were flying. I suppose he did go twenty miles an hour, but it seemed like a hundred would now and we passed a policeman on a horse and the horse got frightened and tried to run away and God! the cop was so mad: he came galloping after us and shouted for us to stop, and Daddy laughed just like a crazy man and said, "Go on, son! Go on! There's not a horse in the world can catch you!"

But the young fellow was scared and he slowed down and then the cop came up and said what did we mean, and where did we think we were, and he'd a good mind to put us all under arrest for disturbing the peace at that hour of night, with "that thing"; he kept calling it "that thing" in such a scornful way, and I got so angry at him, I thought it was so beautiful, it was painted the richest kind of winey red, it looked good enough to eat, and I was so mad to think the man should talk that way.

I don't know why it made me mad, but I think the reason must have been that the car didn't seem to me like a thing at all. It's hard to tell you how it was, but it was almost as if the car were some strange and beautiful and living creature which we had never known before but which now gave to all our lives a kind of added joy and warmth and wonder. And I believe that was the way it was with those first motorcars. Somehow each one of them seemed different from all the others, each one seemed to have a different name, a separate life and personality; and although I know they would look crude and funny and old-fashioned now, it was all different then. We had never seen or known them in the world before, we had only dreamed or heard they could exist, and now that I was riding in one, it all seemed unbelievable and yet gloriously real and strange, as every beautiful thing is when it first happens to you. The car was as magical to me as if it had come out of some other world like Mars, and yet the very moment that I saw it I seemed to have known about it always, and it seemed to belong to that day, that hour, that year, somehow to be a part of all that happened that night; to belong to Daddy and the priests and Mr. Gates, the young mechanic and all the haunted faces of the actors, and to all the songs we sang that year, the things we did and said, and something strange and innocent and lost and long ago.

I can remember now the way the old car looked, so well that I could close my eyes and draw it for you. I can remember its rich wine color, its great polished lamps of brass, the door that opened in its round, fat back, and all its wonderful and exciting smells—the strong and comforting smell of its deep leather, and the smells of gasoline and oil and grease that were so strong and warm and pungent that they seemed to give a kind of thrilling life and ecstasy to everything in the whole world. They seemed to hold the unknown promise of something wonderful and strange that was about to happen and that belonged to the night, and to the mystery and joy of life, the ecstasy of the lilac dark, as all the smells of flowers and leaf and grass and earth belonged to them.

* * *

So I guess that was the reason that I got so mad when I heard the policeman call the car "that thing," although I did not know the reason then. It looked as if the cop were going to run us in, but then Daddy got up out of Father Dolan's lap, and when the cop saw Father Dolan of course he got very nice to us: and Mr. Gates talked to him and gave him some money, and Daddy joked with him and made him laugh, and then Daddy showed him his police badge and asked him if he knew Big Jake Dietz at police headquarters, and told him he was one of Jake's best friends, and then I was so proud to see the way the cop came round.

And the cop said for us all to go into Central Park and we could ride all we damn pleased for all he cared, but you wouldn't catch him in one of those things, they'd blow up on you at any moment and then where'd you all be? And Daddy said he hoped we'd all be in Heaven, and what's more we'd take our own priest with us, so there'd be no hitch in any of the formalities, and we all got so tickled and began to laugh and the cop did too, and then he began to brag about his horse, and God! it *was* a beautiful horse, and he said give him a horse always, that they'd never make one of those things that could go faster than a horse. The poor fellow! I wonder what he'd say now!

And Daddy teased him and said the time would come when you'd have to go to the zoo to see a horse, and the policeman said by that time you'd have to go to a junkshop to see a motorcar, and Daddy said, "The trouble with us is that we're anachronisms." And the policeman said, well, he didn't know about that, but he wished us luck and hoped we all got out of it alive.

So he rode off and we drove into Central Park and

started off as hard as we could go and began to climb a hill, when sure enough, we broke down just as the policeman said we would. I guess the young fellow may have had too much to drink, he seemed wild and excited, but anyway we saw a hansom halfway up the hill in front of us and he cried out, "Watch me pass them," and did something to the car, and just as we got up even with them and were trying to go by, the car coughed and spluttered and stood still. Well, we could hear the people in the hansom laughing, and one of them shouted something back to us about the tortoise and the hare. And I felt so mad at them and so humiliated and so sorry for our driver, and Daddy said, "Never mind, son, the race may not always be to the swift, but even the hare will sometimes have his day."

But our young fellow felt so bad he couldn't say a word. He got out of the car and walked round and round it, and finally he began to explain to us the way it happened and how it could never happen again in a hundred years. And well, you see it was this way, and well, you see it was that. And we didn't understand a word of what he was saying, but we felt so sorry for him that we told him he was right. So he began to poke around inside of it, and then he would turn something here and twist something there, and grab the crank and whirl it round and round until I was afraid he was going to wring his arm off. Then he would get down on his back and crawl in under it and bang and hammer at something underneath. And nothing happened. Then he would get up and walk round and round the car again and mutter to himself. Finally, he gave up and said he was afraid we'd have to get out of the car and take a hansom if we wanted to get home without walking. So we started to get out, and the mechanic

was so mad and so embarrassed at the way his car had acted that he grabbed it and shook it as if it were a brat. And nothing happened.

He gave it one last try. He grabbed the crank like a crazy man and began to whirl it round and round until he was exhausted. And when nothing happened he suddenly shouted out, "Oh, damn that thing," kicked it in the tire as hard as he could, and collapsed across the radiator, sobbing as if his heart would break. And I don't know what that did to it or how it happened, but suddenly the car began to chug and wheeze again, and there we were ready to go, and the young fellow with a grin that stretched from ear to ear.

So we went on up that hill and coasted down the next, and now we really seemed to fly. It was like soaring through the air, or finding wings you never knew you had before. It was like something we had always known about and dreamed of finding, and now we had it like a dream come true. And I suppose we must have gone the whole way round the park from one end to another, but none of us really knew how far we went or where we were going. It was like that kind of flight you make in dreams and sure enough, just like something you are waiting for in a dream, we came tearing around a curve in the road and there before us we could see the same hansom we had tried to pass upon the hill. And the minute that I saw it I knew that it was bound to happen, it seemed too good to be true, and yet I had felt sure all the time that it was going to turn out just this way. And that was the way it was with all of us, we threw back our heads and roared with laughter, we yelled and waved our hands at all the people in the cab, we went tearing by them as if they were rooted

219

to the earth, and as we passed them Daddy turned and shouted back at them, "Cheer up, my friends, they also serve who only stand and wait."

So we passed them by and left them far behind us and they were lost; and now there was nothing all around us but the night, the blazing stars, the lilac darkness in the park, and God! but it was beautiful. It was just the beginning of May and all the leaves and buds were coming out, they had that tender feathery look, and there was just a little delicate shaving of moon in the sky, and it was so cool and lovely, with the smell of the leaves, and the new grass, and all the flowers bursting from the earth till you could hear them grow: it seemed to me the loveliest thing that I had ever known, and when I looked at my father, his eyes were full of tears and he cried out, "Glory! Oh, glory! Glory!" and then he began in his magnificent voice, "What a piece of work is a man! how noble in reason! how infinite in faculty! in form and moving how express and admirable! in action how like an angel! in apprehension how like a god!"

And the words were so lovely, the music was so grand, that somehow it made me want to cry, and when he had finished he cried out, "Glory!" once again, and I saw his wild and beautiful brow there in the darkness, and I turned my eyes up toward the sky and there were the tragic and magnificent stars, and a kind of fate was on his head and in his eyes, and suddenly as I looked at him I knew that he was going to die.

And he cried, "Glory! Glory!" and we rode all through the night, and round and round the park, and then dawn came, and all of the birds began to sing. And now the birdsong broke in the first light, and suddenly I heard each sound the birdsong made. It came to me like music I had always heard, it came to me like music I had always known, the sounds of which I never yet had spoken, and now I heard the music of each sound as clear and bright as gold, and the music of each sound was this: at first it rose above me like a flight of shot, and then I heard the sharp, fast skaps of sound the birdsong made. And now they were smooth drops and nuggets of bright gold, and now with chittering bicker and fast-fluttering skirrs of sound the palmy, honied bird cries came. And now the bird tree sang, all filled with lutings in bright air; the thrum, the lark's wing, and tongue-trilling chirrs arose. And now the little brainless cries arose, with liquorous, liquefied lutings, with lirruping chirp, plum-bellied smoothness, sweet lucidity. And now I heard the rapid kweet-kweet-kweet-kweet-kweet of homely birds, and then their pwee-pwee-pwee: others had thin metallic tongues, a sharp cricketing stitch, and high shrew's caws, with eery rasp, with harsh, far calls— these were the sounds the bird cries made. All birds that are awoke in the park's woodland tangles; and above them passed the whirr of hidden wings, the strange lost cry of the unknown birds in full light now in the park, the sweet confusion of their cries was mingled. "Sweet is the breath of morn, her rising sweet with charm of earliest birds," and it was just like that, and the sun came up, and it was like the first day of the world, and that was the year before he died and I think we were staying at Bella's then, but maybe we were staying at the old hotel, or perhaps we had already moved to Auntie Kate's: we moved around so much, we lived so many places, it seems so long ago, that when I try to think about it now it gets confused and I cannot remember.

The Men
of Old
Catawba

On the Middle Atlantic seaboard of the North American continent and at about a day's journey from New York, is situated the American state of Old Catawba. In area and population the state might almost strike a median among the states of the Union: its territory, which is slightly more than fifty thousand square miles, is somewhat larger than the territories of most of the Atlantic coastal states, and, of course, much smaller than the great areas of the immense but sparsely populated states of the Far West. Upon this area, which is a little smaller than the combined areas of England and Wales, there live three million people, of whom the third part are black. Catawba, therefore, is about as big as England, and has about as many people as Norway.

The state possesses, however, a racial type and character that is probably much more strongly marked and unified than those of any European country. In fact, although America is supposed by many of her cities to be a confusion of races, tongues, and peoples, as yet unwelded, there is perhaps nowhere in the world a more homogeneous population than that of Old Catawba. Certainly, there are far greater differences in stature, temperament, speech, and habit between a North German and a South German, a North Frenchman and a Southern Frenchman, a North of England man and a

Devon man, a North Italian and a South Italian, than between a Catawban from the East and one from the West.

The name "Catawba" is, of course, an Indian name: it is the name of a tribe that is now almost extinct but which at one time flourished in considerable strength and numbers. The chief seat of the tribe was in South Carolina, and there is at the present time a reservation in York County of that state where the remnant is gathered together.

The way in which the state of Catawba got its name rests entirely upon misconception: the tribe that the early explorers encountered were not Catawbas, they belonged probably to a group that is now wholly extinct. Yet, so strong is the power of usage and association that any other name would now seem unthinkable to a native of that state. People outside the state have often said that the name has a somewhat tropical laziness in its sound, particularly when prefixed with the word "old," but there is very little that is tropical or exotic either in the appearance and character of Catawba itself, or of the people who inhabit it. To them, the name Catawba perfectly describes the state: it has the strong, rugged, and homely quality that the earth has.

In the state documents during the period of the royal proprietors, the territory is invariably referred to as "Catawba," or "His Majesty's Colony in the Catawbas": the name "Old Catawba" does not begin to appear in state papers until twenty or thirty years before the Revolution, and for what reason no one knows. The typical American method in naming places has been to prefix the word "new" to the name—*New* England, *New* York, *New* Mexico—to distinguish these places from their older namesakes. But if *New* York indicates the existence somewhere of an *old* York, *old* Catawba does not indicate the existence of a new one. The name undoubtedly grew out of the spirit of the people who had dwelt there over a century, and the name did not come from a sentimental affection, it grew imperatively from a conviction of the spirit. It is one of those names that all men begin to use at about the same time, a perfect and inevitable name that has flowered secretly within them, and that now must be spoken.

Anyone who has ever lived in the state for any length of time is bound to feel this: the word "old" is not a term of maudlin affection, it describes exactly the feeling that the earth of that state inspires —the land has a brooding presence that is immensely old and masculine, its spirit is rugged and rather desolate, yet it broods over its people with stern benevolence. The earth is a woman, but Old Catawba is a man. The earth is our mother and our nurse, and we can know her, but Old Catawba is our father, and although we know that he is there, we shall never find him. He is there in the wilderness, and his brows are bowed with granite: he sees our lives and deaths and his stern compassion broods above us. Women love him, but only men can know him: only men who have cried out in their agony and their loneliness to their father, only men who have sought throughout the world to find him, can know Catawba: but this includes all the men who ever lived.

Catawba got discovered in this way: a one-eyed Spaniard, one of the early voyagers, was beating up the American coasts out of the tropics, perhaps on his way back home, perhaps only to see what could be seen. He does not tell us in the record he has left of the voyage how he happened to be there, but it seems likely that he was on his way home and had been driven off his course. Subsequent events show that he was in a very dilapidated condition, and in need of overhauling: the sails were rent, the ship was leaking, the food and water stores were almost exhausted. During the night in a storm off one of the cruelest and most evilly celebrated of the Atlantic capes, the one-eyed Spaniard was driven in and almost wrecked. By some miracle of good fortune he got through one of the inlets in the dark, and when light broke he found himself becalmed in an enormous inlet of pearl-gray water.

As the light grew he made out seawards a long almost unbroken line of sandy shoals and islands that formed a desolate barrier between the sea and the mainland, and made this bay or sound in which he found himself. Away to the west he descried now the line of the shore: it was also low, sandy, and desolate-looking. The cool gray water of morning slapped gently at the sides of his ship: he had come from the howling immensity of the sea into the desert monotony of this coast. It was as bleak and barren a coast as the one-eyed Spaniard had ever seen. And indeed, for a man who had come up so many times under the headlands of Europe, and had seen the worn escarpments of chalk, the lush greenery of the hills, and the minute striped cultivation of the earth that greet the sailor returning from a long and dangerous voyage—and awaken in him the unspeakable emotion of earth which has been tilled and used for so many centuries, with its almost personal bond for the men who have lived there on it, and whose dust is buried in it—there must have been something particularly desolate about this

coast which stretched away with the immense indifference of nature into silence and wilderness. The Spaniard felt this, and the barren and desert quality of the place is duly recorded in his log, which, for the most part, is pretty dry reading.

But here a strange kind of exhilaration seizes the Spaniard: it gets into his writing, it begins to color and pulse through the gray stuff of his record. The light of the young rising sun reddened delicately upon the waters; immense and golden it came up from the sea behind the line of the sea dunes, and suddenly he heard the fast drumming of the wild ducks as they crossed his ship high up, flying swift and straight as projectiles. Great heavy gulls of a size and kind he had never seen before swung over his ship in vast circles, making their eerie creaking noises. The powerful birds soared on their strong even wings, with their feet tucked neatly in below their bodies; or they dove and tumbled through the air, settling to the water with great flutterings and their haunted creaking clamor: they seemed to orchestrate this desolation, they gave a tongue to loneliness and they filled the hearts of the men who had come there with a strange exultancy. For, as if some subtle and radical changes had been effected in the chemistry of their flesh and blood by the air they breathed, a kind of wild glee now possessed the one-eyed Spaniard's men. They began to laugh and sing, and to be, as he says, "marvellous merry."

During the morning the wind freshened a little; the Spaniard set his sails and stood in toward the land. By noon he was going up the coast quite near the shore, and by night he had put into the mouth of one of the coastal rivers. He took in his sails and anchored there. There was nearby on shore a settlement of "the race that inhabits these regions," and it was evident that his arrival had caused a great commotion among the inhabitants, for some who had fled away into the woods were now returning, and others were running up and down the shore, pointing and gesticulating and making a great deal of noise. But the one-eyed Spaniard had seen Indians before: that was an old story to him now, and he was not disturbed. As for his men, the strange exuberance that had seized them in the morning does not seem to have worn off, they shouted ribald jokes at the Indians, and "did laugh and caper as if they had been madde."

Nevertheless, they did not go ashore that day. The one-eyed Spaniard was worn out, and the crew was exhausted: they ate such food as they had, some raisins, cheese, and wine, and after posting a watch they went to sleep, unmindful of the fires that flickered in the Indian village, of sounds and chants and rumors, or of the forms that padded softly up and down the shore.

Then the marvellous moon moved up into the skies, and blank and full, blazed down upon the quiet waters of the sound, and upon the Indian village. It blazed upon the one-eyed Spaniard and his lonely little ship and crew, on their rich dull lamps, and on their swarthy sleeping faces; it blazed upon all the dirty richness of their ragged costumes, and on their greedy little minds, obsessed then as now by the European's greedy myth about America, to which he remains forever faithful with an unwearied and idiot pertinacity: "Where is the gold in the streets? Lead us to the emerald plantations, the diamond bushes, the platinum mountains, and the cliffs of pearl. Brother, let us gather in the shade of the ham and mutton trees, by the shores of ambrosial rivers: we will bathe in the fountains of milk, and pluck hot buttered rolls from the bread vines."

Early the next morning the Spaniard went ashore with several of his men. "When we reached land," he writes, "our first act was to fall down on our knees and render thanks to God and the Blessed Virgin without Whose intervention we had all been dead men." Their next act was to "take possession" of this land in the name of the king of Spain, and to ground the flag. As we read today of this solemn ceremony, its pathos and puny arrogance touch us with pity. For what else can we feel for this handful of greedy adventurers "taking possession" of the immortal wilderness in the name of another puny fellow four thousand miles away, who had never seen or heard of the place and could never have understood it any better than these men? For the earth is never "taken possession of": it possesses.

At any rate, having accomplished these acts of piety and devotion, the Spaniards rose from their prayers, faced the crowd of Indians who had by this time ventured quite close to all this unctuous rigmarole, and discharged a volley from their muskets at them ("lest they become too forward and threatening"). Two or three fell sprawling on the ground, and the others ran away, yelling, into the woods. Thus, at one blast, Christianity and government were established.

The Spaniards now turned their attention to the Indian village—they began to pill and sack it with the deftness of long experience; but, as they entered one hut after another and found no coffers of nuggets or chests of emeralds, and found indeed that not even the jugs and pots and cooking utensils were of gold or silver, but had been crudely fashioned from baked earth, their rage grew; they felt tricked and cheated, and began to smash and de-

231

stroy all that came within their reach. This sense of injury, this virtuous indignation has crept into the Spaniard's record—indeed, we are edified with a lot of early American criticism which, save for a few archaisms of phrasing, has a strangely familiar ring, and might almost have been written yesterday: "This is a wild and barbarous kind of race, full of bloudie ways, it exists in such a base and vile sort of living that is worthier of wild beestes than men: they live in darkness and of the artes of living as we know them they are ignorant, one could think that God Himself has forgot them, they are so farre remote from any lighte."

He comments with disgust on the dried "stinkeing fysshe" and the dried meat that hung in all the huts, and on the almost total lack of metals, but he saves his finest disdain for a "kinde of weede or plante," which they also found in abundant quantity in all the dwellings. He then goes on to describe this "weede or plante" in considerable detail: its leaves are broad and coarse and when dried it is yellow and has a strong odor. The barbarous natives, he says, are so fond of the plant that he has seen them put it in their mouths and chew it; when his own men tried the experience, however, they quickly had enough of it and some were seized with retchings and a puking sickness. The final use to which the plant is put seems to him so extraordinary that he evidently fears his story will be disbelieved, for he goes on, with many assurances and oaths of his veracity, to describe how the plant may be lighted and burned and how "it giveth a fowle stinkeing smoak," and most wonderful of all, how these natives have a way of setting it afire and drawing in its fumes through long tubes so that "the smoak cometh out again by their mouth and nostryls in such wyse that you mighte thinke them devils out of helle instead of mortyl men."

Before we leave this one-eyed fellow, it is ironic to note with what contempt he passes over "the gold in the streets" for which his bowels yearn. As an example of one-eyed blindness it is hard to beat. For here was gold, the inexhaustible vein of gold which the marvellous clay of the region could endlessly produce, and which mankind would endlessly consume and pay for; and the Spaniard, devoured by his lust for gold, ignores it with a grimace of disgust and a scornful dilation of his nostrils. That act was at once a history and a prophecy, and in it is all the story of Europe's blundering with America.

For it must be said of all these explorers and adventurers, the early ones and the late ones, who came back from their voyages to the Americas embittered because they did not find gold strewn on the earth, that they failed not because there was no gold, but because they did not know where and how to look for it, and because they did not recognize it when they had it under their noses—because, in short, they were one-eyed men. That gold, real gold, the actual honest ore, existed in great quantities, and often upon the very surface of the earth as these men supposed, has since been abundantly shown: it is only one of the minor and less interesting episodes of American history—a casual confirmation of one of Europe's fairy tales. They tried to think of the most wonderful fable in the world, these money-haters, and they evolved the story of gold on the ground.

It was a story as naïve and not as beautiful as a child's vision of the lemonade spring, the ice-cream mountains, the cake and candy forests but, at any rate, America confirmed this little fable about gold in one short year of her history, and then proceeded to unpocket and unearth vast stores of wealth that made the visions of these old explorers look absurd. For she unearthed rivers of rich oil and flung them skyward, she dug mountains of coal and iron and copper out of the soil, she harvested each year two thousand miles of golden wheat, she flung great rails across the desert, she bridged the continent with the thunder of great wheels, she hewed down forests of enormous trees and floated them down rivers, she grew cotton for the world, her soil was full of sugars, citric pungencies of a thousand homely and exotic things, but still the mystery of her earth was unrevealed, her greatest wealth and potencies unknown.

The one-eyed Spaniard, however, saw none of these things. He looted the village, murdered a few of the Indians, and advanced eighty or one hundred miles inland, squinting about for treasure. He found a desolate region, quite flat, with soil of a sandy marl, a coarse and undistinguished landscape, haunted by a lonely austerity, and thickly and ruggedly forested—for the most part with large areas of long-leaf pine. As he went inland the soil deepened somewhat in hue and texture: it had a clayey, glutinous composition, and when rain fell he cursed it. It grew coarse grasses and tough thick brush and undergrowth: it could also grow enough of the pungent weed whose fumes had so disgusted him to fill the nostrils of the earth with smoke forever. There was abundance of wild game and fowl, so that the one-eyed Spaniard did not go hungry; but he found no nuggets and not even a single emerald.

234　The one-eyed Spaniard cursed, and again turned eastward toward the sea. Swift and high and straight

as bullets the ducks passed over him, flying toward
the coastal marshes. That was all. The enormous
earth resumed its silence. Westward, in great hills
that he had never seen, cloud shadows passed above
the timeless wilderness, the trees crashed down at
night athwart the broken boil of clean steep waters,
there was the flash and wink of a billion little eyes,
the glide and thrumming stir, the brooding ulula-
tion of the dark; there was the thunder of the wings,
the symphony of the wilderness, but there was
never the tread of a booted foot.

The Spaniard took to his ship, and set sail gladly.
He was one-eyed and he had found no gold.

The Catawba people are great people for all manner of debate and reasoned argument. Where the
more fiery South Carolinian or Mississippian will
fly into a rage and want to fight the man who doubts
his word or questions his opinion, the eye of the Catawban begins to glow with a fire of another sort—
the lust for debate, a Scotch love of argument. Nothing pleases a Catawban better than this kind of dis-
pute. He will say persuasively, "Now let's see if we
can't see through this thing. Let's see if we can't git
to the bottom of this." A long, earnest, and even passionate discussion will ensue in which the parties
on both sides usually maintain the utmost good tem-
per, kindliness, and tolerance, but in which they
nevertheless pursue their arguments with great
warmth and stubbornness. In these discussions several interesting traits of the Catawban quickly become manifest: the man is naturally a philosopher—
he loves nothing better than to discuss abstract and
difficult questions such as the nature of truth, goodness, and beauty, the essence of property, the problem of God. Moreover, in the development of his

235

arguments the man loves the use of homely phrases and illustration, he is full of pungent metaphors drawn from his experience and environment; and in discussing an ethical question—say, the "moral right" of a man to his property, and to what extent he may profit by it—the Catawban may express himself somewhat in this manner:

"Well, now, Joe, take a case of this sort: suppose I buy a mule from a feller over there on the place next to mine, an' suppose I pay a hundred and fifty dollars fer that mule."

"Is this a one-eyed mule or a two-eyed mule you're buyin'?" Joe demands with a broad wink around at his listening audience.

"It's a two-eyed mule," the first man says good-humoredly, "but if you've got any objections to a two-eyed mule, we'll make it a one-eyed mule."

"Why, hell, no! Jim," the other man now says, "I ain't got no objections, but it seems to me if you're goin' to have a two-eyed mule you ought to have something better than a one-eyed argyment."

There is a roar of immense male laughter at this retort, punctuated with hearty slappings of thigh and knee, and high whoops in the throat.

"'*Oddamn!*'" one of the appreciative listeners cries, when he can get his breath, "I reckon that'll hold 'im fer a while."

The story of the "two-eyed mule and the one-eyed argyment" is indeed an immense success, it is the kind of phrase and yarn these people love, and it is destined for an immediate and wide circulation all over the community. It may even be raised to the dignity of proverbial usage, so that one will hear men saying, "Well, that's a two-eyed mule an' a one-eyed argyment if I ever saw one," and certainly the unfortunate Jim may expect to be greeted for some time to come in this way:

"Howdy, Jim. I hear you've gone into the mule business," or, "Hey, Jim, you ain't bought no two-eyed mules lately, have you?" or, "Say, Jim: you ain't seen a feller with a one-eyed argyment lookin' fer a two-eyed mule, have you?"

Jim knows very well that he is "in" for this kind of treatment, but he joins in the laughter good-humoredly, although his clay-red face burns with a deeper hue and he awaits the resumption of debate with a more dogged and determined air.

"Well, that's all right about that," he says, when he can make himself heard. "Whether he's a one-eyed mule or a two-eyed mule is neither here nor there."

"Maybe one eye is here, an' t'other there," someone suggests, and this sets them off again at Jim's expense. But Jim has the determination of the debater and the philosopher, and although his face is pretty red by now, he sticks to his job.

"All right," he says at length, "say I got a mule, anyway, an' he's a good mule, an' I paid one hundred and fifty dollars fer him. Now!" he says, pausing and lifting one finger impressively. "I take that mule an' work him on my farm fer *four* years. He's a *good* mule an' a *good* worker an' durin' that time he pays fer himself *twice* over! Now!" he declares again, pausing and looking triumphantly at his opponent, Joe, before resuming his argument.

"All right! All right!" Joe says patiently with an air of resignation. "I heard you. I'm still waitin'. You ain't *said* nothin' yet. You ain't *proved* nothin' yet."

"Now!" Jim continues slowly and triumphantly. "I gave one hundred and fifty dollars fer him but he's earned his keep an' paid fer himself *twice* over."

"I heard you! I heard you!" says Joe patiently.

"In other words," someone says, "you got back

237

what you paid fer that mule with one hundred and fifty dollars to boot."

"Egs-actly!" Jim says with decision, to the group that is now listening intently. "I got back what I put into him an' I got one hundred fifty dollars to boot. Now here comes another feller," he continues, pointing indefinitely towards the western horizon, "who *needs* a good mule, an' he sees *my* mule, an' he *offers to buy it!*" Here Jim pauses again, and he turns and surveys his audience with triumph written on his face.

"*I* heard you. *I'm* listenin'," says Joe in a patient and monotonous voice.

"How much does *he* offer you?" someone asks.

"Now, wait a minute! I'm comin' to that," says Jim with a silencing gesture. "This here feller says, 'That's a perty good mule you got there!' 'I reckon he'll do!' I say. 'I ain't got no complaint to make!' 'I'm thinkin' of buyin' a mule myse'f,' he says. 'That so?' I say. 'Yes,' he says, 'I could use another mule on my farm. You ain't thinkin' of sellin' that mule there, are you?' 'No,' I say, 'I ain't *thinkin'* of it.' 'Well,' he says, 'would you consider an offer fer him?' 'Well,' I say, 'I might an' I might not. It all depends.' 'How much will you take fer him?' he says. 'Well,' I say, 'I ain't never thought of sellin' him before. I'd rather you'd make an offer. How much will you give?' 'Well,' he says, 'how about three hundred dollars?'"

There is a pause of living silence now while Jim turns finally and triumphantly upon his audience.

"*Now!*" he cries again, powerfully, and decisively, leaning forward with one big hand gripped upon his knee and his great index finger pointed toward them.

"I'm *listenin'*," Joe says in a calm but foreboding

tone.

"I *got* my money back out o' that mule," Jim says, beginning a final recapitulation.

"Yes, an' you got another hundred an' fifty to boot," someone helpfully suggests.

"That makes *one* hundred percent clear profit on my *'riginal* investment," Jim says. "Now here comes a feller who's willin' to pay me three hundred dollars on top of that. That makes *three* hundred percent."

He pauses now with a conclusive air.

"Well?" says Joe heavily. "Go on. I'm still waitin'. What's the argyment?"

"Why," says Jim, "the argyment is this: I *got* my money back——"

"We all *know* that," says Joe. "You got your money back and a hundred percent to boot."

"Well," says Jim, "the argyment is this: Have I any *right* to take the three hundred dollars that feller offers me?"

"Right?" says Joe, staring at him. "Why, what are you talkin' about? Of course, you got the right. The mule's yours, ain't he?"

"Ah!" says Jim with a knowing look, "that's just the point. *Is* he?"

"You *said* you bought an' *paid* fer him, didn't you?" someone said.

"Yes," said Jim, "I did that, all right."

"Why hell, Jim," someone else says, "you just ain't talkin' sense. A man's got the right to sell his own property."

"The *legal* right," Jim says, "the *legal* right! Yes! But I ain't talkin' about the *legal* right. I'm talkin' about the *mawral* right."

They gaze at Jim for a moment with an expression of slack-jawed stupefaction mixed with awe. Then he continues:

"A man's got a right to buy a piece of property an'

to sell it an' to git a fair profit on his investment. I ain't denyin' that. But has *any* man," he continues, "a right—a mawral right—to a profit of three hundred percent?"

Now Jim has made his point, he is content to rest for a moment and await the attack that comes, and comes immediately: after a moment's silence there is a tumult of protest, derisive laughter, strong cries of denial, a confusion of many voices all shouting disagreement, above which Joe's heavy baritone finally makes itself heard.

"Why, Jim!" he roars. "That's the damndest logic I ever did hear. I did give you credit fer havin' at least a *one*-eyed argyment, but I'm damned if this argyment you're givin' us has any eyes a-tall!"

Laughter here, and shouts of agreement.

"Why, Jim!" another one says with solemn humor, with an air of deep concern, "you want to go to see a doctor, son: you've begun to talk funny. Don't you know that?"

"*All* right. *All* right!" says Jim doggedly. "You can laugh all you please, but there's two sides to this here question, no matter what you think."

"Why, Jim!" yet another says, with a loose grin playing around his mouth. "What you goin' to do with that two-eyed mule? You goin' to *give* him away to that feller simply because you got your money out of him?"

"I ain't sayin'!" says Jim stubbornly, looking very red in the face at their laughter. "I ain't sayin' what I'd do. Mebbe I would and mebbe I wouldn't."

There is a roar of laughter this time, and the chorus of derisive voices is more emphatic than ever. But for some moments now, while this clamor has been going on, one of the company has fallen silent, he has fallen into a deep study, into an attitude of earnest meditation. But now he rouses himself and looks around with an expression of commanding seriousness.

"Hold on a moment there, boys," he says. "I'm not so sure about all this. I don't know that Jim's such a fool as you think he is. 'Pears to me there may be something in what he says."

"Now!" says Joe, with an air of finality. "What did I tell you! The woods are full of 'em. Here's another 'un that ain't all there."

But the contest is now just beginning in earnest: it goes on furiously, but very seriously, from now on, with these two Horatiuses holding their bridge valiantly and gaining in strength and conviction at each assault. It is a remarkable circumstance that at almost every gathering of Catawbans there are one or more of these minority warriors, who become more thoughtful and dubious as their companions grow more vociferous in their agreement and derision, and who, finally, from a first mild expression of doubt, become hotly embattled on the weaker side, and grow in courage and conviction at every breath, every word they utter, every attack they make or repel.

And it has always been the same with the Catawba people. Their character has strong Scotch markings: they are cautious and deliberate, slow to make a radical decision. They are great talkers, and believe in prayer and argument. They want to "reason a thing out," they want to "git to the bottom of a thing" through discussion, they want to settle a thing peaceably by the use of diplomacy and compromise. They are perhaps the most immensely conservative people on earth, they reverence authority, tradition, and leadership, but when committed to any decision, they stick to it implacably, and if the decision is war, they will fight to the end with the fury of maniacs.

Until very recent years these people were touched scarcely at all by "foreign" migration, whether from any of the other states, or from Europe: even today the number of "foreign-born" citizens is almost negligible, the state has the largest percentage of native-born inhabitants in the country. This stock proceeds directly from the stock of the early settlers, who were English, German, and Scotch, particularly Scotch: the frequency with which Scotch names occur—the Grahams, the Alexanders, the McRaes, the Ramsays, the Morrisons, the Pettigrews, the Pentlands, etc.—is remarkable, as is also a marked Scottishness of physique, a lean, angular, big-boned and loose-jointed structure, a long-loping stride, an immense vitality and endurance, especially among the mountaineers in the western part of the state. In fact, during the recent war, it was found by the army examiners that Catawba furnished easily the tallest troops in the service, and that their average height was a good inch and a half above the average for the country. From this it must not be supposed, as some philological pedagogues have supposed, with the mincing and accurate inaccuracy which is usual in this kind of people, that Old Catawba is today a magnificent anachronism populated with roistering and swashbuckling Elizabethans, "singing" (the pedagogues gloatingly remark of the mountaineers) "the *very* songs their ancestors sang in England four centuries ago, in a form that is practically intact," or with warlike and mad-eyed Kelts, chanting the same ballads as when they stormed across the border behind the Bruces.

No. The Catawban of today is not like this, nor

would he want to be. He is not a colonist, a settler, a transplanted European; during his three centuries there in the wilderness, he has become native to the immense and lonely land that he inhabits, during those three centuries he has taken on the sinew and color of that earth, he has acquired a character, a tradition, and a history of his own: it is an obscure history, unknown to the world and not to be found in the pages of books, but it is a magnificent history, full of heroism, endurance, and the immortal silence of the earth. It lives in his heart, it lives in his brain, it lives in his unrecorded actions; and with this knowledge he is content, nor does he feel the need of ballads or armadas to trick him into glory.

He does not need to speak, he does not need to affirm or deny, he does not need to assert his power or his achievement, for his heart is a lonely and secret heart, his spirit is immensely brave and humble, he has lived alone in the wilderness, he has heard the silence of the earth, he knows what he knows, and he has not spoken yet. We see him, silent and unheralded, in the brief glare of recorded event—he is there in the ranks of the American Revolution, and eighty years later he is there, gloriously but silently, in the ranks of the Civil War. But his real history is much longer and much more extraordinary than could be indicated by these flares of war: it is a history that runs back three centuries into primitive America, a strange and unfathomable history that is touched by something dark and supernatural, and that goes back through poverty, and hardship, through solitude and loneliness and death and unspeakable courage, into the wilderness. For it is the wilderness that is the mother of that nation, it was in the wilderness that the strange and lonely people who have not yet spoken, but who inhabit that immense and terrible land from East to West, first knew themselves, it was in the living wilderness that they faced one another at ten paces and shot one another down, and it is in the wilderness that they still live.

The real history of Old Catawba is not essentially a history of wars or rebellions; it is not a history of politics or corrupt officials; it is not a history of democracy or plutocracy or any form of government; it is not a history of businessmen, puritans, knaves, fools, saints, or heroes; it is not a history of culture or barbarism.

The real history of Old Catawba is a history of solitude, of the wilderness, and of the eternal earth, it is the history of millions of men living and dying alone in the wilderness, it is the history of the billion unrecorded and forgotten acts and moments of their lives; it is a history of the sun and the moon and the earth, of the sea that feathers eternally against the desolate coasts, and of great trees that smash down in lone solitudes of the wilderness.

The history of Old Catawba is the history of millions of men living alone in the wilderness, it is the history of millions of men who have lived their brief lives in silence upon the everlasting earth, who have listened to the earth and known her million tongues, whose lives were given to the earth, whose bones and flesh are recompacted with the earth, the immense and terrible earth that makes no answer.

Circus
at Dawn

There were times in early autumn—in September—when the greater circuses would come to town—the Ringling Brothers, Robinson's, and Barnum and Bailey shows, and when I was a route boy on the morning paper, on those mornings when the circus would be coming in I would rush madly through my route in the cool and thrilling darkness that comes just before break of day, and then I would go back home and get my brother out of bed.

Talking in low excited voices we would walk rapidly back toward town under the rustle of September leaves, in cool streets just grayed now with that still, that unearthly and magical first light of day which seems suddenly to rediscover the great earth out of darkness, so that the earth emerges with an awful, a glorious sculptural stillness, and one looks out with a feeling of joy and disbelief, as the first men on this earth must have done, for to see this happen is one of the things that men will remember out of life forever and think of as they die.

At the sculptural still square where at one corner, just emerging into light, my father's shabby little marble shop stood with a ghostly strangeness and familiarity, my brother and I would "catch" the first streetcar of the day bound for the "depot" where the circus was—or sometimes we would meet someone we knew, who would give us a lift in his automobile.

Then, having reached the dingy, grimy, and rickety depot section, we would get out, and walk rapidly across the tracks of the station yard, where we could see great flares and steamings from the engines, and hear the crash and bump of shifting freight cars, the swift sporadic thunders of a shifting engine, the tolling of bells, the sounds of great trains on the rails.

And to all these familiar sounds, filled with their exultant prophecies of flight, the voyage, morning, and the shining cities—to all the sharp and thrilling odors of the trains—the smell of cinders, acrid smoke, of musty, rusty freight cars, the clean pine board of crated produce, and the smells of fresh stored food—oranges, coffee, tangerines and bacon, ham and flour and beef—there would be added now, with an unforgettable magic and familiarity, all the strange sounds and smells of the coming circus.

The gay yellow sumptuous-looking cars in which the star performers lived and slept, still dark and silent, heavily and powerfully still, would be drawn up in long strings upon the tracks. And all around them the sounds of the unloading circus would go on furiously in the darkness. The receding gulf of lilac and departing night would be filled with the savage roar of the lions, the murderously sudden snarling of great jungle cats, the trumpeting of the elephants, the stamp of the horses, and with the musty, pungent, unfamiliar odor of the jungle animals: the tawny camel smells, and the smells of panthers, zebras, tigers, elephants, and bears.

Then, along the tracks, beside the circus trains, there would be the sharp cries and oaths of the circus men, the magical swinging dance of lanterns in the darkness, the sudden heavy rumble of the loaded vans and wagons as they were pulled along the flats and gondolas, and down the runways to the ground. And everywhere, in the thrilling mystery of darkness and awakening light, there would be the tremendous conflict of a confused, hurried, and yet orderly movement.

The great iron-gray horses, four and six to a team, would be plodding along the road of thick white dust to a rattling of chains and traces and the harsh cries of their drivers. The men would drive the animals to the river which flowed by beyond the tracks, and water them; and as first light came one could see the elephants wallowing in the familiar river and the big horses going slowly and carefully down to drink.

Then, on the circus grounds, the tents were going up already with the magic speed of dreams. All over the place (which was near the tracks and the only space of flat land in the town that was big enough to hold a circus) there would be this fierce, savagely hurried, and yet orderly confusion. Great flares of gaseous circus light would blaze down on the seared and battered faces of the circus toughs as, with the rhythmic precision of a single animal—a human riveting machine—they swung their sledges at the stakes, driving a stake into the earth with the incredible instancy of accelerated figures in a motion picture. And everywhere, as light came, and the sun appeared, there would be a scene of magic, order, and of violence. The drivers would curse and talk their special language to their teams, there would be the loud, gasping and uneven labor of a gasoline engine, the shouts and curses of the bosses, the wooden riveting of driven stakes, and the rattle of heavy chains.

Already in an immense cleared space of dusty beaten earth, the stakes were being driven for the

249

main exhibition tent. And an elephant would lurch ponderously to the field, slowly lower his great swinging head at the command of a man who sat perched upon his skull, flourish his gray wrinkled snout a time or two, and then solemnly wrap it around a tent pole big as the mast of a racing schooner. Then the elephant would back slowly away, dragging the great pole with him as if it were a stick of matchwood.

And when this happened, my brother would break into his great "whah-whah" of exuberant laughter, and prod me in the ribs with his clumsy fingers. And further on, two town darkeys, who had watched the elephant's performance with bulging eyes, would turn to each other with apelike grins, bend double as they slapped their knees and howled with swart rich nigger laughter, saying to each other in a kind of rhythmical chorus of question and reply:

"He don't play with it, do he?"

"No, *suh*! He don't send no boy!"

"He don't say 'Wait a minute,' do he?"

"No, suh! He say 'Come with me!' That's what he say!"

"He go boogety—boogety!" said one, suiting the words with a prowling movement of his black face toward the earth.

"He go rootin' faw it!" said the other, making a rooting movement with his head.

"He say 'Ar-rumpf'!" said one.

"He say 'Big boy, we is on ouah way'!" the other answered.

"Har! Har! Har! Har! Har!"—and they choked and screamed with their rich laughter, slapping their thighs with a solid smack as they described to each other the elephant's prowess.

251

Meanwhile, the circus food tent—a huge canvas top without concealing sides—had already been put up, and now we could see the performers seated at long trestled tables underneath the tent, as they ate breakfast. And the savor of the food they ate—mixed as it was with our strong excitement, with the powerful but wholesome smells of the animals, and with all the joy, sweetness, mystery, jubilant magic and glory of the morning and the coming of the circus—seemed to us to be of the most maddening and appetizing succulence of any food that we had ever known or eaten.

We could see the circus performers eating tremendous breakfasts, with all the savage relish of their power and strength: they ate big fried steaks, pork chops, rashers of bacon, a half-dozen eggs, great slabs of fried ham and great stacks of wheat cakes which a cook kept flipping in the air with the skill of a juggler, and which a husky-looking waitress kept rushing to their tables on loaded trays held high and balanced marvellously on the fingers of a brawny hand. And above all the maddening odors of the wholesome and succulent food, there brooded forever the sultry and delicious fragrance—that somehow seemed to add a zest and sharpness to all the powerful and thrilling life of morning—of strong boiling coffee, which we could see sending off clouds of steam from an enormous polished urn, and which the circus performers gulped down, cup after cup.

And the circus men and women themselves—these star performers—were such fine-looking people, strong and handsome, yet speaking and moving with an almost stern dignity and decorum, that their lives seemed to us to be as splendid and wonderful as any lives on earth could be. There was never anything loose, rowdy, or tough in their comportment, nor did the circus women look like painted whores, or behave indecently with the men.

Rather, these people in an astonishing way seemed to have created an established community which lived an ordered existence on wheels, and to observe with a stern fidelity unknown in towns and cities the decencies of family life. There would be a powerful young man, a handsome and magnificent young woman with blonde hair and the figure of an Amazon, and a powerfully built, thickset man of middle age, who had a stern, lined, responsible-looking face and a bald head. They were probably the members of a trapeze team—the young man and woman would leap through space like projectiles, meeting the grip of the older man and hurling back again upon their narrow perches, catching the swing of their trapeze in midair, and whirling thrice before they caught it, in a perilous and beautiful exhibition of human balance and precision.

But when they came into the breakfast tent, they would speak gravely yet courteously to other performers, and seat themselves in a family group at one of the long tables, eating their tremendous breakfasts with an earnest concentration, seldom speaking to one another, and then gravely, seriously and briefly.

And my brother and I would look at them with fascinated eyes: my brother would watch the man with the bald head for a while and then turn toward me, whispering:

"D-d-do you see that f-f-fellow there with the bald head? W-w-well he's the heavy man," he whispered knowingly. "He's the one that c-c-c-catches them! That f-f-fellow's got to know his business! You know what happens if he m-m-misses, don't you?" said my brother.

"What?" I would say in a fascinated tone.

253

My brother snapped his fingers in the air.

"Over!" he said. "D-d-done for! W-w-why, they'd be d-d-d-dead before they knew what happened. Sure!" he said, nodding vigorously. "It's a f-f-f-fact! If he ever m-m-m-misses it's all over! That boy has g-g-g-got to know his s-s-s-stuff!" my brother said. "W-w-w-why," he went on in a low tone of solemn conviction, "it w-w-w-wouldn't surprise me at all if they p-p-p-pay him s-s-seventy-five or a hundred dollars a week! It's a fact!" my brother cried vigorously.

And we would turn our fascinated stares again upon these splendid and romantic creatures, whose lives were so different from our own, and whom we seemed to know with such familiar and affectionate intimacy. And at length, reluctantly, with full light come and the sun up, we would leave the circus grounds and start for home.

And somehow the memory of all we had seen and heard that glorious morning, and the memory of the food tent with its wonderful smells, would waken in us the pangs of such a ravenous hunger that we could not wait until we got home to eat. We would stop off in town at lunchrooms and, seated on tall stools before the counter, we would devour ham-and-egg sandwiches, hot hamburgers red and pungent at their cores with coarse spicy sanguinary beef, coffee, glasses of foaming milk and doughnuts, and then go home to eat up everything in sight upon the breakfast table.

The Web
of Earth

In the year that the locusts came, something that happened in the year the locusts came, ... two voices that I heard there in that year. . . . Child! Child! It seems so long ago since the year the locusts came, and all of the trees were eaten bare: so much has happened and it seems so long ago. . . .

"What say?" I said.

Says, "Two . . . Two," says, "Twenty . . . Twenty."

"Hah? What say?"

"Two . . . Two," the first voice said; and "Twenty . . . Twenty," said the other.

"Oh, Two!" I cried out to your papa, and "Twenty . . . Twenty—can't you hear them?"

"Two . . . Two," it said again, the first voice over by the window, and "Twenty . . . Twenty" said the second, at my ear.

"Oh, don't you hear it, Mr. Gant?" I cried.

"Why, Lord, woman!" your papa said. "What on earth are you talking about? There's no one there," he said.

"Oh, yes, there is!" I said, and then I heard them once again, "Two . . . Two" and "Twenty . . . Twenty."

"There they are!" I said.

"Pshaw, Mrs. Gant," your papa said. "It's something you imagined. You fell asleep, you must have dreamed it."

"Oh, no, I didn't," I said. "It's there! It's there all right!"—because I *knew, I knew:* because I heard it just as plain!

"It's the condition you're in," he said. "You're tired and overwrought and you've imagined it."

Then all of the bells began to ring and he got up to go.

"Oh, don't go!" I said. "I wish you wouldn't go"—you know I had a premonition, and it worried me to see him go.

And then I heard it once again—"Two . . . Two," the first voice said, and "Twenty . . . Twenty," said the other . . . and I *know, I know* —why, yes! Lord God! don't I remember, boy!— the hour, the time, the very year it happened, to the day . . . because that was the year the locusts came at home and all of the trees were eaten bare.

But, say, then!—Ben—Steve—Luke—pshaw! Boy! *Gene!* I mean—I reckon Luke is thinking of me at this moment, that's why I keep calling you his name. Well, now—hah? What say?

"You started to tell me about two voices that you heard one time."

Oh, yes! That's so! Well, now, as I was—say! What was that? Hah?

"Those were the ships out on the harbor, Mama."

What say? Harbor? Ships? Oh, yes, I reckon now that's so. The harbor is yon way?

"No, Mama, it's the other way. You're turned around. It's just the other way: it's there."

Hah? *That* way? Why, no, child, surely not. . . . Are you telling me the truth? . . . Well, then, I'll vow! I *am* mixed up. I reckon comin' in that tunnel did it. But you couldn't lose me in the country; give me a landmark of some sort to go by and I'll be all right. . . . Why, boy, I'll vow! . . . There goes that thing again! Why, Lord! It sounds like some old cow! And here you are right on the edge of it! How did you ever come to such a place? Lord! Listen—do you hear it? I reckon that's a big one gettin' ready to pull out. . . . Lord, God! You're all alike: your daddy was the same—forever wantin' to be up and gone. If I'd let him he'd have been nothing but a wanderer across the face of the earth. . . . Child, child, you mustn't be a wanderer all your days. . . . It worries me to think of you away off somewheres with strange people. . . . You mustn't spend your life alone with strangers. . . . You ought to come back where your people came from. . . . Child, child, it worries me. . . . Come back again.

Well now, as I was goin' on to say, that night I heard it, the first voice—pshaw! there goes that whistle once again. Say, boy! I tell you what—it makes me want to pick right up and light out with it! Why, yes, I'm not so old! I could start out now—I tell you what, I've got a good mind to do it—I'd like to start right out and just see everything—why! all those countries: England, where all our folks came from, and France, Germany, Italy—say! I've always wanted to see Switzerland—that must certainly be a beautiful spot—as the feller says, the Wonderland of Nature. . . .

Say . . . oh, now I hear it! . . . Now I know. . . . Why, yes! It's out yon way. And where's the bridge, then, that we walked across that night?

"It's here—right at the bottom of the street. Here! Come to the window and look out. Don't you remember how we came?"

Remember! Now, boy, you ask me if I can remember! Lord, God! I reckon I remember things you never read about—the way it was, the things they never wrote about in books.

I reckon that they tried to put it down in books, all of the wars and battles, child, I guess they got that part of it all right, but Lord!—how could these fellers know the way it was when they weren't born, when they weren't there to see it: they made it seem so long ago and like it happened in some strange land—what could they know, child, of the way it was: the way the wind blew and the way the sun was shining, the smell of the smoke out in the yard, and Mother singin', and the scalded feathers, and the way the river swelled that spring when it had rained? The way the men looked as they marched back along the river road that day, as they were comin' from the war, and the things we said, and the sound of all the voices of the people who are dead, and the way the sunlight came and went, and how it made me sad to see it, and the way the women cried as we stood there in Bob Patton's yard, and the men marched by us, and the dust rose, and we knew the war was over. Lord, God! do I remember! Those are the things that I remember, child, and that's the way things were.

I can remember all the way back to the time when I was two years old, and let me tell you, boy, there's mighty little I've forgotten since.

Why, yes!—don't I remember how they took me by the hand that day and led me down into the holler—Bob Patton and your Uncle George—and here boylike they had constructed an effigy of Willy and Lucindy Patton out of that old black mud they had there—you could mold it in your hands just like a piece of putty—and how I screamed and all—because I *knew*, I *knew*, I'd seen them both and I remembered them—why! Willy and Lucindy were two slaves that Cap'n Patton owned—oh, Lord! the blackest African niggers you ever saw, as Father said, charcoal would 'a' left a white mark on them, their parents had been taken right out of the jungle —and those white teeth, those gleaming white teeth when they grinned—but oh! the odor! that awful odor, that old black nigger smell that nothin' could wash out, mother couldn't stand it, it made her deathly sick, when they passed through a room they left the smell behind them—and here these two devils of boys had made this effigy with pebbles they had taken from the creek for teeth, and to think of it!—that they should tell a child of two a thing like that—*why*, that it was Willy and Lucindy Patton I was lookin' at—"Look out!" says Bob, "they're going to eat you up," he says, and how I screamed— why, I remember it all the same as yesterday!

And don't I remember taking Brother Will up to the Indian Mound—of course the story went that there were Indians buried there, that's what it was, they said—and here this brook was filled up with this old black oily stuff that came out from the mound—of course, Father always gave it as his opinion there was oil there, that's what he said, you know, that someone would make a fortune some-day if they dug a well there—and Will was only two and a half years old and George told him that the old black oil was squeezed out of the corpses of the In-dians and how Will screamed and hollered when he told him—"Why," Mother said, "I could wring your neck for having no more sense than to frighten a child with such a story."

* * *

261

And yes, now! What about it? Don't I remember
that winter when the deer come boundin' down the
hill across the path and stopped and looked at me
not ten feet away, and I screamed because I saw its
antlers? Lord! I didn't know what to make of it, I'd
never heard of such an animal, and how it bounded
away into the woods again and how when I told
Mother she said, "Yes, you saw a deer. That was a
deer you saw all right. The hunters ran it down here
off the mountain" and—why, yes! wasn't it only the
next spring after that when I was a big girl four years
old and remembered everything—that the Yankees
began to come through there, and didn't I hear
them, didn't I see them with my own eyes, the villains—those two fellers tearing along the road on
two horses they had stolen, as hard as they could, as
if all hell had cut loose after them—why! it's as
plain in my mind today as it was then, the way they
looked, two ragged-lookin' troopers bent down and
whippin' those horses for all that they were worth,
with bandanna handkerchiefs tied around their
necks and the ends of them whipping back as stiff
and straight as if they'd been starched and ironed—
now *that* will give you some idea of how fast they
were goin'—and couldn't I hear the people shoutin'
and hollerin' all along the road that they were
comin', and how the womenfolks took on and made
the men go out and hide themselves? "Oh, Lord,"
says Mother, wringin' her hands, "there they
come!" and didn't Addie Patton come running up
the hill to tell us, the poor child frightened out of
her wits, you know screaming, "Oh, they've come,
they've come! And Grandfather's down there all
alone," she says. "They'll kill him, they'll kill him!"
Of course we didn't know then that these two Yan-

kee stragglers were alone, we thought they were the

advance guard of a whole brigade of Sherman's
troopers. But Law! the rest of them never got there
for a week, here these two thieving devils had broken away, and I reckon were just trying to see how
much they could steal by themselves. Why, yes!
Didn't all the men begin to shoot at them then as
they went by and when they saw they didn't have
the army with them, and didn't they jump off their
horses and light out for the mountains on foot as
hard as they could, then, and leave the horses? And
didn't some people from way over in Bedford
County come to claim the horses when the war was
over? They identified them, you know, and said
those same two fellers were the ones that took 'em.
And Lord! didn't they tell it how Amanda Stevens
set fire to the bridge with her own hands on the
other side of Sevier so that those that were comin' in
from Tennessee were held up for a week before
they got across—yes! and stood there laughin' at
them, you know; of course they used to tell it on her
that she said ("Lord!" I said, "you know she
wouldn't say a thing like that!") but of course
Amanda was an awful coarse talker, she didn't care
what she said, and they all claimed later that's just
the way she put it—"Why," she hollers to them,
"you don't need a bridge to get across a little stream
like that, do you? Well, you must be a pretty worth-
less lot, after all," she said. "Why, down here," she
says, "we'd call it a pretty poor sort of man who
couldn't——across it," and, of course, the Yankees
had to laugh then, that's the story that they told.

And yes! Didn't they tell it at the time how the
day the Yankees marched into town they captured
old man Mackery? I reckon they wanted to have
some fun with him more than anything else, a great
fat thing, you know, with that swarthy yeller com-

263

plexion and that kinky hair, of course, the story went
that he had nigger blood in him and—what about it!
he admitted it, sir, he claimed it then and there in
front of all the Yankees, I reckon hoping they would
let him off. "All right," the Yankees said, "if you can
prove that you're a nigger we'll let you go." Well, he
said that he could prove it, then. "Well, how're you
going to prove it?" they asked him. "I'll tell you
how," this Yankee captain says, calls to one of his
troopers, you know, "Run him up and down the
street a few times, Jim," he says, and so they started,
this soldier and old man Mackery, running up and
down in that hot sun as hard as they could go. Well,
when they got back, he was wringin' wet with per-
spiration, Mackery, you know, and the story goes
the Yankee went over to him and took one good
smell and then called out, "Yes, by God, he told the
truth, boys. He's a nigger. Let him go!" Well, that's
the way they told it, anyhow.

And yes! Don't I remember it all, yes! With the
men comin' by and marchin' along that river road on
their way into town to be mustered out and all of us
ganged together there in the front yard of Uncle
John's place to see them pass, Father and Mother
and all the childern and all of the Patton and Alexander and Pentland tribes and these two black African niggers that I told you John Patton owned, Willy
and Lucindy Patton, and your great-grandfather,
boy, old Bill Pentland that they called Bill the Hat-
ter because he could make them of the finest felt—
learned how to treat the wool with chamber lye, oh!
the finest hats you ever saw, why don't I remember
an old farmer coming to our house in my childhood
to give a hat to Uncle Sam to be reblocked, says,
"Sam, old Bill Pentland made that hat for me just
twenty years ago and it's as good," he says, "as it

ever was, all it needs is to be blocked and cleaned," and let me tell you, everyone that knew him said that Billy Pentland was certainly a man with a remarkable mind.

Now, boy, I want to tell you, I've always said whatever ability you had came from that side of the house, there's one thing sure, Bill Pentland was a man who'd 'a' gone far if he'd had the education. Of course he had no book learnin' but they told it, you know, how he could argue and take sides on any question, hale and hearty, mind you, right up to the hour of his death, sent word down to Sam one day to come up there to see him, says, "Sam"—of course Sam told it how he found him building his fire and singin' a hymn, at peace with the world and without a thing wrong with him—"Sam," he says, "I'm glad you've come. There are matters I want to talk over with you. Lay down on that bed," he says, "so we can talk." Well, that just suited Sam, you know, oh! the *laziest* feller that ever lived, he could spend his whole life just a-layin' round and talkin', "Why," he says, "what is it, Father? What's the matter? Aren't you feelin' good?" he says. "Oh," says Bill, "I never felt better, but I'm not goin' to be here with you much longer," he says, "I've made up my mind it's time to die, Sam, and I want to put my house in order before I go." "Why, Father," Sam says, "what are you talkin' about, what do you mean? There's nothing wrong with you." "No, not a thing," says Bill. "Why, you'll be here for years to come," says Sam. "No, Sam," the old man says, he shook his head, you know. "I've just decided that it's my time to go. I've had a Call. Now, I've lived out my full three score years and ten," he says, "with some to spare and I feel there's nothin' more I can do on

265

earth, so I've made up my mind." "Made up your
mind?" says Sam, "why, made up your mind to
what?" "Why," he says, "I've made up my mind to
die, Sam." "Why, Father," says Sam, "what are you
talking about? You're not going to die," he says.
"Yes," says Bill, "I've made up my mind to die tomorrow," says, "I've made up my mind to die at ten
minutes after six tomorrow afternoon, and that's the
reason I sent for you." Well! they built up a roarin'
big fire and stayed up all night long talkin' together,
and oh! you know, Sam told it how the wind roared
and howled, and how they talked long, long into the
night, and they cooked breakfast, and lay around
and talked some more, and they cooked dinner and
talked some more and that old man was as well and
strong as he'd ever been, at peace with mankind, sir,
and without a worry in the world, but on the stroke
of six, now, boy, I want to tell you the kind of man
he was, on the stroke of six, he turned to Sam and
said, "Get ready, Sam," and at ten minutes after six
to the dot, he looked at him again and said, "Good-
bye, Sam: it's my time, I'm going, son," and he
turned his face to the wall, sir, and *died*—now that's
the kind of a man he was, that goes to show the kind
of willpower and determination he had in *him*—
and *let me tell you something:* we've all had it in us,
that same thing, when it came our time to go, we
knew it. Father went the same way, sir, kept wakin'
up all day long to say, "Is it six o'clock, yet?"—
couldn't seem to get it off his mind, you know—
"Why, no, Father," I said, "it's only noon." Now,
six, six, I kept a-thinkin', why does he keep asking if
it's six? That *very day* sir, as the clock was striking
the last stroke of six he breathed his last, I turned to
Jim and whispered, "Six": he nodded, "Yes," he
said. Of course we knew.

But here he was that day—don't I remember
him? Old Bill Pentland standin' there with all the
rest of us to watch the troops go by, a hale and
hearty old man, sir, oh! married twice and had all
those childern, eight by his first wife, Martha Patton, of course Father was one of *that* crowd and
fourteen by that other woman—well, that's so, there
was that other one, I reckon, that he'd had by that
woman down in South Carolina, of course there was
no record of the ceremony and I reckon what they
said was true, but he brought that child home and
sat her down at the table with all the rest of them
and said to them all: "From this time on she is your
sister and must be treated so," and that's the way it
was all right. And here, to think of it! All these childern that he had went out and had big families of
their own, those that didn't die early or get killed,
until now there are hundreds of them living down
there in Catawba in the mountains, and in Georgia
and Texas and out West in California and Oregon
until now they are spread all over like a web—but
that's where they came from, from that one old man,
he was the only one there was to begin with, the
son of that Englishman that came there back in Rev-
olutionary days to sink those copper shafts out there
in Yancey. Of course they say we've got great estates
waitin' for us in England—I know Uncle Bob came
to Father at the time Bill Pentland died and told
him he ought to do something about it, but they decided against it, said the expense would be too great
—but he was *there*, all right, Bill Pentland was there
with all the rest of us the day they came back from
the war. And here came all the troops, you know, and
you could hear the men a-cheerin' and the womenfolks a-crying, and every now and then you'd see one
of the men drop out of line and then the women

would start crying again, and here comes Uncle Bob
—only sixteen, mind you, but he seemed like an old
man to me—wearing a stovepipe hat I reckon he'd
looted from some store and no shoes on, and here
he comes and we all began to cry.

"Why, Lord!" says Bob, "this is a pretty home-
comin' for a fact," he says, you know, trying to joke
us along and cheer us up. "Why, I thought you'd be
glad to see me," he says. "I didn't expect you all to
bust out cryin'! Why, if that's the way you feel," he
says, "I'm goin' back."

"Oh, Bob, Bob," his mother says, "you've got no
shoes, poor child, you're barefooted," she says.

"No," says Bob, "I wore 'em out in my hurry to
get home," he says, "I just walked them clean off
my feet," he says, "but if I'd known it was going to
be like this, I wouldn't have come so fast," he said,
and of course that made 'em laugh.

But, child, that wasn't the reason that the women
cried. So many had gone off that never would come
home again and, of course, they knew it, they knew
it, and then, didn't we all flock into the house, and
hadn't they all been baking and cooking for a week
and, let me tell you, poor as we were, that was a
meal, no little dabs of stuff such as they give you
nowadays: fried chickens—why we must have
cooked two dozen of them—and boiled hams and
pork and roasting ears and sweet pertaters and
string beans and plates full of corn bread and hot
biscuits and peach and apple dumplings and all
kinds of jams and jellies and pies and cakes galore
and all of the cider you could drink, and Lord! I
wish you could have seen the way that Bob and
Rufus Alexander and Fate Patton put that food
away, why, as Mother said, you'd 'a' thought they
hadn't had a square meal since they went to war and
I reckon maybe she didn't miss it much either.

Why, wasn't I a big girl of five years old at the time, and saw it all, and remember it as well as I'm settin' here yes, and things that happened long before that—and things you never heard of, boy, with all your reading out of books: why, yes, didn't we learn to do everything ourselves and to grow everything we ate and to take the wool and dye it, yes, to go out in the woods and get the sumac and the walnut bark and all the walnut hulls and elderberries for the dyes and rinse the wool in copperas water until we had a hard fast black you couldn't take the shine off—why! it beat the stuff they have today all hollow—didn't I learn to do it with my own hands and couldn't I get the finest reds and greens and yellers that you ever saw, and didn't I learn to spin the flax and bleach it and make fine shirts and sheets and tablecloths myself, why, yes, don't I remember the day—oh! that strong rank smell, you know, of scalded feathers, with Mother plucking the chicken in the yard, and the smell of the smoke, and the fresh pine chips out by the chopping block, and all (that's where you got your sense of smell from, boy!) and the wind that howled and whistled through that old coarse grass, it made me sad to listen to it (that was the year just after Sally died) and I sat there at the wheel spinning away, and I can see it all, I remember just the way it was—when here they came along the river road, and you could hear them shout and holler out "Hurrah! hurrah!" I reckon they'd all been in to town to vote. "Hurrah!" they cried: "Hurrah for Hayes!" one crowd would cry and, "Hurrah for Tilden!" cried the other.

Lord God! do I remember! I reckon that I do! I remember things you never dreamed or heard of, boy.

* * *

"But what about those voices that you heard?"

Well, now, I say—that's what I'm telling you:

"Two . . . Two," the first voice said, and "Twenty . . . Twenty," said the other. "What say?" I said. Says, "Two . . . Two," says, "Twenty . . . Twenty." "Hah? What say?" Says, "Two . . . Two," the first voice said, says "Twenty . . . Twenty," said the other.

Well, then—say! what about it!—I was thinking about it the other day. . . . I don't know . . . but it's pretty strange when you come to think about it, isn't it? Why, that very day, you know, the twenty-seventh of September, I remember because it was on the twenty-fifth, just two days before, that I had the talk with Ambrose Radiker, that's exactly when it was all right, about eleven o'clock in the morning, your papa was back there in his workroom lettering a tombstone he was getting ready to set up for a man out there in Beaverdam whose wife had died, when here he came, Mel Porter. Your papa said he marched right back into the workroom, sir, and stood there looking at him without sayin' a word: he just stood there shakin' his head and your papa said he certainly looked blue and depressed as if some awful calamity had befallen him, so your papa said, "What's the matter, Mel? I never saw you look so sad," he says.

"Oh, Will, Will," he says, and he just stood there shakin' his head at your papa, "if you only knew how I envy you! Here you are with a good trade you can work at and nothing to worry you: I'd give up everything I have in the world if I could just change places with you!" "Why what on earth are you talking about!" your papa said. "You're a first-class lawyer with a good practice and here you want to swap places with a stonecutter who's got to work with his hands and never knows where his next job's comin' from," your papa said. "It's a curse and a care," your papa said, that's exactly the way he talked to him, you know the way he had of talkin', he'd come right out with a thing without mincin' words. "It's a curse and a care," he said, "and it was a bitter day for me when I first took it up: you've got to wait until they die to get a job and then their families, ingrates that they are, will give the work to one of your competitors: if I'd done the thing I was cut out for, I'd 'a' studied law like you did and gone into practice." Well, of course, they all said that, they said that Mr. Gant would certainly have made a fine lawyer, with his fluent command of language and all. "Oh, Will, Will," he said, "you can just go down on your knees and thank God that you didn't," he said. "At least you have enough to eat," he said, "and when you go home at night you can go to bed and sleep."

"Why, Mel," your papa said. "What on earth is wrong with you? Something is worryin' you, that's one thing sure." "Oh, Will," he said, shakin' his head, "it's those men. I can't sleep at night for thinkin' about them!" Well, he hadn't said *what* men, he hadn't mentioned their names, but your papa knew right away who he was talkin' about, it flashed over him all at once that he was referrin' to Ed Mears and Lawrence Wayne and those other three murderers down there in the county jail he had defended. And he had been down there to see them, he'd just come away from there, your papa said he knew exactly where he'd been the moment he looked at him, said his shoes and the bottoms of his trousers were coated with that old red-clay Niggertown dust, that's all in the world it was.

"Why, yes, Mel," your papa said, "I reckon it is pretty hard, but you've got nothin' to blame yourself for," he said. "You did all anyone could expect you to do," he said; says, "You did the best you could for them," he says; says, "I don't see what you got to blame yourself about now," he says.

"Oh, Will," he says, "it's the strain, the awful strain of it," he says. "Here I've done all I could to save them," he says, "and it looks as if there's nothing else I can do," he says; says, "It looks to me as if they've got to hang," he says, "and here are their wives and childern and all of their kinfolk beggin' me to save them and," he says, "Will, I just don't know what else there is I can do," he says; says, "I've racked my brain lookin' for a way out," he says, "and it looks to me as if they've *got to swing.* I tell you what," he says, shakin' his head, and your papa said he looked mighty blue, says, "it's an awful thing when you come to think of it! What about it!" he says. "Here they've got all those little childern dependent on them who have got to grow up now with that awful stigma attached to their name of knowin' they're the childern of men who were hanged for murder. Why, it's awful, that's what it is, Will," he says; says, "I can't sleep at night for thinkin' about it."

Well, when your papa came home to dinner that day he told me all about it, says, "I tell you what, it's pretty hard on him, isn't it? I reckon he's done all he can but he feels like he's in some way responsible for it, that maybe there's somethin' he failed to do that might have saved their lives," he says; says, "I couldn't help feelin' sorry for him," says "he was pale as a ghost: he looked as if he hadn't been able to sleep for a week." "Hm!" I says. "Now you listen to me: there's *something mighty funny* about this *somewheres.* I've never known a lawyer yet," I says,

"who wasn't able to sleep because a client was goin'

to be hanged, and you can just bet your bottom dollar," I says, "that Melvin Porter isn't losin' sleep on *that* account. The only reason they'll lose sleep," I says, "is because they're afraid they're not goin' to get paid or because they're stayin' awake figgerin' how they can get the best of someone, and if he told you *any such story* as that," I says, "you can depend upon it that he wasn't tellin' you the truth—there's a nigger in the woodpile somewheres: that story *just won't wash.*"

"No," your papa says, "I believe you're wrong," says, "I think you're doin' him an injustice."

"Why, pshaw, Mr. Gant!" I says. "I wouldn't be such a goose! There's not a word of truth in that story, all they've got to do is to appeal to your sympathies and you'll believe anything they tell you."

And of course that was just exactly how he was: he'd curse and rave and carry on, and then they'd tell him some big lie to get on his good side and he'd give them everything he had. Why! didn't Mel Porter's own brother, that miserable old rip, Rufus Porter—as the sayin' goes, if there's a just God in heaven he's getting today the punishment he deserves—with his old red face all stewed down like a persimmon with all the licker he'd drunk—why yes! when I was a girl didn't I see him myself march right down the aisle as big as you please, sir, that night at the meeting of the Sons of Temperance, arm in arm with Jeter Alexander to sign the pledge and Lord! as I said later if you took all the rotten old licker they'd poured down their throats since then you'd have enough to float a battleship—come to your papa and got him to sign his note and stand security for him at the bank for fourteen hundred dollars. Pshaw! when I think of it! . . . I said to your papa, *"He's* the one who ought to be hanged! I could

273

spring the trap myself!" I said; says to your papa, in that mealy voice he had, you know, says, "Oh, it will be all right, Will." Says, "You know I wouldn't let you lose a penny," when he didn't have a dollar to his name! "I'll vow, Mr. Gant!" I said at the time. "How on earth were you ever such a fool as to do such a thing!"

"Well," he said, "he swore it was all right—said he'd go down and dig ditches before he'd let me lose a penny."

"Yes," I said, "and you were *just* fool enough to believe him, weren't you!"

"Well," your papa said, "I've learned my lesson. There's one thing sure: I'll never get stung that way again," he said.

"All right," I said, "we'll wait and see."

Well, it wasn't two years before Rufe Porter tried the very same trick on him again; he had the gall to walk right into your papa's office, sir, as big as you please, and ask him to go his note for five hundred dollars. Your papa was so mad he took him by the collar and pitched him all the way out into the square and says, "If you ever come back here again, you Goddamned mountain grill," that's just the way your papa talked to him, you know the way he talked, he didn't mince words when he was mad, "I'll kill you." Why yes! wasn't old Bill Smathers the chief of police at the time standin' right there on the steps of the city hall and saw the whole thing? and he hollered right out to your papa, "Yes, and if I'm here when he does come back, Mr. Gant, I'll help you to do it," he says; says, "you did exactly the right thing," says, "the only pity is you didn't kill him now."

When your papa came home and told me about it, I said, "Yes, and he was *exactly right*! You should

have finished the job then and there. That's exactly
what you should have done. It would have been
good riddance," I said, you know, I reckon I was
pretty bitter, to think of it—here we were with six
childern to support and to think that he would go
flingin' his money away on that miserable old toper:
I could 'a' wrung his neck for being such a fool.
"Now, you look a-here," I said. "Let this be a lesson
to you: don't you ever let him have a penny again,
and don't you go lendin' money out to anyone without consultin' me first. You're a married man with a
family of little childern to support, and your first
duty is to them." Well, he promised, of course—he
said he'd never do such a thing again, and I suppose
I believed him.

Well, sir, it wasn't three days before he went off
on a big spree, he came home roaring drunk, I remember they sent word to us from Ambrose Radiker's saloon that he was up there and that we'd
better come and get him: of course, they said they
couldn't do anything with him and they thought
they'd better let us know. So I went myself. *Oh!*
Lord! . . . Why, child! you never knew him till later
when he was getting old and tired—I reckon you
thought he was bad enough then, but child! child!
You don't know, you don't know. You never *saw*
him! . . . that nigger of Radiker's told me. . . . You
know, that big old pock-marked yellow nigger that
they had—*told me* that he could drink more licker
than any *four* men he ever saw. . . . He *told me*,
mind you, that he'd seen him stand right up at the
bar and drink two quart bottles of that old rye licker
without stoppin'. "Yes," I said to Ambrose Radiker,
"and *you let him! You,*" I said, you know I looked
him right in the eye when I said it and he looked

pretty sheepish, I tell you he did! "Here you are," I said, "a man with a wife and childern of your own, and you've got no more pride nor honor than to take money out of the pocket of a man who needs it to support his family. Why, they ought to tar and feather a man like you and ride him out of town on a rail," I said. I reckon I was pretty bitter but that's just exactly the way I talked to him.

Well. . . . I reckon it stung him. He didn't say anything for a minute, but, I tell you what, his face was a study. . . . Oh! that mortified look, you know, looked as if he'd 'a' been glad if the earth had opened and swallered him up at that moment. Then, of course, he said: "Why, Eliza! *We* don't want his money! We don't need it that bad. Why, your good-will would be worth more to me than that," he says. "There are plenty of people who will come in here and drink and behave themselves," he said. "You know we don't try to lure him on to get him to come in here. Why," he said, "I'd be the happiest man alive if Mr. Gant took a solemn oath never to touch another drop of licker as long as he lived—yes and lived up to it, too. Because he's one man," he says, "that ought never to touch a drop! If he'd take one drink and then go on," he said, "why, he'd be all right, but one drink's no more use to him than a drop in the eye," he says, that's just the way he put it, "he's got to drink up half a bottle before he even feels it and then," he says, oh, shaking his head, "I tell you what, he is a caution. It's just a problem to know what to do with him. You never know what he's going to do next," he says; says, "we've had some terrible times with him.

"Ah, you don't know," he says. "He can get the queerest notions in his head of any man *I* ever saw," he said, "you never know what's comin' next. Why,

one night," he said, "he began to holler and rave
about Lydia. Why," Ambrose says, "he swore that
she'd come back from the grave to haunt him because of the life he'd led. 'There she is,' he hollers,
'there! . . . there! . . . Don't you see her?'—he
kept a-pointin' round the room and then he said she
was looking at him over my shoulder. 'Why, no,' I
says, 'there's no one there, Will, you're just imag-
inin' all that.' 'Yes, she is,' he says, 'and damn you
you're trying to shield her. Get out of the way, or I'll
kill you,' he says, and with that he ups and throws a
quart bottle half full of licker right at my head—
why, it's a wonder," he says, "that it didn't kill me: I
saw it comin'," he says, "an ducked my head just in
the nick of time but it smashed up a whole row of
glasses we had settin' back behind the bar, and
then," says Ambrose, "he got down on his knees and
began prayin' to her and saying, 'Oh, Lydia, Lydia,
say that you forgive me, baby,' and then he started
talking about her eyes—'There! . . . there!' he
says, 'they're glarin' at me—don't you see them?—
Oh, God have mercy on me!' he hollers, 'she's come
back from the grave to curse me!' It was enough to
curdle your blood to hear him," Ambrose says.
"Why, that nigger Dan of mine," he says, "was so
scared that he lit right out of here: I didn't see hide
nor hair of him for two days," he says, "you know
how superstitious a nigger is," he says, "a thing like
that would frighten the life out of him." "Why, of
course," I says, "and let me tell you something: I'm
not so sure it's nothin' but superstition, after all."

Well, he gave me a mighty funny look, I tell you
what, he did, and he says, "Why, Eliza! Surely you
don't think there was anything in all that?" "I
wouldn't be so sure," I says. "I could tell you some
mighty strange things, I could tell you of things I've

seen myself," I said, "and I don't know how you're goin' to account for them unless there is, sure enough, as the saying goes, a voice beyond the grave." Well, his face was a study, I can tell you. In a moment he looked me straight in the eyes and said: "*Who* was Lydia? Did he ever know anyone by that name?" "Yes," I said, "he did. That was before you knew him," I said. "Was it his other wife—the one that died?" he said. "That's who," I said. "Yes, that's exactly who it was. And he's got a lot to remember and be sorry for, too," I said. Well, I didn't say any more, I didn't tell him your papa had had two other wives, I didn't tell him that he had been married and divorced from one woman way down in the eastern part of the state before he married Lydia, of course, Lydia was the only one the folks at home knew about. I reckon I was too proud to let anyone know about Maggie Efird, it was considered a disgrace in those days to have anything to do with a divorced man and as for a divorced *woman*, why, of course, she wasn't considered much better than a chippy. If I'd known about it before I married him I don't reckon I'd 'a' had anything more to do with him: I'd 'a' been too mortified at the thought of lowerin' myself in that way. But, of course, he didn't tell me! Law, no! I'd been married to him almost a year before I knew anything about it.

Of course, he told it then, he had to admit it.

Why, yes! didn't old Mrs. Mason—child! I've often thought of her, that poor old woman, to think what she went through! Here she was, of course, livin' with us about a year after we got married, just to see that he got settled once again and tryin' to restore peace in her own family: tryin' to bring John and Eller Beals together again—of course John and Lydia were her childern by her first marriage, she married a man named Beals the first time, says: "Oh, Eliza, I'll help you any way I can. He'll be all right now if she just keeps away from him. If I can just keep them apart now, if I can just persuade her to go back to John and lead a decent life, I'll consider that my work in life is finished. I'll be able to die in peace," she said, oh, cryin', you know. "You don't know, you don't know," she says, "what I've lived through."

And then she told the whole story, you know, how they came to know him first, how they met him that first time down there in Sidney when he came to their house to live. Of course, he'd just come South to live: here he was workin' for John Arthur as a stonecutter, doin' all that work there on the State Penitentiary and I reckon at first he didn't have many friends; of course, he was a Yankee, and it was back in Reconstruction days, and the feeling was still bitter.

Why, yes! Didn't he tell it himself about how bitter he was against us when he came South from Baltimore? "But my comin' was an accident," he said, "I firmly intended to go West. That was my boyhood ambition, and I'd have gone if John Arthur hadn't written me and told me to come on, that there was work to do," but, oh! he considered us nothing but a set of damned rebels and hangin' too good for us. Why! didn't they want to try Lee and Jefferson Davis as traitors—of course, his oldest brother George had been killed at Gettysburg and here he was all up in arms against us, sir—until he saw it all —and then he changed right over and cursed the government for allowin' it—why the black legislatures—there in Sidney and at that time he helped John Arthur build the penitentiary at Columbus, South Carolina—oh! some of the *blackest* niggers you ever laid your eye on, drinkin' and carousin'

and squanderin' the taxpayers' money, dressed in the finest broadcloth, with big cigars in their mouth, if you please, and their feet stuck up on fine mahogany desks, the nasty stinking things—why didn't we see it all in that picture, *The Birth of a Nation* based upon Tom Dixon's book? "Yes," your papa says, "and every bit of it is true. I saw worse things than that myself." But that's the way he came, all right.

Well, he came there to their house, and they took him in, you know, as a boarder, Lydia and old Mrs. Mason. Of course, the old woman said, she admitted it, says, "Well, we were glad to have him. We were livin' there all alone," she said, "and we needed a man around the house. We felt safer havin' him," she said. "And I tell you what," she said, "Will was certainly a good man to have about the house. I've never known his equal," she said. Well, of course, I had to admit it: you've got to give the devil his due—with all his wanderin' and goin' away, he was as good a family man as ever lived. Now, boy, I want to tell you: he could do anything about a house, he could repair and fix anything, he could make anything with his hands, and let me tell you, sir; when you went downstairs in the morning you always found a good fire burning in the range; now, you didn't have to *wait*, you didn't have to go pokin' around to get a fire. Now he liked to *eat*, and he always had a hot stove waitin' for you. Why, Lord! as I said to him, "The way you make a fire, no wonder. Why anyone could make a fire the way you do," I said, "pourin' half a can of kerosene oil on it every time. Why, mercy, man!" I cried, "you'll burn us all up some day, as sure as you're born!"—child! child! that awful waste! that awful extravagance! Oh, roaring up the chimney till the whole house shook with it, you know.

* * *

Now, boy, here's another thing: we've got to be fair, we've got to be just, and he wasn't *all the way* to blame! It wasn't *all* his fault: of course, the old woman admitted it, I said to her: "But Mrs. Mason, see here! You *must* have known something about him before he came to your house to live. Now, he'd been livin' right there in the same town with you, and surely you must have heard about him and Maggie Efird before he came to your house. Now, livin' in a little town like that, I don't see how it could have been otherwise. *You must have known!*" Well, she had to admit it then, said: "Yes, we knew about it." Said, "Of course, the story was he had to marry her, her father and brothers made him, and I reckon he hated her for it ever after. I guess that's why they got the divorce," she said.

I looked her straight in the eye: "Now," I said, "knowing that, you let me marry him, *a divorced man*, without sayin' a word! Now, why didn't you tell me about it?" I said—of course, she'd never said a word about it, if I'd waited for *her* to tell me I would never have found out. Here it was, you know, months after we got married, and it all came to light by accident. I was cleanin' out the bottom drawer of that old walnut bureau, lookin' for a place to put his shirts, and there it was—a stack of old letters and papers, you know, that he'd put away there, I reckon meaning to destroy them. Well, I picked them up, I didn't intend to look at them, I was goin' to put them in the stove and burn them up. "Now, he's left them there," I said, "intendin' to destroy them," but I had a premonition—I don't know what else you'd call it—it flashed over me all of a sudden, I reckon some providence left them there for me to read, here it was, the final papers of his divorce from Maggie

Efird, and I could see it, I could read it! There it
was! a-starin' me in the face.

Well, I waited for him to come home you know, I
had them in my hand, said: "Here are some old letters I came across cleanin' out your bureau drawer
today. Do you want them?" I didn't let on, you
know, I just looked at him as innocent as you please.
Well, his face was a study, I tell you what, it was.
"Give me those papers," he said, and made a snatch
for them. "Did you read them?" he said. I didn't say
a word, I just looked at him. "Well," he said, and his
face had a mighty sheepish look, I tell you what, it
did, "I intended to tell you about it, but I was afraid
you might not understand."

"Understand," I said, "why what is there to understand? It's all written down there as plain as the
nose on your face: you are *a divorced man* and you
never told me a thing about it. You let me marry you
believin' you were a widower, that Lydia was the
only woman you were ever married to. I understand
that much all right!"

"Well," he said, "that first marriage was a great
mistake. I was led into it against my better judgment," he said. "I didn't want to worry you by tellin'
you about it," he said. "Now," I said, "I'm going to
ask you: I want to know. What was the trouble? Why
were you divorced?" "Why," he said, "the decree
was granted on grounds of incompatibility. She refused to live with me as my wife. She was in love
with another man," he said, "and married me just to
spite him. But from the moment we were married
she never had anything to do with me. We never
lived together for a moment as man and wife."
"*Who* got the divorce," I said, "you or her?" He
spoke right up quick as a flash, "I did," he said.
"The decree was granted in my favor."

282   Well, I didn't let on, I didn't say a word, but I

knew, I *knew*, that he was lying. I had read that paper from beginning to end and the divorce had been given to *her*. Maggie Efird got the divorce, all right: I saw *that* much with my own eyes! But I didn't say anything, I just let him go on, "And you mean to say that she never lived with you as your wife?" I said.

"Not for a minute," he said, "I swear it."

Well, it was too much; that story was too fishy— here they told it on her, you know, old Mrs. Mason told me, that she was a good-lookin' girl, a high-stepper with lots of beaux before she married him, and, of course, they said that was the trouble—he *had* to marry her. I looked at him, you know, and shook my head: "No, sir," I said, "I don't believe you. There's something mighty queer about this somewhere. That story just won't wash. Now, you can't tell me that you lived with that woman eighteen months and never had anything to do with her. Now, I know *you*," I said—you know I looked him straight in the eye—"I know *you*, and I know you couldn't have kept away from her. You'd 'a' got at her somehow," I said, "if you had to bore a hole through the wall!" Well, it was too much for him; he couldn't face me, he had to look away, you know, with a sort of sheepish grin.

"Well, now," I said, "what are you going to do with these old papers? Now, surely you don't want them any more," I said. "They're no use to you that I can see." "No," he said, "I hate the sight of them. They're a curse and a care and I never want to look at them again. I'm going to burn them up."

"Yes," I said, "that's what I think, all they do is bring up memories you ought to try to forget. You ought to destroy them."

"That's what I'll do," he said. "By God, I will!"

* * *

"But still" (I said)—as I was goin' on to say, you know, I said to the old woman, Mrs. Mason—"but still, you must have known all about him when he came there to your house to live. Now, Mrs. Mason, you must have known he'd been married to Maggie Efird and divorced from her. Surely, you must have known that," I said.

"Well, yes," she said, "I guess we did"—admitted it, you know.

"Well, now, I'm going to tell you how it was," she said—and then, of course, she told the story: it all came out. Now, boy, I want to tell you: I want to show you that it wasn't *all* your daddy's fault.

Now, I'm not sayin' a word against Lydia—of course, I knew *her* before I did *him*, when they first came there to live and she opened up a little millinery shop there on that corner of Academy Street where the Greenwood Hotel now stands. I reckon the first real "store" hat I ever owned I bought from her out of my savin's as a schoolteacher that time I taught all winter way back there in Yancey county. I got paid twenty dollars a month and my board and room and let me tell you something: I considered myself *rich*. Why, Lord, yes! didn't I save up enough out of it to make the first payment on the first piece of property I ever owned, that corner lot there on the south side of the square where your daddy built his shop after we got married, that's exactly where it was, sir, why, yes, wasn't I only twenty-two years old at that time I bought it, and Lord! I thought I'd done something *big*, you know! Here I was a property owner and a taxpayer like Cap'n Bob Patton and old General Alexander, and all the rest of 'em (child, child! we were so poor, we'd gone through so much hardship since the war

that I reckon that's what led me on, I reckon that's

what got me into it: I was determined to own something of my own); why, yes: don't I remember how I ran all the way to town the day I got my first tax statement, $1.83, that's all in the world it was then, and the money just a-burning a hole in my pocket! Lord! what a goose I must have been! afraid they'd try to take it away from me and sell me out under the sheriff's hammer before I got there.

Well, then, as I say, I got to know Lydia before I got to know your daddy. Here she was, you know, runnin' this little millinery store there on that northeast corner, and, as I say, the first "store" hat I ever owned I got from her. That's where it was, all right. Now, boy, I'm not saying a word against Lydia: for all I know she was a good, honest, hard-working woman and till she met your daddy she was all right. Of course, she was more than ten years older than he was, and that's exactly what the trouble was, that's where the shoe pinched, all right, that was the rub. Now your daddy was not *all the way* to blame: when he came there to their house to live he was only a young man in his early twenties and Lydia was thirty-six years old. Now, if it had been some young girl he led astray you could blame him more, but you can say what you please, Lydia was old enough to know better. Of course, he was a strong, fine-lookin' man, and all the women were right out after him, but she should have known, a woman that age should have had too much pride and self-respect—why I'd 'a' died before I did a thing like that!—to have follered and thrown herself at him the way *she* did! Why, of course! Didn't old Mrs. Mason admit it? Didn't she *tell* me? "Oh, Lydia!" she said, "Lydia!" shakin' her head, you know. "She went clean out of her head about him."

Here she'd been a decent respectable woman

285

all her life, runnin' a little millinery shop down there, you know, and well thought of by everyone in town—and, of course, I reckon, considered sort of an old maid, and to think she'd go and behave herself like that. "Oh, it was awful," the old woman said; says, "She never gave him a moment's peace, she kept after him all the time," and, of course, that's just what happened. You know your daddy; as the sayin' goes, he didn't stop to say his prayers when there was a woman around. It was the same old story: within a year's time he'd gone and got himself all mixed up again, that woman was goin' to have a child and sayin' he'd ruined her and would have to marry her.

Well, he didn't know what to do. Told me himself, you know, admitted it, said: "I didn't want to marry her. I wasn't in love with her," he said. Well, he studied it all over and at last he decided to send her to Washington to see a doctor. So he wrote to Gil: of course Gil and your Aunt Mary were livin' there at the time—that was before Gil had follered him down South. Gil was workin' there in Washington as a plasterer, and they were brothers and he knew he could depend on him.

She went, he sent her, and I don't know just what happened, Gil never said and I didn't like to ask, but I guess it came before its time: they were riding in the day coach of a train comin' South again, some little town down there in the eastern part of the state, the conductor stopped the train and helped Gil carry her out into the station, and the next day she got up again and went on home. Now, give her her due, that woman had lots of grit: I reckon that's the way it was, all right.

* * *

Well, of course, the whole thing got found out. The story got known and your daddy had to marry her. And, I reckon, the feeling against him in the town was pretty bitter: here he was, you see, a Yankee, as the sayin' went, a damn Yankee, who'd come down there and ruined *two* of their women; of couse, if there'd only been *one* it might have been different, but I reckon *two* of them was more than they could stomach. It got too hot for him; he had to leave. That was the time he decided to come to Altamont: of course Lydia had consumption and he thought the mountain air might do her good and I reckon he was afraid he had it, too—he'd been livin' with her and I guess he thought he had contracted it from her. When I first saw him he looked like a dead man, oh! as thin as a rail and that saller complexion, you know, from all the trouble and the worry he'd been through, I reckon. Well, then, Lydia sold out her stock—what little that she had—and closed her shop, and he sent her on ahead with old Mrs. Mason. Your daddy stayed behind down there a little bit, tryin' to close out what stock he had left in his marble yard, and to get what money he could, and then he came on, too, and that's how I came to know them first: when she was running that millinery shop on the corner there and he'd set up business in an old shack on the east side of the square. That's when it was, all right.

Now, boy, I was going on to tell you about that woman, Eller Beals. Up to this time, mind you, up to the time he moved up there from Sidney, she'd never had a thing to do with him. Of course, she had known him down there—she was the wife, you know, of Lydia's brother, John—but Law! they were too *fine*, you know, too *fine*, to have anything to do with your daddy, a common stonecutter who'd

287

gone and disgraced the family like he had. Oh, they stormed and carried on about it, you know, when he got Lydia into this trouble. They wouldn't speak to him or have anything to do with him: he told me they hated the sight of him and that he hated them. And here within six months she had no more pride than to foller them all up there. Of course, she came because she had to come, I reckon: this John Beals was a shiftless good-for-nothin' sort of feller, and he couldn't support her, so she wrote Lydia and old Mrs. Mason and they told her to come on. Your daddy didn't know she was coming: they were afraid to tell him, and they thought they'd let her come and win him over afterwards. And that's just what happened: he came home one day to dinner and there she was—oh! the fine lady, if you please, all primped and powdered up and dressed to kill— that was the first he knew about it. Well, I guess it brought back bitter memories: he hated her so much he wouldn't speak to her, he picked up his hat and started to leave the house again, but she came up to him—oh, with her fine bonnet and the Langtry bang, and all: that was the way she fixed her hair, and put her arms around him, saying in that sugary voice: "Aren't you going to kiss me, Will?"—Oh! (as I said later) to think of it! the villain! he should have wrung her neck for her then and there, it'd been a good riddance! Says, "Can't we be friends, Will?"—after the way she'd acted, if you please— honeying up to him and takin' him in right there before his own wife and his wife's mother. "Can't we let bygones be bygones?" she says, getting him to kiss her, and all—"Why it served you right," I said, "for being such a fool! A man with no better sense than that deserves anything that happens to him!"

288 And he agreed, admitted it, you know: "You're

right," he said. So that's the way she came to be there with him.

This Eller Beals was a little dark black-and-white sort of a woman: she had this white skin, and hair as black as a raven's and coal-black eyes. She had this easy sugary sleepy way of talkin', all soft and drawly —like she'd just waked up out of a good long sleep. I could a-told him the first time I laid eyes on her that she was no good: she was a bad egg if ever I saw one, a charmer out to get the men and lead them on, you know, and bleed them out of everything they owned. Of course, she was a good-looking woman, there's no denying that, she had a good figger and this creamy-white complexion without a blemish on it. "Why, yes," I said to him later when he'd begin to brag about how pretty she was to look at. "Why, yes, I reckon so, that's true, but then," I said, "a whole lot of us could be pretty if we never lifted a finger to do a lick of work. Some of the rest of us could look real nice," I said, "if we didn't have to cook and wash and bring up childern." Well, he admitted it then, of course, said, "Yes, you're right."

And, here, to think of it! this villain misbehaving herself with him right under his wife's nose, sitting there primping herself and fixin' herself up pretty to entice him day after day, just livin' for him to come home and Lydia dying in that room upstairs, coughing her lungs out with every breath she took, and knowing about it all. Why, didn't he admit it! didn't he tell himself how Lydia said to him—of course, the poor thing knew that she was dying, says, "Will, I'm sick. I know I'm no good for you any more. I know I haven't got long to live and, Will," she said, "you can go where you like. You can do as you please," says, "I don't care, I'm dying, but Will," and then he told it how she looked him in the eye,

289

"there's one thing I can't stand. In my *own* house! My *own* house!" Says, "Will, *you've got to leave my brother's wife alone!*"—Oh! he told it, admitted it, you know, says: "Ah, Lord! It's a crime upon my soul. I reckon if there's a just God in heaven I'll be punished for it."—And that poor old woman doing all the work, cooking and drudging for them all, with this little powdered-up trollop, that's all in the world she was, laying up waitin' for him and never liftin' a hand to help, why, they should have tarred and feathered her.

Well, as I say, when Lydia died, Eller kept right on livin' there: she wouldn't budge. And, of course, by that time he had lost his head about her, he was infatuated, you know, and he wanted her to sta. And that was the time John Beals came up to visit her, and I reckon he sized the situation up, he saw the way things were, and I suppose it went against the grain, it was a little more than he could stomach. Now, I always considered him a pretty poor sort of man: a man who would wink at a thing like that and let his wife run wild—but, give him his due, I reckon he had some spunk left in him, after all: he was out of work but he went down to Johnson City, Tennessee, and got him a job there as a hotel clerk. And then he wrote back for her, telling her to come on.

Well, she wouldn't go. She wrote him and told him she didn't love him and would never live with him again, said she was going to stay right where she was. Oh! she had it all fixed up in her mind, sir, she was going to get a divorce and marry your daddy —and him agreeing to it, if you please, like a moon-struck fool, just a-lavishin' gifts and money on her, with that poor old woman working like a nigger and

weepin' and beggin' her to go on back to her husband where she belonged. But you couldn't reason
with her, you couldn't budge her, oh! crazy in love
with him, mind you, determined to have him.

Well, sir, John Beals wrote to her again, and this
time he meant business, he'd reached the end of the
rope. "Now you can make up your mind in a hurry
what you're going to do," he said, "for I'm not going
to put up with you any longer. You can decide now
whether you're coming by yourself or whether I'm
going to have to come and take you, but I want you
to understand right now that if I have to come and
take you from him, I'll come prepared, and I'm
going to leave a damned dead Yankee behind me in
the house when I do."

Well, she didn't answer him, and let me tell you,
sir, he *came:* he got on a train and came to get her.
And oh! old Mrs. Mason said when she told me
about it, shakin' and tremblin', you know. "Oh, I tell
you, Eliza, it was awful. Here she'd locked herself
in upstairs and wouldn't move, and here was John
with a loaded pistol in his pocket, walkin' up and
down the dining-room floor and saying, 'If she's not
ready to go in half an hour I'll blow his brains out if
it's the last thing I ever do,' and Will, pale as a
ghost," the old woman said, "walkin' back and forth
across the front porch, wringin' his hands, and her
up there refusin' to go with John."

Well, they persuaded her somehow: I reckon she
saw she'd have to go or there'd be bloodshed, and so
she went along with him to Tennessee—but child!
child! she hated it, she didn't want to go, she was
bitter about it, she cursed them all. Well, that's the
way it was, all right, before I married him.

And then, after we were married she kept on writing to him: the letters kept a-coming to him until fi-

nally I considered it my duty to write John Beals and inform him that his wife was misconductin' herself by writing letters to a married man, and that it was his business as her husband to stop her. Well, then, the letter came: she wrote him, you know, and I've never seen the like of it. She told him that I had written to her husband, she cursed him with every name she could think of, and she said: "If I had known you were going to marry her I'd have told her all I know about you, and you can be certain, no woman would have you if I told her all I know. Now she can have you and welcome to you; for no matter how much I may have hated her, her punishment will be greater than anything I ever wished for her."

Well, he brought it home and flung it in my face: "There you are, damn you," he said. "That's your work. Now, I want to tell you that you're setting in her place here at my table because she left me, for you can rest assured if she had never gone, you would not be here—and I want you always to remember it!"

Child! Child—I reckon I was young and proud, and it made me bitter to hear him talk that way. I got up and went out onto the porch and I wanted to go out and leave him then and there, but I was carrying my first baby around inside me, and it had rained and I could smell the flowers, the roses, and the lilies, and the honeysuckle vines, and all of the grapes a-gettin' ripe, and it was growing dark, and I could hear the people talking on their porches, and I had nowhere to go, I could not leave him, and "Lord God!" I said. "What shall I do? What shall I do?"

Well, then, of course, as I was tellin' you, he'd go up there to Ambrose Radiker's saloon, and he'd get to drinkin' and Ambrose told it on him how he'd imagine he was seeing Lydia again, and how she'd come back from the grave to haunt him. "Yes," I said, "and maybe he's not far wrong about it."

"And then," says Ambrose, "that's not all, that's not the only thing. He came in here one time and accused Dan here of being a Chinaman"—of course, you remember that big yellow nigger Dan with all those small-pox splotches, and, of course, I reckon your daddy in his drunken way just took the notion into his head that Dan was a Chinaman. "Why, yes," says Ambrose, "he accused Dan of being a Chinaman and said he'd been sent here by somebody or other to kill him, and all such stuff as that. 'Damn you!' he says, 'I know what you're here for and I'll make an end of us both right now: God damn you!' he says, that's just the way he talked, you know, 'I'll cut your heart out,' he says, oh, laughin'," says Ambrose, "in a crazy blood-curdlin' manner, and then," he says, "he grabbed up a carving knife off the lunch counter and started round the bar to get the nigger. Why, it was awful!" he says. "It almost scared the poor darkey to death," he says; says, "Dan hadn't done anything to him," he says, "you *know*, Dan never done no harm to anyone. Well, we had to do something, so we got the knife away from him, and then," he says, "I tried to reason with him. 'Why, Will,' I said, 'what have you got against Dan? Dan never did no harm to you,' I said.

"So he says, 'He's a Chinaman and I hate the sight of him'—oh, you know, he was crazy, you couldn't reason with him at all. 'Why, no, he's not,' I said. 'Now, Will, you know better than that,' I said. 'You've been comin' in here for years,' I said, 'and you know Dan, and you certainly know by now that he's no Chinaman,' I said.

"'Why, no, sah, Mistah Gant,' says Dan, you know niggerlike, he wanted to have *his* say, 'why you

293

know me,' he says, 'and you know I ain't no China-man.'

"'Yes, he is,' he says, 'and by God I'm going to kill him.'

"'Why, Will,' I says, 'he's not any Chinaman, and besides,' I said, 'even if he was, that wouldn't be any reason for you wanting to kill him. Now, just use your reason a little about this,' I said. 'A Chinaman's a man like anyone else,' I said. 'There's one thing sure, they were put here for some purpose,' I said, 'like everyone else, or they wouldn't be here. Now it wouldn't be right to go and kill a man that never did you any harm,' I said, 'just because you think he's a Chinaman, would it?'

"'Yes, by God,' he said, 'for they're a set of fiends out of hell, they have drunk my heart's blood and now they sit there gloatin' upon my death rattle,' he said.

"And that's not the *only* time either," said Ambrose Radiker, "that he's been that way." "What!" I said—of course, you know, I didn't let on to Ambrose I knew anything about it at all—"do you mean he's carried on that way before?" "Many's the time," he said, "I tell you what, it's a mighty peculiar thing: there's something mighty strange about it somewheres," he says. "He's got some grievance against Chinamen, at some time or other he's had trouble with them."

"No," I said, "you're wrong." I looked him straight in the eye. "Not in *this* life," I said. "Why, what do you mean?" he says, and, let me tell you, he gave me a mighty queer look.

"I can't say no more," I said, "but there are things you don't understand," I said. "Have *you* heard him talk like that?" he said.

"Yes," I said. But I wouldn't tell him any more.

* * *

I could have told him, but I got to studying it all over and "I thought I'd better not," I told your papa; says, "No, I'm glad you didn't: you did right. I'm glad you said no more." "But what is it, man? What's the reason for it?"—I tried to reason with him about it—child, child, he always had it, that awful hatred, that bitterness—"now see here, Mr. Gant, surely you must have some reason that you should feel that way against them. People don't feel that way without some cause: did one of them ever do you an injury? Did you ever know one of them?" He shook his head, says, "No. I never knew one in my life, but I've always hated the sight of them since the first time I ever saw one in my boyhood days in the streets of Baltimore. The first thing that I saw when I came out of the ferry house at San Francisco was a Chinaman—that awful yellow skin," he said, "and I hated the place from that time on! But I don't know what the reason is—by God, I don't! It's a pretty strange thing when you come to think of it—unless," he said, and he looked at me, "I may have known them, as the saying goes, in some former life, some different reincarnation." I looked him straight in the eye: "*Yes*," I said, "that's what I think it was, you've hit the nail on the head, all right. That's exactly what it was, it never came out of *this* world," and he looked at me, and let me tell you, sir, his face was a study.

And yes! why long years after that, you know, at the time of that Boxer Rebellion, didn't he come home one day all excited with the news! "It's come at last," he said, "as I predicted long ago: the pitcher went to the well once too often. They've declared war on China, and I'm going to enlist, by God, I will!" Oh! all up in arms against them, sir, and

wantin' to leave everything, his family and business, to go out there and fight them. "No, sir, you
will not!" I said. "You're a married man with a family of little childern to support and you're not going.
If they need troops you let the others volunteer:
your place is here. Besides," I said, "they wouldn't
take you noway: they wouldn't have you, you're too
old. They want the young men."

Well, I reckon it stung him, callin' him an old man
like that: he flared right up, says, "I'm a better man
than nine-tenths of them this minute, for we are
livin' in a degenerate age, and if you think I'm not
the equal of these nonentities an' nincompoops you
see hangin' around the poolrooms with a cigarette
stuck out of the corner of their mouths, the miserable degenerates that they are, then God help you,
woman, for the truth is not in you and you are like
the bird that fouls its own nest!" Says, "I can do
more work right now than any four of them!"

Well, when he put it that way I had to admit he
was tellin' the truth: of course, your papa was an
awful strong man. Why, Lord! haven't I heard them
tell it on him how they'd go back there in his shop
and find him liftin' up one end of an eight-hundred-
pound stone like it was nothin' with two big black
niggers sweatin' and strainin' at the other end of it
that they could hardly budge, and "Yes," I said to
Wade Eliot that first time that we took him up to
Hopkins, "I'll give you *my* theory now. I'll tell you
what *my* diagnosis is"—and then, of course I told
him, "now my opinion is he helped to bring this
trouble on by just such things as that"—("Why,
what on earth do you mean, Mr. Gant, by doin' such
a thing! You're apt to strain and rupture yourself first
thing you know: let the niggers do that kind of work,
that's what you're paying them for." "Why, Lord!"

he said, "you know I couldn't do a thing like that: if I depended on those niggers I'd never get anything done!") "But that was it, all right," I said to Doctor Eliot. "He was hastenin' his own end by just such stuff as that." "Yes," he said, "I agree with you, I think you're right. That's it exactly," he said—"But *you*," I said, "you have your family to consider, and *you're not goin'*." I put my foot right down, you know, and then, of course, he admitted I was right, he gave in, but *oh!*—child, child, you don't know what it was like—California, China, anywheres! He'd have been up and gone if I'd a-let him: a strange man.

Lord God! I never saw a man like that for wanderin'. I'll vow! a rollin' stone, a wanderer—that's all he'd a-been, oh! California, China, anywheres— forever wantin' to be up and gone, who'd never have accumulated a stick of property if I hadn't married him. Here Truman wrote to him that time from California, this same Perfesser Truman, why, yes! the father-in-law of these two murderers I'm telling you about (and how that night I got the warning, boy: "Two . . . Two—and Twenty . . . Twenty"), Ed Mears and Lawrence Wayne, who married sisters, Truman's daughters, why, yes!—but *oh!* the scholar and the gentleman, you know, no murderer to *him*, I can assure you—oh! too *fine*, too *fine*, oh! too *honorable*, you know: he wouldn't soil his hands with blood, always the finest broadcloth and the patent-leather shoes, wrote to him of course, to come on out there. Says, "The Lord has rained his blessings on this country with a prodigal hand"—oh! the cultured gentleman with all that beautiful English and the flowery command of language, and all— says, "Come on out. This is the Wonderland of Nature, there's riches and abundance here beyond the dreams of avarice, and as yet," he says, "it's hardly been touched. If you come out now you'll be a rich man in fifteen years"—he says—urgin' him to come, you know, says, "Sell out now. Sell everything you got and come on out." "Hm!" I says, "he's mighty anxious to get you out there, isn't he?" "Yes," says your daddy, "a new country and by God I'll do it." Then, worried-like, "What do you mean?" he says.

I didn't tell him: I just looked at him, I didn't speak. I just said, "Says come on out? And what about your wife and childern? What's to become of them?" I said. Says, "Oh, that part's all right," your papa said. "Says bring them with you, 'Sell out at once, bring Eliza and the childern with you,' your papa said. "That's what he said, all right." "I *thought* so! That's what I *thought*," I said. "What do you mean?" he said. I looked at him. I didn't tell him.

I could have told him but I didn't want to worry him. Child! I didn't tell him but I *knew*, I *knew*— that man—now boy, I want to tell you—"I've come to say good-bye," he says—and let me tell you, boy, his face was a study—why! "Oh, we're sorry to see you go!" I said, "We'll miss you." "Yes," he said, and he looked me straight in the eye—oh! that *look*, you know, "and I'll miss *you!*" He looked straight at me when he said it. "Well, now," I said, you know I thought I'd turn it off, "we'll miss you too, both Mr. Gant and I—we'll both miss you. Now," I said, you know I thought I'd jolly him along to cheer him up, "when you get out there, I hope you won't forget us. I hope you'll write us. Why, yes," I said, "if it's the wonderful place they say it is, if you can pick gold up right off the streets *I'd* like to know about it, too,"

I said. "Why, yes, if that's the sort of place it is, I'd
like to live there too—we might pack right up and
come on out," I said. "Well, now," he said, "I wish
you would, there's nothin' I'd like better," and I
could see, child, I could tell—why, yes! now—long
years after when your papa made that trip out there.
(Now, boy, that was a wild-goose chase—what did
he do *that* for? Why did he go out there? Why did he
waste that money?) "Oh," I said, "did you see Perfesser Truman?" the first question that I asked him,
you know. "Yes," he says, "I saw him," and his face
was a study, I can tell you. "Well, how is he? what's
he doin'?" Of course I wanted to find out, you know.
I wanted to hear the news. "Say," your papa says,
"what about it?" and his face was a study. "You
know he did nothin' but talk about you all the time I
was there. Why," he says, "I believe the damned
old fool was in love with you, by God I do." Well, I
didn't say anything, I didn't want to worry him, but
child, I had seen it in his eyes and I *knew*, I *knew*!

I'll vow! I never saw such a man for wantin' to
wander around. Pshaw! I reckon maybe old Amanda
Stevens was right about them. That's what she said,
you know; of course, they told it on her when all her
sons went off to the Civil War—she had eight, and
every last one of them went to war, sir! And, of
course, all of the people were comin' around to congratulate her for sendin' them, sayin' how proud she
must be, and so on. "Send nothing!" she said. "They
all lit out of here in the middle of the night without
sayin' a word to me about it. If I had my way I'd
bring every last one of them back here where they
belong, helpin' me to run this place!" "Yes," they
said, "but aren't you proud of them?" they said.
"Proud?" she says, "why, Lord God"—of course,
you know, Amanda had an awful rough way of

talkin'—"what's there to be proud of? They're all alike! I never saw a man yet that could stay where he was five minutes. Why!" she says, "all of them act as if their tails were full of turpentine," she said. Of course she was bitter to think they should all light out that way to leave her alone to run the farm without tellin' her about it.

But, I tell you what, that was *certainly* a remarkable woman; lived to be eighty-seven and hale and hearty, sir, right up to the end. Yes! and would go anywheres, you know, in the dead of winter to help out anyone that was sick, and all! Of course, they told it on her at the time—whew-w! what about it? —I remember sayin', "Oh, surely she didn't say a thing like that! you must be mistaken," I said—to think that a woman would talk that way to her own daughter—"if that don't beat all!" I said: why, they told it, you know, how her daughter Clarissy that married John Burgin, this same John Burgin I've been tellin' you about all along, boy, your own distant cousin on my mother's side of the house that Ed Mears killed, as I said to your papa at the time when he came home that day tellin' me what Melvin Porter had said, I said to him: "Let them hang! they killed that man in cold blood," I said, "a good upright man with a family of little childern that never did any harm to anyone," I said, "as wicked and cold-blooded a murder as I ever heard of, and hangin's too good for them," I said. Why, they told it of course how Clarissy's first baby came seven months after she was married. Well, it was all right, of course, nobody was blamin' the girl, it never entered their minds that she had done anything wrong, but she began to scream and holler like she'd lost her mind.

300

"Well," the doctor says, "the baby's all right,

there's nothing wrong with the baby, but if something isn't done to stop that girl from cryin' this child won't have any mother before long."

"Well, I'll stop her," Amanda says, "or know the reason why," so she marches right into the bedroom and sits right down beside the girl: "Now you look a-here," she said, "there's nothing wrong with you and I'm not going to put up with your foolishness any longer." "Oh," the girl says, "I shall die of shame! I'll never be able to hold my head up again!"—weepin' and goin' on, you know. "Why, what's the matter?" Amanda says, "what have you done," she says, "that you should feel like that?" "Oh," the girl says, "I haven't done anything but my baby came before its time!" "Why, Lord God!" the old woman says—she came right out coarse with it, you know—"is that all that's troublin' you? I thought you had more sense than to let a thing like that bother you," she said. "Oh," the girl said, "they'll all be sayin' now that I misbehaved myself before I married John!" "Why, Lord God, let them say it, then," Amanda said, "what if they do? Tell 'em your ass is your own and you can do as you please with it!" That's exactly what she said, you know, and of course they told it on her. I know when I told your papa about it, he said, "Lord! you know she didn't say a thing like that!" But that's the story that they told.

Well, I said to him, "You're *not* going." I put my foot down, you know, and when he saw I meant it, he had to give in, of course. But as I say he always had it in him, that desire to go off somewheres, California, China—why, yes, say! what about it, as long as he lived he never got over that feeling he had against them. That time, you know, long after—why

301

yes! you must remember, you were right there with us—no, I guess that's so. You must have been away at college. That was the year before the war ended, and we all went up there with him—Luke and Ben —I tell you what, I've often thought of it, that poor child: here we were all lookin' for Mr. Gant to die at any minute, when he had five more years to live, and *Ben—Ben* was the one! We never *thought,* we never *dreamed* that *he* would be the one, would be dead and buried in the grave within a year! And to think that your daddy would behave as he did— here he was, you know, eaten up with that awful cancer—Lord! how he ever did it! with that rotten old thing consumin' him, sending out its roots, you know, all through his blood.

Wade Eliot said to me, "I don't know what's holdin' him up," he says, "I never thought I'd see him again when he went away the last time," he says; says, "it is certainly a remarkable case," he says; says, "in all my life," he says, "I've never seen the beat of it." "Well," I says, "you must have some opinion," I says. "A great doctor like you who has operated on thousands of people must know all the signs and symptoms," I says—of course, you know, I wanted to draw him out and get him to tell me what *his* theory was. "Now," I said, "surely you've some sort of notion about it, Doctor Eliot, and if you have," I said, "*I want to know!* His family has a right to know," I said, "and I want to *know the worst.* How much longer has he got to live?" I said. I looked him square in the eye.

Well, sir, he just threw back his head and laughed. "Live!" he says, "why, probably, till both you and I are in our graves," he said—and, let me tell you, he didn't miss it much! That man, here he was a fine-looking man in the prime of life, why he'd be the last one anyone would expect to go, the doctor they called in for Woodrow Wilson, and all. . . . Said he'd saved thousands of lives, and here when his time comes he couldn't save his own! They did everything on earth they could to save him—as the sayin' goes, I reckon they exhausted all the resources of medical science but to no avail!—was dead and in his grave, sir, within two years after your papa died. I remember sayin' to McGuire when I read the news, "Well, it only goes to show," I said, "that when your time comes there is nothing that can save you. . . . I don't know what you'd call it," I said, "but there is some higher power, as sure as you're born, and when it calls us," I said, "we've got to go, doctors and all." "Yes," he said, "you are exactly right. There's something there," he said, "that we know nothing of"—and here he had only a year longer to live himself, drinkin' himself to death, you know, just grievin' over the way that woman had acted. Of course, that nigger at the hospital told Luke he'd come in there late at night so drunk he'd have to get down on all fours an' crawl upstairs like some big old bear when he had to operate the first thing in the morning, said he'd get him to put him in a tub of cold water with chunks of ice in it, said he'd seen him that way many a time and put him to bed.

"Well," says Eliot, "I don't pretend to know anything about it any more. I don't know what is keepin' him alive," he says, "but there he is, and I don't want to make any more predictions. He's not a man," he says, "he's four men, and right now," he says, "he's got more real vitality than the rest of us put together"—and of course, it was true: right up to the end he could eat a meal that would put most people in the grave, two dozen raw oysters, a whole

303

fried chicken, an apple pie, and two or three pots of coffee, sir. Why I've seen him do it time and again! with all sorts of vegetables, corn on the cob and sweet pertaters, string beans and spinach and all such as that. Of course, Eliot was honest about it: he came right out and admitted he couldn't say. "Now here," he said, "I want you to look after him until he enters the hospital. I want him to be ready for us when he comes in here," he said, "and you see to it that he behaves himself." "Well," I said, "I think he is going to be all right. He has promised, you know, and of course we are all going to do our best. Now," I said, "what can he eat? Do we have to put him on a diet? Can he have some oysters?" I said. Well, he laughed, you know, says, "Look here, I'd call that a pretty strange diet to put a sick man on." "Well," I said, "you know he's been lookin' forward to it. He's always loved oysters," I said, "he's always remembered how he could eat them by the dozen on the half shell in his boyhood here. He's looked forward to it so much," I said, "that I hate to disappoint him." "Oh, all right," Wade Eliot says, laughin', you know, "let him have them then. You couldn't kill him noway," he said, "but look a-here!" he said, and he looked me square in the eye, "I'm not worryin' about what he eats so much as what he drinks. Now," he says, "you keep him sober. I don't want to have to get him over a drunk when he gets in here," he says. "You put the fear of God into him," he says, "I know you, and you can do it. Now, you tell him," he said, "that if he goes off on another big spree he'll never live to get home. Tell him I said so."

Well, I told him what Wade Eliot had said. "You can have the oysters," I said, "he said that would be all right, but he says you're not to touch a drop of anything to drink, or they may have to send you home in a box." "Why, Lord! Mrs. Gant," your papa said, "you know I wouldn't do a thing like that in my condition. If anyone offered me a drink I'd throw it out the window. Why, the very sight of the stuff makes me sick at my stomach!" Well, he promised, of course, and I reckon we all believed him.

Well, sir, it wasn't twenty-four hours before he went off on a big spree and came home at two o'clock in the morning roaring drunk—I tell you what, I certainly felt sorry for that woman. Why! here we were all stayin' there just across from the hospital at Mrs. Barrett's, a good religious woman, you know, a big churchgoer, and all, with her livin' to make and that grown-up daughter to support whose husband ran off with some other woman— and here he comes in the dead of night howlin' and hollerin' that it was nothing but a bawdy house that he was in and to bring on the women. Why, of course, you might know he waked the whole house up, they all got up to see what the trouble was, and she knocked at the door tremblin', in her nightgown and wringin' her hands. "Oh, Mrs. Gant," she says, "you'll have to get that man quiet or he'll ruin me," she says; "get him out of here," she says, "I've never had anything like that in *my* house before," she says, "and if it gets out I'm disgraced"—and her childern, you know, those two little boys she had, she sent them out on the roof and there they were perchin' up there like monkeys, and all of the people whisperin' together in the halls. Ben was so mortified and bitter to think he would behave himself like that. "By God," he said, "it'd serve him right if he did die. After the way he's acted I wouldn't care."

Well, I got hold of the bottle, I found a bottle of   **305**

licker about a third full in one of his pockets, and pretty soon he began beggin' for a drink: "No, sir," I said. "Not another drop! Now you listen to me," I said. "You're a sick man: if you keep this up you'll never get home alive," I said. Well, he said he didn't care. "I'd as soon get it over with now," he says, "as go through all the torment and the agony." Well, he kept yelling for a drink, but we wouldn't let him have it—I took it and poured it out, anyway—and at last he got off to sleep. Then I took his clothes and locked them up in my trunk so he couldn't get out again.

We let him sleep it off. He slept right through until ten o'clock next morning and when he woke up he seemed to be all right, he wouldn't eat any breakfast, said it would make him sick, but I got him to drink some good hot coffee Mrs. Barrett brought up to him. She was certainly a kind, good-hearted Christian woman and your papa told her he was sorry for the way he had acted. Well, we tried to get him to get up and come with us then, none of us had had any breakfast, and we were going down the street to a lunchroom. "No," he said, "I don't feel like getting up, you go on: I want you to go on and get something to eat," he said.

Well, I knew he didn't have any more licker because I'd poured it out, and I knew he couldn't go out for any because his clothes were locked up, so I thought it'd be all right if we left him alone for a little. Well, we went out and ate and we couldn't have been gone more than an hour, but when we came back he'd been drinkin' again, layin' up in the bed, you know, crazy-like, singin' a song to himself. "Why, Mama," Ben says, "I thought you told us you took his licker away from him and poured it out." "Why, I did," I said. "Well, he must have had another bottle that you didn't find," he said. "There's one thing sure, he's had plenty since we left him." "Well, now," I said, "if he's had anything to drink he's got it while we were away. It wasn't there in his room when we left," I said, "because I searched that place from top to bottom with a fine-tooth comb and you can just bet your bottom dollar there was no licker there." "Well, he's getting it from someone," Ben said, "and I'm going to find out who it is that's giving it to him. Let's ask Mrs. Barrett if anyone has been here to see him." "Why, yes," I said, "that's the very thing."

So we all trooped downstairs and asked her if anyone had been there for him. "No," she said, "no one has set foot in this house since you left it," she said, "I was on the lookout for just such a thing to happen," she said, "and if anyone had been here I'd have known it." "Now there's something mighty strange about this somewheres," I said, "and I mean to get to the bottom of it. You childern come on," I said to Luke and Ben, "we're going to find out where this mystery is or know the reason why."

Well, when we got back upstairs to his room there he was, you know—and you could see it, you could tell it—he'd had something else to drink since we'd been downstairs. He was drunk as a lord. I marched right up to him: "Look a-here," I said, "you've been getting licker somewheres and I want to know who's been giving it to you." "Why, who-o? Me?" he says, in that drunken voice, "why, baby," he says, "you know me, I wouldn't touch a drop," he says—trying to hug and kiss me, you know, and all that. Well, we looked again, the childern and I, we searched that place high and low, but it was no use —there was certainly nothing there, or we'd 'a' found it.

307

Well, I got to studyin' about it, and it flashed over me all of a sudden—I don't know why I'd never thought of it before—"Come on, childern," I said to the boys, winkin' at them, you know; "come on, we'll go downtown and see the sights. Mr. Gant, we'll be back in an hour or so," I said, "you be ready when we come," I said. "We're going to take you to the hospital at three o'clock."

Well, that just suited him, that was just what he wanted, he said, "Yes, go on"—of course he wanted to be left alone so he could get more to drink. Well, we left him, we went right down the hall to my room and I took the childern in there and closed the door, easy-like, behind me. "Why, Mama," Luke says, "what are you talking about? We can't go off downtown and leave him alone like this while he's drinking. No," he says, "he's been getting it somewhere and I'm going to see to it that he gets no more if I have to sit there and watch him," he says. "No," I said, "you wait." "Why," he says, "what do you mean?" "Why, don't you see?" I said—pshaw! I was so mad to think I hadn't thought of it before, that miserable old toper Gus Tolly from Seneca, South Carolina, that used to stop at our house— here, he had the room right next to your papa and was waitin' to be admitted over at Hopkins with the same trouble your papa had, and here the two of them were layin' up together a-swillin' it down as hard as they could—"it's that rotten old Gus Tolly," I said, "who's been lettin' him have it." "Why, damn him," says Luke, "I'll go wring his neck for him," and he starts for the door. "No, you don't," I said, "you wait a minute. I'll fix him."

Well, we waited, and sure enough, it wasn't five minutes before your papa's door opened easy-like

and he came creeping out into the hall, and then

we heard him knockin' at Gus Tolly's door. Well, we heard Gus Tolly say, "Have they gone yet?" and we waited a moment longer until we heard the door shut again, and then we started. I marched right up and knocked and in a moment Gus Tolly says, "Who's there?" "You open the door," I said, "and you'll find out." Well, he opened it, and his face had a mighty sheepish look, I tell you. "Why, Mrs. Gant," he says, "is that you? Why, I thought you'd all gone to town," he says. "Well now, didn't you get fooled that time?" I said. "Mr. Gant is in here," he says in that mealy voice, stickin' his old red nose out that was all covered with warts like a pickle, "we were just having a little talk together," he says. "Yes," I said, "and it looks to me you've been havin' something else besides. If it's only talk," I said, "I'd call it mighty strong talk that gets on people's breath and smells up the place till you can't bear to come near them." Oh! you know, awful, that old rank odor of rye licker, you could 'a' cut it with a knife. "Now," I says, "I've been talkin' all my life and it never had no such effect as that on me." "Yes," says Luke, "and I see you've got a whole bottle of that talk right there on the table before you."

Well, we marched right in on him then, and there he was, sir, sitting right up at the table, if you please, with a whole quart bottle of licker before him fixin' to pour himself out a drink. Well, I reckon if looks could kill we'd have all been dead, for he gave us one of the blackest and bitterest looks you ever saw, and then he began to curse and rave. Well, I got hold of the bottle and then he began to beg me to give him just one drink. "No, sir," I said, "you're going into that hospital, and what's more you're going *now*. We're not going to wait a minute longer." Of course, I knew that was the only way to handle him; I'd seen him too many times before, and I knew if we didn't take him he'd get licker somehow if he had to drill a tunnel to get to it. "Yes," said Luke, "you're going now if I have to drag you over there, and Ben will help me do it." "No," said Ben, "I'll just be damned if I do! I don't want to have anything more to do with him. He can do as he likes." "Well," said Luke, "if we let him stay here he'll drink himself to death." "Well, I don't give a damn if he does," said Ben, "if that's what he wants to do let him go right ahead. Maybe the rest of us would get some peace then if he did. He's always had his own way," he said, "he's never thought of anyone but himself and I don't care what happens to him. I was lookin' forward to this trip," he said, "I thought we might all get a chance to enjoy ourselves a little and here he's gone and disgraced us all and ruined it for us. Now you can look after him if you like, but I'm done." Of course, the child was bitter: he'd been lookin' forward to comin', he'd saved up the money for the trip and had a nice new suit of clothes made before we left home, and here to think your papa would act this way, of course it was a bitter disappointment to us all. We *thought,* you know, we'd get him in the hospital and then have a little time to look around and see things for ourselves but *Law!* the way *he'd* been actin' it would have taken a whole regiment of men to look after him.

Well, he didn't want to go, of course, but he saw we meant business and he'd have to, so he went along back to his room with Luke and I got his clothes out, and we dressed him. Well, I began packin' away a few things I thought he'd need in the hospital, some nightshirts, and his bathrobe and

slippers and so forth, and then I saw he had no clean
shirts: the one he had on was filthy, I was ashamed
to let him go in that, and I knew he'd need some
clean ones after he'd begun to sit up again. "Why,
where on earth are your shirts?" I said, "what have
you done with them? I know that I put in six, you
couldn't have lost 'em," I said, "where are they?"
"Oh, they've got 'em, they've got 'em," he said in
that maudlin tone, beginning to rave and carry on,
you know, said, "Let 'em have them! Fiends that
they are, they have impoverished and ruined me,
they have drunk my heartsblood, now they can take
what's left." "Why, what are you talking about?" I
said, "who do you mean?" "Why, Mama," Luke
said, "it's those Chinamen that run that laundry
down there. They've got his shirts," he said, "why I
took them there myself," he said, "but *that* was a
week ago," he said; said, "I thought he'd gone and
got them by this time." "Well, we'll march right
down there and get them now," I said, "he can't go
to the hospital wearing that thing he's got on. We'd
all be disgraced!"

Of course, that just suited him: he said, yes, go on,
he'd be all ready when we came back—of course,
he wanted to get rid of us so he could drink some
more. I said, "No, sir, when we leave this house
you're coming with us."

So we started out. He went on ahead with Luke,
and Ben stayed behind to go with me. Of course,
Ben was proud and he refused to help him. "I'll
carry his valise and come along with Mama," he
said, "but I won't be seen with him." "What's the
matter?" Luke said, "he's your father as much as
mine," he said, "you're not ashamed to be seen with
him, are you?" "Yes, by God, I am!" said Ben—that

was just the way he put it. "I don't want anyone to think I know him," he said. "Now you needn't expect me to help you," he said, "I'm no damned nursemaid," says, "I've done all I intend to do."

Well, then, we went on down the street to this laundry; it was down there a block or two below the hospital on the corner in a little old brick building and, of course, when we got there we could see them, these two Chinamen inside, just a-ironing away for all they were worth. "Well, this must be it," I said. "Yes, this is it, all right," said Luke, "this is the place." So, we all went in, and this Chinaman asked him, says, "What do you want?" "Why, God-damn it," your papa says, "I want my shirt." "Well," the Chinaman says, "Tickee, tickee"—kept sayin' "tickee," you know. Well, of course, Mr. Gant had been drinkin' and he didn't understand him. He got excited, you know, says, "Tickee, hell! I don't want any tickee. I want my shirt!" "Well, now, you wait," I said to your papa, "now don't you worry," I says, "*I'll* talk to him. If your shirts are here, I'll get them for you." Of course, I knew I could talk to the Chinaman and reason with him about it. "Now," I said to him, winkin', you know easy-like, "you tell *me* about it. What is it you want?" I says. "Why," he says, "tickee, tickee." Now, I thought to myself, the man's all right—I could see it, you know—he's tryin' to say something, he's tryin' to explain something to us with this tickee. "Now," I says, "do you mean you're not finished with them yet?" I thought, of course, he might not have them done—but no, I thought, that can't be, he's had a whole *week's* time to do them in. Surely, I thought, he's had time enough. "No," he said, "tickee, tickee," and then, of course, he began jabberin' to the other feller and then they both came and they both began to shout and holler at us in that awful outlandish tongue. "Well," your papa says, "I'll make an end of it all now, by God I will! Little did I reck," he says, "that it would come to this." "Now, Mr. Gant," I said, "you be quiet and I'll get to the bottom of this. If your shirts are here I'll get them." Well, these two Chinamen had been arguin' about it together and I reckon the other one had told him that we didn't understand because he got one of those slips of paper then that they used—as I said to Luke later, it looked exactly like it was covered by old hen tracks —and he pointed to it, you know, and said, "Tickee, tickee."

"Oh!" I cried—of course, I caught on then, it flashed over me all of a sudden, I don't know why I'd never thought of it before! "Why, of course!" I said, "he means *ticket*, that's what he's trying to say." "Yes," he says, beginning to smile and grin, you know, *he* understood that much all right, "tickee, tickee." "Why, yes," I said winkin' at him, "that's just it—tickee." Of course, I suppose, with your papa hollerin' and goin' on I'd got confused, and that was the reason I hadn't understood before. "Why, Mr. Gant," I said, "he says he gave you a laundry ticket and he wants to see it." "No, I haven't got any ticket," he says, "I want my shirt." "Why, surely, you've got a ticket," I said, "what have you done with it? Surely you haven't gone and lost it." "I never had one," he said, you know—drunkenlike. "Why, yes, he has," Luke said, "I remember giving it to him now. What did you do with the laundry ticket I gave you?" he said, "where is it? Speak, speak!" he says, shakin' him—the child was excited and upset, you know, to think he'd go and do a thing like that. "Don't stand there mumbling like an idiot! Goddamn it, where's the ticket?" Well, sir, we

313

searched his pockets, we went through everything
he had, and there was no ticket to be found, it wasn't
there! "Well, now," I said to the Chinaman, "Mr.
Gant has mislaid that ticket somewheres but I tell
you what you do: you just let us have his shirts anyway and as soon as I find the ticket I'll bring it to
you myself"—you know, tryin' to humor him
along. "Oh, *no!*" he says, he couldn't do anything
like that, and he began to jabber away, I reckon
tryin' to tell us he didn't know where the shirts were
and couldn't let us have them noway until we
brought the ticket. Well, sir, the trouble started then
and there: your papa grabbed him by the neck and
says, "Goddamn you, I'm goin' to kill you," hittin' at
him over the counter, you know, says, "fiend that
you are, you have impoverished and ruined me, you
have hounded me to the gates of death," he said,
"but I'll make an end of you now before I go," says,
"I'll take you with me."

Well, Ben and Luke got hold of him and pulled
him off, but the damage was done: the other feller
had gone screamin' and hollerin' out the door and
he came back now with a policeman. "What's the
meaning of all this?" the policeman says, "what's
going on here?" he says, sizin' us all up, you know.
"They have robbed me," your papa says, "and now,
fearful, awful and bloodthirsty fiends that they are,
they stand there plottin' my destruction." Why, he'd
'a' ruined us all, if he'd gone on: Luke shook him,
you know, says, "Now you be quiet or you'll land in
jail. You've made trouble enough." "No, now, officer," I said to the policeman—of course, I knew I
had to be diplomatic—"there's been a little misun-
derstanding, but everything's all right." "Why," he
says, "what happened?" "We're takin' my husband
here to the hospital," I said—of course, I thought

315

I'd let him know your papa was a sick man—"and we just came by to get some shirts we left here to be laundered." "Why, what's the matter?" he says, "won't they let you have them?" "Well," I said, "it seems they gave Mr. Gant a laundry ticket and I reckon he's mislaid it. At least, we haven't been able to find it yet. But the shirts are here," I said, "they're bound to have them: my son here brought them himself a week ago."

Well, he began to eye Luke then, and I tell you what! That child certainly made a good appearance. Of course, he was all dressed up nice in his sailor clothes—you know he'd got leave of absence to come up there from Norfolk and as Mrs. Barrett said, says, "That is certainly a fine-looking boy. I tell you," she says, "it does you good to look at him—makes you feel that no harm can come to a country as long as it's got boys like that to defend it," she says.

"Why, yes, Captain," Luke says—you know, callin' him that, I reckon, to make him feel good—"it's all right. The shirts are here all right," he says, "because I brought them myself but I guess my father accidentally mislaid the ticket." "Well," the policeman says to me, "would you *know* the shirts if you saw them?" "Why, Lord!" I said, "you know I would! I'd know them in the dark, I'd be able to pick them out by the size of them. Why, you *know,*" I said, lookin' him straight in the eye, "you can use your own reason," I said, "they wouldn't have another shirt in the house that would fit a man like that," I said. Well, he took one look at your papa, and then he began to laugh. "No," he said, "I reckon you're right. Well, I tell you what to do," he said, "you go around there yourself and pick 'em out," he said, "and I'll stay right here until you find them."

And that's exactly what he did. I marched right around behind the counter and that man stayed there until I found them. "Here they are!" I sang right out—way down at the bottom of a pile, you know, why I must have opened up fifty packages before I came to them and I tell you what! those two Chinamen didn't like it either, the looks that they gave us were oh! bitter, bitter. If that policeman hadn't been there to pertect us, I'll tell you what, I'd been alarmed, of course, there's no telling what people like that might do, especially with your papa ravin' and stormin' at them the way he did. I know I said to Luke later, after we'd taken him up and put him in the hospital, "I tell you what," I said, "I was glad to get out of that place. There was a look in the eyes of those men I didn't like; it made my flesh crawl!" "Yes," he said, "I felt the same way. Damned if I don't believe papa was right about them: I wouldn't trust one of them as far as I could throw an elephant," he said. "Well, child," I said, "he's had it a long time, that feelin', you know, and you may rest assured there's something there, something we can't understand," I said.

And, of course, that's just what I told Ambrose Radiker, that day in his saloon long, long ago! "It's something," he said, "sure enough—and he's a terror when he has it. I don't know what to do with him when he gets that way." "Well, I tell you what to do," I said, "don't sell him any licker when he asks for it. Now, the best way to keep out of trouble," I said, "is to avoid it." "That's right," he said. "Well, what do you want to put up with it for?" I said. "Now, surely, you've got strength of mind enough not to be forced into a thing against your better judgment. You've got more sense than that," I said.

"Why, what can I do?" he said. "Why, you can re-
fuse him the next time he comes here after licker," I
said, "that's exactly what you can do." "Why,
Eliza," he said, "what good would that do? He'd
only give that old Rufe Porter the money and send
him in here to buy a bottle, and I'd rather see him
spend his money on himself," he says, "than squander it on that old toper." "Why, you don't mean to
tell me he ever did that," I said. "Yes," says Ambrose, "that's exactly what he's done, many a time.
Rufe comes and buys the licker for him and they
drink it up together over at the shop." "Well, that ex-
plains it then!" I said. "The cat's out of the bag at
last!" Of course, I knew then—I could see—just
how that villain had got him into his power, gettin'
him to go his note, and all: he'd get him drunk, of
course, an' then your daddy would do anything he
told him to.

"*Yes!*" I said, that day he came home and told it
how Mel Porter had been in to see him and was so
upset because those men were going to hang. "Let
them hang—and I wish that miserable old brother
of his was going to be hanged with 'em." "Oh, you
mustn't talk like that," he said, "I hate to hear you
say such things." Of course, I was bitter against him.
"Well," your papa says, "I couldn't help feeling
sorry for Mel. I reckon he's been under a great strain
and now he's all worried and grieved to think that
all of them have got to hang." "Not a bit of it," I said,
"if you swallered any such story as that you're more
gullible than I am, you don't know Mel Porter as
well as I do. Now you can mark my words," I said,
"it's something else that's troublin' him." "No," he
says, "I think you're wrong." "All right," I said,
"you wait and see."

Well, he didn't have to wait long, either. That very

night, sir, they made that break from jail. They got away scot-free, all five of them, and none of them was ever caught. "Ah-hah," I said to him, "what did I tell you? And you were just fool enough to think Mel Porter was worryin' about their bein' hanged, weren't you? You see, don't you?" "Well," he said, "I reckon you're right! I guess that's what was troublin' him. He knew about it!" "Knew about it! Why, of course!" I said. "That's just it!"—of course, we could see then that he'd known about it all along, he knew they were going to make the break that night, and in his heart he was dreadin' it—he was afraid something would go wrong and there'd be more bloodshed, for they were a set of desperate bloody men and they wouldn't have hesitated to kill anyone who got in their way, and so, of course, the thought of it was weighin' on Mel Porter's conscience. "Well," your papa says, "it's an awful thing and I hate to think about it."

"What about it?" says Mr. Gant. "Dock Hensley came in to see me the other day and tried to give me two tickets for you and me to see it. To think of it!" he says, "here they were all boon companions six months ago, and now Dock is just waitin' for the moment when he springs the trap on them." "Why, yes," I said, "they were all thick as thieves together"—and, of course, that was true. Ed Mears and Lawrence Wayne and Dock Hensley had been bosom friends for twenty years—"and let me tell you something," I said, "I don't know that any of them are any worse than he is. Now," I said, "they're all tarred with the same brush: they are all violent men, and Dock Hensley has shed as much blood as any of them, and I reckon he knows it. The only difference," I said, "is that he has worn a badge and has always had the authority of the law to per-

319

tect him." Why, of course! didn't they tell it on him
that time he was being tried for the murder of Reese
McLendon—of course they freed him on grounds of
self-defense and an officer in the performance of his
duty, but I said at the time to your papa: "Now, you
know as well as I do that that was nothing but a deliberate cold-blooded murder if ever there was
one." Of course, Reese was an awfully strong man,
and when he got drunk he was a holy terror—and, I
guess, he'd killed plenty, too—but here he and
Hensley were close friends, you know, had always
got along fine together, and then they arrested him
for bein' drunk and disturbin' the peace. Well, the
story goes that he got to making so much noise that
they had to take him out of the cell. Oh! they said
you could hear him howlin' and hollerin' the whole
way across the square, and they put him downstairs
in what they called the dungeon; of course, it was
nothing but an old cellar basement with a dirt floor
that the city had used one time as a stable. Well, that
was Hensley's defense: he said he went down there
to see if he couldn't reason with him and do something to quiet him down, and of course, his story
was that McLendon had picked up an old horseshoe
that he'd found laying around down there and when
he came in, he said, McLendon jumped on him and
tried to brain him with the horseshoe.

So his claim was that it was either his life or
McLendon's and he got the horseshoe out of his
hand and gave him a lick across the forehead with it
that killed him. Well, the rest of them told it when
they tried him that he came back upstairs all covered with blood and said: "You'd better get a doctor
for Reese. I'm afraid I've killed him." Well, of
course, when the doctor got there he saw there was
nothing he could do, said McLendon was dead, you

know. Why, the doctor said it looked as if he'd hit him a hundred times with the thing, said the whole side of his head was bashed into jelly and he lay there welterin' in his blood. Oh, they said it was awful.

Your papa went to that trial and he came home and told about it: "I tell you what," he said, "in all my life I've never heard anything to equal Zeb Pentland's address to the jury today"—of course, your cousin Zeb was prosecutin' him— "It was a masterly effort," your papa says, "I wish you could have heard it." "Well," I said, "what are they going to do? Will they convict him?" "Why, Lord, no!" your papa said, "he'll go free. He'll get off on grounds of self-defense, but I tell you what," he said, "I wouldn't have been standing in his shoes today for a million dollars. You can mark my words," he said, "he'll never be able to forget what Pentland said to him as long as he lives. His face turned pale as he listened," he said, "and I reckon he'll carry it with him to his grave." Of course, it came out in the trial—Zeb Pentland proved it—how Dock Hensley had shot down and killed eighteen men since he had been an officer of the law, and your papa said he turned to the jury and told them, "You have given a policeman's badge, you have armed with the full authority and pertection of the law a man without mercy and without pity, to whom the shedding of human blood means no more than the killing of a fly, you have given him a loaded pistol and yet some of you," he said, "would set this mad dog free again to ravin and destroy, and take the lives of innocent and defenseless people. Look at him as he sits there before you!" he said, "cowerin' and tremblin' with the mark of Cain upon his brow and with his hands

321

red with the blood of all his victims! The accusing fingers of dead men are pointed at him from the grave," he said, "and their blood, could it have a tongue, would cry aloud for his conviction as do the tongues of all the widows and orphans he has made —"Well, Mr. Gant said it was a powerful effort, said Hensley turned pale and trembled as if the spirits of the dead had come back to accuse him, sure enough. But of course they acquitted him like everyone predicted.

But, Lord! as I said to your papa, I could never stand to go near the man after that time they had us to their house for dinner and here he was, sir—he had it on the table right where everyone was going to eat!—to think of it, I said!—why, the skull of a nigger he had shot and killed—that he should have no more refinement, I said to your papa, than to do a thing like that right there with guests comin' to his house for dinner and before his own childern, usin' it, mind you, as a sugar bowl! Oh, braggin' about it, you know, like he'd done something big, with the top of the skull sawed off to make a lid and a place in the forehead for the sugar to pour out where the bullet hole was. Why it was enough to turn your stomach, I couldn't touch a bite. When we got out, your papa said, "Well that's the last time I'll ever go to *his* house," he said, "I don't want to have anything to do with a man who's got no more mercy in him than that. It's enough to curdle your blood," he said, and from that day on he never set foot in his house again. Oh! he couldn't endure him, you know. But they say that's exactly why he killed himself in the end—I know Gilmer who was stayin' at the house brought me the news, came right back to the kitchen, you know, says, "Well, it was a terrible sight." Says, "I was the first one there. I heard the explosion," he says, "right behind the new courthouse, and when I got there—there he was," he says, "all sprawled out behind a pile of brick"; says, "they couldn't tell who it was for a while, the whole top of his head blown off so they couldn't identify him. Oh, *awful,* you know."

"Well," I said, "I'm not surprised. Those who live by the sword will perish by the sword," and, of course, that's just what happened, I reckon his conscience got too much for him, he couldn't face it any longer. Why, didn't Amy tell Daisy way back there when they were both in high school together, "Oh, daddy!" she says—the child came right out with it, you know—"oh, we don't know what to do with him. We're afraid he's goin' to lose his mind," she says. "He wakes up in the middle of the night screamin' and hollerin' and we think he's goin' crazy," she said. "Ah-hah!" I said to your papa when I heard it, "you see, don't you? 'The guilty fleeth when no man pursueth.'" "Well," he said, "I reckon he's got a lot to forget. He's got all those crimes upon his soul and he can't forget them. It's the torment of a guilty conscience as sure as you're born. It wouldn't surprise me if he committed suicide some day," he said.

But, of course, for a long time there he seemed to get all right. He quit the force and became a sort of religious fanatic, a pillar of the Methodist Church, and all, right down there among them in the amen corner every Sunday and yes! what about it! in the real estate business, if you please, swellin' it around town in a big car, promotin' *Hensley Heights,* and all such stuff as that, and of course I reckon for a time there like all the rest of us he made some money or *thought* he did.

I know when I bought those lots from W. J. Bryan

he told me Hensley had acted as agent in a couple of deals for him, and I reckon Bryan was feelin' pretty good about it, he began to brag about him, says: "I tell you what: Hensley is certainly a fine upright sort of man," he says. "In all my dealin's with him," he says, "I don't think I've ever heard him make use of a coarse expression, or utter a word that couldn't be spoken in the presence of a lady." Hm! I thought to myself, times have certainly changed, I thought, but of course, I didn't say anything, I just let him go on. "Yes," he says, "I've found him honest and upright in all my dealin's with him and what's more, you'll find him right in his seat in church every Sunday morning. And for a man who says he never had any schoolin'," he says, "his knowledge of the Scriptures is profound," says, "I've tried him out myself on texts from all parts of the Bible and I haven't managed to trip him up yet." Says, "It's a rare thing that you'll find a businessman in this day and time with so much interest in spiritual matters," says, "he is certainly a credit to the community." "Why, yes," I said, "I reckon you're right but then there are a whole lot of things about this community you don't know, Mr. Bryan. Of course," I said, "you're a recent comer and there may have been a time when Dock Hensley wasn't such a credit as he is now." "Why, when was that?" he said. "Well," I said, of course I wasn't going to tell him anything, winkin' at him, you know, "maybe we'd better let dead dogs lie. I reckon it was a long time ago, for a fact," I said, "about the time you first began to run for president."

Well, sir, he just threw back his head and hahhahed. "Why, yes!" he said, "I reckon that was a long time ago, sure enough. Well, maybe you'd better say no more," he said; says, "but I'll bet you if there was anything I *did* want to know," he said, "you'd remember it." "Why, yes," I said, "of course, I don't believe in anyone braggin' on themselves, but I've always been considered to have a pretty good memory," I said. "Well, I should say you have," he said, "I was tellin' my wife the other day," he says, "that it was remarkable to find a person who took as keen an interest in all that's goin' on as you do. Why," he says, "I said to her I believe you remember everything that ever happened to you." "Well, no," I said, "I wouldn't go so far as that. There may be a few things that I don't remember very well before I was two years old, but there hasn't been much I've missed out on since then." "Well, I just bet there's not," he said, laughin', you know, as big as you please. But, of course then I said to him—you know I didn't want to do the man an injury, I thought I would give him credit for his good points—said, "Well, Mr. Bryan, there are things we could say against anyone," I said, "for there is no one alive that hasn't got his faults. 'Judge not lest ye be judged,'" I said. "That is certainly true," he said. "We must all be charitable." "And I suppose if I wanted to," I said, "that I could tell you things about Dock Hensley that might not be exactly to his credit, but," I said, "you may rest assured on one score: he has certainly been a home-lovin' man and he has stuck to his wife and childern: no matter what else he has done he has never been guilty of no immorality or licentiousness, no one has ever been able to say that about him," and of course, that was true: they tried to prove *something* like that on him in that trial, in order to discredit his character, they tried to show that he'd gone running around after other women besides his wife, but they couldn't do it, sir—they had to give the devil his due—his morals were pure.

* * *

325

"Why, Dock," your papa said, "you've been good friends with those men for twenty years," says, "I don't see how you've got the heart to do it." "Yes, I know," he says, "it's an awful thing, but someone's got to do it. That's part of my job, that's what the people elected me for," he says, "and besides I believe Ed and Lawrence would rather have me do it anyway. I've talked it all over with 'em," he says— of course, they told it that he'd been goin' down there to the jail to see them, and that they were all as thick as thieves, sir, laughin' and carryin' on together—says, "they'd rather have me do it than some stranger." "Yes," Mr. Gant said, "but I should think it would trouble your conscience. I don't see how you'd be able to sleep at night after doin' such a thing." "Why, pshaw! Mr. Gant," he said, "it wouldn't bother me at all. I've done it many a time," he said, "all I've got to do is spring the trap. Why, I think no more of it than I would of wringin' a chicken's neck," he said. "What about it!" your papa says to me, "did you ever hear of such a man? Why it seems that all human feeling and mercy has been left out of him," he says.

Well, we never could find out if Dock Hensley was in on it or not—if he knew they were goin' to make that break—but if he did, it looked mighty funny that— "I tell you what," says Mr. Gant a day or two after it happened, "I believe we misjudged Dock Hensley," he says, "I believe he knew they were goin' to make that break all along and that's the reason," he says, "he was takin' it so easy." "Well, now," I said, "there's something mighty funny about it somewhere. If he knew about it why did he come to your office with those passes? Why was he so anxious to have us come and see it?" "Well," he says, "I reckon he did it in order to turn suspicion away from him." "No, sir," I said, "I don't believe a

word of it. He was just waitin' his chance to hang
'em—yes, and gloatin' about it." Well, of course,
Mr. Gant didn't want to believe it of him, said he
didn't like to think that any man could be so callous.

Of course, they said later that the whole thing had
been arranged for weeks: that was the story, you
know, that John Rand, the jailer, had been fixed, as
the sayin' goes, to let them make their getaway.
Now they weren't able to prove anything on the
man and he *may* have been an honest all-right sort
of feller—but there was something mighty queer
about it somewhere: here they found him, you
know, in Ed's cell all trussed up as slick as a whistle
and without a mark upon him, sir, to indicate he'd
ever made the least resistance. Well, the story he
told was that he'd gone in there to take Ed and
Lawrence their supper and that they overpowered
him and tied him up as soon as he came in, said they
took his keys and unlocked the other three and
skipped right out. Of course, those other three had
nothing to do with Ed and Lawrence, they were just
plain ordinary murderers, mountain grills, as your
papa called them, down there waitin' to be hanged,
and the story goes that Ed said to Lawrence, "Well,
we'll just turn them loose, too, while we're about
it."

Well, there was something funny about John
Rand's story. People didn't like the look of it. And
then, within six months' time John Rand goes into
business for himself, opens up a great big plumbing
shop on South Main Street with a stock that must
have cost him thousands of dollars. "Look here,"
your papa said, "do you know what they're saying?
They're saying that John Rand was bribed to let
those men escape." "Well," I said, "they may be
right. It's mighty funny," I said, "that a man who

327

never earned over fifty dollars a month in his life
gets money enough all of a sudden to start up a big
business of his own. Now *where* did all that money
come from: you've got to admit it looks fishy."
"Yes," your daddy says, "but who bribed him?
Where did the money come from?" he said. "Why,"
I said, "it came from Yancey County where all their
kinfolk and relations live—that's exactly where it
came from." "Why," he says, "are their people well-
to-do?" "They've got *plenty*," I said, "plenty—and
they'd 'a' spent every last penny they had to see
those men go free." Of course, I knew what I was
talkin' about. "Look here," I said, "I've lived here
all my life and I know those people better than you
do. I grew up among them," I said, "and I want to
tell you they'd 'a' stopped at nothing." Why, they
said the money poured in there like water, said
thousands of dollars were spent in their defense,
why, yes! didn't they tell it that old Judge Truman
alone—the brother of this same Perfesser Truman,
of course, Ed Mears and Lawrence Wayne married
Perfesser Truman's daughters, they both married
sisters—didn't they tell it that Judge Truman alone,
one of the biggest lawyers that they had in Yancey,
spent over ten thousand dollars in defendin' them,
"and you can rest assured," I told your papa, "that
that wasn't a drop in the bucket. Wherever they are
today, they're well provided for," I said, "and you
needn't waste your pity on them." "Well," he said,
"I'm glad they got away. There's been enough
bloodshed already. I don't see any use in adding to
it."

I shook my head. "No," I said, "you're wrong.
They should have been hanged and I'm sorry they
didn't get what was comin' to them, but," I said,

"I'm glad *we* acted as we did. I shouldn't have cared

if they'd been caught, but I don't want the blood of any man, guilty or innocent, on my conscience." "No," he said, "nor do I." "But *you know*," I said, "*you know* as well as you're standin' there that those men were guilty as hell"—that's just the way I put it—why, *murder*, of course, as deliberate and cold-blooded murder as anyone was ever guilty of. Here they told it at the trial that both of them walked into that mica mine on Saturday afternoon when they were payin' off, and they were spoilin' for a fight—that's all in the world it was. Why! I said to your papa at the time, if it had been money they were after, if they'd wanted to hold up the place, you might have seen some reason for it—but no! they were out to start a row, and they'd come ready for it. Of course, they'd both been drinkin' and when they drank they were always up to devilment. And here, of course, they began to abuse that pay-master—a decent law-abidin' man, they said—and to hinder him from payin' off and, of course, that was when John Burgin stepped into the office. "Now, boys," he said, "I don't like to see you act like this. Why don't you go on off now," he says, tryin' to reason with them, you know, "before you get your-selves in trouble?" "Why, damn you," says Law-rence Wayne, "what business is it of yours what we do?" "Why, it's no business at all," John Burgin says, "only I don't like to see you act this way. I don't want to see you get into any trouble," he said, "and I know when you wake up tomorrow morning you're goin' to regret this thing." "Well, now," says Lawrence Wayne, "don't you worry how we're goin' to feel tomorrow morning. You worry about yourself. It's people like you," he says, "who don't wake up at all. Why, damn you," he says, "I never did like your face noway. Now you'd better go on," he says,

329

"while you're still able to walk." "All right," John said, "I'll go. I don't want to have no trouble with you. I was just tryin' to reason with you to behave yourselves for the sake of your wives and childern, but if that's the way you feel about it, I'll go on." And they said he turned his back on them and was walkin' away when Ed Mears shot him, turned to Lawrence, they said, with a kind of a drunken grin, says, "Lawrence, do you reckon I can hit him?" and he shot that man down that never did him no harm, through the back of his head—and then, of course, they both cut loose on the paymaster and that man he had assistin' him—killed them all, and then skipped out. "But to think of it!" I said to your papa, "there was no excuse, no provocation as far as I can see—they were *simply out to kill,*" I said, "and hangin's the only treatment they deserve." "Yes," he said, "but I'm glad we acted as we did."

Now, boy, I want to tell you:

"Two . . . Two," the first voice said, and "Twenty . . . Twenty," said the other.

I know exactly when it was—I'm goin' to tell you now: it was on the twenty-seventh day of September, sir, at twenty minutes to ten o'clock in the evening. The reason I know is—well, that's what I'm goin' to tell you—but it was just two days before that on the twenty-fifth day of the month, sir—that I'd had that talk with Ambrose Radiker in his saloon, that's exactly when it was. That was just after Mr. Gant had been off on that spree and they'd had to send for us to get him and bring him home. Now, I thought, I've had as much as I can stand, I won't put up with it any longer, and I marched right in there by myself to have it out with him.

Well, I could see that Ambrose was telling me the truth—that was the time of course he told me how your daddy raved and carried on in his delirium against the Chinese and how much trouble they'd had with him—give the devil his due, of course— saloonkeeper though he may have been, I believe he told the truth and was being honest with me. "Now," he said, "I've done everything I can but if there's anything more I can do to persuade him to stop drinkin' you tell me what it is and," he says, "*I'll* do it!"—and yes! didn't he stop in to see us that very evening on his way home, we were sitting there after supper, you know, your daddy reading the paper to me, and all, and says, "Will, I want you to promise me that you'll try to cut out drinkin'. I hate to see you do it," he said, "a man with your mind and your command of language and all—why there's nothing you couldn't accomplish if you set yourself to it!" "Why, yes," I said, "he's smart enough, all right. I don't believe there's a man in the community with half his natural ability," I said, "and he could go far if it wasn't for that accursed cravin' for licker. There's one thing sure," I said, "he never learned it from any of my people—you know, my father, Major Pentland," I said, "never touched a drop in his life and never allowed anyone to come inside his house if he thought he drank." "Yes, I know," says Ambrose, "he is certainly a fine man and a credit to the community," he says, "and, Will," he says, "here you are with everything it takes to make a man happy—with a fine wife and a family of childern and a good business and, Will, for *their* sakes," he said, "you oughtn't to do it, you ought to cut out drinkin'." Well, your papa admitted he was right and he promised, you know, said he'd never touch another drop and Ambrose went on then—that was the very night it was, all right, the twenty-seventh of September.

Well, then, I heard it! "Two . . . Two," said one,

and "Twenty . . . Twenty," said the other. "Why, Lord, woman!" says Mr. Gant, "there's no one there!"—went to the window and looked out, you know, says, "It's something you imagined. You don't hear anything," he said.

"Oh, yes, I do!" I said—of course, I was as sure of it as I was sitting there—"there it is again!" I said, and of course I heard it just as plain, "Two . . . Two," the first one over by the window said, and "Twenty . . . Twenty," the other one kept whispering in my ear.

And that was the time the bell began to ring—that courthouse bell, you know, banging it out as hard and fast as it could go. "Oh, Lord!" I said, "something's happened. What do you reckon it can be?" You could hear them the whole way to the square shoutin' and hollerin' and smashing in the windows of Curtis Black's hardware store to get the guns, that's what they did, all right, and then manlike, of course, your papa wanted to be up and gone, grabs his hat, you know, says, "I think I'll go and see!"

"Oh, don't go!" I said, "don't go! I wish you wouldn't go. You oughtn't to leave me while I'm in this condition," I said. "Why, Lord," he said, "I'll be back in half an hour. Why you're all right," he said, "there's nothing can happen to you." I shook my head—I had a premonition, I don't know what else you'd call it—but something *awful, awful,* some approachin' calamity. "I wish you wouldn't go," I said—but he was up and gone.

I looked at the clock as he went out the door and the minute hand stood just exactly at twenty minutes to ten o'clock.

So I waited. I felt it, you know, I didn't know what it was, but I knew that it was comin', and I listened to that old wooden clock there on the mantel—tock-tock, tock-tock, it said, ticking the minutes off, and let me tell you: that was the longest time I ever waited, each of those minutes seemed an hour. The clock struck ten.

And then I heard it—creepin' along the alleyway above our house, and then I heard the fencewires creak outside the window, and then it dropped down on the flowerbeds outside the house—and then it crept up soft and easy and began to crawl along the porch outside the sitting-room door. "Oh, Lord!" I said—it flashed over me all at once, the meaning of it—"they've come! they're here! What shall I do," I said, "left all alone here with the childern to face them, these bloody men?"

Of course, I saw it then—the meaning of that warning—"Two . . . Two," and "Twenty . . . Twenty"—they'd tried to warn me and your papa that they'd be there in twenty minutes. "He should have waited, he should have listened," I said, "that was what they were trying to tell him."

I went to the door—how on earth I ever mustered strength and courage in my condition, I don't know how I ever did it, but child! child! I must have been given strength and courage to face them by some higher power—and I flung it open. It was a pitch-black night along toward the beginning of autumn. It had been raining but the rain had stopped and Lord! it seemed that you could cut the darkness with an axe, everything still and heavy, frosty-like— that was the reason we could hear them all so plain up on the square, but not a sound, sir! not a word now!

"All right!" I sang right out into the dark, you know, like I wasn't afraid of anything. "I know you're there, Ed! You can come on in." He didn't speak. I listened. I could hear him breathing, heavy-like. "Now, surely," I said, "you're not going to be afraid of me. I'm all alone," I said, "I'm nothing but a defenseless woman, and you've got nothing to be afraid of"—of course, I knew that that would agger-vate him.

Well, it stung his pride, he got right up and walked into the room: "I'm not afraid of anyone," he said, "man nor woman." "Well, no," I said, "I reckon you're not. At least they all said you weren't afraid of John Burgin when you shot him in the back when he was walkin' away from you and surely," I said, "a man who's killed as many people as you have is not going to be afraid of one lone woman who's been left alone in the house without pertec-tion. Now I know better than that," I said, "I know you're not afraid of *me*."

"No, Eliza," he said, "I'm not, and that's the rea-son that I'm here," he said. "You've got nothing to fear from me," he said, "I came here because I knew that I could trust you and you wouldn't give me away. I need your help," he said. Well, I reckon the look of the feller was too much for me, he looked like a hunted animal and *let me tell you*, I never want to see no such look in anyone's eyes as I saw in his that night: if he'd been to hell and back it couldn't have been worse. It was too much for me, I couldn't have told on him then no matter what he'd done. "It's all right, Ed. You've nothing to fear from me, I won't give you away. And you can tell Lawrence," I said, "to come on in. I know he's out there."

Well, he gave me a mighty funny look. "Why, what do you mean?" he said, "Lawrence isn't here. He's not with me." "Yes, he is," I said. "I *know* he's there. I'm *sure* of it. And you can tell him so, and to

334

come on in." "Why, how do you *know* he's there?"
he said, worried, "What makes you so *sure* of it?"
"Well, I tell you," I said, "I was *warned* about it,
Ed. I knew that you were both coming." "Warned?"
he said, beginning to get excited, you know, "Why,
who warned you? Has anyone been here? How did
anyone know?" he said. "No," I said, "you needn't
get excited, Ed. Someone was here to warn me, all
right, that you and Lawrence were coming, but it's
no one you've got to be afraid of in *this* world. The
next world is a different matter, of course," I said, "I
can't tell you about that. You'll have to face that for
yourself." Well, he looked at me and his eyes were
sticking out of his head. "*Spirits?*" he said. "Yes," I
said, "that's what they were, all right! Now I don't
know *who* they were, but they came here to warn
me, whisperin' in my ear, and they said you and
Lawrence were on your way and would be here in
twenty minutes."

Well, his face was a study, and at last he said: "No,
Eliza, you're wrong. I don't want to alarm you," he
said, "but if they were here they came here to warn
you about something else. It wasn't me and
Lawrence," he said, "I'll swear to that!" "Why, what
do you mean?" I said. "I've told you," he said,
"Lawrence isn't with me. We parted company outside the jail; we decided that was best and he lit out
toward South Carolina. I'm going across the mountain," he said, "and if we get away we hope to meet
again out West." "You look me in the eye," I said,
"are you telling me the truth?" Well, he looked
straight at me: "Yes," he said, "so help me God, it's
true!"

Well, I looked at him and I saw, of course, that he
was telling me the truth. "Well," I said, "it was

335

something else, then, what it is I don't yet know, but
I'll find out. Now," I said, "why did you come here
to my house? What do you want?" I said. "Why," he
said, "Eliza, I've got to get away across those mountains tonight, and I've got no shoes, I'm barefooted," he said. And then, of course, I saw, I reckon
I'd been too excited to notice before, but there he
was, ragged and bleeding, in his bare feet, and let
me tell you he was a sight to behold and marvel at:
here he was with no shoes and no coat and nothing
to wear but an old ragged pair of pants that looked as
if he'd been sleeping in them all the time he'd been
in jail, and a dirty old flannel shirt that had been all
ripped out beneath the shoulder, and here his hair
was all matted and tangled up like a bird's nest,
hanging down over his eyes and he must have had a
six weeks' growth of beard upon his face—why it
looked as if he hadn't had a shave or haircut since he
went to jail, the very sight of him was enough to
scare the life out of a grizzly bear. Why, as I told
your papa later, they'd thought of everything to help
him make his getaway except the things he needed
most: here they'd given him a pistol and cartridges
to kill people with—as if he hadn't killed enough
already—but they didn't have sense enough to give
him shoes to walk in or a coat to keep him warm. "If
that don't beat all I ever heard of!" I told your papa.

"I've got to get them somehow," he said. "If I
don't I'll cut my feet to pieces going across the
mountains and then," he said, "if I can't walk, I'm
done for. They'll catch me sure." "Why, of course,"
I said. "Well," he said, "that's why I came here to
see you, Eliza. I knew you wouldn't give me up and
I could depend on you to help me. Now," he says,
"you can see for yourself I've got an awful big foot
and the only man I know," he says, "who wears a

shoe that would fit me is Mr. Gant. Now if you'll
only let me have a pair of his old shoes—anything
you've got—I'll pay you for them. I've got plenty of
money," he said, and he pulled out a big roll of bills,
he had certainly come well heeled, "and I'll pay you
anything you say they're worth." "No, Ed," I shook
my head, "I don't want your money"—of course, I
couldn't have touched it, it'd been like taking blood
money—"but I'll give you the shoes." So I went to
the closet and got them out, a fine new pair, sir, that
your daddy had bought only a couple of months before, in good condition, for he certainly took good
care of all his clothes. "Here they are," I said, "and I
hope you'll be able to use them." Well, he put them
on then and there, and they fitted him, sir, as if
they'd been made for him. Well, you know, murderer that he was, he showed he still had feeling left
in him, he took my hand and began to cry, says: "I'll
never forget what you've done as long as I live. If
there's ever anything I can do to pay you for it," he
says, "I'll do it." "Well, you can do something," I
said, "and you can do it here and now." "What is
it?" he said. "I don't want your money," I said, "I
wouldn't touch it. You can have the shoes, Ed, and I
hope they help you to escape—you need the
shoes," I said, "but you don't need that pistol you're
carryin' in your hip pocket." I could see it, you
know, making a big bulge when he walked. "Now
you've shed enough blood already," I said, "but
come what may, whether you escape or not, I never
want to hear that you've shed another drop of blood.
You give that gun to me," I said, "and go on. If they
catch you it won't do you any good."

* * *

337

Well, he looked at me a moment as if he couldn't make up his mind, and then he gave it to me. "All right," he said, "I reckon you're right. I don't suppose it'd do me much good noway and besides, if they do catch me I don't care. I've committed so many crimes in my life," he said, "that I don't care what happens to me now. I'd just as soon be out of it," he said. "No," I said, "I don't like to hear you talk like that. You've got a wife who's stuck by you through thick and thin and little childern, and now," I said, "you must begin to think of them. Go on off somewheres," I said, "where no one knows you and make a fresh start, and when you are ready, send for her and I *know* her," I said—I looked him in the eye—"I *know* her, and she'll come."

Well, it was too much for him. He couldn't speak, he turned his head away, said, "All right. I'll try!" "Now, you go on," I said. "I don't want them to find you here," I said, "and I hope that all goes well with you." "Good-bye," he said, "I'm going to try to lead a different life hereafter." "Yes, that's what you've got to do. You've got to try to atone for all the harm you've done. Go," I said, "and sin no more."

Well, he went. I heard the fence wires creak and I saw him going up the street, I reckon toward the mountain. He got away, all right. I never saw him again.

Well, he hadn't been gone ten minutes when here he came, you know, your daddy, all excited with the news he *thought* he had to tell.

"Well," he said, "they got away, all five of them. Hensley and a big mob have smashed the windows of Black's hardware store to get guns and he's out after them now with a posse."

"Yes," I said, "and you had to run all the way to town to find *that* out, didn't you? The next time you go chasing off like that bring me back something I don't know about." "Why," he said, "how did you hear? Do you know about it?" he said. "Know about it!" I said, "why I know more about it than you'll ever know," I said. "I got my information at first hand," I said, "and I didn't have to stir out of this house to get it, either." "Why," he says, "how was that? What do you mean?" "I've had a caller since you went away," I said. "Who was it?" he says. I looked at him. "Ed Mears was here," I said. "Good God!" your papa says, "do you mean to tell me that murderer was here—in my house? Have you given the alarm?" he says, "have you told the neighbors?" "No," I said. "Well, I'm going to," he says, "this very minute." And he started to go again. I stopped him. "No," I said, "you'll do no such thing. You'll stay here. Now, I gave him my promise not to give him away, and we're going to stick to it. You keep quiet." He studied about it for a moment. "Well," he said, "I reckon you're right. Maybe it's the best way, after all. But that's the strangest thing I ever heard about," he said. "By God it is!"

Well, they got away, all right. None of them were ever caught. Of course, years later when your daddy made that trip to California, Truman told him that both Ed and Lawrence had come to his house in Colorado when he was living there and, of course, the girls both follered them within six months or so. Lawrence's wife, who was Mary Truman, died out there in Colorado of consumption a year or two later, and I don't know for certain whatever became of Lawrence. The story went that he settled down in Kansas and got married again and had a big family of childern and is living there right now, sir, a well-to-do man and highly respected in his community.

339

Of course, we *know* what happened to Ed Mears. I got the whole story from Dock Hensley. Truman told your papa that Ed had come out there to Colorado and went up into the mountains to some mining camp to work, and, of course, when he was ready he sent for Addie, and she follered him. Well, Truman said, she lived with him up there a year or so and then she came down to her father's house again. Oh! he told it, you know! Said it was awful, she couldn't stand no more of it, said Ed was going crazy and would go out of his mind sometimes screaming and raving that the spirits of the dead men he had killed had come back from the grave to haunt and torment him. "You see, don't you," I said to your papa when he told it, "you see what happens, don't you? I've never known it to fail," I said. "'The guilty fleeth when no man pursueth.'" "Yes," he said, "that's it. A guilty conscience as sure as you're born," he said. "So I took her away from him," said Truman. "I sent her back East where she would never see him any more. Of course," he said, "he threatened me—he threatened my life, but I could see that the man was goin' crazy, and I wouldn't let her go back to him," he said.

Well, Addie came home again and got a divorce: of course, Cash Jeter took the case for her—that was long before he got elected to the Senate, he was nothing but a practicing attorney at the time—and the story goes, in the course of the proceedings he fell in love with her, and marries her, if you please, within a month's time after she got the final papers. "Well, they didn't wait long, did they?" I said to your papa! "Now it does seem to me," I said, "that they might have waited a decent length of time." "Ah, Lord!" your papa says, "'the funeral baked meats did coldly furnish forth the marriage tables.

'Twas thrift, Horatio, with a vengeance,'" he says. "That's so," I said, "that's what it was, all right."

Well, then, they sent Dock Hensley West to get a man who'd killed someone, and, of course, when he came back he told it how he had run into Ed Mears in Mexico. Said he was on a boat somewheres going from Texas into Mexico follerin' on the trail of this murderer he'd been sent to get, I reckon, when here he saw him, face to face—Ed Mears. Dock said he'd grown a beard, but said he'd recognized him, "but I want to tell you," he says, "he's changed a lot. He's not the same man that you knew," he says. Dock said he looked like a dead man, said he was nothing but a shadder of his former self. "Why," he said, "he was only a bundle of skin and bone, he didn't have no more meat on him than a squirrel," he says. "Well," I said, "did he know you? Did he speak to you?"—of course, you know, I wanted to hear the story. "Why, Lord, yes!" Hensley said. "We roomed together for four days down there, hail-fellow-well-met and boon companions," he says. Then, he went on to say, you know, "Of course," he says, "when he first saw me on the boat he thought that I had come for him, he stepped right up," he said, "to surrender himself." "All right, Dock," he says, "I know you came down here to take me back and," he says, "I'm ready to go." "Why, no, Ed," I says, "you're wrong. I'm here for someone else. You're not the man I'm lookin' for," I said, "I don't want you—and besides," I said, "even if I did I've got no authority to arrest you, I've got no warrant for you." "Well," he said, "I'm comin' back anyway someday. I've one more killing to do yet before I die," he said, "and then they can take me and do what they like with me." "Why, who's that?" Dock says—asks him, "who do you want to kill?" he says. "Cash Jeter," he says. And then Dock told it how bitter he hated him for getting the divorce and marrying his wife.

So Dock said that before he left for home again Ed handed him a letter and asked him to deliver it to Jeter when he got back—and he said he *saw* that letter with his own eyes, mind you, and that in all *his* life he never read the like of it: "I may have been a murderer," Ed wrote, "and I've got many a crime upon my soul to atone for but in all my days I have never sunk so low as to steal a man's wife away from him. Now," he said, "you can set your house in order and get ready for me because I'm coming back. It may be a month, or it may be a year, or it may be ten years, but I'll *be* there," he said. "I've got a score to settle with you, and you get ready." Well, Dock said when he handed that letter to Jeter he opened it and read it and Dock said his face turned pale and you could see him tremble and I suppose, of course, his life was hell on earth from that day on until the news got back to them that Ed was dead—because, of course, Ed never lived to get there, the story went that he got killed in a saloon in Mexico. But you can rest assured that he'd 'a' come.

Well, that's the way it was, all right: that's just what happened.

But still and all—the thing was puzzlin' me, you know—"Two . . . Two," and "Twenty . . . Twenty"—what could it mean?

"Why, Lord," your papa said, "it didn't mean a thing! It never happened anyway," he said, "it's something you imagined."

"You wait," I said, "you wait and see."

It wasn't long. We didn't have long to wait.

It started in along some time before dinner, about

one o'clock. Oh, Lord! it felt like something had tore

loose inside me. And he was there, he'd come home
early, here he was, you know, out in the backyard
rendering the lard out of some hogs he'd bought.
"Why, what on earth!" I cried. "What ever made
you buy them?" Child, child! that awful waste, that
awful extravagance! Why, as I told him, if it hadn't
been for me he'd have spent every penny he earned
featherin' the nests of the butchers and the farmers
and the saloonkeepers—he couldn't resist 'em, you
know. "Why, man alive!" I said, "what ever persuaded you to go and do a thing like that!" Here we
were with hams and bacon in the pantry that he'd
bought, six smoked hams, if you please, and here he
comes with this whole hog. "Why, man, you'll kill
us all with all this hog meat!" I said—yes! with lots
of chickens of our own and a twelve-pound roast
he'd sent down from the market—"Why, we'll get
down sick," I said, "you'll have the childern all in
bed! So much meat isn't good for people." To think
of it! the waste, you know—child, child, many's the
time I've sat down and cried about it, to think he'd
go and squander away his money in that way. "Why,
Lord!" I said, "I never saw such a glutton in my
life!" I thought I'd appeal to his pride, you know.
"Why, all you think of is your belly! Now stop here
and consider for a moment: how do you ever expect
to accumulate any property if everything you earn
goes rolling down your gullet to feed your gut?
Why, I'll vow! man! I believe all of your brains are
in your belly!" Why, yes! he'd meet up with some
old farmer who had a whole wagonload of stuff he
wanted to get rid of so he could get out of town and
hike for home again, and he'd buy him out, sir. Why,
didn't I tell you! What about it! to think that he
could be such a dunce—the time he sent this man
home with forty dozen eggs—Lord! I could have

thrown them at him I was so aggervated!—when here we had hens of our own layin' us fresh ones every day as hard as they could. "Why, what ever prompted you to do such a trick as that?" I said. "Well," he says, sheepish-like, "he let me have the lot at seven cents a dozen. It was such a bargain," he says, "it seemed a pity not to buy them." "Why I don't care," I said, "if he let you have them for two cents a dozen, it was money thrown away," I said, "we'll never use them." "Oh, we can use them," he said. "We'll give 'em to the childern." "Why, Lord, man, how you talk!" I said, "you'll get the childern so sick of eggs they'll never look one in the face again. They'll never eat 'em," I said, "they'll all go bad!" And he looked pretty sheepish about it, I tell you what he did! "Well," he says, "I thought I was actin' for the best. I guess I was mistaken," he said.

And yes! Didn't he come home one time with a whole load of cantaloupes and watermelons—twenty-seven watermelons, if you please, and the Lord knows how many cantaloupes, hundreds of 'em, I reckon. "To think you had no better sense than that!" I said. "Oh, we'll eat 'em, we'll eat 'em," he said. "The childern will eat 'em up," he says. Yes, didn't Luke get down sick from eating them, "and there's a doctor bill to pay," I told him . . . and all the other times he'd come with wagonloads of roastin' ears and termaters and string beans and sweet pertaters and onions and radishes and beets and turnips and all kinds of garden vegetables and all sorts of fruit, peaches and pears and apples and plums, when here we had a big orchard and garden right behind the house growin' everything we needed. Why, it kept me busy thinkin' up ways to keep it all from goin' to waste, said, "how do you ever expect me to look after the childern if you keep dumping this stuff in here on me?"—here I was in that condition, you know, putting up preserves for all I was worth and him out there rendering the lard out. Oh! the smell of it, that old strong smell of fat, you know—right up to the very time, four hundred and thirty-seven jars of preserved cherries, peaches, apple, grape, and plum jelly, quince honey, preserved pears, termater ketchup, chowchow, pickled cucumbers, and all such stuff as that, why you couldn't get into the pantry, it was stacked up to the ceiling, and *let me tell you, now,* he could *eat:* now I've seen some good eaters in my day and time but I've never seen anyone who could poke it away the way *he* could. I reckon he got it from that crowd he came from up there, told it you know how they'd come in from the fields in his boyhood and sit down to a meal that would stall an ox. Why didn't I see the old woman myself, when we were up there that time, eat a whole chicken and three big hunks of pie—says to Augusta, you know, "Daughter, fill my plate again," she says, and she was in her seventies then—that's exactly how she got her death, sir. "To think of it!" I said when I heard the news—in her ninety-sixth year and fell out of her chair and broke her leg while reachin' for an ear of corn: of course it killed her, she was too old to recover from the injury, her bones wouldn't knit together again, "but if that don't beat all!" I said.

Why, I'll vow! It's a wonder his constitution stood it as long as it did—brains and eggs and bacon and fried steak and oatmeal and hot biscuits and sausage and two or three cups of coffee for his breakfast, and two or three different kinds of meat, liver and roast beef and pork and fish and chicken, and a half-dozen different vegetables, beans and mashed pertaters and succotash and turnip greens and preserved peaches and pie, and all such as that, for dinner and supper. "Why," I said to Wade Eliot, "I believe that's what helped bring on this trouble. He's been diggin' his grave with his teeth." "Well," he said, "he's been diggin' a long time, hasn't he?" and, of course, I had to admit it, but I'll vow! I sometimes think he might be alive today if he'd only used more judgment!

Well, then, I say, it hit me, those awful stabbing pains. I went to the window and called out to him, "Come! come quick!" And let me tell you, he didn't *wait:* he came a-running.

"Oh, it can't be!" I said. "There hasn't been time enough."

"That's what I think it is," he said. "I'm going for the doctor."

And he went.

That was the year the locusts came: it seems so long ago since the year that the locusts came, and all the earth was eaten bare, it seems so long ago. But no (I thought) the thing kept puzzlin' me, you know —it can't be that, there hasn't been time enough for that, it was only the year before in January—Lord! Lord! I often think of all that I've been through, and wonder that I'm here to tell it. I reckon for a fact I had the power of Nature in me; why! no more trouble than the earth takes bearing corn, all of the childern, the eight who lived, and all the others that you never heard about—all of the childern and less married life than any woman that I knew—and oh! to think of it, to think that he should say the things he did—cursin' and tauntin' me and runnin' wild with other women, when he had done it all, and like a devil when he saw what he had done. Lord! Lord! he was a strange man, a wild and savage man; sometimes it seemed I never got to know him: there was a devil in him somewhere, something wild and strange we never got to know about—the things he did and said were more than I could stand, they made me bitter and I prayed that God would punish him, but Lord! it was so long ago since the year that the locusts came, and I think of it all, the orange trees, the fig trees, and the singin' and all of the times we knew together. Oh! the good, the bad times, all of the happiness and bitter weepin', and there is something now that can't be said, I tried to hate him but now I have no words to say against him: he was a strange man but where he was no one was ever cold, no one was ever hungry, there was enough for all, and now when I remember him it seems so long ago since the year when the locusts came, and there's something that I want to say that can't be spoken.

That year—it was the year the childern had the typhoid and Steve and Daisy were just gettin' well again and I had taken them—Lord! how did I ever do it all alone—down to St. Augustine—and he came, he couldn't stay, of course, he follered us, and began to drink—I tried to find it but he got Steve to hide it in the sand up underneath the house—and to curse and rave when he had seen me, says, "Damn you! if you bring it back with you I'll kill you both!" And child, to think that he should talk like that, it made me bitter and I didn't stop to think: I walked the floor, I walked the floor and then I went out on the porch and leaned against a post—we were livin' in a cottage that I'd rented from some Northern people—and there was no rail—there was nothin' but that old loose sand there anyway, and I knew the childern wouldn't hurt themselves if they fell off— and Lord! What shall I do! What shall I do! I thought. . . .

The next day he had sobered up again and was all   347

right and so toward sunset of that day we took the childern with us and set out for old Fort Marion, the Spanish Fort, down by the Ponce de Leon, and here were all the people in their finery and the soldiers' band a-playin' and then you heard the gun and the bugle blowin' as the flag came down—yes— Toodle-oo! Toodle-oo!—that was the way the bugle blew and all the little childern put their hands up to their mouths to see if they could do it too, and the birds flyin', the palm trees and the music and the smell of water and the orange blossoms, and that old black fort—why Lord! the walls were fourteen feet in places—with the sun goin' down behind it like some big orange, and the people listenin' to the music. In January of that year the locusts came at home, and then I felt as if the whole thing had torn loose inside me.

"Come on," I said. "We've got to go," and he says, "What is it?" "Oh, Lord!" I told him, "it's tearin' me in two. Oh, Lord! We'll never get there! Come!"— and we went, the childern and all, and my feet slippin' and sinkin' in the sand, until I thought I'd never get there, and that great hunk of a thing tearin' away at me, and he picked me up and carried me the last part of the way into the house, and I said, "You see, don't you? You see what you've done. That's your work!" and he was frightened and his face turned pale and he trembled as he looked and he said, "My God! My God! What have I done!" and he walked the floor, and it got dark, and I lay there, and all of the childern were asleep around me, and he went out into the yard, and we had a fig tree there, and I lay there in the dark listenin' to people comin' by, and I could hear music playin' somewheres and hear their voices laughin' and singin', and smell all of the blossoms—oh! the magnolias and the lilies and the roses, the poinsettias, and all the other

flowers they had there and the orange trees and all,
and the little childern sleepin' in the house, you
know, and see the sky all full of stars and Lord God!
I thought, what shall I do, what shall I do?—and
that was the year the locusts came at home and now
it seems so long ago.

But Lord! I reckon Nelson got it right that time,
said, "You've got the power of nature in you for a
fact. I've never seen the like of it," he said. Why,
yes! didn't I have them all, and couldn't I make
things grow by touchin' them, and wasn't it that way
ever since I was a child—termaters and flowers and
corn and vegetables—and all kinds of fruit. Why
Lord! it seemed that all I had to do was stick my fingers in the earth and they'd come up for me. "Oh,"
says old man Shumaker, workin', you know to all
hours in his garden till it looked like a checker-
board, everything standin' up straight and neat
without a weed among it, like I reckon he'd been
taught to do in Germany, says, "Oh! you mustn't let
your garden go that way. You've got to weed it out or
things will never grow." "You wait," I said, "you
wait and see! They'll grow," I said, "they'll grow for
me, and I'll have things as good as yours for all your
work and grubbin'." And didn't I have onions and
radishes and lettuce and termaters that beat him out
of sight—why Lord! you could see them poppin'
from the earth! and let me tell you, if the worst
comes to the worst, I wouldn't starve, if I didn't
have a penny I could live, I'd make the earth produce for me. I've done it and I could do it yet.

Why, yes! didn't I go in to the Catawba Coal Company here one day last winter to pay my bill and talk
to him just two days before he dropped dead from
that heart attack, and see him, you know, Miller
Wright, not a day over seventy, pale as a ghost and

trembling and shaking all over like a leaf? "Why,
Miller," I said, "it worries me to see you in this condition. What is it? What's the matter?" "Oh," he
says, trembling and shaking, "Eliza, it's the worry,
the awful worry! I can't sleep no more for thinkin' of
it." "Why, what is it?" I said; says, "Oh, Eliza,
everything I ever had is gone! I'm penniless. Most
of it went in real estate," he says, "and now that miserable bank has closed its doors. What am I going to
do?" he said. "Do?" I said, "why you're going to do
the same as me—profit by your mistakes and start
all over." "Oh, but Eliza, Eliza," he said, shakin' his
head at me, "it's too late—we're both past seventy
and we're too old, too old," he said. "Old!" I said,
"why, Lord God, I could start right out tomorrow
and earn my living with the best of them." "Yes," he
said, "but Eliza, what are you going to do?" "Do!" I
said, "why, I tell you," I said, "I'm going to pitch
right in and work hard till I'm eighty and then," I
says, winkin' at him, you know, "I'm goin' to cut
loose and *just raise hell*," I said—that's exactly
what I said, you know, I thought I'd jolly him up a
bit and, of course, he had to laugh then, says, "Well,
I reckon that's as good a plan as any." "Now, look
here, Miller," I said, "you ought to know better than
to give in like this. We've both been through the
mill, and we've seen some mighty rough times—
why, these people that they've got today don't know
anything about it, they don't know what hardship
is"—why, didn't we both grow old within five miles
of each other and don't I remember it all, yes! every
minute of it like it was today, the men marchin', and
the women cryin', the way the dust rose, the times
we went through and the way we had to work, the
wool, the flax, the wheel, the things we grew and
the things we had to make, and a thousand things
you never dreamed or heard of, boy, the summer-

time, the river and the singin', the poverty, the sorrow, and the pain—we saw and had to do it all—
"And *you*!" I said to Miller Wright. "You! You did it,
too," I said, "and you remember!"

Well, he had to admit it then, you know, says,
"Yes, you're right, I remember. But," he says—you
know, he brightened up a bit, "could you do it
now?" "Do it?" I said. "Why, I could do it like a
flash. Now, Miller," I said, "suppose we did lose
out. We're in the boat with lots of others. We all
thought we were doing the right thing and I reckon
we lost our heads," I said. "We allowed ourselves to
be swept off our feet against our better judgment"—
pshaw! when I think of it! I had my mind all made
up. . . . If I'd only known. . . . Why, I was just
going to make another trade or two and then get out.
Pshaw! I'll vow, I believe if it hadn't been for all
these sharks and New York Jews and easy-money
grafters that came in there overnight . . . *that* was
the time I should have sold if I'd only had the sense
to see it . . . and as for all that stuff we bought in
Florida, I believe we'd have been all right today if
that hurricane hadn't come along and hit us like it
did, and then on top of it these lying villains out in
California spread that story about the Mediterra-
nean fruit fly down in Florida. Why, Lord, there was
no more fruit fly there than at the North Pole—it
was all part of a lying story they put out to ruin and
injure Florida because they couldn't stand to see us
get ahead of them, and Hoover and all his crowd
playin' right along with them and abettin' them in
their villainy because *he* came from California, if
you please—that's all in the world it was, but Florida will come back in spite of all the lies they told
about her, you can't down Florida!—"And Miller,"
I said, "the banks haven't got everything," I said.
"They may think they have, but now," I said,

winkin' at him, "I've got a secret that I'm goin' to tell you. I've still got a little patch of land out in the country that no one knows about and if the worst comes to the worst," I said, "I won't starve. I'll go out there and grow my food and I'll have plenty. And if you go broke you can come on out," I said. "You won't go hungry, I can make things grow." "Oh, but Eliza," he said, "it's too late, too late. We're both too old to start again, and we've lost everything." "No," I said, "not everything. There's something left." "What is it?" he said. "We've got the earth," I said. "We've always got the earth. We'll stand upon it and it will save us. It's never gone back on nobody yet."

Well, here they came, you know, tearing along for all they were worth, your papa and old Doctor Nelson. I lay there with those awful pains rending me as if they were going to tear me in two.

"But no," I said to Doctor Nelson. "It can't be that. I'm not ready for it yet. It's not been time, it's two weeks before my time," I said.

"No matter about that," he said. *"You're ready.* It's *your* time," he said. "It's *your* time, sure enough."

And, sure enough, it was. Why! that was it, of course!—that's what I've been telling you, boy!— that explained it all.

"Two . . . Two," the first voice said, and "Twenty . . . Twenty," said the other:

Twenty days later from that evening that Ed Mears came there to our house, to the minute, at twenty minutes to ten o'clock on the seventeenth day of October, *twins* were born—Ben and Grover were both born that night.

The next day as I lay there thinkin', it flashed over
me, the meaning of it, of course I saw it all. The
mystery was explained.

And that's the story, sir, that's just the way it happened.

"Two . . . Two," the first voice said, and
"Twenty . . . Twenty," said the other.

I've told you now.

"What do you think of that?" I said to Mr. Gant.
"You see, don't you?"

His face was a study. "It's pretty strange when
you come to think of it," he said. "By God, it is!"

Lord, boy! What's that I hear now on the harbor?
Hah? What say? A ship!—Now it will soon be April,
and I must be going home again: out in my garden
where I work, the early flowers and blossoms will
be comin' out, the peach trees and the cherry trees,
the dogwood and the laurel and the lilacs. I have an
apple tree and it is full of all the birds there are in
June: the flower tree you planted as a child is
blooming by the window where you planted it. (My
dear child, eat good food and watch and guard your
health: it worries me to think of you alone with
strangers.) The hills are beautiful and soon it will be
spring once more. (It worries me to think of you like
this, alone and far away: child, child, come home
again!)

> O listen! . . .
> Hah? What is it? . . .
> Hah? What say? . . .
> (Lord God! A race of wanderers!)
> Child, child! . . . what is it?
> *Ships again!*